The GIRL WITH STARS IN HER EYES

XIO AXELROD

sourcebooks
casablanca

Published by Sourcebooks Casablanca, an imprint of Sourcebooks
P.O. Box 4410, Naperville, Illinois 60567-4410
(630) 961-3900
sourcebooks.com

Library of Congress Cataloging-in-Publication Data

Names: Axelrod, Xio, author.
Title: The girl with stars in her eyes / Xio Axelrod.
Description: Naperville, Illinois : Sourcebooks Casablanca, [2021] |
    Series: The Lillys ; book 1 | Summary: "Growing up, Antonia "Toni" Bennett's
guitar was her only companion...until she met Sebastian Quick. Seb was a little older,
a lot wiser, and he became Toni's way out, promising they'd escape their small town
together. Then Seb turned eighteen and split without looking back. Now, Toni B is all
grown up and making a name for herself in Philadelphia's indie music scene. When
a friend suggests she try out for the hottest new band in the country, she decides to
take a chance...not realizing that this opportunity will bring her face-to-face with
the boy who broke her heart and nearly stole her dreams."-- Provided by publisher.
Identifiers: LCCN 2020046663 (print) | LCCN 2020046664 (ebook)
Subjects: LCSH: Women guitarists--Fiction. | Rock groups--Fiction. | GSAFD:
    Love stories.
Classification: LCC PS3601.X46 G57 2021 (print) | LCC PS3601.X46 (ebook)
    | DDC 813/.6--dc23
LC record available at https://lccn.loc.gov/2020046663
LC ebook record available at https://lccn.loc.gov/2020046664

Printed and bound in the United States of America.
SB 10 9 8 7 6 5 4 3 2 1

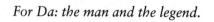

For Da: the man and the legend.

It isn't where you came from,
it's where you're going that counts.

—Ella Fitzgerald

PROLOGUE.

ANTONIA: 12 YEARS OLD

ANTONIA BENNETTE WOKE FROM HER after-school nap to the sound of a guitar. It was coming from somewhere inside the small dressing room in the back of Ginny's Jazz House where her mother was gigging tonight. She listened for a while, searching for something familiar amid the improvised notes, giddy with anticipation.

The tenor of Mary Bennette's prized old Gibson was unmistakable. Softer than the Fender or even her other, newer Gibson. Antonia loved the way its tone could change note to note—from the sound of water dripping from the roof when it rained to the crunch of loose pavement under her shoes. And the way her mother could make it sing, make it harmonize along with her own voice, gave Antonia goose bumps. Audiences loved Mary Bennette too. They packed small clubs in Chester, Baltimore, and even Philadelphia to hear her. Antonia's mother was a star.

After another few bars, Antonia was able to pick out the melody to Stevie Wonder's "Happy Birthday." Her mom had remembered and must have something special in store for her. Maybe she'd even let Antonia stay for the show and not send her off to stay with one of her play-aunts across town.

Slipping off the tiny cot in the corner, Antonia padded around the wardrobe and into the main area.

Mary Bennette sat on the edge of the old, striped sofa against the wall. Wrapped in her dressing gown, and her hair in rollers, she had the cherry-red guitar propped on her right knee, her left foot tapping along.

Antonia watched her mom vamp on the melody for a while longer before finishing it off with a flourish. Then she looked up at Antonia, her dark eyes flashing. "I wondered if you was gonna sleep the whole night," she said with a smirk. "Happy birthday, Sweet Potato."

"Thanks, Mommy!" Antonia walked over to sit on the footstool by her mother's side. She was only allowed to call her Mommy when they were alone. In public, she was Mary. Her mother said it was better for her image, as people sometimes thought they were sisters rather than mother and daughter.

Mary pursed her lips and brushed the hair back from Antonia's forehead. "You're practically grown. Almost as big as me."

Antonia beamed as Mary started playing a different song, one she recognized from her nightly performances.

If you don't like my ocean, don't fish in my sea.
Stay out of my valley, let my mountain be.

Her mother's voice was sweet and smoky, and Antonia loved when she sang, especially when it was just for her.

She eyed Antonia. "Go get the Fender."

Antonia jumped up and went to the corner to grab the newer instrument. It was styled like the guitars from the 1940s that her mother had once shown her in photos. The body was solid wood and its body wasn't as rounded as the Gibson, but Antonia liked its buttery finish. She was usually afraid to even breathe too close to Mary's guitars, and only touched them when her mother told her to.

"Go on, pick it up," Mary commanded, and Antonia obeyed. "Bring it here. Careful, now."

Antonia gingerly carried the Fender over to her mother and sat on the stool when Mary pointed at it.

"Wanna learn this tune?"

"Yes!" Antonia answered breathlessly. "Please." She placed the guitar in her lap and her mother handed her a pick, the lamplight glinting off her polished crimson nails.

"Starts in F7," Mary said. Antonia could feel her mother's eyes on her as she positioned her fingers on the fret board. "Good, now B-flat, back to 1, then 2. Repeat that. Now go to E-flat-7."

Antonia followed her mother's instructions, picking up the 4/4 rhythm of the song easily. She'd heard standard blues enough to understand what was expected.

"Gimme that again with some feeling," her mother instructed. "Now, where do you think it goes?"

Antonia thought as she played. "To the B?"

Mary's dimples popped as her mouth curved into a grin. "Diminished B, you're right. You sure have a good ear."

Antonia looked up at her mother. "Like you?"

Mary huffed out a laugh. "Someday, maybe. Those big hands were meant to hold a guitar, though. That's for certain."

At school, Antonia had been teased for being so tall and so developed for her age. Her hands were especially noticeable, with long, spindly fingers that looked more alien than human to her. She'd hated them until the first moment she'd picked up a guitar.

"Okay, girlie, I laid out a new dress for you. Clean up and put it on. I'm on in an hour, and I need to work the room," Mary said, setting the Gibson aside.

"A dress?" Antonia dutifully wiped down the Fender with a cloth and put it away. "Aren't I going to Aunt Dot's or Aunt Jean's?"

"You're staying with me tonight," her mother replied as she sat in the dressing room chair. She spun to the mirror and started removing the rollers from her hair. "Ginny said since it's your birthday, you can stay for my set tonight."

"Really?" Antonia ran toward her mother, wanting to hug her, but Mary held out a hand.

"Don't muss me up!" Antonia froze, and Mary turned back to the mirror. "You sit on the side of the stage and you don't move, you hear me?"

"Yes, I promise," Antonia replied, eager. "Can I get a Shirley Temple?"

"Only from the waitress."

"Aww, I want to order it at the bar," Antonia complained as she slipped the dark-red cotton dress over her head.

When she emerged from the fabric, Mary caught her gaze in the mirror. "What part of 'Sit on the stage and don't move' did you not understand? The last time I let you do that, the club almost got shut down for serving a minor. Thank goodness the cop on duty was a fan of mine and let Ginny off the hook, or I'd have lost a string of gigs at this place." She shook her head. "Maybe I should get Dot to watch you."

"I'll stay put, I promise," Antonia said, hands clasped.

Mary stood and dressed, her rich brown skin perfectly complemented by the deep plum of her own dress. With her figure, her thick mane of black hair, and her pearly white teeth, she was so pretty. Antonia wanted to grow up to be just like her.

"Why you standing there gawking?" Mary asked. "Grab the Fender and let's go."

When they left the dressing room, her mother led her down the short hallway. Straight ahead lay the door to the bar. To the side, another door led to the kitchen.

"Wait here," Mary instructed before slipping into the main bar.

It was dark, and the hall smelled like week-old garbage. Antonia could've sworn she saw a rat or two scurrying around in the dim light. Wearing the thin cotton dress—basically a long T-shirt—she shivered, but not from the cold. After what seemed like forever, Mary returned. She pulled back a curtain, revealing a short set of steps that led to the stage.

"Get on up there, Sweet Potato." Mary pointed, and Antonia picked her way across a tangle of cords and cables to the opposite wall.

It wasn't a big space and close enough to the kitchen that the smell of grease and smoke nearly choked her. Antonia swallowed it down, not wanting to give Mary any reason to send her away.

Mary gestured toward a big black Marshall speaker. "Stay there and don't move."

"Okay, Mommy."

She pointed a stern finger in Antonia's face. "What'd I say?"

"Sorry, Mary."

Her mother scowled but then smiled, shaking her head. "I'll tell Corinne to bring you your Shirley Temple, but behave. This is a big night for me. There's a man here from Atlantic City that saw my show and wants to talk."

"I will, Mom...Mary."

"Good girl."

Antonia watched from the wings as Mary worked the room. She seemed to know everyone, and everyone knew her. It was like watching a queen hold court. Men, especially, seemed to be taken with her, and she paid a few of them a little extra attention.

Several waitresses wove in and out of the packed crowd, moving from table to table with trays full of drinks. One of them stopped and whispered something to Mary. Her eyes lit up and she nodded before glancing back at Antonia. Mary held up one finger and Antonia nodded.

"You Mary's kid?"

A pale man with bulging eyes and yellowing teeth stood at the open stage entrance. He was dressed in a suit that didn't quite fit him, but it was clean and looked expensive.

He stepped closer, and Antonia gripped the edges of the amp. She realized she hadn't answered his question. "I'm... Yes, sir." She blinked up at him and he narrowed his eyes, deep crinkles at their corners.

Was she supposed to tell people if they asked her directly? Should she have lied?

"Well, now," the man drawled. "She didn't tell me you was so pretty." He crouched down and Antonia moved as far away from him as she could, which earned a chuckle. "Don't worry, darlin', I won't bite ya." He flashed a broken smile. "Unless you want me to. I'm Mr. Allen."

Not knowing how to respond, Antonia looked out at the crowd, hoping to catch a glimpse of her mother, but she'd disappeared.

Mr. Allen circled behind her, way too close for comfort. "How old are you?"

"Today's my birthday. I'm twelve." Antonia didn't turn around to answer him, her eyes glued to the room looking for any glimpse of her mother's purple dress. She didn't care if she was being rude; the man was practically breathing down her neck. Antonia could smell his cologne—and the scent, combined with the odors in the bar, was enough to make her want to gag.

"No way." His voice rumbled like a freight train. "I was about to ask if I could buy you a drink."

Antonia did turn to him then, shocked.

He laughed low in his throat, and suddenly she was terrified. She'd seen men look at her mother the way he was looking at her.

"Do I scare you, sweetness?"

"I—I should go find my mom." Antonia scooted forward on the speaker.

"No need to be skittish," he said, backing away with his hands up. "It's all good."

"Ray." The sound of Mary's voice brought a wave of relief so sharp that Antonia nearly lost her breath. "I was looking for you."

Antonia got up and practically ran to her mother's side.

Mary gave her a funny look.

"I was right here," Mr. Allen—Ray—responded. "Introduced myself to your lovely little girl."

Mary cut a sharp look at Antonia. "Antonia, Mr. Allen is—"

"I own a club in AC, just off the main drag," he said, talking to Antonia. "But I also manage one of the casino lounges. I'm gonna make your mom a star."

Antonia looked at her mother. "Are we going to Atlantic City?"

Ray laughed under his breath.

Mary glanced at him and then back at Antonia. "I'm going, but I can't take you with me."

For the second time that night, Antonia was breathless. "Wh-what?"

"Your mom is going to be very busy—" Ray began.

"Ray," Mary cut him off. "Why don't you go to my table? It's the one just there." She pointed at a table offstage and to the right. "Order whatever you want. It's on me."

Ray eyed them both but nodded. "Don't worry, little one. I'll take good care of your mommy." His smile made Antonia's skin crawl.

"What do you mean, you can't take me with you?" Antonia asked as soon as Ray was gone. The members of Mary's backing band for the night entered the stage and began to settle in for the show.

Mary grabbed Antonia by the arm and pulled her down the steps and into the hall, checking around them before she spoke again. "This is the big break I've been working toward. I can't let any...distractions get in the way."

"But..." Antonia's breath hitched. This couldn't be happening.

"Ladies and gentlemen," a voice boomed over the PA. "Ginny's is proud to welcome back to the stage the fabulous Mary Bennette!"

"Mommy—"

"We'll talk later," Mary snapped, her grip tightening. "If you can't sit still and stop looking at me like I shot your dog, then go back to the dressing room and wait."

The band started the first song, Mary's cue to go on.

"Please don't leave me," Antonia pleaded.

Mary's expression hardened. "Go. Wait. I won't tell you again."

She spun Antonia around and shoved her toward the dressing room before mounting the steps to the stage.

"Hey, Chester!" Antonia heard her mother say to the crowd, sunshine in her voice. "How it do, how it do?"

"Oh, stop your blubbering. You'll be fine," her mother had said as they arrived at the bus station in Center City Philadelphia. "Besides, it won't be forever—you can even take my old Gibson with you."

"You're giving me your guitar?"

"Hold onto it for me, and I'll send for you both as soon as I get established," Mary had promised. "Imagine it, Sweet Potato! My name on a billboard over I-95. Ray's gonna make that happen. We'll be set!"

"What if Mo doesn't want me there?" Antonia had asked.

She'd been about to board a Greyhound bus bound for Bordon, Pennsylvania, a town she'd never heard of, to stay with a man she'd never met.

Mary had seemed to think about it. "He probably doesn't," she'd said, handing Antonia her backpack. "But I've carried you all these years. It's his turn."

Her mother had kissed her cheek, told Antonia to be good, and walked away. Antonia had fought tears the whole trip, and they threatened to spill over when the driver said they'd reached Watertown, Pennsylvania—their final destination, and the closest bus stop to Bordon.

The transit station was small, dusty, and gray, but it was a welcome sight after being stuck on a bus for five hours. Antonia retrieved her mother's guitar and her small suitcase, and looked for a taxi stand. Few others had gotten off at this stop, so it was easy enough to get a cab.

"You visiting family?" The driver was chatty and had offered continuous narration as they made the trip from downtown Watertown to its outskirts.

Antonia didn't know how someone she'd never laid eyes on could be "family". Mary Bennette was all she'd ever known. From everything Antonia's mother had told her about Mo, she'd been lucky not to grow up around him.

Didn't stop her from shipping me off to live with him, though.

What would happen to her if Mo turned her away? A heavy weight settled on Antonia's chest, making it hard to breathe.

"Kid?"

"Yeah?" Antonia answered.

She met his gaze in the rearview mirror. He seemed friendly enough, but she hugged her backpack to her chest and went back to staring anxiously out the window. "I asked if you traveled all by yourself?" he said.

"Y-yeah." Antonia touched the outside pocket of her bag, relieved when she felt the outline of the prepaid cell phone her mother had given her. For emergencies.

"Can you put the radio on?"

The driver turned the knob, and a twangy voice emerged from the speakers. "I'm bettin' you don't like country."

Antonia shrugged. "I haven't heard much, but probably not."

"Well, I'm not listening to any rap," the guy groused. He fumbled with the tuner until a familiar set of chords caught Antonia's ear.

"Leave that on? I love this song."

"Sure, kid." He gave her a quick glance in the mirror. "You're a little young to know about these guys, though, aren't you?"

Antonia stuck out her chin. "I love classic rock. And I'm *not* a kid."

The man chuckled. "Yes, ma'am."

They passed a quarry and a stretch of farmland that softened the gray landscape, and Antonia thought maybe living there wouldn't be so bad. After all, it was only for a little while.

But they kept driving. Past the large farmhouses and green spaces. Past the colorful barns and the roadside diner and the old-timey gas station.

They drove until the streets narrowed and became uneven. Great dips in the asphalt shook the chassis, and the driver—who said his name was Arnie—would take a breath and apologize before continuing his narrative on the significance of the insignificant scenery.

"This area's where they have the farmers market."

Arnie explained that it was one of the oldest outdoor markets in the state, but to her it looked like one big dump. Wooden pallets lay stacked along the rows, topped with what looked to Antonia like garbage. Matted straw and rotting food.

Not a place she'd want to visit.

Despite its fresh air and open spaces, Bordon had rows and rows of boarded-up buildings and empty, overgrown lots. It wasn't home and would never be. Home was with her mom, one hundred and fifty-three miles south.

Once Mom gets everything worked out, she'll send for me.

The thought comforted Antonia a bit. Life would return to

normal, and this ugly, broken place would be nothing but another weird story to tell the kids at school. Why not? They already thought she was pretty weird anyway.

Arnie turned onto a street lined with buildings that had definitely seen better days. White vinyl siding covered most of the brick facades. On the corner sat a three-story building with a sign over the door that read MO'S TAVERN & BAR. The upstairs windows were dark.

Antonia had seen plenty of places like Mo's before. And though it was a slight step up from the crab shack she and her mom had been living above for the last few months, she'd give anything to go back there.

"Here you are, young lady." Arnie popped the trunk and got out to retrieve her stuff.

She hesitated, staring at the bar from the back seat of the taxi, unsure of what she'd find when she went inside. Memories of the night before flashed through her mind, and fear had her hand tightening on the door handle. Antonia considered telling Arnie to take her back to the bus station, but she didn't have enough money for a ticket back to Chester. After everything that had happened, she wasn't even sure if her mom had stayed there.

"Out you go," Arnie said, opening her door. Her bags sat waiting on the sidewalk. "I've got time for another long-haul fare before I quit for the day."

Antonia grabbed her backpack from the back seat and stepped gingerly onto the crumbling sidewalk. The air smelled different here. Metallic. She scrunched her nose.

"We're close to the train tracks—that's what you're smelling," Arnie provided. "Factories and trains. All that metal exposed to the moisture in the air means lots of rust."

Antonia's ears perked up. "We're near the water?"

"Walk six blocks in that direction, past the abandoned train tracks, and you'd have to swim across Lake Tasker." Arnie hooked his thumb toward a clump of trees in the near distance. "Not good for much more than dipping your toes in, though, unless you want to grow a third arm."

He held out his hand and Antonia looked up at him, confused.

Arnie's expression turned suspicious as he eyed the building. "You do have money, don't you? Or do I gotta go inside?"

"Oh!" Antonia reached into her book bag and pulled out one of the twenty-dollar bills her mom had given her. "Is this enough?"

The cabby groaned, but took the crumpled bill. "Hardly, but I'll cut you a break. You look like you could use one." He shoved the cash into his pocket and rounded the car, slamming the door once he was inside.

Antonia watched the cab pull away, her stomach tightening more the further the taillights got in the distance. A cloud of dust had kicked up in the cab's wake, and she had to shield her eyes. They stung and watered—because of the dust and *not* because she was crying. She was twelve, not two.

When the air cleared, Antonia wiped her eyes with the hem of her shirt and blinked. Wiped them again.

It didn't matter; the tears kept falling.

Her mother had really shipped her off to some weird little town that looked like the set from a dusty old movie. She half expected a tumbleweed to come rolling down the street. For the first time in her life, Antonia felt truly alone. But she didn't want to meet her father like this, wet and weepy and desperate.

Antonia rifled through her backpack for something to use on her dripping nose, relieved when she found a clean napkin. Balling it up, she shoved it back inside when she was done. She fished out her brush and tried to tackle her hair, determined not to go into the bar looking like an urchin.

"Hey."

Antonia shot up straight. Across the street, a boy stood staring at her. He wore ripped jeans and a T-shirt that read *Caspian's Ghost* in faded gold letters. With long, dark hair that fell into his eyes, he looked like a rock star, like he'd stepped right off the pages of *Rolling Stone*. He hadn't been standing there the whole time. Had he?

"You okay?" he asked as he walked slowly across the street without even bothering to look for traffic.

"I'm fine," Antonia replied, lifting her chin.

His gaze slid over her, sizing her up when he got closer. "Never seen you around her before."

Freckles dotted his nose and cheeks, and there was a small white scar across his left eyebrow. But that's not why Antonia smiled.

"Who are you, and what are you grinning at?"

"Antonia Bennette," she answered, the tight feeling in her stomach loosening a bit as she stared at the guitar strap slung across his chest and caught a peek of the lacquered wood resting against his back. "And you?"

The boy stopped in front of her, his gaze landing on the guitar case at her feet. He cocked his head to the side and looked up at her from under thick lashes. The corners of his mouth lifted, one green eye squinting.

"Sebastian Quigley," he said. "Nice to meet you, Antonia Bennette."

"Nice to meet you," she replied. "I like your shirt. They're pretty awesome."

He grabbed the hem and glanced down as if he'd forgotten which one he'd put on that morning. "What do you know about Caspian's Ghost?"

"I know they should have won the Grammy for Best Rock Album

this year." This was good. This was something familiar Antonia could latch onto. She breathed a sigh of relief.

Sebastian's eyes widened excitedly. "Right? They were robbed!"

"At least they picked up a bunch of new fans from their performance."

"Man, they killed it." Sebastian gave her an assessing look. "How old are you, kid?"

Why did everyone keep calling her that? "I'm not a kid, I just turned twelve."

"Well, I'm thirteen and a half," he said sagely. "Practically an adult."

"Thirteen doesn't mean you're an adult, Sebastian," she scoffed. "Just means you're a teenager."

"Whatever," he said dismissively. "Anyway, call me Seb. Everyone does—well, except my dad. What do your friends call you?"

The question hit her like a slap, and her easy smile dissolved. Antonia didn't have any friends. Her mother had moved them around too much.

"I'm just Antonia."

"Okay, *just Antonia*," Seb said with a teasing grin.

She rolled her eyes but found herself relaxing again despite everything. "What does your dad call you?"

Seb snorted. "Asshole."

"Oh. Well, are you one?"

He tapped his chin, thinking. "What's today?"

"Tuesday," Antonia supplied, frowning a little.

"Lucky you," Seb said, his eyes full of mischief. Reaching behind him, he pulled his guitar around—a weathered black Gibson acoustic. "I'm only an asshole on Mondays." He began strumming softly, tuning as he played. He nodded toward the case at her feet. "You play?"

"Yeah," she said. "A little."

Seb strummed a few chords.

"You need to tune that D."

"Yeah," he said, turning the peg for that string. "Good ear."

The sound of laughter split the air. Antonia glanced over her shoulder to find a man and woman walking out of the bar. She caught a glimpse of its dark interior before the door shut again.

"You going in *there*?" Seb asked, sounding skeptical. "You know that's a bar, right?"

"My...uh...my dad owns it," Antonia replied, turning back to him. "I'm moving in, I guess."

His lips twisted into a grimace. "Bummer." He looked up at the building and back at her. "You don't gotta go in right away, do ya?"

It only took a second for Antonia to decide. "No, not right away."

Seb's grin made her insides go all funny. "C'mon," he said, stowing his guitar and reaching for her suitcase. "I'll show you where I hang out. We can jam." At her hesitation, he paused, his brow furrowing. "Trust me?"

Antonia didn't know why, but she did trust him. She shouldered her backpack and handed him the suitcase. "Sure, but I'll carry my own guitar."

CHAPTER 1.

A MUSTY COMBINATION OF CAKED-ON blackout paint and well whiskey filled Toni's nostrils.

The Electric Unicorn was little more than a double-wide row-home in the Fishtown section of Philadelphia. The first floor had been transformed into a dive bar sometime during the 1960s. It wasn't much different than the run-down places Toni had grown up around.

Cheap drinks, faceless musicians, and loyal locals haunted the poorly lit tables and booths. Somehow, the Unicorn had survived the rash of gentrification that had transformed the neighborhood from a pockmarked, blue-collar holdout into a thriving hipster wonderland, complete with organic biergartens and vegan pizzerias.

"Hey, Toni."

She raised her head in time to see Axel Page step into the room. He was a regular on open mic night. Axel twirled the e-cigarette in his left hand and hoisted his backpack on his shoulder with the other.

"Not playing tonight?"

Axel shook his head. "Nah. Can't. I've got an audition for this theater gig in Old City."

"Theater?" Toni lifted an eyebrow.

"Yeah, some sort of one-man show."

"Sounds cool."

Axel nodded. "I thought so. Listen," he began, running long fingers through his shock of brown hair. "That asshole from last week is back."

Toni cursed under her breath. "I thought he'd been banned."

Axel grunted, his expressive blue eyes flashing. "You know Elton has a three-strike rule."

"'Unless they get physical,'" she quoted.

"Unless they get physical," Axel echoed. "Ignore him. Okay?"

Toni nodded, already backing off from her decision to try out some new arrangements.

"Have a good night, Toni."

"You too." She offered him a thin smile, her brain working overtime.

Hecklers came with the territory, but Toni loved the Unicorn because they didn't frequent the place. They weren't encouraged here, as they were in other venues. The Electric Unicorn was a safe space.

Well, usually.

The multicolored lights were hot and bright in her eyes, but she smiled at the smattering of applause that greeted her introduction to the tiny stage.

Toni lifted her weathered Fender and looped her guitar strap over her head. It settled into its usual place on her shoulder. She shifted it with her thumb to stop her bra strap from digging into her skin and tried to stretch the tension out of her neck. She could feel every pair of eyes on her, ready to pass judgment. On her skills. Her appearance. Her everything. *Ugh.*

Taking a moment to collect herself, Toni stared over the heads of the patrons. She focused on the bar's logo—a mural of an anthropomorphic unicorn rocking out on an electric guitar—and turned up the volume on the guitar enough to strum out a few chords and check her tuning. After a quick run to warm up her fingers, she was good to go.

"Freebird!"

A few patrons laughed, and Toni gave a small salute because it was *such* an original joke. Maybe he'd take it easy on her tonight.

"You gonna play some Tracy Chapman for us? Or...or how about some Beyoncé?" he called out. "Show us some moves, sister thang!"

Or not.

Toni squinted in the direction of the disruption and caught the exasperated glower of Elton Pepple, the Electric Unicorn's owner-slash-manager. His scowl, and a very stabby finger, were aimed at a guy sitting at the bar.

The guy held up his hands, apparently pleading his case.

Elton looked at her and shook his head. She offered him a wan smile, once again questioning why she'd accepted his offer of a residency. Oh, right. The money. There weren't many steady gigs in Philly with a guaranteed payday. Toni knew how lucky she was, but every time she stood under the lights, they burned a little.

"Now or never," Toni muttered to herself as she stepped up to the microphone. "Uh, hey, Unicorn."

On cue, a screech of feedback burst from the speakers. Toni jumped back, shielding her eyes as she squinted in the direction of the sound board tucked in the front corner of the bar.

Luca, the sound person, waved and gave her a thumbs-up.

Heckler dude's laugh rang out. Great. Not that she needed to impress him, but it would be nice to shut him up.

Approaching with more caution, Toni stepped back to the mic and smiled. "Let's try this again."

A few people laughed with her, and Toni exhaled some of the apprehension that had coiled at the base of her spine. The idea of performing in front of a room full of strangers always filled her with dread. Toni loved to play, and she played often—in the studio, or sometimes for a few friends. But situations like this unnerved her because, once she was under the lights, it was too easy to get caught up in it. Too easy to accept the adoration, even to expect it. Too easy to let the audience get under your skin and tear you down when things didn't go their way.

Toni took a deep breath. She was too much in her head tonight, and she didn't want to let Elton down. She had this.

"What's up, Electric Unicorn? My name is Toni B."

"Tone-eeee!" A man yelled her name from the back of the room and lifted his glass to her. Ah, that would be Sticks, one of the Unicorn's regulars.

This place wasn't much, but it was hers.

Toni tried on another smile, which quivered at the edges. *Ugh, stupid nerves.* She nodded at Sticks and twisted the volume knob on her guitar up to seven with shaky fingers.

Strumming a fat F-sharp chord, Toni closed her eyes and let it ring out for several seconds before stepping on the pedal of her loop station.

A bass drum track she'd recorded earlier in the week thumped out a 4/4 beat, and Toni launched into the opening riff of Alice in Chains' "Man in the Box," a move that seemed to make Sticks sit up a bit straighter in his seat. Recording the guitar loop, she pressed the pedal again and layered another guitar part over it, something that never failed to draw the audience in.

Sure enough, when Toni let her gaze sweep over the Unicorn's crowd, many—including the heckler—were leaning forward, their heads bobbing. She had their attention. Good.

Toni sang her version of the melancholic rock anthem, using the smoky quality of her voice to infuse it with a bit of soul and turning it into a pseudo torch song. By the time she finished, a few people had abandoned their seats altogether in favor of standing at the foot of the stage.

She fought against her need to put more distance between her and these strangers, completely fine with them loving the performance. After all, it's what she'd come to give them. But so often, people wanted more. And more wasn't something she was willing or able to give.

For the next forty-five minutes, Toni let the songs breathe for her. She let her guitar be her voice, let the music put her soul on display for a little while. And then, before she knew it, it was over.

After her set, Elton was all smiles. Applause and whistles filled the air, and Toni gave the small crowd a wave.

"Fuck me, little girl, you sure can play!" Elton grabbed Toni's shoulders as soon as she stepped offstage. "I keep telling you this hole-in-the-wall is too tiny for a talent as big as yours."

"Hey! Don't bad-mouth the Unicorn." Toni headed back up the steps toward the club's only storage-slash-dressing room. "This is home, you know."

Elton grinned and wrapped an arm around her shoulders for another quick squeeze. "It warms the cockles of me heart to hear you say that, love. It really does." His grip on her tightened with his enthusiasm, and Toni couldn't hide the grimace this time.

Elton immediately loosened the embrace and let her go with an apologetic smile.

Toni was *not* a hugger.

Fortunately, Elton had picked up on that pretty quickly and had stuck to awkward back pats and shoulder squeezes since. More often than not, he refrained from touching Toni at all. She appreciated that about him, which was why she put up with his delusions about her grandeur.

"I keep telling ya, you're too good for this place," Elton said again as he wrapped up a stray cord and set it on top of a speaker.

"Not that I'm complaining. I love having you here, but it's only a matter of time before you realize you're cut out for more."

"I bet you say that to all your regular acts."

Elton opened the door to the back room. "Only the pretty ones who can shred as well as you do, darling. I swear to God, if I wasn't watching you with me own eyes, I'd think you were a bloke."

Toni stopped and gave him a pointed look.

Backing into the room, Elton held up his hands in surrender. "Now, before you go and lecture me on girl power, I'm only saying. In the twenty-three years I've been in the pub biz, I've never heard a…" He paused, as if searching for the right words. "Lady, especially one as young as you, rock as hard as you do. Except maybe that one who plays in the Lillys. Candi something or other? Now, there's a real rock guitarist," he gushed. "Usually, you girls only play—y'know—strummy bits."

Toni smirked. "Strummy bits?"

"Quiet folk songs and the like. I can't think of too many women that can wail."

Her jaw dropped. "Uh, Sister Rosetta Tharpe?" Tony held up a hand and started ticking off her influences. "Barbara Lynn? Lady Bo?"

Elton frowned with obvious confusion. Of course, he had no idea who they were.

"Sister Rosetta practically invented rock and roll," Toni informed him. Elton looked skeptical. "Okay, how about Joan Jett?"

"Ah, well, she's an exception, isn't she?"

Shaking her head, Toni dropped onto one of the ottomans. "YouTube is your friend, Elton." She pulled a cloth from her back pocket and began to wipe down her guitar. "Anyway, I heard the Lillys aren't real musicians. I bet it isn't even Candi playing on their EP. They probably brought in a bunch of hired guns."

"Hired guns don't get multi-record deals with YMI Records, my dear," Elton scoffed.

"If they look like that, they do," Toni bit back before her brain caught up. "Wait, they signed with YMI?"

He walked over to the mini fridge, muttering something about Toni not keeping up with the industry, and grabbed two bottles of water. He tossed one to her, and she caught it with one hand.

"Rumor has it, they were discovered in a no-name place like this," he said.

Toni wiped her mouth with the back of her hand and squared off to face him. "Yeah, well, I'm no Cinderella, if that's what you're trying to get at. No Prince Charmings in my future."

"Stranger things have happened," Elton said sagely.

"Not to people like me."

"Talent is talent, even when you try to hide it under a bushel," Elton countered.

Toni was over this conversation. She set the bottle aside and picked up her guitar strap to fold it.

"Fancy," Elton commented, pointing at the braided leather strap. "Looks older than you. Where'd you get it?"

"It was a gift from...a guy I used to play with," Toni said. "I thought I'd lost it, but I found it in a box the other day."

"S'nice. Can I see it?"

Toni wordlessly handed it over. Forty-six inches of braided cowhide, the strap was the only thing Toni really had left of her old life—that and the 1963 Gibson ES-335 that still hung on the wall of her father's bar.

When she'd arrived in Bordon, Mo had taken one look at the guitar and ripped it right out of her hands. He called it his insurance policy. The cherry-red semihollow body was worth a nice chunk of change, and Mo seemed to think her mother owed him. Or maybe he thought Toni did.

Toni worried he would sell Minx—the nickname she'd given the Gibson—and would sneak the old guitar out of the bar and use her to try out a new solo or work out an old one.

"By the way, was that a Caspian's Ghost song you snuck into your set tonight?" Elton handed the strap back to her. "Surprised you even know them. They're well before your time."

"What can I say? I grew up on the classics," Toni offered absently as she stared down at the braided leather relic that still triggered memories of rusting railroad ties, broken, weed-riddled asphalt, and...him.

ANTONIA, AGE 15—SEB, AGE 16

"Play that again."

"What?" Antonia continued to noodle on the guitar, a random solo from an old Ghost song.

"That riff." Seb bent his knee to turn toward her. The sun was high in the sky and danced in the highlights of his long, dark hair.

Antonia stared at him. Gosh, he was pretty.

"Well?" He nudged her, eyes searching her face. "That's one of Christian K's solos, isn't it?" he asked, oblivious as always.

Blinking, Antonia tried to focus and retrace the steps her fingers had made on the strings.

Closing her eyes, she let muscle memory take over.

"That right there," Seb said after she made a simple run up the fretboard. "Play it again."

She did.

"Slow it down a little."

As she did, the song coalesced into the familiar tune. Antonia opened her eyes to find Seb smiling, his gaze trained on her fingers and the guitar cradled in her hands as she repeated the phrase over and over, each time with more feeling than the last, recalling every bit she could of the famous solo.

"Goddamn, Nia," Seb whispered, his voice full of something like awe. His green eyes flashed up to meet hers. "That's amazing. How do you *do* that? You're...amazing." He picked up his own guitar and nodded toward hers. "Teach me?"

Toni had thought Seb might be her Prince Charming, until he'd left town without a word. So much for their dream of getting out of Bordon together.

"Those girls remind me of the Ghost a bit, actually." Elton's voice snapped Toni back to the present. "It's that raw edge they have. Like they don't give a toss what you think, they're gonna play."

She frowned at him. "Who?"

"The Lillys." Elton gave her a quizzical look. "She may be a bit dodgy, but that Candi can play the hell out of a guitar."

"Hmmm," Toni mused, shoving the strap, and the memories it had conjured, into her case. "If that's true, I may have to rethink everything I thought I knew about them."

"You do have a tendency to judge a cake by its frosting," Elton chided. Maybe he had a point.

The band's namesake, Lilly Langeland, looked more like a Nordic runway model than the lead singer of a rock band, but Toni could appreciate her raw vocals and intensity. And Candi's flaming-pink hair and over-the-top, sexually suggestive way of playing made her something of a cliché. But if it really *was* her playing the more intricate songs on the band's rough recordings, then Candi Fair, actually Candace Fairmount, socialite and heiress to one of the country's biggest oil fortunes, might be one of the best guitarists Toni had ever heard.

"The Lillys don't really fit in with what YMI's been doing lately."

"Maybe they're hoping to return to form," Elton replied, shrugging. "Not a bad way to start, bringing those girls on board. Introducing them—that sound—to the rest of the world."

"Huh," was Toni's eloquent reply. She made a mental note to take a closer listen to the Lillys. Maybe she'd incorporate one of their songs into her set.

"They've got that *it* factor," Elton proclaimed as he perched on the arm of the beat-up, mismatched sectional that occupied most of the space. "Mark my words, they'll go far."

Better them than her. "You're probably right, as always," she offered begrudgingly.

Elton nodded, evidently confident in his role as armchair talent scout. "You've got it, too, love."

Toni laid her guitar in the case and fastened it shut. Shrugging out of her denim jacket, she grimaced at the dampness in the material. She needed a shower. "Yeah, well, I'm good where I am, for now."

He looked affronted. "Why? You have everything it takes to be a star."

Toni sighed. "For the hundredth time, I'm not interested in being front and center."

"Nonsense," he scoffed. "You're on my stage three nights a week."

"Because *I like it* here," Toni reminded him. "It's comfortable. Like an old pair of socks."

"How flattering," Elton deadpanned.

Toni smiled and gave his arm the briefest of touches to show her sincerity. "I mean it. I don't need throngs of adoring fans or the pressure that comes with their expectations. Fame is a...a trap."

The truth was that it terrified her. Fame was as addictive as any drug. She'd seen firsthand what her mother had done in its pursuit, dragging her kid to dive bars and one-star motels. Doing anything to see her name at the top of the bill, including tossing aside her own daughter in exchange for a shot at stardom. Little Antonia had bought into her mother's dream, but it had shattered the moment she set foot on that bus bound for Bordon. Toni wanted no part of it now.

She offered Elton what she hoped was a conciliatory smile. "Not everyone wants to be a household name."

Elton gave her a begrudging nod, but Toni could see he wasn't convinced.

"If a band like the Lillys can be handed a golden ticket, why not you? Whatever you want to tell yourself, you come alive when you're on my stage. You were born for this, my darling."

Toni shrugged. It wasn't anything Elton hadn't said to her before.

"I do like performing," she admitted. "But I *love* recording. I love arranging, producing. That's what I want to do. In fact, I have my first big-label session coming up. And you know my goal is to own my own studio."

"One doesn't preclude the other," Elton said. "In fact, getting a little notoriety might help you achieve that goal. You could earn a wad of cash and use it to fuel your dreams."

"Maybe," Toni conceded, if only to get him to back off. Having lived with a father who couldn't have cared less what she did with her life, she'd often wished for someone who gave a damn, but Elton was a lot to take at times.

"One of these days," Elton said, "you're going to see yourself the way I do. The way most people do when they hear you play." He placed a gentle hand on the top of her head, giving it a light pat before dropping his arm to his side. "I only hope I'm still alive to see it."

"Oh, please," Toni huffed as she got to her feet, pulling him into a quick, tight hug. "You'll outlive us all, you silly Brit."

Elton laughed and ran a hand over the silvering coils of his once-dark-brown hair. "You're probably right. I'm far too old and saggy to die young and pretty."

CHAPTER 2.

TONI HAD LEARNED, HARD AND fast, the rules of being a session musician. A hired gun. Learn the songs, nail the gig, and keep your damn opinions to yourself. This was not her first time playing in someone else's sandbox.

So why, *oh why*, had she opened her big stupid mouth?

"I don't hear it." Jerry Gant, a veritable icon in Philadelphia's tight-knit folk-rock scene, folded his arms and looked at Toni as if she'd pulled out a can of lighter fluid and set fire to his custom-made Gibson. "Run it back again."

Tossing a look of sympathy her way, Richie Michaelson—engineer and heir apparent of Phactory Sound Studios—hit Play and turned up the volume on the monitors.

Shit, shit, shit. She really couldn't fuck this up. A hired gun was supposed to be a fixer, a clutch musician who could step into any situation and deliver on demand. She'd spent the last few years working her way onto the studio circuit. Hard for any musician, but even harder for someone like her.

Richie had brought her in for several local sessions, and not once had the words *not bad for a girl* ever dropped from his mouth. Toni held her breath as he pressed Play. Again, something sour hit her ear. She looked at Jerry, but he seemed steadfast. Was it possible he really couldn't hear it? She glanced at Richie, whose face remained impassive, as always.

"I could be wrong," Toni hedged. She wasn't, though. Something on the track grated on her ears like nails on a chalkboard.

"It's worth another listen," the engineer said. Toni knew what he was doing, and she was grateful for the silent support.

The intro to the midtempo, alt-folk ballad poured through the speakers for the third time in a row. It reminded Toni of the songs her mother used to sing in bars and small clubs up and down the East Coast, back when Toni traveled with her as a child, but with a contemporary twist. The song didn't really fit what she knew of Jerry's legendary sound.

Acoustic guitars were richly layered over a muted upright bass, cycling through the opening chords until the vocals kicked in. It was that transition, from intro to verse, that had caught Toni's attention. Something wasn't quite right, but she couldn't yet put her finger on it. Despite that, she'd called the room's attention to it. That had brought the entire session to a halt—a session that was already well over time and budget.

This was bad. But Toni couldn't let it go, not if her name was going to be attached.

"There. Stop it there," she instructed Richie with a light touch on his shoulder. In for a penny. "Something's clashing."

"Again," Jerry barked, striding over to peer at the screens.

Richie played the track from the beginning. This time, Toni saw his head cock to the side when the song got to the part that had been bugging her. He stopped the playback.

"Right there." Toni pointed to a spot on the large display monitors. The sound waves etched up and down each track showed the spikes and valleys of each instrument. "Someone's guitar is out of tune."

"Yeah, it's one of the acoustics," Richie said. "Good ear."

Jerry turned and looked at Toni as if seeing her in a new light, his gaze narrowing as he studied her.

This was another thing Toni had learned to take with grace. People didn't expect much from her, especially when they first met. She was attractive enough, sure. Toni wasn't so naive as to think she didn't luck out in the genes department. With her thick black hair, light-brown eyes, and dimpled cheeks, Toni knew she had some appeal. But cute, curvy girls were a dime a dozen in the music industry.

Cute, curvy Black women who could play the guitar like Prince and knew the difference between Matchbox Twenty and Twenty One Pilots? Not so much.

So, yeah. Toni understood the expression on Jerry's face.

"Well, *I* don't hear anything," he sneered.

Screw it. It was his goddamned song.

"Could be me," Toni offered, glancing down at Richie.

His mouth twisted into the barest of grimaces, but Toni could see the wheels turning behind his ice-blue eyes.

"How about I drop out each of the acoustic guitar tracks and we play the intro on a loop?" he suggested. "I'll add them back in one at a time, just to be sure."

Richie was one of the good guys. Yay for that.

Jerry groaned. "Whatever, hurry up. I'm not made of money."

Ironic coming from a guy who had just signed another multimillion-dollar deal with YMI.

Jerry stalked over to the plush suede sofa that sat against the longest wall of the control room and plopped down next to his bassist, producer, and sometime mouthpiece Elias Crown.

"Go on, loop it," Elias said. He was old school, from an era when the labels and studios were like automated factories, churning out hit after hit, and the casting couch was a rite of passage for aspiring artists. His eyes raked over Toni in a leer. "Let's see if there's anything there," he added. "Or if this…young woman is angling for more time to get her bearings."

Toni's eyes flashed to Elias's. Cretin. She didn't want to give him the satisfaction of knowing he'd gotten to her. The song was simple, easy to navigate, and in desperate need of some flavor. Flavor she could provide without even breaking a sweat.

"I don't need more time," she said, keeping her voice as even as she could.

Elias must have interpreted her disgust as something else entirely because a slow smile spread across his chapped lips. "You sure?" He thought he'd caught her out.

"I can knock it out, no problem, if you mute the other guitars," Toni challenged, keeping her gaze locked with Elias's. "That *off* chord is distracting."

"Whew! I'm sure glad Jerry here isn't too put out to hear you say his guitar is out of tune." Elias grinned.

Oh, hell.

Toni felt the blood draining from her face. "I never said—"

"Let's do that, then. Shit," Jerry complained loudly, pointing to Richie. "Have her do Vinny's part so we can wrap this up. Christ," he added under his breath. "Damn fool has already cost us a day, and now we've got to pay this little girl to do his job. The label wants the rough tracks tonight."

Toni bit her tongue and turned to Richie. "You want me in the booth?"

"Yeah." Richie stood and gestured for her to lead the way.

Toni picked up her guitar and made her way into the tiny room. It was perfectly suited for a vocalist or single instrument. "This is new," she said as she leaned her guitar against the carpeted wall. The lingering odor of sawdust and varnish greeted her deep breath.

"Yeah, sorry about the state in here," Richie offered. "I finally convinced my dad to let me repurpose one of the disused storage rooms into an iso booth."

Richie set an amp in the corner behind a floor mic that would capture her performance. It hummed in anticipation.

"No worries." She took the headphones he handed to her and hung them on the music stand.

Richie plugged her in and made some final adjustments. "I know I normally set you up in the live room or even in the control room…" He nodded toward the men in the other room. "But there are fewer assholes in here."

Toni smiled. "Thanks."

"Listen, don't pay the old guard any mind." Richie returned her smile but there was a note of bitterness in his words. "That was a good catch. It would have been hell to fix tonight, with the teeny bit of time I have. You've made my job a little easier, as always."

"Cool." Toni exhaled a sigh of relief. "I'm glad. I sure don't want to screw things up for you, or for the Phactory."

"Speaking of making my life easier, you give any more thought to my offer?"

"You were serious about that?"

"You think I'd joke about asking you to be my partner?" Richie asked, grinning.

Wrapping up a late session, Toni had rambled on to him about her dream of owning a place like the Phactory. Richie had surprised her with the offer. For a measly fifty grand, she could buy her way into living history. Too bad it was about thirty-five grand more than she had to her name.

"When my dad retires—*if* he ever retires," he added, adjusting the overhead mic, "I want to make the Phactory my own, you know?"

"Sure, I get that," Toni assured him. "It's one thing to inherit a legacy, and another to make one of your own."

"Speaking from experience?"

Toni dropped her gaze. "Something like that."

"Let me guess… You're the secret love child of your namesake." He smirked at Toni's confused expression. "Tony Bennett?"

"Ah," she said, rolling her eyes. "Good one, and actually kinda original. Usually, people just ask if it's my real name or if my parents were some kind of weird superfans."

"Is it?"

"Yep, well, Antonia."

"Pretty," Richie said, smiling. He pulled a cable from the wall and uncoiled it, seemingly on autopilot. "Being a Michaelson in Philly, in music, they always ask about the Phactory. Tell me what a legendary space it is, as if I didn't know. Or they wax on and on about my dad."

"I bet," Toni said as she checked her tuning. "And he's not eager to kick back and relax? Let you take over the reins?"

Richie groaned. "He doesn't think I'm ready."

"Seriously? You?" Toni frowned. "You've been doing this forever. And you're good—not that I have a ton of in-house experience."

"Thanks. I learned at the foot of the master," Richie said as if quoting someone. He plugged a lead into the monitor station and double-checked the connection. "You'd think he'd trust that he's trained me well enough, since he taught me almost everything I know."

"You'd think," she agreed.

"Well, fucking this gig up would have set me back years with him," he said, smiling. "So, thanks for saving my ass."

"Happy to help."

"You could help even more by coming on board. Save me from having to team up with someone just like my dad." He looked so hopeful.

"Trust me, I'm…I'm flattered that you would even make me an offer like that. And I wish I could," Toni said.

"Don't say no yet. We'll talk more about it later, okay? Anyway..." After checking the setup one more time, Richie turned to go but looked back. "I know we're on the clock, but don't rush it. I can go fiddle with some knobs for a few minutes if you need time to get your head in the track."

"Nope, I'm good to go." She wasn't. She needed to calm her racing thoughts. Part owner of Phactory Sound? Her? In what universe?

Richie stared at her for a long moment and Toni began to squirm. "What?"

He squinted at her. "Sorry, I'm curious. Did you know it was Jerry's guitar you called out in there?"

Toni shook her head. "Not at the time."

"Didn't think so," Richie said, scratching the stubble on his chin. He had a youthful face, but his pale-olive skin crinkled a little around his eyes and mouth. "Jerry can be a bit of a prima donna, but don't let him intimidate you. I doubt he'd blacklist you or anything like that."

Toni's stomach dropped. *Holy crap*. That possibility hadn't even crossed her mind.

What had she done? Because that was *totally* something a person like Jerry would do. Or Elias. *Shit, shit, shit.*

Perhaps sensing her panic, Richie slowly and lightly touched her shoulder, giving her plenty of time to object to the contact. Toni was grateful for it and put a mental green check next to Richie's name. She'd felt like she was about to fly out of her skin. The simple touch grounded her.

"Don't sweat it." Richie's smile was kind. "You were absolutely right. And if I'd sent it up to New York like that, it would have cost me. Old Jerry in there would have to book more studio time, spending even more of the label's money. And my dad would have had my head."

He squeezed her shoulder before letting go.

"We've all got someone to impress," he added. "You did good."

"Er, thanks." The volcano bubbling in Toni's stomach eased to a simmer.

"You sure you're good to go?"

She exhaled a heavy breath. "Yeah. Let's finish this."

Richie's smile widened. "Cool, cool. See you on the other side."

He winked and left the booth, closing the two doors behind him and sealing her in a sudden silence.

It's not enough to be good. Seb's voice echoed from a long-lost memory. *You gotta be unforgettable.* Ever since her conversation with Elton, Seb had crowded Toni's thoughts. She wasn't sure how to feel about that.

She ran her fingers along the leather strap that had once been his. Toni had kept it both as a reminder of where she'd come from and as a warning of who to trust.

Lifting her guitar, she slipped the strap over her head and settled it comfortably on her shoulder. The guitar itself wasn't anything special—just an old Stratocaster she'd picked up at a pawn shop—but Toni knew she could make it sing.

She waited for Richie to turn on her monitor. After a quick tune-up, she fit the headphones over her ears, leaving one half off so she could hear herself in the booth.

For now, there was only the hum from the amp and the sound of herself swallowing down her nerves. She stared through the double-paned glass that separated the control room from the isolation booth and waited.

"All set?" Richie's voice in the headphones startled her out of the recurring daydream.

After giving him the thumbs-up to start the track, Toni tried to clear her mind of any distractions.

The song was pretty standard, but the chorus was hook-laden and sticky. An undeniable earworm. With the acoustic guitars muted, the rest of the instrumentation was tight. Toni closed her eyes and gave herself over to it.

Over the next thirty minutes, she earned her three-hundred-dollar session fee. She let her instincts take over, finding spaces between the other instruments to leave her mark. A riff here, a run there. Toni got lost in the music and knocked out take after take, giving them all the variation they could possibly need or want.

Spent, and damp with sweat, Toni opened her eyes and looked through the glass.

Jerry's nose was buried in his phone, and Elias's back was to her. The only face she could see was Richie's, and his expression was inscrutable. Finally, he looked up from the console and gave her a thumbs-up accompanied by a half grin.

Toni unplugged her guitar and made her way back to the control room. When she pushed through the door, Elias and Jerry were whispering furiously in the far corner.

Richie smiled at her.

"I'll run what I think was your best take, so you can listen." He slid his chair across the hardwood floor to the other end of the expansive console.

Toni tried her best not to eavesdrop on the conversation across the room, but a few words caught her ears.

Amateur.

Chick.

Toni's shoulders sagged. She'd blown it. Her first big-label session would likely be her last. Worse, she'd messed things up for Richie. Goddammit. When would she ever learn to shut up?

The beginning of the song washed over her, and it wasn't until her first solo riff kicked in that Toni tore her attention away from Jerry and Elias.

It wasn't a bad take. Actually, it was pretty freaking good.

Richie let the entire song run, and each time Toni's guitar chimed in, a little kernel of pride burst in her chest.

"Good stuff," Richie murmured loud enough for Toni to hear.

She knew the caliber of people that had recorded at the Phactory. To have a Michaelson engineer's approval and admiration was no small thing, but Toni was yanked out of the moment by Jerry's ever-increasing volume.

"I don't fucking care. Get her out of here!" He whipped out his phone and stabbed furiously at the keyboard.

Elias patted Jerry on the back and walked over to Toni.

Standing, Richie positioned himself near her side, grabbing a bottle of water from the counter behind her as a cover for what was clearly a protective move.

Part of Toni bristled at the idea of needing his protection, but another part was grateful for the show of solidarity.

Elias held out his hand for her to shake, his palm clammy when she reluctantly accepted. "Thanks *so much* for coming in on such short notice."

He pulled his wallet from his back pocket and thumbed off a couple of twenty-dollar bills. Folding them, he grabbed her wrist and pressed the money into Toni's hand. "You can go," he said. "Buy yourself something pretty."

Confused, Toni looked back and forth between Elias and Richie before peering over Elias's shoulder to where Jerry stood on the other side of the room, his phone to his ear.

"You're dismissing me?" Toni looked at Elias, caught somewhere between rage and desperation. "If you didn't like that take, we could listen to another." She turned to Richie and he nodded, already set to back her up. "Play the fourth one, maybe. It felt good."

"It won't be necessary," Elias said, a smug smile on his face.

"We've decided to go with someone else. In fact, he'll be here in a few minutes."

He'll be here in a few minutes. Not only were they replacing her; they were bringing in a guy.

Because of course they were.

Toni bit the inside of her cheek.

"Are you sure we have time for that?" His face reddening, Richie crossed his arms and faced Elias. He spoke loudly enough that Jerry could definitely hear him. "I need to at least get some rough mixes done before I send these files up to New York, and they want them by the open of business tomorrow."

"You'll just have to work through the night," Elias offered, sounding like he couldn't care less. "I can probably get you an extension 'til noon."

Richie carded his fingers through his light-blond hair. He stalked around Elias and went over to Jerry. "Toni's parts were perfect," he said, clearly fighting to keep his tone neutral. "There's plenty there to choose from, and the track sounds good except for a few spots. Which I can easily clean up. I honestly don't think you need to waste time and money bringing another body in here."

Jerry narrowed his eyes as he pulled the phone away from his ear. "I'm sorry. Are *you* producing this album?"

Richie's lips thinned into a taut line. Toni watched as his hairline turned white as the blood rushed north. A vein at his temple throbbed visibly.

Then, with a furtive, apologetic glance toward her, he took his seat at the board and made the only decision he could. "Just an observation."

"Quick will be here any moment," Elias informed him. "I'm sure we'll get a take we can actually use out of him."

Jerry finally turned to Toni, and she fought not to flinch. There was honest-to-God malice in his eyes. "Sorry, sweetheart," he said, his voice saccharine sweet. "You simply don't have what we're looking for."

A dick, you mean.

Toni gave Jerry a quick nod. Swallowing her retort burned like acid. "Thanks for giving me the chance," she forced herself to say.

She packed up her stuff, eager to get the hell out of there. Screw this. Screw him. And screw Quick, whoever that was. *Ugh.* She was never going to get anywhere in this world, not with people like Jerry and Elias holding the keys to the kingdom.

Gathering her things as fast as she could, she thanked Richie for trying.

"Sorry," he said as he walked her to the door. "Jerry's an asshole, but I didn't think it would go down like this. I should have. I'd tell him to fuck off, but..."

Toni gaped at him. "No! No, don't do that. No use in both of us getting kicked to the curb."

"If it makes you feel any better, Jerry apparently threw a fit when he found out I was running his session and not my dad." Richie's jaw flexed, the color rising in his cheeks again. "My fucking *dad* had to convince him I was up to the task. I'm thirty-three years old! Been behind the desk since I was in grade school."

"That's ridiculous." Though it did make her feel marginally better.

"Tell me about it," he huffed. "Can't wait 'til I have full control over this place. Then I can tell people like Jerry Gant to go fuck themselves. Bring the Phactory into the twenty-first century. You know?"

Toni nodded. "You're living my dream."

Richie eyed her. "You could be living it too." Toni chuckled. "I'm serious."

Toni gestured around them. "There's so much magic in these walls, I'd live here if I could, but I don't have that kind of money."

"How much you got?" Richie was still smiling, but Toni could hear a hint of desperation in his voice. "Seriously, though, being a partner at the Phactory would shut assholes like Jerry Gant up real fast. Get your name out there."

It was such a dangling carrot, and she did have her savings. Maybe... "Would twenty thousand dollars get me in?"

Richie winced. "Sorry. I need at least fifty. I'd have to bring in one of Dad's people otherwise."

Hope, which had flashed its boarding pass and was ready to take flight, came crashing down in a ball of fiery disappointment. Still, the idea of owning a piece of Philly's musical legacy lit a different kind of fire inside her. Forget moving in on the ground floor, this would be like moving straight into the penthouse.

There's always Minx. Toni's stomach soured at the mere thought of selling the Gibson. She wasn't sure she could part with her. Too many dreams were tied up in that hunk of wood and metal. Too many memories. "Let me see what I can do," she heard herself say, not knowing what the hell she could possibly do, short of robbing a bank.

Richie's entire face lit up. "Really? Oh man, we would make an awesome team."

"No promises, but I'll definitely look into it." She was relatively healthy. How much did kidneys go for these days?

Richie nodded. "Understood, but don't take too long. We've had offers to buy into the place, though none from anyone that shares my vision."

"You really think we'd make a good team?"

"Hell yeah." He grinned and held up his hand for a high five.

Buoyed by his enthusiasm, Toni lifted her hand to smack Richie's palm. "All right," he said. "I'm psyched. This'll help me get through the rest of this session."

Behind her, the door chimed.

Richie's grin melted away as he looked over Toni's shoulder. "Speak of the devil, looks like that Quick guy is here."

This was her cue to leave. She bent to grab her gear.

"Are you here for Jerry?" Richie asked the newcomer.

"Yeah, I got here as soon as I could," a deep, rumbling voice answered.

Toni froze.

Straightening, she slowly turned around and had to swallow the hysterical laughter that wanted to burst from her throat. Because of course.

She'd managed to go seven years without so much as a glimpse of Sebastian Quigley. It was as if that stupid guitar strap had conjured him up from her memories.

Seb hadn't changed much. A little taller, a little broader, and a little worn around the edges, he was still inequitably, infuriatingly handsome. Relief flooded her veins. Seb was alive! And, by all appearances, hale and hearty. But that relief was quickly burned away by white-hot rage because he'd left her in Bordon without so much as a backwards glance.

Toni stared unblinking as all the color drained from his face. He looked like he'd seen a ghost.

Seb's mouth went slack. "Ni...*Nia*?" It was barely above a whisper, but he may as well have slapped her. That nickname...

His eyes roamed her face, taking her in. She hadn't seen that expression in years but recognized it immediately. It was the way his nostrils widened ever so slightly, the way he searched her gaze.

When he inched forward, Toni jerked back as if she'd been stung by a wasp. She crashed right into Richie, and the engineer put a hand on her back to steady her.

"You okay?" He gave her a gentle push until she got her feet under her.

"Sorry," she sputtered. The guitar case in Seb's hand brought her back to the reality of the situation, and a sudden realization struck her.

"You?" Toni cursed the waver in her voice. "*You're* my replacement?"

Seb's brow furrowed. He looked up at Richie and then back down to her.

"I'm, uh… I'm here for Jerry Gant," he spluttered.

"They're waiting for you through here." Richie opened the door and gestured at Seb. "If you don't mind, we need to get moving on this."

A combination of outrage and embarrassment made her want to melt into the floor. Years had passed since the day he'd abandoned her, and now he had shown up—only to take her place.

Seb narrowed his eyes, then looked at Toni. "Wait, were you supposed to…?" He exhaled a labored breath as if he'd run a few blocks to get there. "I didn't know. Nia, I swear, I…"

Oh hell no. This was not happening. Not right now, and not right here.

Toni tightened her grip on her gear and strode forward, using her guitar case to steer Seb out of the way.

"Wait!" he called after her as she power-walked down the hallway. "Can we talk for a sec?"

Nope. That was definitely not happening. Toni went as fast as her legs could take her without breaking into a sprint. "C'mon, man, we're on the clock," she heard Ritchie call out to Seb.

Toni burst through the Phactory's front doors and stopped on the sidewalk to catch her breath.

Richie's stalling tactics didn't work for long, and Seb pushed through the door after her.

Toni frantically hailed a passing cab, thankful when it immediately swerved over to the curb.

"Nia!"

Toni yanked open the door and shoved her gear into the back seat before the car had come to a complete stop.

"Drive," she gasped as she squeezed into the seat next to her stuff.

"Whoa there," the driver said. "Where's the fire?"

"Can you please wait a second?" Seb said, grabbing the door before Toni could shut it in his face.

"You better get back in there," she spat out, tapping at her empty wrist. "You're on the clock, remember?"

Seb crouched down. "Just...gimme a minute, will ya?"

"If we're going to sit here, I gotta start the meter," the cabby said.

"We're not," Toni said at the same time Seb piped in with "That's fine."

He pulled some crumpled bills from his jacket pocket and stuck them through the opening in the partition. With a shrug, the driver took the cash. Sellout.

Toni glared at Seb. "I don't need your money." Her voice sounded icy to her own ears, and Seb flinched. *Good.*

He rubbed the back of his neck. "Nia, I didn't know you were working with Jerry. Hell, I had no idea you were even here! I got a call to come salvage the session."

Toni rolled her eyes. Salvage indeed. "Why *would* you know I was here? Why would you know anything about me?"

He sighed and cast his gaze down the street.

Without Toni's permission, her eyes wandered over him. From his artfully tousled hair, down the too-tight white tee, over the painted-on jeans and the distressed leather jacket that was probably brand new and cost a fortune. He looked good.

The realization that she could still think that after the way he'd abandoned her just made her angrier.

Seb turned to look at her, and there it was—the intense green gaze that had haunted her dreams every night for years. But instead of her blood running hot as it had when she was a teenager, a chill snaked its way through her veins.

"Can you stick around for a bit?" he asked, his expression so achingly familiar she had to turn away. "I'd really, uh…"

"I have to go."

Out of the corner of her eye, she saw Seb nod. "Okay, but—"

"Do me a favor," Toni cut him off. She turned to look at him, choosing to ignore the impulse to read him for filth. She wasn't that lonely little girl anymore, and he no longer had any power over her. "Get back in there and wrap up the session so Richie doesn't get blamed for the delay."

There were more important things than *Sebastian Quigley* at stake.

Seb's dark brows crinkled. He searched her face for a breath and then nodded. "Yeah, sure. Of course, but Nia, we should—"

"Thanks," Toni snapped, pulling the seat belt across her body. She fastened it and fixed her gaze firmly on the windshield and the street beyond.

Seb had taken a job away from her—a woman—in a business where it was hard enough for someone like her to get work. A fact he knew very well, since he'd drilled it into her skull when they were kids.

"*Wherever you go, whatever you're asked to play, you better come in firing,*" he'd said, way back when. "*Be the best in the room. Always. They're gonna look for excuses to write you off. Don't give 'em one.*"

Never in a million years had Toni thought *he'd* be the one screwing her over. Then again, it wouldn't be the first time.

"If you don't mind?" she said. "I've got somewhere to be."

Seb's sigh disturbed the air around her.

"Okay." He pulled a business card out from somewhere. "If you want to talk, you can reach me at this number."

When Toni didn't take it, Seb set the card on the seat beside her. He stood. "It's really good to see you, Nia."

She bit the inside of her lips to keep them together.

Seb closed the door and rapped the roof of the car twice.

The driver caught her eyes in the rearview mirror. "Where to?"

"I dunno. Anywhere. Please go."

Chuckling, the man ran a hand over his beard. "And here I thought that sort of thing only happened in the movies."

When they finally pulled away from the curb, Toni sank down into the seat, refusing to let herself look back to see if Seb was still standing there. He was in Philly? And working *her* circuit? Since when? And why hadn't she seen him? And what the actual hell?

It was a complication. Toni *hated* complications. Especially ones with flashing green eyes and a metric ton of baggage.

The business card he'd left on the seat bounced and shifted with every bump in the road. Toni wouldn't allow herself to even look at the thing, too tempted to slip it into her bag. She had questions, but the thought of dealing with Seb on top of Elias and Jerry's boys' club fuckery was enough to make her break out in hives. Besides, nothing Seb could say could erase the last seven years of silence. Nothing he could say would have any lasting effect on what Toni wanted for her future, a future he'd erased himself from long ago. If he was horning in on her territory, she'd just have to make herself irreplaceable.

She was always a better player than him anyway. Screw Sebastian Quigley. She wanted nothing to do with him.

And yet Toni's heart had still stuttered in her chest at the sight of him. Like she was seventeen all over again. Like some small part of her had never let go of the hope that one day...

Her gaze fell on the business card just as they hit traffic. It slid onto the floor, out of sight, and Toni exhaled with relief. The universe had saved her from herself.

"Look, I'm all for running up the meter, but do you have a destination in mind yet?" The driver's tone hung somewhere between amused and annoyed.

"Um…" Toni didn't want to sit home and stew.

Outside the windows, most of the shops were closed. A woman dragged the chairs of a sidewalk café into a stack, startling a few pigeons. A few doors down, a man rolled down the front gate of his grocery store. The sad remnants of the day's offerings sat in sagging cardboard boxes at his feet.

A little girl bounced excitedly alongside her mother as they exited yet another shop, a sparkly unicorn on her adorable little dress.

Toni sat up and peered through the plexiglass divider. "Hey, what time is it?"

"Coming up on seven."

"Could you take me to the Electric Unicorn?"

"Sure, I know the place." He hooked a thumb over his shoulder toward her guitar. "You playing there tonight?"

Toni slouched back and stared out the window. "We'll see."

She pulled out her phone and shot Elton a text.

TONI: Got room for one more tonight?

He responded immediately.

ELTON NOT JOHN: For you? Always.

Toni needed something to ground her. A touchstone. What better place than under the lights?

CHAPTER 3.

SEB WASN'T SURE HOW CANDI had managed to talk him into coming out tonight of all nights. He guessed those shots of tequila that accompanied their afternoon jam session had played a big role in the decision.

He had made a number of questionable choices over the last few days, ever since he'd run face-first into the biggest regret of his life. What was one more?

"Worst idea ever," he said as photogs and reporters formed a wall between their car and the hotel.

"It'll be fun!" Candi flashed a brilliant, practiced smile. "Don't be such a wuss."

This part sucked. It was the part of his job he could do without, where vultures with cameras shouted at them like auctioneers. It was inevitable with Candi.

"Relax." She pulled a compact from her purse and checked her reflection. "You always complain, and we always have a blast."

Seb thumped his head against the seat rest. "I thought we agreed you were going to lay low for a while."

"This *is* laying low," she retorted, running a wand of gloss across her lips. "Kurt's an old friend. It'll be nothing but my true peeps there. A teensy gathering." She turned to him. "Cross my heart."

Her face was half in shadow, but Seb didn't need to see her bright-blue eyes to know she was full of shit. He closed his, images of Nia immediately flooding his brain. *Ugh*. Seeing her had been a kick in the teeth.

The plan had been to play nice with Jerry and head back to New York. No pit stops, no detours, and definitely no surprise trips down memory lane.

He had known it was possible Nia still lived in the area, but there were six million people in the Philly metro, and dozens of studios.

When he walked into Phactory Sound, Seb had wondered if he was drunk. Or high. Or tripping. Or, shit, had a brain tumor. Anything that would explain why the reality of an all-grown-up and disturbingly beautiful version of Antonia Bennette had greeted him. Not that the daggers in her deep, brown eyes could be in any way interpreted as a greeting.

If looks could kill, he'd be enjoying the afterlife. But at least he wouldn't have to go to yet another one of Candi's fucking parties.

As soon as the SUV pulled up in front of the swanky hotel, it started. *Toni would hate this*, he thought to himself as a barrage of flashes greeted them, but he got out of the car and reached back to take Candi's manicured hand.

"Seb! Candi! Over here!"

Immediately, bodies bandied them back and forth. In the chaos, someone shoved a camera in Seb's face, clipping him on the chin.

"Fuck!" He grabbed the sore spot, checking for blood as he shoved away the man closest to him. Seb had a job to do. He needed to get his head out of the past. "Back the hell up!" he barked at the offending photog, putting himself between the guy and Candi.

"Only doing my job, dude," the man yelled back. He was short, pale, and thin, with wiry red hair and a bad case of rosacea.

Seb had seen him before. He worked for *Celeb Watch* and was particularly aggressive. Even for a pap. "If you broke my camera—"

"You'll sue me," Seb finished for the asshole. He'd heard it before.

Seb lost sight of their black Suburban as two members of their security detail tried to clear a path for them from the curb to the door.

Candi grabbed his wrist and pulled him toward the entrance of the Royal Something-or-Other like she was on a mission. The partying had taken center stage with her lately. It usually did when she had a run-in with her family and their not-too-subtle disapproval of her life choices. Seb seemed to be the only person who could keep Candi from doing irreversible damage to herself or her career with these outings, since she was adept at giving her security detail the slip. He couldn't let things get out of hand tonight.

As the camera shutters clicked, flashes popping like rapid fire in an urban war zone, Candi preened and winked like the pro she was.

Seb knew this had been daily life for her, growing up an heir to the Fairmount family fortune, but she seemed to thrive on it. "Hey, Candi, who are you wearing?" someone called out.

"Dolce, darling," she purred in response. "Seb went for something vintage, per usual."

"Well, you guys look hot!"

The skin of her bare waist was warm against Seb's palm as Candi turned in his grip to blow a strawberry-tinted kiss at the man who had called out.

Pop-pop-pop.

One of the few female reporters in the bunch pushed her way to the front. "Ms. Fairmount, do you think your family will cut you off?"

Candi rolled her eyes. "Don't care."

"Are you here for Kurt Rappaport's birthday party?" the woman asked.

"Candi, are you and Seb staying here tonight?" This from Herbie, one of the guys that followed Candi fairly regularly.

He was a balding, late-fifty-something with thick, meaty hands and a paunch that hung over legs that looked too skinny to support it. Judging by the way he maneuvered the pushing and shoving of the others around him, he'd been in the game a long time.

"You angling for an invitation to join us, Herbie?" Candi always seemed to feast on banter.

"Trying to give me a heart attack?" Herbie replied, clearly used to Candi's brand of charm. His mouth curved into an amused smile as she preened for him, though he continued to shoot with the camera resting on his belly.

Seb figured Herbie got a lot of his trademark candids that way, engaging his mark in actual conversation so they'd turn his way.

Candi propped one hand on her hip and stepped away from Seb, gliding over to the bank of photographers. They had been sectioned off behind a barricade by the front doors. She stopped in front of Herbie, his camera now dangling from the strap around his thick neck. He pulled out a notepad.

"What does your family really think about you becoming a pop star?"

Candi rolled her eyes again, playfully this time. "Baby, I am *not* a motherfucking pop star. Trust me, I know more than one way to rock your world." She lifted the credentials hanging from his lanyard with one shiny pink nail before letting it drop.

The explosion of camera shutters sounded like a swarm of locusts about to descend. Their security detail fought alongside the hotel's own doormen to stave off the people closing in from the crowded New York sidewalk. The air thickened with shouts and demands as the small mob surged.

"You're a terrible tease, Candi," Herbie said with some affection.

"Say the word," Candi somehow managed to purr over the din, "and I will show you things you've only ever speculated about in that greasy rag of yours." She licked her lips and traced a finger down her sternum to the valley between her breasts, setting off another volley of flashes.

"Candi," Seb warned, careful to keep his voice low.

She glanced back at him and winked, the tip of her tongue teasing along the edges of her perfect white teeth. The cameras went bananas, clicking so fast it sounded like an alien language.

From the moment he'd met her, Seb knew the trajectory of his life would change. The woman was powered by lip gloss and rocket fuel, with a mind as sharp as anyone he'd ever known and a tongue to match. And she could play the fuck out of a guitar. Seb had said yes to her from the first second their eyes made contact and their smiles clashed.

And when he'd introduced her to Lilly, another not-of-this-world creature he'd fallen in with when he moved to New York, her bright, cold flame and laser-focused energy had complemented Candi's unpredictable nature in a way that seemed predestined. Seb knew they would be explosive together. That the three of them would make magic. Make history.

And he still believed that despite everything.

The lines had gotten blurred somewhere along the way. Too many booze-soaked sessions when they'd jammed late into the night, cementing the sound Lilly had been searching for since he'd met her. Too many mornings when he'd woken up sandwiched between Candi and Lilly, lips and hands straying into dangerous territory.

But where Lilly had pulled back, retreating into the music and the business of the band, Candi had followed Seb home one night and demanded he "stop pussyfooting around and fuck me already."

He had known right away that it had been a mistake.

He'd ended their extracurricular activities not long after they began, but a seismic shift had occurred between the three of them. Things had changed, dramatically, and now he was Candi's glorified babysitter, keeping pace with her as best he could so she'd always have someone by her side she could trust. Tomorrow was a big day, probably the biggest in the Lillys' short career. Judging by tonight, Candi didn't seem to grasp the importance of the showcase performance YMI had arranged for them.

Or maybe she was just too angry with her family to care.

Candi blew a kiss to the *CelebWatch* cameraman following them to the door.

"Hey, Seb! Is it true you and Candi are moving in together?"

The hell?

"Wouldn't you like to know?" Candi supplied, giving him a sly grin.

Seb groaned under his breath. They had agreed to let the press think they were together. After all, it was better than having them speculate about where she spent her nights. But the media's relentless desire to catch famous people in the act of something—anything—grated on him.

Walking, talking, eating, sleeping, fucking, fighting, or brushing their damn teeth, it didn't matter. The paparazzi were scavengers, praying for the next nip slip or overdose. It was all Seb could do sometimes to keep himself from knocking one of them on their asses.

"Candi, is it true you had a threesome with YMI's new owners, Andreas and Daniel Herbots? Is that how the Lillys got the deal?"

Candi stopped, tilting her head at the reporter. "What? No, I..."

"What the hell kind of question is that?" Seb asked, stepping between them. "Whoever's spreading that bullshit will find themselves in court."

The man pushed forward. "I don't hear a denial," he said to Candi. "It wouldn't be the first time a chick has used her goods to get the goods. No shame in it."

Seb did the one thing you should never do when dealing with this kind of press attack—he stepped into the guy's personal space, his fists clenched, ready to unleash holy hell. "You wanna repeat that?"

The asshole grinned and shoved the camera right in Seb's face. He knew what he was doing, and Seb had played right into his hands. Seb cursed under his breath when Candi grabbed his arm.

"Don't," she said.

"Let's keep it moving," a deep voice said in his ear as a strong hand cupped his shoulder and pulled him away.

"Seb, over here! Any plans to make it official between you two?"

Seb pushed his sunglasses up his nose and gave a noncommittal wave in response, grateful when he and Candi were finally ushered through the gleaming glass doors. The quiet descended upon Seb like a mist, and the air-con caressed the back of his neck with cool fingers. For one blissful moment, this was his favorite place in New York.

Hooking his arm across Candi's shoulders, Seb drew her to his side. The mob may have been held at bay outside, but there were still plenty of people in the reception area. The place was money, though, dripping in purple velvet, Italian marble, and gilded everything.

Candi's bright-pink hair tickled his nose as she pressed close to him, their legs tangling as they tried to walk. She was already on something—Seb knew it—and she kept giggling every time they nearly tripped over each other's feet.

"This place is fabulous!" she exclaimed, gliding her fingers over every shiny surface they passed. "Do you want to go to the bar? I want to go check out the bar. Ooo! Let's go check out the rooftop bar, baby. I hear they have a pool. We could give them some shots of us together, you know, having fun."

"There are no cameras to perform for in here, so knock it off."

Candi buried her face in Seb's chest and laughed, nearly toppling them both to the polished marble floor when their knees clashed. "But you're so much fun to play with."

Seb saw a few people take out their cell phones, not at all subtle about filming them. Great. He'd get shit from Jordan and Lilly for letting her be seen in public like this again. Flirty drunk Candi was fine. Sloppy drunk Oil Princess was not.

"Come on," Seb urged her. "Let's get you to the penthouse. Okay? To...uh..." *Who was it again?* "Kurt's party."

Flanked on either side, the pair were finally ushered to the elevators.

"I'd like to restate, for the record, that this is a very bad idea." Eric Masturini had been on Candi's security detail since Seb had met her. He was promoted to full-time bodyguard shortly after news got out that the Lillys had signed with YMI two months ago. The deal had skyrocketed the band to the top of the New York indie rock scene but it was Candi's involvement that had landed them on the front page of the *Post* and made them all shiny new targets for the national press.

Fortunately, Eric knew how to handle difficult situations, having been with Candi's family for most of his post-military career. He was as no-nonsense as they came, but he seemed to understand the need to give Candi room to spread her rebellious wings. Put too many restrictions on her, and she would go out of her way to annihilate every one.

Seb liked him, even though the guy could out-worry a doting grandmother.

"Clear." The other bodyguard on her detail, a man Seb had seen before but had never spoken to, gestured for them to board the elevator he'd procured.

Finally releasing the death grip she had on Seb's arm, Candi snorted.

"These guys."

She giggled, turning her cheek to Seb's for a kiss. He pecked her quickly, unable to see her eyes behind the enormous sunglasses she insisted on wearing most of the time.

"I'm not the fucking Queen of England, boys. Relax."

"You're a five-foot-and-change woman who is already worth a small fortune and about to break into the international spotlight," Eric rebutted smoothly. He used his body to block the entrance to the elevator, shaking his head firmly at the couple trying to get a peek of Candi.

When the doors slid shut, Seb took a deep breath. Eric wasn't wrong; this party was a bad idea. But when Candi got it in her mind to do something, not even Seb could talk her out of it. The best he could do was tag along and try to keep her out of the worst of the trouble.

Candi moved away from him and shoved her glasses up to rest in the dirty-blond roots of her hot-pink waves. She rummaged through the small handbag she carried. "Where the fuck are my happy pills?"

Seb glared at Candi.

She made a face. "What?"

Seb nodded at the two men crammed inside the elevator with them.

Candi rolled her eyes and resumed the search of her small clutch purse.

Lifting his gaze to the numbers above the doors, Seb watched them climb. The higher they went, the tighter the knot in his stomach twisted.

Toni wouldn't do this. She'd probably want to grab a burger somewhere instead of hitting up a party.

And *why* was he thinking about Antonia Bennette? Ever since their encounter, Seb couldn't seem to exorcise her from his thoughts.

Not for the first time, Seb wondered what Lilly would think of her, or what Toni would think of Lilly. He wondered if he'd ever get the chance to find out.

But if he'd ever hoped time had healed any of Toni's wounds, he'd found out the answer pretty quickly. She'd given him no quarter. No way in.

Seb didn't know much, but he knew it was a flashing neon sign when someone dismissed you the way Toni had. It had put to rest any thoughts of reconciliation. It hurt more than it should, but it was nothing less than he deserved.

"You really need to relax," Candi said, nudging his shoulder. He hadn't even realized she'd moved.

"I *am* relaxed," Seb groused, feeling anything but. "Let's… take it easy tonight, okay? We have to be at the Meridien at eleven tomorrow morning."

"God." Candi let out an exaggerated sigh. "You're worse than Lilly. We are going to nail that showcase, and all those promoters will be *crawling all over* each other trying to book us." She slid her arm around Seb's waist, pulling him against her. "YMI will quit nagging once we start booking. Stop worrying, old man."

He looked down at her. Candi barely came up to his chin, but she was the textbook definition of the phrase *larger-than-life*.

Her blue eyes, rimmed in smoky charcoal, were a little blood-shot but they were bright and assessing.

Candi stuck out her tongue and placed a tiny white pellet on the end of it.

Seb startled and drew back, but Candi tightened her grip on his waist.

"What's wrong?" Her brow crinkled.

"What part of 'Let's take it easy tonight' did you not understand?"

Candi smirked and released him, keeping her eyes on his as she swallowed. "What's got you so distracted lately?" she asked. "You meet someone?"

Seb frowned, uncomfortable with the way she could read him. "No."

Candi narrowed her eyes. "Well, something's going on with you."

"I'm anxious. About tomorrow," he added. "That's all."

Candi pulled out another pill and held it out to him. "All the more reason for you to chill."

Seb folded his arms. "I'll *chill* when we're on the other side of the showcase."

Shrugging, she stuck the tablet back in her clutch.

After what seemed an interminable amount of time, the elevator came to a halt. Ears popping uncomfortably, Seb stepped out as soon as the doors opened. A thumping bass drum vibrated the air around them.

"You can wait for us out here," Candi instructed as Eric and his partner led the way to the penthouse suite.

Eric stopped and turned to her, his jaw clenched. "That is not a good idea."

"Why? Seb can look after me," Candi countered. She wrapped a hand around Seb's bicep and used her other hand to pat his chest. "He'll protect me from any big bads. Won't you, Seb?"

Candi grinned up at him, and Seb gave a stiff nod. The words of reason and protest that sat lodged in his throat never made it to his tongue. After all, this was their arrangement, even if he was still reeling so hard from that unexpected run-in with Toni that he wasn't sure he trusted himself to keep his own head on straight. The earth had shifted under his feet. He needed to find some solid ground.

Eric gave him a decidedly unconvinced look. "If there's any trouble, call us in."

"I've got this," Seb said, summoning his confidence. "Two or three hours, and I'll get her out of there."

Famous last words.

The party was an absolute shitshow, and Seb had wanted to leave as soon as they'd set foot inside the suite. It was hot, loud, and wall to wall with people with enough wealth to run a medium-size country and every vice imaginable available at their fingertips. Booze, drugs, sex—all on display.

Joy.

Seb needed a drink if he was going to get through this.

A man walked by them, carrying a tray of cocktails. Seb stopped him, because his mouth was a desert and his nerves were shot. He was ready to down the icy, clear liquid in one go.

Before he could bring the glass to his lips, Candi grabbed his wrist and took it out of his hand.

"The fuck?" He scowled at her. "What're you doing?"

Candi led him to a bar in the corner, pushing her way to the front of the line.

"Candi…"

"He'll have a gin and tonic," she instructed the beleaguered bartender. Turning, she shook her head at Seb, concern etched in her features. "Never take a drink from one of Kurt's trays unless you want…a little extra kick."

Frowning at his own stupidity, Seb accepted the G&T from the bartender with his thanks and tucked a bill into the woman's tip jar. "Shit. Thanks."

Candi clinked the glass she'd swiped from him against his fresh cocktail. "Cheers." She took a few gulps before he could say anything and hummed. "Oh, yeah. That's the good stuff."

"Can...just... Take it easy on that stuff. Please?"

Candi blinked slowly up at him. "You know, it's sweet the way you worry about me."

"I'm your friend," he said. "I'm only looking out for you."

"Since I can't look out for myself?" Her gaze turned steely. "I don't need a nanny, Seb. I'm a grown-up."

Seb sighed and took in the room. Clumps of people gathered along the edges. Their conversations were reduced to a buzzing chatter, drowned out by the music pouring out of the enormous speakers set up by the windows.

Their host held court on the sectional. Kurt was surrounded by doting onlookers, enraptured by whatever anecdote he was sharing. But it was what was in front of him that snagged Seb's attention.

At least a dozen crystal bowls covered the surface of the coffee table, each one filled to the brim with party favors—drugs of every conceivable variety and indulgence. And people were indulging. Snorting, popping, huffing...

Christ.

Candi leaned up to yell over the music, which had cranked up several decibels. "I'm gonna go blow off some steam."

Seb looked down at her. "Tomorrow is a big deal. You get that, right?"

Candi met his gaze. For a moment, Seb caught the uncertainty in her eyes.

"I know," she said. "I need...I need to get out of my head for a while. But you'll look out for me, right?" She pointed at the glass in his hand. "It's what we do, look out for each other."

Seb could only nod as she slowly backed away, lifting her glass to her lips as her smile returned.

Candi turned and wandered toward the makeshift dance floor in the center, weaving her way through a sea of writhing bodies.

He watched her dance alone for a while, eyes closed, and could tell whatever she'd taken had really kicked in when she started grinding on the first body she came in contact with. That fast, any notion of restraint had gone right out the window.

Fucking fantastic.

Seb knocked back his drink.

"Another?" The bartender, a petite South Asian woman with a dimpled smile, poured a glass of red wine for another customer as she eyed him.

It was tempting, but Seb set his glass on the bar. "Thanks, no. I'm on duty."

Seb found Candi at the center of a group of people. Each held a shot of amber liquid in their hands. After counting down from three, they all drank. Candi bent over with laughter, looking freer than he'd seen her in a while.

She had a lot of pressure on her. Seb got that, and he wanted to be a friend and give her the space she needed. But the line between distraction and escape was thin. He needed to be the kind of friend who kept her from pushing the self-destruct button.

It's what we do, she'd said. *Look out for each other.*

Before he could reach her, a svelte, deeply tanned brunette—dressed in an oversize napkin that probably cost more than Seb's rent—wrapped her arms around Candi and pulled her into a sloppy hug.

A couple of onlookers took out their phones. Any one of them could be looking for photos of the Oil Princess to sell to the tabloids.

Seb strode forward, ready to intervene, when the woman released Candi. He recognized her. Naya Broward, heir to the Broward Cosmetics fortune and Candi's on-again, off-again BFF.

Naya caught his eye and gave him a slow smile.

Seb nodded. He wasn't a fan, but at least Candi had someone she knew well by her side and not some rando. He relaxed a little. "Naya."

"It's the boy toy!" she said, a challenging gleam in her eye. "Sam, right?"

"Yaya," Candi said, laughing. "Don't be a bitch. You know Sebby."

"Sorry, *Sebby*," Naya replied, sounding not sorry at all. She held his gaze while Candi buried her face in her neck, nuzzling into her. She was so gone.

"Nice to see you again," Naya said, her voice flat.

"Likewise," Seb said, giving her the same amount of ice she'd dished out. Yeah, not a fan.

Naya turned her attention to Candi. "Let's grab a seat and catch up, babes. I haven't seen you since Mykonos."

"Oh, *fuuuuuck*!" Candi drawled. "Mykonos was the shit. We have to go back, like, now."

"We have a gig in the morning," Seb informed Naya, who looked at him as if she'd forgotten he was there.

Her brow quirked. "We?"

"The Lillys," he gritted out.

Naya smiled and it was not friendly. "Ah, well, we'll park ourselves somewhere and chill. Keep out of trouble."

"Don't worry, Seb," Candi said, blinking up at him. Her pupils were saucers. "I'm in good hands."

Naya steered them to a love seat in the corner and Candi fell into it, giggling.

Seb thought maybe they should call it a night.

"God*damn*!" a man shouted in a familiar SoCal drawl. "Do mine eyes deceive me, or is it really you?"

Seb turned around. "Holy hell, Finn? What are you doing here?"

He smiled into the hug that Finn Costa wrapped him in, thumping the guy on the back when breathing became an issue. Years of surfing the world's best waves had carved him into a wall of muscle. He didn't seem to know his own strength.

"I was about to ask you the same." Finn released him, giving Seb a slap on his shoulder. "Last I heard, you'd fled LA for Europe or something."

Seb snorted. "You need to find a new source. Nah, I was in Miami for a bit. I'm here now. You?"

"YMI called me in to produce the debut of a sixteen-year-old they plucked off of YouTube," Finn said. "The kid's not bad. I think they could make a splash, if YMI gives me full control over the production and song choices. Speaking of which, would you be interested in writing one or two for me?"

"Sure," Seb agreed. "Let me know what you're looking for."

Candi's giggle broke above the din of the party, and Seb looked back to check on her. She and Naya were clinking glasses of champagne, heads together as they peered down at something on Naya's iPhone.

"Which one is yours?"

"The one with the pink hair," Seb replied before amending himself. "Well, she's not *mine*, but yeah. I manage her band."

Finn squinted in Candi's direction. "Isn't that Candi Fairmount? Wait, are you the guy behind that all-girl cover band she's in, the one YMI inked to that huge deal? What's their name, the Daisies?"

"The Lillys."

Finn snapped his fingers. "Right, right. I knew it was something flowery." He gestured toward Candi. "Is she any good?"

"She's fucking phenomenal," Seb said without hesitation. "The Lillys are more than a cover band, and they're going to blow everyone's minds. Trust me."

"Well, I hope it works out for you," Finn replied with a grin. "You have a good ear for talent, so I can't wait to hear them." He raised a hand to wave to someone across the room. "I've been looking for him all night. Catch you later, man."

Seb watched Finn greet a man on the other side of the room. Feeling like an island at the center of an ocean of partygoers, he found a seat in the corner by the window and pulled out his phone to text Eric Masturini.

An hour. He'd give Candi an hour and then get them the hell out of there.

There was a Google alert in his notifications, a new video by Toni B. Seb's heart stuttered.

It was too loud to hear anything, but he clicked the link anyway. Jesus. There she was—all five feet sevenish inches of her—onstage in what looked like a small club.

Her smile, God. It knocked the wind out of him and brought back all sorts of long-buried memories. She seemed happy. She always had, whenever she played.

Seb had forgotten the way her eyes could light up a room. He couldn't stop staring at the small screen, mesmerized by her every movement. When the video ended, he restarted it.

"Champagne?"

Seb looked up, feeling as if he were in a daze. A waiter leaned down with a tray of flutes and Seb absentmindedly took one of the glasses, Candi's warning only a hazy memory.

"Thanks," he said, draining half of the glass in one sip.

The man nodded and walked away.

Seb hit Play again.

Something had crawled inside his ear, shredded his brain, and then died inside his mouth. That was the only logical explanation for the way Seb felt when he came to. How many hours had passed? Had it been a day? A year?

Bright light beat against his eyelids, demanding entrance. Rolling over onto his stomach proved to be a horrible idea as something pointy stabbed him in his side.

Seb blindly fumbled for the offending object. He cracked open one eye to glare at the mostly empty bag of microwave popcorn he'd apparently...taken to bed?

At least it was his bed, but how the fuck had he gotten home?

Groaning, Seb rolled onto his back, his head protesting painfully.

He shielded his eyes with one hand as he carefully opened them, one by one. His eyelids were so dry that they scraped his eyeballs. Seb blinked a few times, trying to will his tear ducts into production.

He took a moment to assess. He was still fully dressed, so there was that. And he was alone, or so he assumed.

"Hello?"

Seb's voice rang out in the empty apartment. The rancid smell of his own breath hit his nostrils, and his stomach roiled in protest. He stank of good whiskey and bad cigarettes. And popcorn. He scraped a smooshed kernel off his cheek and gave it a weak toss to somewhere in the vicinity of the floor.

"Jesus," he muttered, throwing his arm back over his eyes. "I'm getting too goddamned old for this."

After taking a few minutes to claw his way to full consciousness, Seb stretched his limbs. Luckily, the only soreness was in his head. He'd get some real food in his belly, maybe a bagel and some eggs, then he'd be fine for the—

"Ah, shit!"

Seb bolted upright and immediately regretted it. The dull throb in his brain ramped up to a stabbing pain. He squeezed his eyes shut and waited for the worst of it to pass. He patted his pockets for his phone before spotting it on the floor next to the bed.

Gingerly, Seb reached for it, nearly losing the contents of his stomach as he bent over. He really was getting too old for this fuckery. Unlocking the screen with his thumb, he winced at the number of notifications, but froze at the image that greeted him.

Apparently, he'd been busy when he'd gotten home last night...this morning. Whenever. There on his phone, paused mid-song, was a video of Toni.

Seb remembered stumbling across the clip at the party and playing it on repeat. He must have watched it when he'd gotten in, before passing out.

Unable to help himself, Seb restarted the video. This was as close as he was likely to ever get to her again.

The quality was grainy, and he couldn't quite make out her features, but the voice was unmistakable. And something about the way her mouth twisted to the side and the determined set of her jaw as she played a song he'd heard her play a hundred times before. Memories he'd kept locked away came flooding back.

SEBASTIAN, AGE 18—ANTONIA, AGE 16

Jesus. Seb had never known Nia to be this nervous. She couldn't seem to stop shaking.

"Why did I agree to do this stupid talent show," she griped. "They're gonna laugh me off the stage."

"Look at me," Seb said. He cupped her shoulders lightly.

They were backstage in the auditorium, and Nia's gaze kept darting around.

"Hey." Seb shook her gently. "Don't worry about them, worry about me."

Nia focused on his mouth. Her eyes slid up to meet his and held there.

Hers were a deep, soulful brown and unfairly pretty.

"You know 'Solace' inside and out," Seb said with utter confidence in her ability. "Own it. It's yours. Go out there and show them what you're made of."

"Maybe I should have gone with the Coldplay?"

Seb snorted. "Are you kidding? Caspian's Ghost all the way. You've totally got this, Nia."

She nodded, her eyes dropping to his chest. "You're staying, right?"

As if he'd ever leave her. "I'm not going anywhere." Seb pulled her into his arms and dropped a kiss on the top of her head. She felt so slight, but solid as she wrapped her arms around his waist. "Nowhere else I'd rather be."

———

As the song ended, Seb's finger hovered over the replay button until his brain caught up with the present. He winced when he finally realized the time.

It was after three.

He'd missed the fucking showcase. Seb rolled to his back.

Okay.

Not ideal, but since Candi wasn't with him, he crossed his fingers that she'd had the good goddamn sense to get there on time and play her heart out, as only she could. That hope was squashed pretty quickly when he squinted at the screen again.

There were nine missed calls and several texts from Jordan that were enough to make Seb wince. But the blood drained from his face entirely when he noted the text from Lilly.

Lilly never texted. She'd call or occasionally send him a direct message on Twitter or Instagram, but she never, ever texted.

He read through a few of Jordan's messages first.

JORDAN IGWE: [10:16AM] Heard Kurt's party was epic. I'm stopping by Java Bomb, I'll grab you something. 20 oz diablo with an extra shot of espresso. Right?

JORDAN IGWE: [10:33AM] I'm at the Meridien. Bring Candi around to the side entrance, there's a media circus out front. We have a leak?

JORDAN IGWE: [10:41AM] Please tell me you're on your way.

JORDAN IGWE: [10:54AM] Where are you, mate? Getting nervous. The suits are getting antsy.

JORDAN IGWE: [11:07AM] What the fuck? WHERE ARE YOU GUYS???

Shit, shit, shit!

Lilly's unopened text stared up at Seb from his phone. He closed his eyes, pinching the bridge of his nose as he tried to work out what she might say. What he could say to her.

LILLY L: [11:39AM] I trusted you.

Ah, fuck. He'd messed up.

Bad.

CHAPTER 4.

SEB STOPPED OUTSIDE THE POLISHED wood-grain door next to the brass plaque that read *Jordan Igwe, Attorney-at-Law*. As he stared at his blurry reflection, he tried to anticipate the temperature of the room. Jordan was his best friend, but his text hadn't given Seb much to go on.

JORDAN IGWE: Band meeting in my office. 4 p.m.

The brevity didn't bode well.

After confirming that Candi had failed to show, Seb had tried to reach out while he nursed his hangover, to no avail. The radio silence was disturbing. It wasn't like anyone in their group to not vent their anger.

Seb absentmindedly toyed with the braided leather bracelet on his left wrist. Old and weathered, it had been a touchstone for him for years. He hadn't removed it since it had been fastened there on his eighteenth birthday, gifted by someone who should have known better than to put their faith in him.

He would never forget Antonia's dark amber eyes, wide with anticipation as he'd opened the small box. She'd blown half of one of her measly paychecks on the gift. He'd promised her they'd get out of Bordon together. See the world. Make music.

Standing in the shadow of Jordan's office, having failed to maintain even a tenuous connection to that faraway dream, Seb was almost glad he'd broken that promise. Whether she'd said it to his face or not, Antonia deserved far better than him. Than this life.

Shit. Even Candi hadn't returned his calls. He was supposed to be the anchor grounding her. Keeping her from floating too high up into the poisoned clouds of celebrity. Instead, he'd gotten lost in his own head.

If he were a better man, he would walk away now.

Seb took a deep breath.

Fuck it.

Stepping inside, he spotted Jordan through the open door to his private office. Seb made his way there, fighting every urge to flee and leave the others to carry on without him. It wasn't like they actually needed him. No one ever really had.

Jordan offered him a curt nod.

The best thing Seb had done for the band was to bring Jordan in to represent them. The first guy he'd hired turned out to be a snake-oil salesman. Jordan was the money man, the fixer, and Seb knew he was ridiculously lucky to call him his best friend.

This, though, was band business.

Jordan Igwe did not fuck around when it came to money. Friend or not, Seb knew Jordan wouldn't hesitate to tell the Lillys to fire his ass.

Seb surveyed the room. Jordan stood by the window behind his desk, looking down over West 56th Street. The band members were scattered around the spacious room. Drummer Mikayla Whitman sat at the small conference table, a stack of papers spread out before her, while bassist Tiffany Kim stood behind, peering over her shoulder. Neither Tiff nor Kayla acknowledged Seb's entrance.

Great start.

Candi lay reclined across the small leather love seat, her legs dangling over an armrest. She wore her big, Bono-esque sunglasses, her face turned toward the ceiling.

Seb would have thought she was asleep if the heels of her Converse sneakers weren't rhythmically thumping against the side of the sofa. She looked...bored.

Lilly sat perched on the edge of Jordan's desk, one foot propped on the windowsill behind it. She was dressed in leggings and a workout top, which made Seb wonder how last-minute this meeting had come together.

She looked up at Seb, her expression unreadable. Unfolding herself, she put her foot on the arm of the chair in front of the desk and spun it to face him, nodding her head toward it.

Feeling like he was at the center of a tribunal, Seb obeyed Lilly's silent command. He slinked over to the chair and sank into it, like a kid about to be suspended from school. Seb had plenty of experiences to draw from.

Slowly, Lilly withdrew her leg and crossed her ankles. Being that close to her when she was in kill mode was usually a thrill for Seb, but this time he was the one up shit creek, not some hapless sound guy.

"I got your message," he said.

Lilly looked away, and a sliver of ice crept into Seb's gut. He hated the disappointment on her face.

Jordan finally turned around. "Thanks for coming on such short notice," he said, all business.

Someone snorted.

Seb glanced around the room.

Candi unwrapped a piece of bright-pink gum and popped it into her mouth, making loud, smacking noises as she began to chew. Kayla wouldn't look at him, but the knot in Seb's gut eased a little when Tiff gave him an encouraging nod.

At least he hadn't lost them completely.

"Can we get the You've-been-a-naughty-Candace speech over with? I have a spa appointment at five," Candi sniped, cracking the silence in two.

"Okay, sure. You're fired," Lilly said, managing to sound both bored and fed up as she got to her feet. She pinned Candi with a look that could only be described as dismissive.

The room went even more eerily quiet as everyone seemed to hold their breath waiting for Candi's response.

"Yeah, right," she muttered, laughing to herself. When no one else made a sound of protest, she sat up and looked around the room, her expression disbelieving. "You dragged me in to tell me I can't play on your playground anymore?"

Jordan rubbed his hand over his short, black hair. Seb could see the muscles in his jaw twitching as he stared at the window frame, presumably searching the wood grain for some patience.

"Really?" Candi was incredulous. She turned to Seb, and he gave her a slight shake of his head. *Don't make things worse*, he wanted to say.

Sighing heavily, she stood and walked over to Lilly, who eyed her warily.

Candi moved in close, so close Seb didn't know if she meant to hug her or shove her. She only blinked up at Lilly, searching her face. For what he didn't know.

"Is this really what you want?" Candi's voice was quiet. Cajoling. She took one of Lilly's hands in hers and laced their fingers together. "You and me against the world, wasn't that how it was supposed to go?"

Behind them, Jordan turned his back to the spectacle, muttering something under his breath.

Unlike the others, Seb had seen this dynamic play out between the two women before, but there was something about this instance that made him uneasy. Especially when Lilly's shoulders drooped as if in defeat.

Her eyelids fluttered, lips moving as if she was having trouble forming words.

Candi pulled Lilly's hand up to her mouth and placed a kiss in the center of her palm before pulling it up to her face.

"I know you're mad, but don't be like this," she said as she closed her eyes and leaned into the touch, her voice almost sickeningly sweet. "Don't ruin everything we've built together."

It was the wrong thing to say because Lilly yanked her hand back and took a giant step away from her. Seb watched as the ice settled back in place.

"Seriously?" Candi scowled up at her, her whole demeanor changing before his eyes. Gone was any hint of remorse. She glanced around the room. "Fine. Fuck all y'all. You honestly think you'll get anywhere without me? *I'm* the draw. *My* name is what keeps us in the press."

"True, you do get the most press, but it's not the good kind," Kayla said, fatigue weighing her words down.

"Press is fucking press!" Candi snarled at her. She snatched up her bag and strolled over to the door. Stopping, she turned to Seb, her expression questioning. Expectant.

But if he left with her, it might blow any chance he had of smoothing this over before it spiraled out of control. He gave her the barest shake of his head, hoping she'd understand.

Pain flashed across her face, so quick it was like it had never happened.

"Whatever." She stormed out, her bracelets jingling in her wake.

The front door slammed behind her, rattling the framed degrees Jordan had on the walls.

Seb looked around at the others, waiting for someone to say something. Anything. *Shit.* Was this really happening?

He got to his feet.

"Stay where you are," Jordan said.

At his tone, Seb shot him a questioning look.

Jordan cut his eyes to Lilly before looking away.

Seb wondered how things had gone to hell so fast. "Let me get this straight. Everyone's cool with letting Candi go? Just like that?"

Kayla shrugged as if to say *it is what it is*. Next to her, Tiff seemed even less sure of what to do. Biting her bottom lip, her gaze flicked over to Lilly.

Seb finally turned back to Lilly, and the expression on her face immediately made him wish he'd followed Candi out the door.

Her cool gaze swept over him before she met his eyes and he wondered what she saw.

A litany of apologies sat heavy on his tongue.

"She brought it on herself," she said, at long last. "We're here to decide whether you need follow her out."

Seb's heart lurched uncomfortably in his chest. "Look, I..." he began, not knowing what to say. "It was my fault. You shouldn't blame Candi."

There was another snort, louder this time, and this one had definitely come from Kayla.

Seb turned to her and she cocked her head, twirling an ever-present drumstick between the fingers of one hand.

"Don't be an idiot," Kayla said, in the same tone you'd use to soothe a kid who'd skinned their knee. "You can't keep taking credit for Candi's shit, man. You have enough of your own to fix."

"We need to be able to depend on you," Tiff added. "You're more responsible for this ride than she is. You brought us all together."

Seb gave her a grateful smile. He couldn't lose this. These people were all he had. And they were his only real connection to the world. He loved them. If they were willing to keep him, he would be stupid not to do anything he could to fix this—for himself *and* for Candi.

"You *can* depend on me," he said, cursing the catch in his voice. "I promise. Nothing like this will ever happen again. I had...some things on my mind, and I let that distract me."

"Mate, you brought me in to fix the mess with YMI and the contract, and to take you guys to the next level," Jordan said. "With the label under new ownership, we have to be extra careful. We don't have the clout to fuck up and still expect them to keep us around."

"Those Silicon Valley guys don't know anything about music," Kayla said. "The only reason they bought the label was because they could."

"And it makes them look cool in front of all their tech friends," Tiff added. "Plus they can make easy money off YMI's legacy catalog."

"Like they need it," Kayla said, disgusted. "They're those twins, right? Inherited a ridiculous amount of money from their mom and turned it into, like, a bazillion dollars? Developing cloud storage software or whatever?"

"Data compression, but it really doesn't matter," Jordan cut in. "Any of it. They're your bosses, for all intents and purposes. And if all they care about is the bottom line, how much do you think they're willing to put up with from an asset that's been nothing but trouble in the short time since they were acquired? Candi is great for free publicity, but the headlines haven't been kind. It's overshadowing the talent."

"It doesn't help that they made us wear those skimpy little cheerleader outfits," Kayla grumbled. "We looked ridiculous."

"Maybe Candi did us a favor, not showing up," Tiff added.

Jordan moved toward the center of the room, ready to focus

the conversation, as always. He faced Seb and spread his hands wide. "This is a family, Seb. You're the one who said so when you lot all started out on this journey together."

Seb released a slow exhale. "I still believe that," he assured them, shifting his focus to Lilly and doing his best to convey his sincerity.

She ran a tongue across her straight white teeth, pondering his fate perhaps.

Seb wasn't sure which was worse, the words he guessed she wanted to say or her stony silence.

"I know you do," Jordan continued, drawing Seb's attention back to him. "That's why I can't for the life of me understand why you would let Candi jeopardize everything we've all worked so hard to get."

Seb sank back down into the chair. He wanted to tell them Candi was a grown woman and he wasn't responsible for her actions. Only, he had taken on that responsibility. Willingly. He couldn't shirk it now that things had gone wrong.

Jordan was right, and they all had every right to be pissed. Seb was pissed too. At himself. At Candi.

"Needless to say, the label isn't interested in investing time and money in an act that can't do something as simple as show up for the most important gig of its fledgling career," Jordan stated. "This could all have been over before it even started, had I not done some fancy dancing."

"I know, and thank you. I'm really sorry."

"This didn't merely make the band look bad," Jordan continued, ignoring Seb's apology. "It made the label look bad. They've been talking the Lillys up to these promoters."

"Yeah" was all Seb could say. He got it.

"We should have gone on and done it without her," Kayla grumbled. "Piped in her guitar, or something."

"Like no one would miss her stage-hogging antics." Kayla shoved the papers in front of her to the side with disgust. "Whoever we get to replace her better be more about the music than the fucking spotlight. No more trust-fund babies, please. We're having a hard enough time getting rock radio to take us seriously."

"Back to your point about the cheerleader getup," Tiff said. "That doesn't help."

"We want to make music, not spectacle," Kayla replied. "She's turning us into a fucking joke."

Seb narrowed his eyes and scanned the room. "So, you're all really done with her?"

Jordan shifted uncomfortably and glanced at Lilly, but her big blue eyes were still trained on Seb. He could feel their cold flames licking the side of his face.

She resumed her perch on the edge of Jordan's desk. "Candi's been voted out."

"Permanently?" Seb couldn't wrap his head around it.

Lilly shrugged. "That's up to her."

"I didn't get a vote," Seb argued. "Or am I out too?"

Lilly tossed her straw-blond hair over her shoulder and leveled her gaze at him. "You think you deserve a vote after today?" Her voice sent a chill down Seb's spine. "Besides, we all know how you would have voted. You're blinded by her charms. You can't see that this is all about fucking over her parents. And she's taking you—*us*—down with her."

Despite her hard tone, Seb could hear the pain. She was wrong, though. He knew the band meant more to Candi than a way to stick it to her family.

"I want it to be permanent, but it seems I'm alone in that," she exhaled, sounding tired.

Seb drew a sharp breath. When he spoke again, his voice nearly failed him. "But... It's *Candi*."

"It was the last straw, really," Jordan offered.

"She made her own bed," Kayla said, sounding every bit as if she needed to convince herself.

"Now she has to live with the consequences," Lilly added, her voice as sharp as broken glass. She lifted her chin in defiance of the hurt Seb could see in her eyes.

Seb got up and stepped close to Lilly. He needed to look her in the eye. Needed her to look into his. Needed to understand how she could so easily shut Candi out of everything they'd built together.

Her lips were dry and chapped, as if she'd been chewing on them. A clearer sign of her state of mind than anything. There were dark circles under her eyes, but they were clear and bright. Assessing him.

"She's family." Seb was close to pleading.

"Chosen family can be as shitty as any real family," she replied, her emotions betrayed by the prominent curl of her accent around the words.

Seb couldn't imagine the Lillys without Candi, or her without them.

"*Dammit*, Seb. You knew how important that showcase was to us." Lilly's voice shook as she jumped to her feet. It pained him to hear it. She was the most stoic of them. It took a lot to break her.

Fuck. What had he done?

Seb closed the distance until only inches remained between them and was relieved when Lilly didn't back away. She met his gaze and her silent questions practically flashed like neon signs above her head. He tried his best to answer them, nodding as he took a deep breath.

"I am so fucking sorry," he rasped.

Lilly pursed her lips, cocking her head to the side. Even in sweaty gym clothes, she was stunning. Intimidatingly so. All the black eye makeup and ripped clothing she wore onstage made her seem even more untouchable than she was. Dangerous and sexy, a combination that enthralled her fans.

Hers was a cold beauty, all pale skin, high cheekbones, and devastatingly blue eyes. Lilly Langeland could kill you with a look, and the one she leveled at Seb while he awaited his sentence made him want to run and hide. Or give her anything she asked for.

"Let me make it up to you," he pleaded softly. "I'd just spin my wheels without you to guide me." Words meant nothing to Lilly, only actions. And Seb's actions of late had been shitty as hell. He just needed a chance to prove himself to her.

"Candi needs us," he said, gesturing to the others as well. "Sometimes she forgets that. Sometimes she...lashes out at everyone—especially when she feels cornered. You know how she gets."

"He's not wrong," Tiff interjected. "She is the Tantrum Queen."

Seb appreciated the help but wished Tiff had chosen her words more carefully.

Lilly frowned. "She is selfish."

"I know, but please don't write her off just yet," Seb said, close to begging. "Give her one more chance. Give *me* a chance to keep the family together."

Lilly held his gaze for a long moment. "Jordan?" Her expression gave away nothing.

Seb held his breath.

"Yeah, love?" Jordan sounded as nervous as Seb felt, his South London roots on full display.

"We'll say Candi is...on hiatus. Draw up a new contract for Sebastian, adding the one-strike rule." Lilly's lips twitched when Seb exhaled a cautious sigh of relief. "And the no-fraternization clause you use for your road crews."

Ouch. But he was still here, so he'd take it.

"Fair?" She arched a brow, challenging Seb.

"More than fair. *Takk*," he thanked her, using one of the three or four words she'd taught him in her native Norwegian. It was a manipulative tactic, and amusement crept into her gaze as she saw right through it.

"*Broren min*," she said, patting his cheek with the flat of her palm hard enough for it to sting. Lilly leaned in close to Seb's ear, sending an involuntary shiver down his spine. "Fuck up again, *brother*, and you can ride off into the sunset with your girlfriend."

"Candi's not my…" There was no point in arguing right now. Seb pulled back to meet Lilly's eyes. "She's one of us."

Lilly sighed heavily, the fire dying in her eyes. "I know."

"And I know she's partied a bit too much. I'll take the blame for indulging her too much, but you know how she is."

"I do, yeah." Her voice hardened again. "I know she signed that endorsement deal with Barrow guitars when she knows I hate their business practices."

"It's not like she signed with them to spite you."

With the barest shake of her head, Lilly briefly closed her eyes. It was then that he noticed the redness rimming her pale lashes and the tension in her jaw as she swallowed. When she looked at Seb again, exhaustion and resignation were written across her face.

"You don't think so?"

She walked around him, leaving Seb to ponder what the hell he had missed. And how he'd allowed himself to get caught in the middle of whatever it was.

"Look, it's not a completely done deal," Jordan hedged. "We told the label Candi had a health emergency last night. Kept the details vague. They've agreed to give us an evening during music week. A lot of those same promoters will be there. It'll give us time to find someone to…sit in for her until this situation…er… resolves itself."

"We'll hold tryouts," Tiff said, her cheery tone transparently artificial. "See if anyone can fill Candi's thigh-high boots for a while."

"It'll be a closed audition," Jordan added. "Invitation only. We don't want to add to the gossip that her not being there will already create."

Seb nodded, but this was all wrong, all of it. And it was his own damn fault. But there was still a window, a chance to salvage things. If he kept his head on straight and found a way to get through to Candi, maybe they could get through this.

CHAPTER 5.

"YOU BROKE YOUR OWN CARDINAL rule, bruv," Jordan said as Seb drained the last of the liquid in his glass. "Don't shit where you eat."

It was too early in the afternoon to be sitting in the dark corner of a dive bar in Hell's Kitchen, finishing off a bottle of Wild Turkey, but there they were. Seb had needed a drink after the day he'd had, and Jordan wasn't the type to let a friend wallow alone in self-pity.

Jordan pushed Seb's freshly revised contract across the table. "Everything's the same except the no-frat and one-strike clauses."

Seb gave the packet a cursory glance before taking the pen Jordan held out for him. "I trust you."

What a colossal clusterfuck it all was, but at least he hadn't been tossed out on his sorry ass. Seb signed and pushed the papers back toward Jordan. As much as it stung, he had to think of this as a chance to right the ship.

There was still a path to healing the rift between Candi and the rest of the band. A narrow one, but Seb could work with that.

He had been mentally kicking himself for hours. "How did I let this happen? And how the hell do I fix it?"

"I did warn you." Jordan signaled the bartender.

The second bottle came quickly, since Seb and Jordan made up roughly half of the bar's clientele.

"Do you know what really went down between them?" Seb couldn't wrap his head around the idea of Candi not being in the group, even temporarily. "Does Lilly really think she can round up some other guitarist to take Candi's place? I mean, what the fuck?"

Jordan nodded. "You can't honestly tell me you didn't see something like this coming."

Seb frowned. "Hell no. How could I? There's no band without Candi."

"Jesus, Seb. Are you really that blind?" Jordan set his glass down so hard a cube of ice bounced out and landed on the table's sticky wood-grain laminate. "I mean, I never thought of you as particularly stupid, but maybe I was wrong."

The wan sunshine filtering through the front window did little to help the pitiful number of overhead lights illuminate the room. Jordan's face was filled with shadows and Seb was having a hard time reading him.

"Do you have anything constructive to say? Or are you just going to pile on and keep dragging me?"

Jordan sighed and leaned his elbows on the table.

"Look, Baz," he began, relaxing into his native Brixton accent, "I know you're clueless when it comes to relationships, but you do know musicians. You know band dynamics. Lilly and Candi may have hung the wallpaper together, but Lilly built the house. This is her gig, despite the narrative YMI wants to push."

"No," Seb argued. "You know that's not how it went down."

"I'm not saying it's a dictatorship," Jordan insisted. "Lilly isn't like that."

"Yesterday, I would've agreed with you. After that shit back there, though…?" Seb hooked a thumb in the general direction of the office.

Jordan's gaze dropped to the tabletop. "When you brought me in on this, I wondered how you could have been conned into getting the girls to sign that original fucking contract. The terms were…are…abysmal. Now I see why."

"Meaning?"

"Meaning you'd do anything for them, especially Lilly and Candi. They're your people. I get it. You were so eager, you weren't thinking. And you're doing it again. Not thinking."

"Hey, I brought you in, didn't I?"

Jordan nodded. "Good bloody thing too. I've got a big mess to clean up, and I will. But you really do need to trust me."

Seb took a large swallow from his drink, downing nearly half. The alcohol burned, but not enough to dissolve the boulder lodged in his chest. He'd need a hell of a lot more to get rid of it. Getting drunk probably wasn't the best response to nearly losing his place in the only family he'd ever really had, but Seb was running on empty.

"I trust you, but… Candi? No longer in the band?" Seb shook his head.

"You know it was our only option, and anyway it's a temporary fix," Jordan said, more to himself than to Seb. He looked up. "No label wants to throw away money on an unreliable act. Kayla was right—the twins are all about the bottom line. Besides, our fearless leader made some promises."

"Lilly?"

"Who else?" Jordan gave him a look. "You know they're pushing to sign her as a solo act instead. If they can't have the Lilly and Candi show, they'll settle for her alone."

"She'd never go for that," Seb replied without reservation. "She wouldn't do that to the others."

"Not voluntarily," Jordan agreed. "But thanks to Candi's antics—and yours, I might add—we're no longer in the driver's seat. This showcase was Lilly's way of showing them why YMI signed the band in the first place. Show 'em the appeal of four badass women playing badass rock and roll. The energy between Lilly and Candi, how they can work a crowd, blah, blah, blah. Their whole act."

"It's not an act. It's who they are."

"I know, and it's partly what made them go viral, yeah? So... Not a good look for half of the wonder duo not to bloody show up. Candi knew what was at stake. How do you know she didn't conveniently forget, mate? That this wasn't some sort of power play?"

"Okay," Seb conceded. "Yeah, okay. I get how it might look like that but... Shit..."

"You can't see the writing on the wall because you're in her bed," Jordan said, his tone grave.

"Fuck off." Seb knocked back the rest of his bourbon and crunched on some of the ice before it could burn through his chest. "Besides, I'm not. Not anymore."

Jordan eyed him suspiciously. "She's out of the band, so you've lost interest?"

"Jesus, no. We haven't...not in a while." Seb glared at him. "Fuck, Iggy, that's what you think of me?"

"Nah, bruv." Jordan pulled out his wallet. "Though I'm surprised Candi went after you in the first place."

"Meaning?"

"No shade against you." He shrugged. "I figured she knew the score."

"What score?"

Jordan studied Seb for a long moment before chuckling to himself. He sat back in his chair, tipping it up on its two hind legs, and grinned. "So, blind, then."

The back-and-forth and innuendo were beginning to grate.

"Dude, what the fuck are you talking about? Blind about what?"

Jordan held up his hands. "Not my place to say." He dropped some money on the table and stood, tucking his wallet away.

"Anyway, I need to go dot some i's and cross some t's. See you at the auditions. Should be a blast."

"Oh yeah," Seb replied, his head already pounding as he stood to follow Jordan to the door. "Hella fun, I'm sure."

CHAPTER 6.

TONI DROPPED BY THE ELECTRIC Unicorn to pick up her
weekly earnings.

After the fiasco with Jerry and Elias, she'd lost out on five
callbacks. Five sessions gone, just like that. And she knew Jerry
was behind it. At this rate, she might as well look for a new career.

Richie still planned to work with her, but her dream of buying
into Phactory Sound, or owning anything at all, seemed completely out of reach now.

At least she had Elton and the Electric Unicorn. Being in residence there had put enough change in her pocket to keep her in
guitar strings and cover her portion of the expenses for the one-
bedroom, fourth-floor walkup she shared with her best friend,
Yvette.

The Unicorn's magic lost its potency in the middle of the day.
Sunlight was not kind to its dusty black walls and painted cement
floors. Even the neon signs showed their age, grime pooling in
their brightly colored loops and swirls.

Elton sat on a stool at the bar, accounting ledgers, receipts,
and invoices spread out in front of him. He looked older, more
tired, but he brightened when Toni approached.

He handed her an envelope and Toni counted the cash. It
wasn't that she didn't trust Elton, but he was prone to overpaying

her. Despite having lived in the States for years, he still didn't seem to have a great grasp of American currency, or so he claimed.

"It's all there." A note of humor colored his voice as he stood and walked by her to the other side of the polished wooden bar.

"There's an extra hundred in here," Toni informed him, removing the bill from her pay and slapping it on the counter. Despite her situation, she didn't want to take advantage.

"We were busy this week," he said, shrugging. "You earned it."

Toni smiled. "You're too good to me."

Elton returned her smile, but his wobbled at the edges.

She stuffed the envelope in her backpack and leaned against the counter to better look Elton in the eye. "What's up with you?"

"Me?" He jerked back, covering his obvious discomfort with a sudden preoccupation with a stack of pint glasses. "Nothing, why?"

"You're being weird."

"I'm always weird, love." Elton's smile brightened. He reached for one of the glasses, snatching up a dish towel to clean it. It was odd enough since Elton rarely worked behind the bar anymore. Even more so since the glass was spotless.

"Something on your mind?" Toni's suspicion turned to concern when Elton averted his gaze and reached for another clean glass to polish. "Why do I feel like you're about to drop bad news on me? Are you shutting this place down or something?"

His eyes went wide. "What? No! God, no. Nothing like that. I…" He cleared his throat. "You… Well, I got a call about you."

Toni frowned. "What sort of call? From who?"

"Whom," he corrected her. He often did.

Unease made his joke fall flat. "Seriously not the time, Elton."

"Right. Sorry." He turned his back to her and opened the register. After pulling out a piece of paper, Elton turned to face her.

Toni waited but Elton remained silent, staring at her and clutching the paper in his hand.

"Is it my dad?" Despite their strained relationship, Toni's heart lurched in her chest at the thought that something might have happened.

"No, it's… It's nothing bad." His demeanor suggested otherwise as he handed over the scrap of paper.

On it he'd written a name and a number.

> *Jordan Igwe, solicitor*
> *Calling about an audition for the Lillys*
> *Call back before Wednesday.*
> *213.555.6344*

"I debated whether or not to give that to you."

"Elton." Toni spoke slowly because her heart was suddenly pounding. "This is about the Lillys."

"You might remember we spoke about them a while back?"

"It was, like, less than a week ago. Of course I remember."

"Ah, right. Of course. Well, a woman from this man's office called a bit ago and asked about you."

Toni blinked. At least she thought she blinked—it could have been an aneurysm.

"What do you mean, 'asked about me'? Why would they do that? Did you call them?"

"No, no," Elton protested. "I swear, it's pure coincidence."

"You're telling me someone just *happened* to call here a few days after we talked about the Lillys to ask me to audition for them."

"Yes. Complete coincidence. I am as surprised as you are. But that's neither here nor there."

"An audition for what? They already have a guitarist. Do you think it's session work?"

Elton grinned and pulled out his phone. After a bit of navigation, he handed it to Toni and pointed at the screen. His browser was opened to a New York celebrity gossip website.

BITTERSWEET SYMPHONY? OIL HEIRESS-TURNED-ROCKER CANDI FAIR REPORTEDLY OUSTED FROM THE LILLYS! RUMORS SWIRL ABOUT POSSIBLE REPLACEMENT.

Toni eased herself onto a barstool, fairly sure she was in danger of stroking out.

Holy hell.

After sleepwalking through her evening shift at the coffee shop, Toni needed a sounding board. Her roommate, Yvette, had filled that role since Toni landed in Philly six years ago with a few hundred dollars in pocket money saved from tips at Mo's bar, odd jobs she'd taken around Bordon—and the small amount Seb had left behind in their Escape Bordon fund.

Toni had overestimated her ability to earn quick cash in Philly. Busking was virtually nonexistent, which had surprised her. Despite living frugally—sleeping in hostels or on the couches of musicians she met—Toni had burned through her savings pretty quickly.

Aimless and alone, she'd stumbled into Little Paulie's one night. The twenty-four-hour diner served as kitchen, rehearsal space, and a safe place to catch a few z's.

She'd often play for Yvette and the rest of the graveyard crew, then doze a little, only to awaken a few hours later to a breakfast of over-easy eggs, home fries, scrapple, toast, and coffee that Yvette would serve her at the end of her shift.

They became fast friends. And when it became clear that Toni couldn't afford a place in Philly on her own, Yvette had offered her pull-out sofa.

"You have to do it," she declared, when Toni told her about the call from the Lillys' manager. "What's there to think about?"

"It's an LA number. I can't afford to fly to LA."

"What about your savings?"

"What about them? You know I'm not going to dip into that account and mess up my interest rate. If I have any shot of buying into the Phactory, I can't touch it."

"Even if it helps you get the future you want?"

Toni grasped at the edges of reason. This was beyond implausible; it was laughable. Her? Auditioning for the freaking Lillys? She'd barely gotten used to playing for the smattering of people that showed up to her gigs at the Unicorn.

"Fine, I'll give you the money."

Toni's brow furrowed. "You just finished telling me that your tips have sucked lately."

Yvette slid her gaze away. "Okay, I'll lend you the money. It happens I have a little saved up for this exact thing."

"Oh, really? You saved up so I could fly across the country to chase a pipe dream?"

"You can pay me back when you make that Lillys bank," Yvette said, grinning. "You know this will be the biggest gig of your little life. You want that studio money, don't you?"

Toni exhaled a heavy breath. The mere thought of going through with something like this was enough to set her teeth on edge. The Lillys were on the cusp of breaking big. Everyone knew it. Toni had seen what even a tiny taste of fame could do to people. She'd watched her mother chase the spotlight for most of her childhood, doing anything to grab onto it. Toni wanted no part of that.

Yvette crossed her arms, her braided bob swinging forward to brush over her shoulders. "I know what's going on in that head of yours right about now. You're thinking *I don't want to play in front of a stadium filled with strangers.*"

Toni groaned and fell back into their lumpy old couch. "You know I'm not about that life."

"It doesn't have to be the end, just the means to it," Yvette said.

Do what you have to do in order to do what you want to do.

Seb's words echoed in Toni's head. God, she hadn't been able to get him out of her head since the night he popped up in Philly. Toni figured his fame-thirsty ass would love this whole situation. He would have pounced on this opportunity without a second thought, like it was his due.

Yvette seemed to share the sentiment.

"Doubt I'd even get a chance to play," Toni grumbled, sounding pathetic even to herself. "They'll take one look at me and my beat-up guitar and point me right back out the door."

The sofa cushions billowed as Yvette plopped down, enveloping Toni in the scent of cocoa butter with an underlying note of stale beer, fried food, and buffalo wings.

"Oh, please," Yvette said, waving her hand. "The false modesty thing doesn't work on me. They're gonna want you and you know it."

"No, I don't."

"Well, you should," Yvette stated, leaving no room to argue.

Clearly, when it came to her friends, Toni had a personality type. Supportive, caring, and pushy as hell.

"Maybe I should make you my manager," Toni teased.

"Oh! I'd so be down." Yvette was such a rock. Toni didn't know what she'd do without her.

She hadn't had many people in her life she could depend on. Once upon a time, Seb Quigley *or whatever he was calling himself now* would have been on that list.

She never would have survived her first five years in backwater, small-minded Bordon, Pennsylvania, without him. He'd made the town home for her, and then he'd left it behind and Toni along with it.

But that was almost eight years ago. She'd been a kid.

Despite his recent…visit, Seb was far from her mind now. Clearly.

"They are gonna *love* you, trust me."

Despite the conviction in Yvette's voice, Toni heard a note of sadness.

"Then why do you make it sound like a death sentence?"

Yvette's smile was forced but heartfelt. She exhaled on a heavy sigh. "I kinda knew this day would eventually come."

Toni sat up. "What day?"

"The one where you left Philly and never came back."

Toni folded her knee under her and turned to face her best friend, needing to reassure her. "I'm not going anywhere." At Yvette's skeptical look, Toni continued. "Let's say I get the gig. The most that'll happen is I'd go on the road with them or something, for a bit, and make a nice stack of cash. It's not like they're asking me to join the band for real."

"Isn't it, though? According to *CelebWatch*, they're looking for a permanent replacement. There's an official statement about Candi injuring her arm or her hand or whatever, but *they* think she and Lilly had a serious falling-out."

Toni waved her off. "I'm pretty sure that's just a gossip rag doing whatever gossip rags do. No one in their right mind would replace *Candi Fair*. Even if she couldn't play for a little while, her name alone would sell tickets."

"But what if it's true?" Yvette's eyes sparkled.

Toni patted her hand. "See, this is why I never read those things. It's all clickbait, or made-up nonsense to sell ad space. I may not follow the tabloids, but even I've heard all about how Candi and Lilly are joined at the hip. A package deal. Besides, I wouldn't want to be in a band. Not permanently. Too much drama."

"Okay," Yvette said, settling back. "Then think of this as an opportunity to flex your muscles for a bigger audience. Make a name for yourself outside Philly. It can only help you get what you want, right?"

"Maybe." Toni bit her lip, thinking about the potential money a gig like that could bring. "It'll probably be me and a couple of guys in suits. Maybe Igwe's assistant or something."

Her best friend looked at her as if she'd lost IQ points. "You said Lilly and Candi are tight, or were. You don't think Lilly will be there to approve Candi's replacement?"

"Again," Toni said, groaning. "Not a replacement."

Yvette rolled her big, light-brown eyes. "Fill-in. Whatever. Geez. Focus, girl. The point is Lilly will probably be there. Even if they're half-assing this whole audition thing, you'll still have the ears of her manager. Her bandmates too. Maybe even a few record execs."

She was right. Of course she was right. She often was, though Toni would never admit it to her face.

"You know I'm right," Yvette added.

"Stop reading my mind. You're not wrong," Toni conceded. "It is a possibility."

Yvette didn't even try to hide her smug expression. "When do they want you in LA?"

"I haven't actually called them yet," Toni hedged.

Yvette gawked at her. "What the hell are you waiting for, a gold-plated invitation?"

Jumping up, she snatched up Toni's phone, which she had stupidly left sitting unlocked on their thrift-store-find coffee table. Grabbing the slip of paper, too, she dialed the number before Toni could protest.

"What are you doing?" she exclaimed, fear flooding her system.

Yvette danced out of her reach.

Toni tried to grab for her phone only to have it suddenly thrust at her.

"It's ringing." Yvette's grin was evil.

Panic rose in Toni's chest, but she snatched the phone and brought it to her ear in time to hear someone say hello.

"Uh, yes. Hi. This is Toni?" Yvette glared at her and Toni shook her head. "I mean, I'm Toni. Antonia Bennette. Someone left me a message at the Electric Unicorn here in Philly. Philadelphia. From your office. This office. Mr. Igwe's office. For me. I'm Toni Bennette."

Toni slapped her hand over her mouth. Jesus, she was a wreck already.

A soft chuckle came across the line. "Hi, Toni. I'm Brenna, his assistant. We called to invite you to a closed audition. You're the guitarist, right? The one who performs as Toni B?"

Brenna's voice was kind, which eased Toni's frayed nerves a little.

"Yes, I am. What's the audition for, again?"

Yvette moved in close and nudged Toni to turn the phone so she could hear.

Toni glowered at her but complied.

"I'm sure you've heard the rumors, Toni." Brenna said her name as if she were scolding her. "Are you interested or no?"

Yvette nodded so fast, Toni thought her head might pop off.

"Sure. Yes, of course. When do you need me?"

"Good," Brenna replied. "Friday morning, ten o'clock."

Yvette's eyes widened. She mouthed the words *oh shit*.

Oh shit was right. It was already late Wednesday, and there was no guarantee she could get someone to cover her shifts at the coffee shop that quickly. Not to mention the fact that a last-minute flight to Los Angeles would cost a ridiculous amount.

"Could we make it early next week? I don't think I can get out to the West Coast before then."

"Oh, no. Sorry for the confusion," Brenna replied. "The audition's in New York."

Yvette threw her arms in the air and let out a silent cheer.

Toni grinned at her. "Oh, okay. Yeah, that's totally doable. What's the address?"

"I'll send you all the info," Brenna said. "At this number?"

"Yeah, this is my cell."

"That's great. They'll be so glad to hear it."

Toni could hear the smile in Brenna's voice.

"Oh, before I forget, make sure you bring an ID with your legal name." She paused. "Is Toni Bennette your real name?"

Toni let out a breath of a laugh. "Yeah. Well, Antonia is my first name."

"I bet you get asked that all the time," Brenna said.

Yvette grinned at Toni, and Toni returned it.

"Yep. Never gets old."

CHAPTER 7.

AFTER THE DUSTUP, SEB DID the only thing he could think to do—he threw himself into work. His inbox was full of people wanting to audition, and he responded to the people he thought might make a good fit. Or at least a good enough impression on the label that they wouldn't trigger the out clause in the band's contract.

Jordan had been right about one thing. It was unhealthy, this…thing Seb had cultivated with Candi.

He needed to get away from her for a while. It wasn't like he'd been much help to her lately anyway. Maybe her break from the band was a blessing in disguise.

Seb had just finished a call with SAGA, the studio they'd use for Friday's auditions, when his laptop pinged with a Google alert for Toni B, the name Antonia used onstage. Like Pavlov's dog, he clicked on the link in the email and navigated to YouTube.

Toni B—Man in the Box @ the Electric Unicorn, Philly

Seb felt the corners of his mouth turn up at the choice of songs. She always did go for nineties grunge. Once again, he cursed the quality of the video, barely able to make out her face.

Seb's mind filled in the details he'd filed away after seeing Nia in person.

He still couldn't believe that had happened.

Back at the Phactory, he'd listened to what she'd done on Jerry's track. It was good, inventive while still in the pocket. He'd tried to get Jerry to keep her work. The guy was a dick.

Staring intently at the video, Seb frowned. Something about Toni's playing was too tentative. He knew how uncomfortable she used to be onstage, and it didn't appear that much had changed.

Toni kept her eyes closed, her head down, despite absolutely owning that Alice in Chains number. She had the crowd in the palm of her hand but didn't seemed to realize it. Didn't know how to handle it. Or simply couldn't.

He wanted so badly for her to look up.

Toni and Candi couldn't be more different in that respect. But Toni was one of the few guitarists Seb had come across who could easily step in for her.

It would be a gigantic mistake to bring her in. He knew it, but that didn't stop him from fantasizing. Just a little.

It was a once-in-a-lifetime opportunity. Should he reach out to her? Would she even come? Maybe then they could find a way to...

He exited the video and sank back into his sofa. Best to nip that impulse in the bud.

On cue, Seb's cell phone rang, cutting short his inevitable downward spiral. Candi's named popped up on the screen, and Seb seriously considered ignoring it. Talk about bad timing. Instead, he slammed his laptop shut and answered.

"I was thinking," Candi said as soon as he connected. She had him on speakerphone, and her voice reverberated across the line.

"About?"

"I should be there for the auditions, don't you think?"

Seb couldn't have heard her right. "Come again?"

"I know everyone's pissed at me, that *Lilly's* pissed at me," she rushed to say. "But it'll blow over once I mend my wicked ways or whatever. Right?"

She didn't sound like she believed anything needed to change at all. Her words slurred a bit, and Seb made a mental note to have Eric check in on her. Normally, he'd already be halfway out the door, keys in hand, but he fought the urge. That's what had landed them in the shit in the first place.

In the background, he could hear her noodling on the guitar. It was the bridge of a song they'd been working on recently. Whatever he'd been about to say dried up in his throat as he listened to Candi play.

Hers was a rare gift, and it reminded him why he and the others had stuck by her. That and, deep down, she really was a good person. Or had the potential to be—they both did.

"Sounds good."

"It's missing something," she sighed.

Seb listened more closely and tried to imagine Lilly's voice weaving through the chords. His fingers itched to grab his guitar and tell Candi he was coming over, but good sense prevailed.

After a short while, Candi stopped midphrase and huffed. "I'm all tense. I need something to relax me."

"Sounds like you're already pretty relaxed."

"Why do you hate fun, Sebastian?" she whined. "And when did you get so fucking *boring*? I cracked open that ginormous bottle of Cîroc we bought. Remember? Made some nice cocktails with it this afternoon. Shame you weren't here, but I had a little company."

Seb's fingers tightened on the phone. "What company?"

"No one you know." She was baiting him, and he knew it.

Seb could practically hear the pout in her voice. He rubbed his eyes, begging the universe for patience. "You do realize you spent the afternoon doing the exact thing that got you sidelined and me nearly fired, right?"

"No, silly," she protested. Seb heard the unmistakable tinkle of ice in a glass. "I spent the afternoon right here, cozy in my own home with a few close friends, rather than out at a party or club where the paparazzi could catch me. No one to embarrass myself in front of here. Not even you."

Her words held more than a hint of bitterness, but Seb wasn't about to call her on it. She was making a tiny bit of sense, and he wanted to hear where she was going with it.

"Fair point," he granted. "But it's only part of the problem. You're drinking too much, even for you. What's really going on?"

There was a long pause. Candi drew a breath and let it out slowly.

"Nothing! I'm...I'm having fun. Living my best life," she said with a giggle that sounded forced. "Listen. I'll clean up my act. Play nice, lie low or whatever, and stay out of the scene for a while."

"All good so far." Seb wanted to believe her, for all their sakes.

"Who knows? Maybe it'll add to my mystique. And I'm serious about coming to the audition."

Seb opened his mouth to object.

"I should be there to help them choose the person who's going to step in for me while I'm..." She hummed in thought. "We'll go with the whole medical leave thing."

"Okay," Seb hedged. "What do we say is wrong with you?"

Candi sighed with clear disgust. "You're missing the point."

"Could you stop dancing around it for once?"

She groaned this time. "Fucking listen. As long as I behave for a while, and the newbie knows it's a temporary position, everything will be aces in no time."

She might have been on to something, but her phrasing stuck in Seb's gut.

"You keep saying 'for a while.' You'll play along 'for a while.' To what, get back in Lilly's good graces? And then what?"

She took another deep breath. "Don't make it sound like I have some nefarious ulterior motive. I just want my girls back."

He could easily imagine Candi's smile, but listened closely for the truth behind her words.

"You promise you won't cause trouble?"

"You'll help me?" Her voice brightened.

"I'd do anything for the band, you know that," Seb replied, trying to keep his voice as even as possible. "But I worry your being there will make an already tense situation even worse. Plus the press will likely follow you there."

"They're easy enough to ditch," she hurried to say.

"You always say that, and it never works," Seb countered. "Really, Can. If you're serious about doing right by the band, you might want to give them some space. Let things settle down with the label."

"Maybe," she said quietly. Seb thought he heard genuine remorse in her voice. "Okay, yeah...maybe. I'll think about it."

"Don't get me wrong, I appreciate that you're willing to try."

"You don't think I want to do what's best for *my* band?"

Seb knew Candi loved being a part of the Lillys. "I do, yeah. Of course I do."

When she spoke again, she sounded more like the Candi Seb knew. The one that worried the shit out of him. "Good answer," she said.

Seb wasn't so sure.

CHAPTER 8.

TONI DIDN'T KNOW WHAT TO expect when she arrived at SAGA Friday morning. She'd heard of the place, of course. As she stepped through the glass doors and into the darkened lobby, she knew she was walking in the footsteps of giants.

Everyone who was anyone had done a live recording in one of its spaces, rehearsed for a tour there, worked on an album or even a Broadway show. This was hallowed ground. Toni's impostor syndrome had never hit her so hard.

Snap out of it, Bennette.

Toni made her way to the reception desk. After showing her ID and getting directions to room 4B, Toni checked the time.

She was early.

Taking a moment to compose herself wasn't the worst idea, so Toni stopped in a hallway restroom. Thankfully, it was empty. No one there to witness her embarrassing mirror pep talk which consisted of: *Keep your shoulders relaxed* and *Remember to tune up before you go in* and *Don't forget to let the G chord ring on the second half of the last chorus, if they let you get that far in the song, but also don't hold it too long or it will sound cheesy.*

Toni closed her eyes and shook out her arms. She was so freaking tense!

"Come on," she whispered to herself.

Opening her eyes, she reapplied her lipstick, a muted plum that Yvette said complemented her skin tone. After adjusting the cups of her bra and smoothing her hair, Toni stared at her reflection and tried to muster some conviction.

"You've got this." Her voice sounded scratchy, bouncing off the tiled walls.

She so didn't have this.

When Toni reached the waiting area, there were two other women lounging about, along with one dude and someone who seemed to embrace every gender.

Everyone there was stunning, unique in a way Toni knew she was not. One of the women was decked out in punk-rock gear, complete with a Sex Pistols tee. The lone guy wore black leather pants that fit him like a second skin and a matching vest. Some sort of modern-day Dave Gahan.

Toni noted the bright-purple hair on one striking fair-skinned woman, a shade lighter than the temporary coloring Toni had streaked throughout her own black hair.

Hers were also the most emerald-green eyes Toni had ever seen. She had such a presence that Toni found it hard to tear her gaze away until a petite East Asian woman began to practice runs on her guitar. Her hair was a silky black curtain, so long it almost reached her knees.

She couldn't have been more than eighteen and wasn't much bigger than her instrument.

Toni didn't know where to look, torn between the girl's eighties-inspired outfit—complete with fishnets and gel bracelets—and her guitar, which probably cost upward of twenty grand.

Toni's grip tightened on her pawn-shop hard case. She found a spot on the end of one of the couches and nodded to those who acknowledged her, feeling their gazes graze over her skin as they sized up the competition.

The guy, an obvious veteran of these sorts of things, flipped through a copy of *Billboard* as he sat in a chair in one corner. He looked bored but Toni wondered if it were an act. She knew it was when she caught him watching the woman dexterously work over the fretboard with a speed that made Toni feel like an amateur. Though the instrument wasn't plugged in, Toni could hear every note she played.

She recognized the phrase immediately, an old Led Zeppelin riff that Seb had taught her years ago.

Strange how he kept creeping into her thoughts. Not that he didn't every so often, but lately it had been excessive. Last night, she'd dreamed about him for the first time in a year or more.

In it, they were backstage at the talent show her junior year in high school. Toni had begged Seb to help her prepare for it. But when the day arrived, she didn't want to go on. Hadn't thought she was good enough. Was absolutely sure they would hate her.

Seb had taken her by the shoulders and tipped her head up with a finger under her chin. She had looked up into his liquid green eyes and tried to soak up all the confidence she'd seen there.

Dream Seb had also smiled and whispered to her, words Toni hadn't been able to make out as he'd inched closer and closer, his eyes on her lips and his hand cupping her face. His mouth had brushed gently over hers and then... And then...

And then Toni's alarm had gone off.

She'd woken up, her heart pounding and her lips tingling with the kiss that had never really happened. The alternate ending she hadn't fantasized about in years. Years! God.

Toni blamed the fact that she was about to audition for one of the hottest new acts in music. This had been Seb's dream, to get a shot at that life, his dream for both of them. Their ticket out.

And the first chance he got, he left me behind.

Toni closed her eyes. She'd worked hard to separate her love for music, for playing, from her feelings for Seb. It had been eight years, for shit's sake.

She sometimes wished she could hate Seb, but she couldn't. He'd given her so much, had been so much *to* her.

Toni's gaze drifted to the guitar case at her feet. If only she had Minx instead of this pawn-shop beater. Okay, *beater* was a strong word. Her Stratocaster wasn't a bad instrument, and she took excellent care of it. But it wasn't Minx, wasn't the kind of instrument to help her stand out. Not like the ones scattered around the waiting room. If she added it up, Toni thought there was probably a hundred grand worth of hardware in the room. A hundred and one, if she included her Strat.

"Haven't seen you around."

Toni looked up to find Purple Hair Girl standing behind her, looking over her shoulder. She had to strain her neck to meet her eyes, the woman stood so close.

"No, I, uh, don't usually come to New York." Toni wanted to stand up. She felt tiny enough next to this Amazon of a woman that it was intimidating. Luckily, Purple Hair walked back to her chair, folding herself into it like a foal.

"Where're you from?" Long Hair Woman asked from her seat across the room. She set her guitar gently in its case, as if it were made of glass. Her hands were small, with thin fingers, and Toni wondered how she could even reach the notes on the fretboard.

"Not New York," Magazine Guy said, peering at the trio from over the copy of *Guitar Magazine* he now held. He snapped it shut and tossed it on a nearby end table. "My guess is Jersey."

"Nah," Purple Hair Girl said. "She's a city girl, look at those boots."

She pointed at Toni's eight-eye, leather Doc Martens. She'd gotten five good years out of them, but they'd definitely seen better days.

"Let the girl speak," Long Hair said as she got up and walked over to Toni. She offered a small smile. "Let me guess. Long Island?"

"Philly," Toni replied.

Purple Hair rolled her eyes and shifted her body away from Toni.

"Country bumpkin."

"Shut up, Lena. Philly's not the country," Magazine Guy said, chuckling. "Besides, didn't you grow up on a commune in California or some shit?"

Purple Hair—Lena—scowled at him. "I'm from *Sacramento*," she ground out.

Magazine Guy nodded. "Right, like I said."

"Shut up, dude, you're from Hackensack."

Magazine Guy held up his hands in surrender. "Newark, but close enough. Point is, Philly is legit." He looked at Toni. "I've done a few sessions down there. You a studio rat? Ever done any work up here?"

"I've worked on a few projects in Philly, but nothing anywhere else." Toni tried not to shrink under their scrutiny.

Long Hair dropped down onto the chair next to Toni. She marveled at the woman's ability not to sit on her own hair. "Who brought you in for this?"

Toni shrugged. "Not sure. Someone left a message for me. I called. Here I am."

"You didn't get a name?" Magazine Guy stood and stretched his arms over his head.

Toni could hear his joints cracking from across the room. He was older than she'd originally thought, maybe early forties. "Nope, only that they were from Jordan Igwe's office."

Lena snorted and started packing up her gear. "Guess this really is for show."

"You don't know that," Long Hair protested.

"Look at the bunch of us." She pointed to Magazine Guy. "This one's a relic."

Unfazed, Magazine Guy nodded. "Pretty much."

"Not to mention you're a dude." Lena turned to Long Hair. "You're way too metal for a band like the Lillys."

"Hey, I'm versatile," Long Hair protested.

"It wasn't a diss, May. I'm just saying. You're way too technical for a pop-rock outfit. This one, I don't know what her deal is, but she looks…" Lena eyed Toni for a moment, giving her a long once-over that made Toni's back straighten. "I dunno, *sweet*." It wasn't a compliment.

"And you?" Toni wasn't about to give this woman an inch. "Why wouldn't you fit in?"

"Oh, I'm sure I would. But if they're not bringing in the big heavy hitters—Bucci, Cox, B.B. Mac, you know, the ones every tour manager and producer in New York and LA have on speed dial—then they're not serious about replacing Candi. I bet this is all to teach her a lesson."

"I don't know." Magazine Guy gestured at the space around them and the hallowed ground that was SAGA. "Expensive lesson."

"YMI's got deep pockets, and Lilly's band is a potential cash cow for them. You think they're about to let anything rock the boat? The fans love Candi. They'll get her to toe the line."

Lena was right. Toni felt so stupid sitting there waiting to play for people who were only using her to make a point. Not that it should matter. She wasn't there to join the band, not permanently. She *was* hoping to use them to make some cash and, maybe, get her name out there. Still, she didn't like the idea of being a pawn in someone else's game.

"Whether that's true or not," May countered, "it's still a chance to be seen by the label execs, and whoever else might be in that room."

Lena picked up her case and slung her bag over her shoulder. "Ain't nobody in there that hasn't seen me before. I'm out."

With that, she left.

May rubbed her hands together with unreserved glee. "And then there were four."

Toni frowned at the math until she realized that she'd forgotten the fourth person in the room. Tucked away in the far corner, they hadn't said a word throughout the whole exchange.

They sat quietly, eyes closed and headphones in place, clearly in the middle of some sort of last-minute prep. Their long, slender fingers worked ceaselessly at an imaginary guitar.

"Who's that?" Toni whispered.

"That's Zeph," Magazine Guy provided.

"Zeph is a phantom. No one knows anything about them, not really," May supplied.

"I don't even know if it's a guy or a girl," he groused with barely disguised disdain.

May turned to Magazine Guy, a sour expression on her face. "Don't be a neanderthal, Gary," May hissed. "Zeph is neither. They're NB."

"Enby?"

At her question, May turned to Toni. "Nonbinary."

"Ah." Toni nodded. Zeph was stunning.

"They're a fucking brilliant guitarist," May continued. "Classically trained. Went to Julliard, I think."

"Been on some big tours too," Gary added, a hint of petulance in his voice.

Zeph had an unattainable but undeniable appeal about them, with flawless dark-brown skin, short platinum hair, and sharp features. If they were as in demand as these two had said, Toni didn't think she stood a chance. Hell, all three of them were more seasoned than she was. All of them stunning in their own way.

She stared down at her thrift-shop blouse, her faded jeans, and her Docs—then at the double doors on the other side of the room, already calculating her commute back to Philly.

What the hell was she doing there?

Getting exposure, Elton and Yvette would say. She was there for the experience. And the potential money.

Over the next hour, all Toni experienced was the desperate need to get it over with as each player went before her. Her only consolation was that no one came out of the room and said *Pack it up, kid. We have what we want already.*

Gary surfaced from his audition in a foul mood. He mumbled something about "that bitchy blond" before storming out the door.

May was smiling when she emerged. She winked at Toni, pressed a business card into her hand, and wished her luck before she left.

Zeph was the next to go. They hadn't acknowledged the rest of the group at all, so it was a shock to Toni when they came out of the audition room and stopped in front of her.

"Don't let them get to you," they said in a voice that was mostly a purr. "Go in, play for your life, and be grateful for the moment. Let that nervous energy move through you. Don't try to force it away. Use it."

Dumbfounded, Toni nodded before she could find her voice. "Uh, thanks."

Zeph smiled, and Toni felt like she'd somehow been anointed.

"Really," she said, feeling the need to express how grateful she was. "Thank you so much."

Zeph left without another word, headphones back in place. If asked about it later, Toni would swear their feet never touched the ground.

"Antonia Bennette?"

Toni hadn't noticed the guy standing in the opposite doorway. She jumped to her feet and then told herself to calm the hell down.

"Yeah, that's me. Toni's fine."

He looked skeptical but smirked. "Toni Bennette? Ohh-kay. Follow me, yeah?"

The guy wore an SAGA Studios T-shirt the same color as his mousy-brown hair. He was shorter than her, which somehow put Toni at ease. She caught up with his brisk stride and he smiled at her, revealing braces.

"Relax and be yourself. I've worked with these guys before. They're cool. Lilly can be moody, but she seems to be okay today."

"You're not with their, um, entourage?"

He shook his head, chuckling. "No, I work at SAGA." They'd stopped at another set of doors and he extended his hand to Toni. "Todd."

She shook it, grateful to see a friendly smile before throwing herself into the lion's den.

"You need anything? Water? Soda? Some weed? I've got some CBD oil in my vape."

"Uh, no. I'm good, but thanks."

The corner of his mouth quirked up as he watched her. "You're freaking out a bit, eh?" A soft Canadian accent curled through his words. Was anyone in New York *from* New York?

"A little bit. I still don't know what I'm doing here." She hadn't meant to voice the thought, but Todd offered her a comforting grin.

"Clearly you've got talent, or you wouldn't be here."

"I don't know—one of the others said this is probably all for show."

Todd frowned, then shrugged. "I guess that's possible. Either way, you're here." He opened the door. "Best to jump right in."

From where she stood, Toni could see Lilly Langeland. The

statuesque blond leaned gracefully against a baby grand piano as a man played a tune Toni couldn't quite make out.

"Ready?" Todd's voice was close to her ear.

Toni nodded, took a deep breath, and strode, chin up, into what could turn out to be a big step toward fulfilling her wildest dream.

No pressure.

It wasn't anything like she'd imagined. Toni had pictured a club-like setting, with a small stage that faced a row of chairs where people would sit, clipboards in hand, ready to pass judgment.

Instead, the room was full of random equipment that had been pushed to the perimeter to leave just enough space for a baby grand piano, an amp, and a microphone.

Lilly was deep in conversation with a dark-skinned man in a bespoke suit. He had attorney written all over him. Maybe someone from YMI? Or Igwe himself. How was this her life?

The two other women moved to a set of low midcentury accent chairs that sat along the wall. Both sets of eyes followed her as Todd led her to the front of the room.

"I've got Toni here for you all."

"Welcome to the jungle," the bassist called out.

Dressed in cutoff shorts and a pullover, her skin was a coppery-russet, and she'd piled her long, ink-black hair atop her head in a cascade of curls.

Next to her, the drummer gave Toni a one-stick salute before she resumed twirling it between her fingers.

Toni offered both women a smile and a wave. They tipped their heads together, chatting—undoubtedly about her.

As she approached the awaiting amp, Lilly looked up from her conversation and swept Toni with an impassive gaze. The suit turned and offered Toni a brilliant smile.

"Don't be nervous," Todd said, drawing her attention back to him as he adjusted the microphone stand to her height.

"Should I introduce myself?" Toni glanced around the room. All eyes were on her, but no one made a move toward her.

"They know who you are."

Toni set down her bag and crouched to lay her case on its back. She popped the locks and sighed. They were going to think she was a goddamned amateur, showing up for a thing like this with such a basic guitar. At least her recently reconfigured pedal board was impressive.

Beside her, Todd chuckled. "Geez, relax. They don't bite."

"Says you," Toni muttered, double-checking her pedals before handing him the lead. She glanced up to find Lilly's icy-blue eyes on her. "She hates me already."

Todd frowned and followed her gaze. "Lilly? Nah. She's just... different. But she's cool, you'll see."

"Why is everyone so quiet? It's like a church in here."

Todd took her guitar lead and plugged it into the amp for her. She didn't need his help, but she appreciated the company. He could probably tell how out of her element she was.

"It's a bit unusual," Todd agreed. "But they prefer to let you settle in without any distraction."

Toni arched a brow at him. "They don't think this silence is distracting? I expected them to ask about me. Where I'm from. What I've done."

He chuckled. "You think they don't already know?"

Point. She was probably the only person in the world who didn't google everyone she ever met or heard of, though she'd been tempted to search for Seb after their encounter. But nothing good lay at the bottom of that particular rabbit hole. She hadn't even mentioned running into him to Yvette.

And why was she thinking about him now?

Toni squeezed her eyes shut. She needed to focus.

Getting to her feet, she settled the guitar against her body and adjusted her brand-new purple paisley strap until it sat comfortably. She dug into the front pocket of her jeans for a pick, glad she hadn't forgotten to grab some on her way out the door.

"Deep breath," Todd muttered.

"I can do this."

"You're a strong, independent woman." His tone was teasing, and he winked at her when she turned to look at him.

"Is it part of your job to handhold the newbie?"

"Today it is," he said. "You sure you don't need a bottle of water? A shot of Jack, maybe?"

Toni laughed, some of the tension draining from her spine. "I'm good, thanks."

"There she is." Todd nodded to himself and made a few more adjustments. "I'm rooting for you, kid."

He walked away, much to Toni's chagrin. Why couldn't he stay?

"Whenever you're ready, no rush." This was from the suit. His voice was warm, and it served to ease a little more of her apprehension.

She *could* do this.

Toni settled the Strat across the front of her body and closed her eyes, willing her breaths to even out and her pulse to settle down into something more manageable than a gallop. She summoned that bit of herself that was her mother. Called upon her ability to draw in an audience, one she'd learned at Mary Bennette's knee.

But what to play first?

She turned the dial on the loop station, and stomped on the pedal, playing the opening bass line of a song she'd seen the band perform on YouTube, "Juliet's Got a Gun." Closing her eyes, she powered through the first half of the simple but intense rock-noir piece, pleased that her voice had decided to cooperate despite her nerves.

Toni stuck as close to their arrangement as she could, keeping some of Candi's flourishing runs between the rhythmic chords. She wanted them to know she'd done her homework. By the time she hit the instrumental section, Toni had forgotten all about the when, where, and why of it all. She let go.

Her fingers felt nimble, sure of their purpose, and she sailed through the solo, her skin damp enough to make her drop her pick. She quickly retrieved another and kept going until she lost track of time. It was just her and the loop in an endless dance.

"Yeah!" a voice called out after she made a particular run.

She opened her eyes to find everyone staring. Toni flubbed the next chord, but quickly recovered. She ended the loop and let the chord she'd just played fade away.

The applause surprised her.

"That's what I'm talking about," the drummer—Kayla?—cheered as she clapped. "Fuck yeah!"

Toni blinked, startled by how quickly the group had come to life. The energy in the room had shifted. As she looked around, she found nothing but appreciative smiles and appraising looks.

Standing in the doorway, Todd gave her two enthusiastic thumbs up.

"Thank you," Toni said, breathless as she positioned her fingers for the next song. She lifted her chin and smiled. She *so* had this. "Now for something completely different."

CHAPTER 9.

SEB WAS LATE BUT AT least he'd made it in one piece.

Midtown traffic was brutal, even for a weekday afternoon. He was glad he'd stayed at his place the night before, rather than at Lilly's. They'd worked late into the night, poring over headshots and listening to demos, and she'd offered to let him crash in her guest room.

With Candi occupying the bulk of his time of late, Seb hadn't realized how much he'd drifted away from Lilly and the others. It had felt good, amazing, to just *be* with Lilly, doing the thing that had brought them together in the first place.

Seb felt responsible for the rift between them, at least in part. And he knew Candi needed someone to be the voice of reason. To be her sounding board.

Of course, Seb had cast himself in that role, so he could hardly complain. Despite everything, she was his friend and he cared about her. Worried for her. But he couldn't let himself get caught up in her schemes. Well, *more* caught up.

Seb's phone buzzed before he could reach the entrance to SAGA. He hit the button, sending the phone to sleep without even looking at the number.

"Ignoring my calls?"

Seb turned to find Candi striding toward him, phone in hand

and Eric hot on her heels. They'd arrived in a nondescript silver sedan that pulled off the moment Eric closed the back door.

"What are you doing here?" Seb asked, incredulous. Then he noticed the sling on her left arm. Concerned, he stepped toward her. "What happened?"

Candi put a palm against his chest, holding him back.

"Calm down, Papa Quick. It's for show." She waggled her eyebrows. "Medical leave, right?"

Seb's jaw dropped.

"And before you get all bent out of shape, I thought long and hard about what you said. If I'm still part of our little family, I should at least be here to help them pick out my stepsibling."

Candi removed her sunglasses and looked at him, her expression sober.

Seb swallowed his arguments. She had a point. "A sling, though?"

One of her pale brows flicked up. "Genius, right? This way, no one will question why we're doing all this."

It sounded reasonable, and Seb knew from experience there was no way to stop Candi from doing anything once she set her mind to it.

He still couldn't shake the feeling that this was a colossally bad idea. "When we get up there, please don't start anything."

Candi pressed her free hand over her heart. "I promise. Best behavior."

Seb searched her face for any hint of deception but found none. "We can't afford to fuck this up, Can."

"I know. And I know I've been a lot to handle lately." She offered a soft smile. "Have a little faith, Sebastian."

From what Seb could hear as they approached the end of the hall, the tryouts were in full swing. Ironically, someone was playing the hell out of a song that had always reminded him of Toni. He smiled. She was everywhere lately, and he was finding it harder and harder to ignore the urge to go back down to Philly and seek her out.

Candi pushed the door and strolled on through, clearly certain she belonged there, but Seb skidded to a complete stop inside the open door.

Front and center, picking the last notes of the outro, Toni powered through "Hysteria" with all the finesse and poise of a seasoned pro. Pride swept over him so fast and pure that, for a moment, Seb forgot to breathe.

She was there. In the flesh. Had she looked him up online? Discovered his connection to the Lillys? Why hadn't she called or texted him? Why show up like this?

Whatever the deal was, she was fucking magnificent. Her feel for the tune was organic, her phrasing crisp and precise.

Seb tucked himself in a shadow by the door, out of her line of sight, and took the opportunity to really look at Antonia Bennette.

She'd changed and yet she hadn't, still petite as ever. But where his Nia was practically skin and bones, Toni was all curves. Her complexion was the same flawless medium-brown the girls in their high school had not-so-secretly envied, and she'd added a little makeup to accentuate her already full lashes and high cheekbones. Her lips were stained a deep plum color.

Seb only let his eyes linger there for a moment.

Toni swayed as she tore through the song, her hair covering one side of her face in a thick, luxurious fall of black velvet, straighter than when he'd last seen her.

He smiled, remembering the long, frizzy braid he used to tug on whenever he teased her.

The way she used to look at him, like he was the center of her universe, like he had worth... It had always confused and amazed him that anyone could see him that way. Some small part of him wondered if she ever would again.

Toni finished to applause, and Seb blinked to clear his head.

"Well, now," Candi said, plopping down on the arm of Tiff's chair. "She's got promise."

"What are you doing here?" Kayla hissed in a whisper.

Candi pouted at her. "Am I not a part of this?"

"Of course you are," Tiff interjected, giving Kayla a look that said *don't be a dick*. She wrapped an arm around Candi's waist. "Not the same without you, boo."

Kayla glared at both of them, opening her mouth to—no doubt—tell them exactly what she thought of the situation.

This could get ugly.

Before Seb could intervene, Toni launched into another familiar intro, effectively shutting everyone the hell up.

He was impressed—with her, not the relic in her hands—and he wondered what happened to the killer Gibson her mother had given her.

Seb had spent too many afternoons at a corner table in Mo's bar, staring up at the cherry-stained beauty. He'd memorized every scratch and ding and had even offered to sneak in and steal it for her, if she'd wanted.

She shouldn't have needed to; it was hers by right.

Surely Mo wasn't still keeping it from her.

"Good song choice," Candi said. She watched Toni closely, and Seb could see her wheels turning.

"I don't know it," Kayla admitted.

Toni had chosen an old PJ Harvey track, "Dress." It was a raw, sometimes raucous, occasionally delicate number that showcased both her guitar skills and her vocals, which were also unreal.

She had a pure alto voice and a natural falsetto that made the hair on Seb's arms stand up when she hit the higher notes.

"Fuck...me..." Kayla whispered, all of her attention on Toni.

From what he could see, Lilly and Jordan were equally rapt as they watched from their positions over by the baby grand.

Seb was unreasonably proud. Toni's skills were light years beyond what he remembered from their days back in Bordon.

When she finished, Seb wanted to march across the room and yank her into a hug, hold her until his arms grew tired. Then beg for every single detail of her life over the last eight years.

But, fuck. What then? He hadn't been there to hear the earlier candidates, but from what he'd heard just now, Toni had to be a front-runner for the gig.

"Where on earth did she come from?" Kayla asked as Toni pulled her strap over her head and rested her poor excuse for a guitar against her hip.

"Bumfuck, PA," Seb muttered without thinking, his eyes tracking Toni's movements as Jordan and Lilly walked over to chat with her.

He drank in the sight of her bright smile. Her nervous fidgeting, so familiar to him. The space around his heart ached with a longing he hadn't allowed himself to feel in years. Eight of them.

"Okay, she is a rock star," Tiff said. "But that ax is a piece of shit. Imagine what she'd do with one of yours, Candi."

"Yeah," Candi answered absentmindedly. She climbed to her feet.

Jordan and Lilly walked over to Toni, Jordan smiling big and toothy when Toni turned to him.

Lilly seemed...intrigued. Seb watched her size Toni up before she looked over at him, Kayla, and Tiff. Her jaw tightened when her gaze landed on Candi.

"Oh boy," Tiff said. "That's a look. Mommy's pissed."

"It'll be fine," Candi assured her, though she didn't sound too sure. Straightening her shoulders, she walked over to them.

"This should be fun," Tiff muttered, trailing after her.

The four of them surrounded Toni, apparently peppering her with questions or comments that had her fidgeting.

Seb caught some of Jordan's words of praise, and he wholeheartedly agreed. Toni was the whole package, everything they were looking for.

Not to mention everything he'd been missing. God... She was...

Shit, he was staring. Seb looked away, and caught Kayla's questioning look.

"What?"

Kayla shrugged, her eyes hard. "Oh, nothing."

Seb opened his mouth to ask what her problem was.

"Seb, Kayla, come meet this little phenom." Jordan's voice boomed across the room. Beside him, Toni was already packing to leave.

Kayla frowned at whatever expression Seb had on his face. Fear? Panic? He wasn't sure, but he followed her over to them.

The smile on Toni's face faltered as Seb approached, eyes wide with disbelief. She banged the sharp edge of her guitar case into Jordan's leg, and he made a pained sound.

Toni winced. "Oh God! I'm so sorry."

Jordan laughed it off. "It's okay. Seb has that effect on people."

Her hair had fallen into her eyes, hiding her from him. It wouldn't do. Seb itched to reach over and brush it back. After so many years apart, he needed to see her, to look into her eyes.

He needed to apologize, though no apology would ever be enough for what he'd done.

As if steeling herself, Toni took a deep breath and raised her head to meet his gaze.

Seb watched as confusion morphed into suspicion before giving way to unmistakable anger, which coalesced white-hot as her gaze narrowed.

After a few moments of awkward silence, Jordan cleared his throat.

"Toni Bennette, this is Sebastian Quick," he said. "Seb, Toni the phenom."

Lilly nodded to Seb in greeting and pulled Tiff over to the piano, where a pile of headshots lay spread out on its ebony top.

Seb's heart hammered in his chest. He opened his mouth, but nothing came out. The connection between his brain and his vocal cords had been severed, which was just as well. He had no idea what to say.

"Nice to meet you." A flush spread across her cheeks, but the ice in her voice sent a chill down Seb's spine and made his jaw snap shut.

Nice to meet you?

Despite the greeting, Toni made no move to shake his hand, clutching her phone in one and her guitar in the other. Her eyes were steely and there was a clear statement in them: *I don't know you.* Or, maybe, *I don't want to.*

Seb managed to nod. He wasn't sure how to play this but thought maybe it was best to follow her lead. He owed her that.

Jordan arched an eyebrow as if to say *What the fuck is wrong with you?*

From his left, Seb could feel Candi's stare burning into the side of his face.

He needed to get his shit together.

"Nice to meet you, too," he finally said. And kudos to him for not screwing that up. "Nice stuff."

"*Nice stuff,*" Candi repeated, mocking his stiff tone. She stuck her hand out to Toni. "You know your shit, missy."

Toni held Seb's gaze for a beat before she turned to her, giving her a warm smile as she shook her hand.

"Thanks so much. You're Candi, right?"

"The one and only," Candi replied pointedly before dropping her hand and walking over to Lilly.

Again, Toni's smile faltered.

"Okay," Jordan said loudly, his eyes still on Seb. He turned to Toni. "We'll definitely be in touch."

"That's great, thanks," Toni replied, her eyes kind for Seb's best friend. "I'll keep my phone charged."

Jordan gave Seb one last look, sent Toni a little salute, and jogged over to the others.

Seb found Toni studying him again, her expression indecipherable. Finally, she rolled her eyes with a huff and moved toward the door.

Before he could think better of it, Seb followed. Grabbing the door before it could close behind her, he trailed Toni into the hall. She was moving fast, giving him a healthy dose of déjà vu.

"Wait up!" He caught up to her in front of the bank of elevators. Seb watched her shoulders rise and fall on heavy breaths.

Despite her distress, Toni's voice came out even. Measured. Glacial. "You're the last person I expected to see. Again."

"Yeah, well…" Seb rubbed the back of his neck.

Slowly, Toni turned to face him, and they stared at each other for a long moment.

Seb couldn't read her at all. "You sounded good in there. Great, actually." His words were so fucking inadequate.

"Thanks."

Now that she was in front of him, Seb floundered. He needed to organize his thoughts. Figure out a way to approach her that didn't cause her to shoot daggers out of her eyes.

"I, uh… How—?"

The elevator doors opened, interrupting whatever Seb thought he might say.

Lifting her eyes to his, Toni walked slowly backward until she was inside.

"See you around," she said, dropping her gaze. "Maybe."

That *maybe* was enough to spur him into action. He stuck out a hand in time to stop the doors from closing.

"Can we at least talk this time?"

Toni's eyes flashed to his. She jerked her chin toward the audition room. "Shouldn't you be getting back?"

There was a slight tremor in her voice that Seb hated to hear.

"Give me two minutes. That's all I'm asking. I wanted to… I need…" Seb exhaled slowly as he stared into her wary eyes. She flattened herself against the back wall of the elevator, her grip tight on the handle of her guitar case. "There has to be a reason we keep running into each other. Right?"

Toni looked away, but he could practically see the war raging inside her.

"Aren't you even a bit curious?"

She pursed her lips. "Curious?"

The word landed like a bullet and Seb realized he'd already stepped in it. Great.

"Sure," she spat out. "I'm curious why the hell you keep turning up. Did you come to audition, too?"

Seb didn't know where to start, and the itch of an irrational anger surfaced in the back of his mind. What was *she* doing auditioning for a major label act? It went against everything she ever claimed to stand for.

He had questions, too, goddammit. And zero right to any answers.

"Let's not get into this here. Come on." Seb moved aside

enough to give her room to step out of the elevator, which had started to beep in protest.

After the space of a dozen heartbeats, Toni let out an exasperated sound and strolled past him.

Seb ushered her toward an empty rehearsal room, flicking on the lights as he followed her inside.

Toni paused to take in the room. She walked over to a skeleton drum kit that had been left in the center of the room. The cymbal stands were mostly empty, but a couple of tom drums and a worn snare were still attached to the frame.

Toni drummed her restless fingers along one of the toms. The room now had a pulse that matched the one racing through Seb.

To have her right there in front of him *again* so soon... It had to be some sort of sign.

"It's nice to see you."

Toni turned and looked at him, her jaw clenched.

"'Nice' isn't the word I'd use," she replied after an uncomfortable silence. "'Surprised' doesn't really cover it either. You keep popping up. Like a zit on prom night. Not that I'd know anything about *that*."

Seb's laugh caught him by surprise. "Tell me you're not still mad at me for skipping out on your junior prom."

She met his eyes, not an ounce of humor in hers. "There's a long list of things I'm mad about."

"Yeah," Seb agreed, sobering. "I'm sure there is."

Toni set down her gear and pushed up the sleeves of her shiny satin blouse. It was a deep plum color, and only then did he notice the tips of her black hair had been dyed to match. It was subtle but lovely.

Toni couldn't seem to hold his gaze for long. It darted around the room and then returned to his face. Looked around, and then took in his hair, his body. She was cataloging him, he realized.

Perhaps comparing Seb now to Seb then, now that the shock was gone and they actually had time to size each other up.

He'd been guilty of the same.

Standing in the spotlight of her anger and disbelief, Seb withered. Guilt gnawed at his insides, a guilt that had been there for years but which suddenly had teeth.

He cleared his throat. "I, uh…"

Having run out of real estate in the room, and apparently patience, Nia—Toni—squared her shoulders and finally faced him.

"I didn't get a chance to tell you before… You look awesome. All grown up."

Toni hooked her thumbs in the pockets of her jeans and cocked an eyebrow at him, a move so familiar it made him smile. "How long have you been keeping tabs on me?"

Seb drew back in alarm. "What? No. I haven't."

It wasn't a total lie, and Seb didn't dare read too much into the disappointment that flashed across Toni's face. He went for honesty.

"I mean, I did for a while, up until you left Bordon. Then I kinda…" *Stopped because I'd turned into a cyberstalker.* "I knew you might still be in Philly, but I didn't know you were going to be at the Phactory that day. Jerry was throwing a fit. I was in the area, sort of, so the label sent me to appease him."

Toni crossed her arms and stuck out a hip, yet another move so reminiscent of their childhood that it brought a reluctant smile to Seb's face.

God, he had missed her.

She scowled at him. "Apparently, I didn't have the right equipment for the job."

White-hot anger flashed through him, remembering the argument he'd had with Jerry and Elias. Seb took an involuntary step forward. "That was complete bullshit. The work you did was fucking stellar."

Surprise widened her eyes, but Toni nodded, her gaze drifting away for a moment. She squinted back at him. "You realize they're an all-girl band, right?"

Confused, Seb frowned. "Huh?"

"The audition." Toni looked at him like he was an idiot, and Seb thought maybe he was. "I assume that's why you're here. There was another guy here, too, but he was in and out pretty quickly."

"Oh!" He *was* an idiot. Toni didn't seem to have had the compulsive need to google him as he had after he'd seen her. Seb grabbed roughly at the curls at his nape. "I, uh… I work with them, actually. The Lillys."

Another flash of surprise crossed Toni's face. She quickly schooled her expression, curling her long fingers around her biceps. It was a protective stance that dislodged another memory from Seb's mental vault, this one not so pleasant.

"Now I get it. This is your way of making it up to me?"

"What?"

Toni dropped her arms to her sides as if she didn't have the strength for this conversation. "Me being here. Calling me up to audition. That was you, right? Some sort of…consolation prize for the Phactory session and…everything?" She waved her hand between them. "Because I think we all know YMI's not going to let you pull in some unknown to replace Candi Fair, even if it is only for a short time," she said, her words speeding up as she went. "There are people way more qualified than me, not to mention more talented and better cut out for all of this. And I don't need your pity. Or your charity. I have—"

"Whoa, whoa, whoa." Seb held up his palms. "It wasn't me, I swear. And that's some bullshit about better musicians than you.

You wouldn't be here if they didn't think you were on the same level."

Toni's shoulders relaxed a bit. "Okay." She let out a slow breath. "If you didn't bring me in, then...how...?"

"How did you end up here?" he asked, because he was dying to know how Toni had landed on the band's radar. "I'm wondering the same."

"Mr. Igwe called—or rather, someone from his office. They left a message with Elton." At his blank stare, she added, "He owns a club I play at regularly."

"They called for you? Specifically?"

"Yeah. And I'd never laid eyes on him before today, so I have no idea how he even knows I exist." Her gaze narrowed again.

Seb held up what he thought was a scout sign, not that he'd ever been one. "Again, not me. I didn't even know you were in the circuit."

"I didn't even know you were on the East Coast," Toni snapped back. "Last I heard, you were in Southern California."

Seb stiffened a bit at the anger crackling in her voice. He deserved every bit of it, but it still stung. "Did you look me up?" He tried for teasing.

Toni wasn't having it. She let out a bitter laugh. "Don't flatter yourself. Your dad said something to my dad a few years ago about you bumming on Sunset Boulevard, or something."

Bumming on Sunset. His fucking father.

"I lived in LA for a while, then Chicago," he said, the need to fill in their blanks almost overwhelming. They'd missed so much of each other's lives. "Spent my first summer after I, uh..."

He swallowed.

"Cut out of Bordon and left me behind with little money and even fewer prospects?" Toni's eyelids fluttered with emotion. He watched her swallow it down, nostrils flaring.

"Nia..."

"Don't," she said, the word splitting the air in two. "LA, Chicago, where else?"

"I..." Fuck, this was hard. And it felt wrong, doing it here. Like this. Seb felt like there was a timer ticking on his chance to explain things. "I spent that first summer down in Miami," he finally finished.

Toni's brow creased. "Never took you for a snowbird."

There was an almost teasing lilt to her words, and Seb latched onto it like a lifeline. "Yeah, well, I didn't have much money. Florida let me get away with wearing the free T-shirts I scored working in clubs and stuff."

At the mention of the money, Toni stiffened but gave him a sharp nod before another awkward silence descended.

"Look, Ni...uh...Toni, I..." Seb's voice petered out. He had no idea what to say. He'd told himself he would never impose. Never should. He'd been a mess at nineteen and he was probably an even bigger mess now, but he felt he owed her something. An apology. Something.

He opened his mouth again, not even sure what would come out.

"Why did you say yes?" He hadn't planned to say *that*.

Toni frowned. "To what?"

"To the audition," he clarified. "You do realize the Lillys are about to break big, right?"

Toni's gaze cut back to the drum kit. She ran the pad of her index finger along the lone cymbal someone had left behind. "I'm still not interested in being a rock star."

"And yet here you are." Seb realized a part of him was disappointed. Antonia had always been so strong in her convictions. It was one of the things he'd admired in her the most, though it hadn't stopped him from trying to change her mind.

Seb could almost see the thoughts moving behind her eyes.

"I thought I'd try something new. I don't know..." She shrugged. "Seemed like an opportunity to...step out of my comfort zone."

Seb got that. And, if it were true, he was damned proud of her. But he didn't buy it, not entirely. She was holding something back. Too bad he had given up the right to ask.

"Anyway, I don't know what I was thinking. And I borrowed a friend's car." She picked up her case and hoisted her bag over her shoulder. "I should hit the road before traffic gets ridiculous."

Seb wanted so badly for her to stay that he could actually feel his heartbeat in his fingertips. Having her in his life again was like waking up from a coma. He wasn't ready to lose her so soon.

"Hey," he said, and she looked at him. "Just so you know, I made sure you got credit for Jerry's song. And full payment," he added. "Rich? He filled me in on what happened."

Toni blinked, her mouth going slack before she pressed her lips together. She nodded. "Thanks for that."

"Least I could do," he replied. Understatement of the fucking century.

"Okay, well..." Toni strode toward the door, finality in every step.

"Wait." Seb lurched forward, catching himself before he reached for her. At this rate, he might have to get that word tattooed to his damned forehead.

She stopped, thank God, her hand flat against the door. The overhead lights glinted off the deep-purple polish on her nails, chipped in places.

Toni turned to regard him over her shoulder, and Seb swallowed past the apologies in his throat. He'd have to find another time for those. Maybe after the shock of seeing him again had worn off and some of her anger had mellowed.

"Will you please stop running from me?" Seb hoped that had come across light, teasing, and not as desperate as he felt.

Despite her lips curling up into a smile, the resignation in Toni's eyes cemented Seb's tongue to the roof of his mouth.

"I'm not. Running away was always more your style than mine."

Before Seb could recover enough to formulate a response, Toni was out the door. This time, he knew enough not to follow.

CHAPTER 10.

"WELL, AIN'T THAT SOME SHIT?"

In five words, Yvette had managed to sum up both of Toni's surprise encounters with the ghost from her past. Her best friend had spent twenty minutes chewing her a new one for not telling her about the run-in at the Phactory.

The thing was, Toni couldn't even say why she'd kept it from her.

After running into Seb—again—Toni had needed to vent. She'd called Yvette on the way home, relaying the shortest version of events she could.

She rarely did the happy hour thing, but after getting blindsided at the audition, Toni had needed alcohol. Lots of it. And the one friend she knew could talk her down from committing homicide was Yvette.

The beer was cold and fresh, not that Toni could taste anything as it went down. She couldn't shake the image of Seb's green eyes searching hers. For what, she didn't know.

"Did he at least say he was sorry for ditching you all those years ago and yanking his cash out of your collective piggy bank?" Yvette swirled the toothpick in her dirty martini.

"Not explicitly." Not that she'd given him the chance. She thought he might, though, if given the chance. He seemed so…contrite.

"Asshole," Yvette hissed. She drained her martini and signaled for another, her eyes lingering on the bartender. "Not one measly excuse for breaking your teenaged heart?"

"For the last time, he didn't break my heart. It wasn't like that between us."

Yvette smirked. "Sure, Jan."

Hot Bartender Guy set a fresh drink in front of her, and Yvette dialed up the wattage on her already gorgeous smile.

"Let me know if you need anything else." The man winked, grinning as he went back to his duties.

Yvette's gaze tracked the guy as he walked to the other end of the bar, humming with appreciation when he bent over to fill a bucket of ice from a machine.

"I know what I need," Yvette said just loud enough for Toni to hear. "Too freakin' cute, that one."

The guy was attractive. Smooth brown skin with a shock of red hair atop his head and the body of a swimmer.

"I thought you were seeing that film student. The blond. Sana something?"

"Unfortunately, that didn't work out." Yvette stared down at her glass.

"Why not? I thought you were into her."

"She was incredibly sweet, a lot of fun too." Yvette's tone turned wistful. "Alas, when school ends for her, she'll be moving back to Ohio. She got a job offer she couldn't refuse." She shook herself and picked up the glass. "And I don't do long distance."

"Bummer," Toni offered. "I liked her."

"Me too," Yvette confessed, her gaze drifting back toward the bartender. "But life doesn't always go the way you want."

No kidding.

"Back to your long-lost not-the-love-of-your-life-but-he-so-is. If he didn't grovel, what did he say?" Yvette asked.

"He wanted to talk," Toni said, trying to put her thoughts into words. "I guess I'm not ready to listen. What could he even say? *Sorry I ditched you to follow* our *dream on my own?*"

"You have every right to still be pissed," Yvette said as she plucked an olive from her glass. "I'd be more than a little salty if my...whatever he was to you...ditched me and ran off with our cash."

"He left my share," Toni corrected her, unsure why she felt the need to defend him. She searched for a way to explain the storm raging in her head. "I thought he was the one who'd set up the audition for me, you know. After the whole Jerry Gant thing and...the rest."

Yvette brightened. "You said you nailed it, though. Right? The audition?"

Toni thought back to a few hours before, how good it had felt to play in a place like SAGA, in front of those people, and walk away with more than her pride intact. She'd held nothing back and they'd seemed genuinely impressed. "Unless..." Yvette continued, frowning. Her gaze flicked to Toni's. "You know what? Never mind."

"No, tell me," Toni pleaded, bracing for the worst. "I'm going in circles here."

Yvette eyed her warily. "Well... Maybe he did tell them to call you up there after all, and he denied it because he didn't want you to feel obligated, or whatever. Maybe he thought he was doing you a solid, putting you in front of that crowd after screwing up the studio gig."

"He claims he didn't know I was going to be there. I don't know why he'd lie about that."

Yvette's mouth twisted. "Baby girl, you don't know that man," she reminded Toni. "No telling who he's become after all these years."

Toni didn't want to believe Seb could lie to her face, but Yvette had a point. "I suppose."

"The important thing," Yvette continued, "is that you brought your A game. I don't doubt you left their jaws on the damn floor." She grinned.

"Maybe. I hope so," Toni said. "Candi was there."

Yvette's eyes went wide. "Really? Was it awkward? It had to have been."

Candi hadn't been there when Toni arrived, but she was the first person Toni had noticed when she finished the PJ Harvey tune. That bright-pink hair was hard to miss. But it was the expression on her face that had stuck with Toni. Unguarded admiration and maybe a hint of concern, at least before she'd schooled her features.

"A little, but she was…nice." Toni toyed with the condensation dripping down the side of her beer. "She had her arm in a sling, so the medical leave thing must be legit."

"Huh," Yvette said, her attention drawn back to the bartender as he walked down to them.

"You ladies doing okay?"

"Yes, perfect. Thank you," she singsonged, making the guy blush. She held out her hand. "I'm Yvette."

"Ben." He shook Yvette's hand, a grin tugging at his lips. "Nice to meet you. How's the martini?"

"Kudos to you for not asking me if it's dirty enough. That line is older than you." She was in full-on flirt mode. Meanwhile, Toni was in the middle of an existential crisis. Ben's shy smile was a nice distraction, though.

He turned his chestnut eyes on her with a soft "hello."

"Toni," she supplied, conjuring up a smile from her reserves.

"I know, I've seen you play," Ben said, surprising her. "You're really good."

Toni hadn't realized how much she'd needed to hear that from someone without a possible agenda. The whole audition experience had her rattled. If she'd been summoned to New York as part of some grand apology from Seb, she wondered if all their praise was because of him and not because she had the chops.

Then again, if he were telling the truth, how would the band have known she even existed? It made her head hurt to think about it.

"Ouch." Toni rubbed her arm where Yvette had pinched her. "What was that for?"

"Where are your manners?" Yvette shook her head at Toni. "Ben paid you a compliment."

Oh.

"Sorry, thanks." Toni offered what she hoped was a warmer smile. "I don't remember seeing you here before."

Ben's smile dimmed a fraction. "I've, uh, been here about six months."

Geez. "Sorry." Toni shoved Yvette's hand away from where it had been slapping against her thigh. "I'm usually pretty focused on playing when I'm here."

"I get it," Ben said, waving her off. "I mostly work lunch and happy hour anyway."

Grateful, Toni took the out for what it was. "And I don't usually come in this early."

"I know," Ben said before nervously shifting his focus back to wiping down the bar he'd just cleaned.

Yvette grinned like the fool she was and leaned her folded arms against the bar. "You do make the dirtiest martinis, Benjamin." She popped her dimples for him when he turned back to her. "Keep 'em coming."

Ben nodded, returning her grin. He was flagged by another customer but gave Toni a furtive glance before walking away.

"Someone's got a crush," Yvette said before draining her glass. She speared the remaining olive and popped it into her mouth.

"Liquid dinner?"

Yvette scoffed at that. "This is the appetizer. I'm taking you out."

Toni shook her head. "Nah, I think I'll hang here."

"You already spend way too much time in this bar. Come on." She tugged on Toni's barstool until it turned.

"I'm fine. Really."

Yvette cupped her hands over Toni's shoulders and pulled her close, touching their foreheads together. "I know you far too well to accept your bullshit, Antonia whatever-your-middle-name-is Bennette." Leaning back enough to look her in the eyes, she paused. "What *is* your middle name?"

"It's none of your business," Toni said. "And I'm really fine. Trying not to get my hopes up, you know?" And determinedly *not* thinking about how good Seb looked. As confusing as all of this was, she hadn't failed to notice. Time had been more than kind to him.

"You need to get your mind off of everything. Get some perspective," Yvette offered. "Then you can make a rational decision on whether or not to accept the Lillys' offer when they make it."

"If."

"When," Yvette countered with an intense stare.

"If!" Toni couldn't allow herself to think that way.

Yvette sighed. "*When* they offer it to you, I think you should take it."

Toni rolled her lips between her teeth. Taking it would mean commuting back and forth to New York for who knew how long. Taking it would mean giving up key recording gigs in Philly and possibly missing out on something more in line with her goals. Taking it would mean seeing Seb again. Regularly. For the foreseeable future.

It would also mean putting a sizable dent in her studio fund, and possibly taking Richie up on his incredible offer. Another tidbit she hadn't shared with Yvette.

Man. She sucked as a bestie.

"How could I accept it, even if they were to offer it to me?" She held up a hand to stop Yvette's protest. "Which they won't anyway, so…"

Yvette regarded her and seemed to come to a decision. "Change of plan. We're going home. I'll have Ben put a six-pack in a bag for us. We'll order Thai food, sit on the couch, and binge something on Netflix."

Toni arched an eyebrow.

Yvette returned it, hers arching impossibly higher in a silent challenge.

"Fine." Toni exhaled. "But I pick the show."

"As long as it isn't anything depressing," Yvette insisted.

"When do I ever?"

"Toni, hey."

She glanced over, surprised to find Richie standing behind her.

"Hi!" Toni swiveled to face him. "Richie, this is Yvette. Yvette, Richie. He's the engineer from Phactory Sound I told you about—we worked that nightmare session." Toni silently cursed herself. "Shit, sorry. I didn't mean *you* were a nightmare," she added, turning to Richie, her face on fire. "You weren't. You're always great."

Richie smiled. "Nice to meet you, Yvette."

"Likewise." Her best friend checked out the newcomer like he was on the menu at her favorite restaurant. Sometimes she had a one-track mind.

"I was kinda hoping I'd find you here." Richie gestured toward the stool next to Toni.

"Oh?" She pushed it out for him and Richie eased in beside her.

Ben appeared at that moment. "What'll you have?"

Richie took a quick look at the colorful row of taps behind the bar. "Hmmm, you got any Downeast?"

"Let me check," Ben replied and left.

"A cider man," Yvette said, grinning. "I like this guy."

Toni swore she saw a blush creep into Richie's cheeks. Yvette was such a freaking flirt!

"Did you come for open mic night?"

"God, no," Richie said before he seemed to realize what he was saying. "Not that, you know, there isn't some real talent that comes through. Case in point." He gestured toward her.

Toni smirked.

"Smooth." Yvette chuckled into her hand.

Ben rescued Richie by bringing his cider, and the engineer took a long pull from the can. He seemed flustered.

"What's up?" Toni asked. "You looking to moonlight as a sound guy for local dive bars? Not sure there's much money in it."

"Nah, it's been a rough week." He ran a hand through his hair. "My dad arranged an impromptu meeting between me and one of his buddies, a guy who wants to buy into the Phactory."

Toni cringed on his behalf. "Not your top choice, I take it?"

He tilted his head. "You already know who my top choice is."

"Are you struggling for cash?" Yvette asked him. "From what Toni tells me, your studio is *the* place to be in Philly."

"Used to be, yeah," Richie said. "Not so much these days but I'm trying to fix that. Bringing it up-to-date with the latest technologies—top-of-the-line software, hardware, instruments, etc."

"It's incredible," Toni told her, not for the first time. "My favorite place to work."

Richie smiled brightly. "Glad to hear it. Does that mean you're considering my offer?"

He looked so hopeful, Toni hated to disappoint him. As much

as it broke her heart, she just didn't have access to that kind of cash. "Richie... The Phactory is, like, hallowed ground to me," she said. "I wish I could, but—"

"Hold on a sec. What offer?" Yvette directed a pout at Toni. "Woman, have you been holding even more stuff from me?"

Perhaps sensing an opportunity, Richie jumped in. "Toni's easily one of the best guitarists I've ever worked with," he said. "But she's also got a natural ear for production. I'm hoping she'll come on board. To be honest, I'm not above begging."

"Wow," Yvette breathed. "High praise indeed. And you are not wrong. Our little Antonia is one of the best to ever pick up an ax." She squinted. "That's guitar lingo, right? *Ax?* Either way, Toni is a queen." She raised her glass and Richie lifted his can in a toast.

"Guys," Toni said, squirming under the weight of all the accolades. She turned to Richie. "I'm flattered. Really. I just don't know how I can raise that much capital."

Yvette set her glass down, her tone serious. "What's the offer? How can I make it happen?"

"You can't," Toni said, loving her for even offering. "Not unless you have thirty-five grand lying around."

Yvette choked on her next sip. "Holy hell. That's a lot of money."

"No shit." Toni sagged against the bar.

Yvette pursed her lips, cocking her head to the side in thought.

"On the other hand, this is your dream," she said. "And where there's a will, there's always a way. Right?" She turned to Richie with a determined glint in her eye. "We'll find the money."

Richie brightened. "You really think you can?"

"Hold on," Toni said, glaring at Yvette. "I don't have access to that kind of cash. Neither of us do."

"There's always Minx."

Toni cut her off right there. "Even thinking about that gives me hives. Besides…" She addressed Richie. "I'm sure there's some-one with more experience you could ask."

"Experience isn't everything."

"Someone with actual cash, then," Toni countered.

A shadow crossed Richie's face. "Fuck. Working with one of Dad's guys would be like working under him all over again. I know it."

"Can't you take out a loan against the property?" Yvette asked. "In a neighborhood like that, the value must be through the roof."

"That would only reinforce his idea that I can't do this with-out putting the studio in jeopardy," Richie replied. "He bought the building outright in 1986. In all this time, he's never taken a loan out against it. It'd be admitting failure before I even got started."

"Sounds familiar," Toni said.

"In all seriousness, I think we'd make a great team. If there's any way you think you can swing it, any way at all, please…say yes."

He paused, gauging her reaction.

Toni couldn't help but picture it.

The idea of playing for the Lillys was exciting. She could admit that to herself since it was almost certainly not going to happen. This, owning a piece of a legendary place like Phactory Sound… It wasn't the kind of opportunity that would come again soon. If ever.

What if there was a way?

Yvette bumped her leg. "Go get Minx. It's yours anyway, and it's not like you're using it."

"What's Minx?"

Toni bit her lip. "It's…an old Gibson. Vintage."

He frowned. "Worth some money?"

"Some," Toni replied carefully. She thought of her mother's guitar, about why she was so reluctant to sell it. There was no real reason to hang on to the past. Running into Seb had taught her that much, at least.

Added to what she had in savings, the money she could get for Minx should be more than enough. Assuming she could pry it out of Mo's greedy, spiteful hands.

"You could set your own hours. Do session work," Richie said, as if sensing an opening. "Charge whatever you want. I think you'd be in high demand."

Toni wanted so badly to say yes. Everything in her screamed *yes!* But it was Minx. It felt...wrong to sell her. Almost like a betrayal.

"Can we get back to you?" Yvette said.

Toni turned to look at her. "We?"

"Sure," Richie said, exhaling as if he'd been holding his breath. "But don't take too long. If I don't come up with a solution in the next few weeks, I'll have to do something drastic. Like give in to my dad."

"And that would be a damn shame," Yvette said.

Richie nodded soberly. "It sure would."

He checked his watch, took another gulp from his can, and set it down. "I better get going," he said, standing. He fished out some cash and left it on the bar. "I'm recording a string quartet tonight."

He reached back into his pocket and removed a business card, offering it to Yvette. "My cell's on here."

Yvette blinked at it. Slowly, she lifted her hand to take it.

Richie's smile was positively wolfish. "Use it if you want, no pressure."

With that, he walked away, leaving behind an amused Toni and an apparently bewitched Yvette.

"I like him," she said, surprising no one.

"He's pretty cool. I can't believe he's serious about all this, about me," Toni admitted as she watched him through the window. "Ugh!" she groaned. "I don't know what to do."

"Yes, you do."

Toni took in Yvette's shrewd gaze. She was right, of course, but it made her stomach lurch.

"Time to pay a visit to your dear old daddy." Yvette finished her drink and signaled for Ben. "Forget the beer. We're gonna need something stronger to prepare you."

She was right about that, too, damn her.

CHAPTER 11.

"ARE YOU NERVOUS?"

Toni's hands tightened on the wheel of Yvette's ten-year-old Corolla as she drove up Route 22. She had borrowed the car for the two-and-a-half-hour trip from Philadelphia, a drive that crossed the socioeconomic diaspora of Pennsylvania. This part of the state was a world away from Philly's gleaming high-rises and high-end boutiques and bucolic university enclaves. "Nervous about seeing Mo?" Toni sucked her teeth, hoping to express her indifference. "Why would I be?"

She'd been unable to find a decent radio station once she got out of Lehigh Valley and had resorted to calling Yvette at work to pass the time.

"Because he's your dad, and you haven't seen him in two years?"

"Three," Toni corrected. "And he's only my dad in terms of our shared DNA. Even that's debatable. It's not like he ever gave a crap about me. Asshole was glad when I left."

"You don't know that," Yvette protested, but it was weak.

Even over the phone, her disapproval was tangible. Yvette had lucked out in the parents department. Hers were loving and supportive, everything Mo was not.

Yvette couldn't conceive of a set of parents as distant and callous as Maurice Robb and Mary Bennette.

"Maybe he's changed, and he'll be happy to see you," Yvette said, ever the optimist when it came to family.

"Mo made it pretty clear, practically every day, that I was a strain on his resources," Toni finally replied. "He hated being responsible for me. Did you know I started working at the bar when I was thirteen?"

"I thought it was to save money so you and he-who-shall-not-be-named could get out of there."

"No," Toni replied, her tone sharper than she'd meant it to be. "I had to, quote-unquote, earn my keep. I got a part-time, under-the-table job at the music store so I could eat something other than frozen chicken wings and government-cheese nachos. Just so I could pick up some decent clothes from the local Goodwill for school. Hell, so I could afford tampons."

Yvette cursed quietly into the phone. "You never told me all that."

Toni shrugged before she remembered Yvette couldn't see her. "Not much to tell. It's not like I was abused or anything."

"There's more than one kind of abuse, babe." Yvette's voice had softened.

"Yeah, well." Toni flipped on her turn signal and took the exit off the highway. "God."

"What?"

"This place is so depressing."

Even on a sunny autumn day, the light in Bordon appeared watered down. As if it had passed through a filter of misery and misanthropy. With the town's population of just under six thousand people and unemployment rate of over 30 percent, it wouldn't come as a surprise to anyone that the citizens of Bordon lived largely unhappy lives.

Philly had its own share of poverty and blight, but at least there were opportunities, or the promise of them. Out here, there was nothing. Your only options were to either find a way to live above the hopelessness—likely with drugs or alcohol—or to sink into it. Music was supposed to be her ticket out, hers and Seb's.

"Don't let it get to you," Yvette reminded her. "Get to the bar, demand that Mo hand over Minx, and get out."

"Something tells me it won't be that easy."

Yvette's sigh echoed from the car's speakers. "I wish you'd have taken it when you left the first time."

"Yeah, right. I didn't know where I was going or where I'd end up. Someone probably would have robbed me. Or I would have been stupid and sold it out of desperation when I didn't have enough money for food."

"You never would have sold Minx."

"Don't forget, I was pretty destitute until you came to my rescue."

"Nah." Yvette made a dismissive sound. "It would have taken more than a hot meal and a warm shower for you to part with her."

Toni hummed in agreement.

Yvette grew quiet for a moment. "You think *he* ever went back there?"

"Who?" Toni knew exactly who Yvette meant.

"Your high-school-crush-turned-stalker."

"He was never a crush. It wasn't like that." She'd learned the hard way that Seb hadn't seen her that way. She'd focused on what they had shared, rather than what they hadn't.

The only things that had kept Toni sane while she served out her sentence in the Sunderland County school district had been her music and her friendship with Seb. They were inextricably intertwined.

But somewhere between them learning to play songs off the radio, commiserating over their shitty home lives, and planning their escape, Toni had experienced her first flush of love.

Turned out, having the one person you thought you could count on skip town without a word was an effective cure for lovesickness. Toni had realized no one was going to rescue her—she had to rescue herself. It had taken longer, but she'd done it. On her own.

Still, driving through town, she saw Seb everywhere she looked. She blamed his sudden reappearance in her life for the nostalgia currently plaguing her.

"How much farther you got to go?" Toni was startled to hear Yvette's voice as she turned onto Mo's street. She'd forgotten the call completely.

"I'm here."

Toni pulled up to the curb and killed the engine.

"Good luck," Yvette said. "And remember, you're not a kid anymore. Don't let him treat you like one. If he gives you shit, you give it right back."

"I will."

"And don't leave without the guitar."

Toni adjusted the rearview mirror so she could see her reflection. "I'll try not to."

"There is no try, there is only do."

Toni laughed. "Okay, Yoda."

"Call me when you're on your way back."

Toni grabbed her bag and opened the car door. "Don't you ever do any work at work anymore?"

"Lucky for me, this place practically runs itself," Yvette replied. "Love you."

"Love you more."

———————

"Never thought I'd see you again." After staring at her for the briefest of moments, Toni's father grabbed a rag and began to wipe down the bar with focused intent. "You finally got some meat on those bones. Been eating those greasy cheesesteaks or whatever down in Philly?"

"Hello to you, too, Pop." Toni dropped her bag on the floor and climbed into one of the empty barstools. The place was deserted, even for a weekday afternoon.

Mo gave his back to Toni and grabbed a stack of dirty glasses from a shelf. He carried it to the bar sink and started washing them, one by one.

Toni watched her father, wondering what she had done that was so horrendous he'd hated the very sight of her. It wasn't a new thing, but still.

She looked down the length of the bar. Not much had changed. "How have things been with you?"

Mo grunted. "If you came here for money, I ain't got none to spare."

"Never did," Toni muttered to herself.

His head snapped up, and he trained narrowed eyes on her. "What did you say?"

Instinctively, Toni looked away. "Nothing."

No use getting him worked up before she told him the reason for her visit. That conversation would be rough enough.

Toni pointed at the transom above the front door. "You got a new Bud sign?"

His shoulders relaxed a bit with the subject change, but Toni knew he was still on edge. Always seemed to be when she was around. He stared up at the new sign like he'd only just noticed it.

Toni didn't get why she made him uneasy. She had been a good daughter. Well, the best one she knew how to be. Stayed in school, got good grades. She had even gotten into college—not that she could afford to finish. Even from a young age, she had paid her own way. She'd never asked Mo for a single dime.

"Old one was busted," Mo answered at last. He filled one of the stainless-steel sinks and squeezed a scant drop of dishwashing liquid into the water. Not nearly enough to clean anything. Spendthrift. "I told my delivery guy half the lights had gone out. Next thing I knew, they was in here installing a new one. Free too."

"Nice."

Mo grunted again, his standard answer. "It's bigger than the old one. And too damn bright, but it didn't cost me nothing, so…" His voice trailed off.

Toni couldn't tell if the sign was too bright or not, but the shiny neon and brushed metal was incongruous with the Great Recession chic of the rest of the bar.

Mo's was a no-frills, cheap-beer-and-well-whiskey kind of joint. Every night, disenfranchised locals filled its battered booths and wobbling stools, gathering to bitch about their factory jobs, or lack thereof.

The place ran on an endless loop. Week in, week out, you found the same beer selection on tap and the same food on the yellowing laminated menu.

As if on cue, Sallyanne—a waitress who had already been there for fifteen years when Toni moved to Bordon—walked in and sat in the corner to write up the daily specials that Toni still knew by heart.

Monday—25¢ Wings
Tuesday—Loaded Mac-N-Cheese
Wednesday—Chicken Finger Basket…

It was Thursday, which meant meat loaf.

Sallyanne waved when she saw her.

Toni waved back, wondering if the woman planned to die on her feet, serving chili made of mystery meat one rainy Friday night.

"You want something to drink? A pop? Water?" Her father's offer forced her to focus on the task at hand.

"Sure, a Coke." Toni pulled out a dollar bill, knowing the soda wasn't on the house. It never was.

Mo returned from the glass-front fridge with an ice-cold bottle of cola.

Toni put the dollar down and Mo's weary black eyes met hers. "Buck fifty."

Toni pulled out another dollar and slapped in on the counter.

Satisfied, for the moment anyway, Mo put the bottle down and took the money.

Toni watched as he rang up the sale on the old register she knew had a sticky drawer and a missing pound key.

"Keep the change," she said to his back. "For Sallyanne."

His only acknowledgment of her words was a slight pause before he dropped the fifty cents into the tip jar he kept by the register.

"Look at you!" Finished with the menu, Sallyanne walked over to Toni, a wide smile on her thin lips. "All grown and lady-like. I love your hair like this." She swept a hand in the air over Toni's blowout. "Though you had the prettiest curls. You get tired of them?"

"No, ma'am. This was just for a gig."

"Listen to her!" Sallyanne beamed. "A gig. You sound like a professional. Always said you had talent."

Toni returned her smile, marveling at the peach lipstick that had managed to both pool in the corners of the waitress's mouth and stick to her top teeth.

"How've you been, ma'am?"

Sallyanne waved Toni off. "Oh, please, with the ma'am stuff. I've known you since you were in pigtails. You can call me Miss Sallyanne now, honey."

"Thanks, Miss Sallyanne."

"Much better."

In her mid-to-late fifties, Sallyanne was an attractive woman. Born and raised in Bordon, she'd apparently never found a reason to leave.

Toni couldn't imagine that level of complacency. She'd wanted to leave as soon as she'd arrived.

"You haven't aged a day, Miss Sallyanne," Toni told her truthfully. "What's your secret?"

Sallyanne grinned and patted at the cloud of bottle-black hair that hovered above her shoulders. "Oh, go on. You're the one. I mean, look at you!"

She took Toni by the shoulder and spun her around on the barstool.

Toni bit the inside of her cheek. Sallyanne was always a tactile person. Hug attacks, tickling, kisses on the cheek. It was one of the many reasons why, if she wasn't off somewhere walking in Seb's shadow, Toni stayed in her room as a kid. When her father put her to work in the bar, it had been harder to escape the unwanted affection.

Toni's mom had understood. She may have even been the same way, averse to physical contact. Maybe it was inherited. Maybe it was learned behavior.

"You're pretty as an angel, you are."

"Thanks, ma'...um, Miss Sallyanne. You really do look fantastic."

Sallyanne leaned in, dropping her voice to a loud whisper. "Cayenne pepper, hon. I put it in everything. Keeps me fitting in my old prom dress."

Toni laughed, but covered it with a cough when Sallyanne gave her a strange look.

"Well, whatever you're doing, it's working."

Sallyanne seemed satisfied enough with that. She reached into the front pocket of her denim skirt and pulled out a small apron. Tying it around her waist, she glanced at Mo, who was busy ignoring them both. "What brings you back to little old Bordon, Miss Thing? Last I heard, you were living it up in the big city."

Toni's gaze flicked to the wall behind the bar. She looked at Sallyanne, whose smile quickly disappeared. Her forehead scrunched into a frown like she knew what Toni was about to say.

"I, uh, I came to get my mom's guitar." Toni spared a glance at her father and immediately regretted it.

With one look, he was able to lower the temperature of the room by several degrees.

Mo straightened from where he'd been working behind the bar and walked slowly over to where she sat. Above his head hung Mary Bennette's Gibson, encased in yellowing plexiglass as if it were a trophy.

Toni wanted to weep. She could see the years of dust and oil buildup from where she sat.

"It's *mine*, not that woman's, and it sure as hell ain't yours," Mo spat out, indignant. He pointed one knobby finger at the instrument. "You know how much that thing is worth?"

"Thirty thousand dollars," Toni answered matter-of-factly. "Give or take." At least, that's the figure she found when she researched the instrument online. She wouldn't have a real sense of its worth until she got it appraised. And restored.

Mo's eyes widened. He scratched at the scruff on his chin. More gray had mixed into his permanent five-o'clock shadow over the years. His rich brown skin was surprisingly unmarred.

"Was twenty the last time I checked." He narrowed his eyes at Toni. "That what you want it for? The money? 'Cause it's my due."

For what? Toni was dying to ask, but she'd been down that rabbit hole with him before.

"I need it...for a gig," Toni said evenly. "I want to play it."

Not a lie, she did want to play it for a while before she sold it. *If* she could go through with selling it.

Mo barked with laughter, a sound she hadn't heard often, growing up. "A gig?" Still laughing, he walked back to where he'd left off cleaning the barware. "Girl, is that what you've been doing out in Philly? All that education and not a lick of sense."

Toni gritted her teeth. She couldn't let his bullshit get to her.

"Mo!" Sallyanne chastised him. "That ain't no way to talk to your only child."

He sniffed with disdain. "I don't even know for sure that she's mine," he mumbled loud enough to be heard over the sports talk radio blaring from the one working speaker in the bar. "Always took precautions when I was messing around, especially with this one's mama."

It shouldn't have hurt. After all, it wasn't anything Toni hadn't heard before, any number of times. Still, it took a moment for her to catch her breath.

Before she could speak, Sallyanne cut in again, the color high in her pale cheeks. "Maurice Robb, I know your own mama raised you better than that. Even if it were true." She paused to turn sympathetic eyes on Toni. "And I'm not sayin' it is, honey."

She turned back to Mo, who had busied himself with polishing the splotchy brass of the beer taps.

"This girl didn't have no say over who brought her into this world," Sallyanne stated firmly. "Didn't have a say over who raised her neither. And considering she had a mama who couldn't keep a steady roof over her head, and a daddy who saw fit to raise her *above a dank old watering hole,* I think she's turned out to be a mighty lovely young woman."

Toni gaped at Sallyanne as she walked by on her way to hang the specials board, surprised and grateful for the unexpected show of support. She'd never heard her speak to Mo like that.

For his part, Mo seemed sufficiently chastised. He grunted and tossed the rag in his hand onto the counter.

Toni watched him take a moment to remove his glasses and clean them on his faded flannel shirt. Finally, he braced both hands on the wood and looked at her. It was then that she saw the weariness in his eyes. Not for the first time, Toni wondered why Mo had chosen this life. If he'd had a choice at all.

He stared at her for a full minute before he sighed and straightened up.

Toni prepared herself for another insult or barb. Instead, he bent over and pulled out a small stepladder.

Mo dragged it over to the guitar and climbed up to retrieve it.

Toni's heart lurched into her throat. She held her breath as she watched Mo lift the plexiglass cover, revealing the rich cherry-stained maple veneer that Toni remembered. He took Minx off the wall and made his way down the ladder, and grabbing the rag, he used it to clean the instrument. To her surprise, there didn't seem to be much to clean. It was immaculate.

Rather than hand it to her, Mo propped the guitar on his knee, turning the tuning pegs with one hand and plucking at the strings with the other.

Even without amplification, Toni could tell the strings were relatively new. She'd expected Minx hadn't been touched since she left town, but that wasn't the real surprise. That would be her father's clear ability to play.

Mo held Minx like he'd done it a thousand times.

Not for the first time, Toni realized how little she knew about the man or even his relationship with her mother.

Mo began to play, bending and soloing his way through a D-minor scale as he launched into a standard four-chord blues.

Toni sat, transfixed, as he ran through some fast licks before bringing it all home, ending with a lovely vibrato.

He laid his hand across the strings to quiet them. "I guess it's time," he said, more to himself than to anyone else.

Toni felt like she was intruding on a private moment. She edged closer to her father.

"You play?"

Her quiet voice seemed to startle him. Mo looked up, his eyes widening as if he'd forgotten she was there. His features had softened. Gone was the permanent scowl. There was genuine regret in his eyes. It was the most open, honest expression Toni had ever seen from him.

Mo straightened and cleared his throat. "I don't, not anymore."

"I didn't know you ever did."

"Yeah, well, the amount of stuff you don't know could fill a church." There was no bite to his words—his voice merely sank with resignation.

Lifting the guitar above the counter, he handed the instrument to Toni. His eyes remained on its lacquered surface long after his hands fell back to his sides. Then he squatted behind the counter.

Toni examined the body. The bridge showed a few signs of deterioration. The pick guard would definitely need replacing. And though the paint on the body was worn down almost to the wood underneath in one spot, Toni didn't want to change that. It had been earned through years of practice and performance, her mother's and whomever had come before her. Maybe even from Mo himself.

"Don't sell it," her father warned as he emerged with Minx's case, no heat in his voice. He set it on the bar and opened it.

Toni nestled the guitar into its cushy shag interior before they latched it shut.

Mo flattened his hands on the surface. "If you need the money, you come and you sell it back to me."

Shocked, Toni could only nod.

Shit. Now what? Her whole reason for the trip was to sell Minx and buy into the Phactory.

Maybe I could borrow against it instead.

The idea of disappointing Mo didn't sit right somehow. Minx was the one thing they seemed to both care about. "I won't," she heard herself say.

"Well, don't." Mo snatched up the stepladder and put it back, his scowl back in place.

"I said I wouldn't," Toni replied, a little annoyed even though she was possibly lying. He didn't know that.

"You also said you wouldn't mess around with the Quigley boy, but that promise didn't hold much water."

"Seb and I weren't *messing around*, Pop. He was my friend, that's all."

Mo scoffed. "I ain't blind, child. I saw the way you'd be looking at him, prancing around in those little tops and shorts."

"It gets stupid hot here in the summer," she argued, heat rising up her neck.

"Following him around like a lost puppy," Mo continued, ignoring her protestations. "Trying to get him to notice you."

Okay, that part was true. Seemed the only person who noticed was Mo.

"I guess you got it honestly. Your mama was a—"

"I am not my mother." Toni had to shut him down. Right. There.

After a short standoff, Mo nodded and resumed his bar prep. "Well... You best get going. I ain't got time to stand around and talk. Some of us got to work."

Toni hopped off the stool, guitar in hand. "All right, yeah."

Grabbing a cocktail napkin, she fished a pen out of her bag. "I'm writing down my address, in case… Well, just in case." She slid the napkin across the counter, avoiding the wet ring left by the bottle.

Mo didn't acknowledge her.

Typical. She moved to go and stopped. "Hey…Dad?"

"What now? You got what you came for," Mo asked as he reached into the cooler and brought out a bottle of Bud. He leaned heavily against the counter, as if his energy had been drained from his body.

Toni sighed. Whatever momentary thaw there had been in the ice between them was gone. It was just as well.

She pushed open the door and walked out of Mo's Bar, probably for the last time.

CHAPTER 12.

SEB TOOK THE ONLY OPEN table at Flick Café and sat stiffly in the wooden chair. He hated places like this. The room was too small for the number of tables that occupied it, and every one of them was surrounded by artsy hipster types, up-and-coming models, and heirs to Manhattan's corporate wealth.

At least the coffee was halfway decent.

A woman walked by, brushing against his arm, and Seb raised his eyes to scowl at her but ended up doing a double take. It was the hair. It reminded him of Toni.

Everything did.

Days had passed and Seb could not stop thinking about her. The vault that had contained all things related to Antonia Bennette had been cracked open, and Seb couldn't get the damned thing to shut. Toni was everywhere.

She was in his earbuds when he worked out to his old Caspian's Ghost playlist. She was in his morning coffee where he'd begun to add a little cream again, something he hadn't done in years.

Most importantly, she was in his conversations with Jordan and the band. She was on their short list... How could she not be? She was exactly what the Lillys needed.

But Seb was terrified, both of never seeing her again and of having her around twenty-four seven, which would happen if the band got its way.

None of the others knew of his connection to Toni, and if they did, they'd probably move on to someone else.

He should've told them.

He probably should tell them.

That would solve a few things.

One, she was as good as Candi, if not better. And having someone that good as a stand-in wouldn't do, not if Candi was serious about regaining her place in the group.

Two, Seb wouldn't have to deal with all the shit being around Toni was bound to dig up. He wouldn't have to examine the last eight years of his life and wonder why he'd been such a coward. Why he had never reached out to her to say sorry or even a simple *Hello, glad you're doing okay after I broke my promise to always look after you.*

But speaking up would also ruin Toni's chance at what could be a life-changing opportunity, the kind of opportunity she deserved. One he had the ability to take away from her with one word to the others.

Jesus.

Candi breezed into the café, dressed in a white crop top with MOSCHINO splashed across the front in big block letters, and faded black skinny jeans that Seb knew were already ripped when she bought them.

He shook his head at the matching MOSCHINO sling on her arm.

Spotting him, she strolled across the room like she owned it, a cloud of whispers rising as she passed.

"Why did you choose this place?" he asked when she sat down. "You know the paps have a permanent camp outside."

Candi's mouth curved into a grin as she removed yet another pair of designer sunglasses. "Silly Sebastian, you answered your own question."

"What is your obsession with being splashed all over Page Six?"

"Oh, Seb. Haven't I taught you anything about how this works?" Candi dropped the sugary tone from her voice. "You're here. This way they'll know I'm not completely cut off from my girls."

"So, you're using me," he stated flatly, surprised at how unfazed he was by the concept.

Candi's eyes twinkled. "Aren't I always?"

Seb had to laugh at that. He shook his head and looked out the window, easily spying the telephoto lens of a camera peeking out from behind a parked car. Their attempts at subtlety were laughable.

"Don't pout, you'll get wrinkles," Candi purred, sliding her hand across the table to cover Seb's. "Anyway, it's not like you never used me."

Seb was not about to touch that one. Instead, he shook his head and looked away. "You're ridiculous."

"Maybe, but that's what my fans love about me." Candi sat back in her seat and scanned the room.

"It's also what'll make them turn on you if you don't stop acting like a spoiled brat."

"Never stopped them before," she retorted, winking.

Candi turned her head toward the window. She didn't look directly at the camera, but gave the photographer a clear shot of her face. Such a pro.

Seb watched as even more press appeared outside the café. Word had apparently gotten out about Candi's arrival. She'd been there for less than two minutes. It had to be a record. Seb turned his back to the window.

Candi's eyes snapped to him. "What are you doing?"

"It's you they want," Seb answered, thumbing through the notifications on his phone.

The front door opened, and a few more local celebs wandered in.

"Fuck, this is better than I hoped," Candi whispered.

"Glad it's working out for you." He moved to stand. "Okay, I'm out."

Candi grabbed his wrist, her nails digging into his skin. "No, stay. Please?" It was the *please* that stopped him from yanking his arm away.

"Can't you stay a little longer?" There was a hint of desperation in her voice, but she smiled up at him, hopeful. "I want a few more background shots."

"Being seen in the right place?"

Her smile widened. "With the right person. Sit. Please?"

Against his better judgment, Seb sat back down. "At least order something."

Candi raised her hand and snapped her fingers at a passing waitress.

Seb was incredulous. Entitlement had a poster child, and she was sitting across from him, completely clueless.

The young woman hustled over, obviously frazzled but smiling, nonetheless. "Sorry, what can I get you?"

"I'll have a double latte, almond milk, with a sprinkle of cinnamon, and he'll have an Americano. Black."

"I already had my morning coffee."

Candi looked affronted. "I can't sit here and drink while you just sulk at me."

Seb managed to turn his grimace into a smile before ordering. "Make mine a latte, please. Whole milk."

"Sure, I'll put those in," the server said. "Anything to eat?"

Candi perked up. "Ooo! Some of those yummy toasted chickpeas, if you have any."

The woman frowned. "I'm not sure we do, but I'll check for you. Anything else?"

"No, doll, that's it." Candi shooed her away. "Thank you," she sang after her.

Seb stared at her, caught between disgust and bemusement.

"You really are a piece of work."

Candi nudged the inside of his thigh. She'd kicked off her sandal and rested her foot on his thigh.

Seb jumped in his seat. "What are you doing?" He barely managed to contain it to a whisper.

She tsked softly. "Giving them something to chew on."

"I'm not here to be your tabloid fodder."

"Fine," Candi huffed, settling back in her seat, feet back on the floor where they belonged. "What did you think about the auditions?"

He'd known the question was coming and could tell Candi had been itching to ask. To stall, Seb pulled out his phone and thumbed through his notifications again. "They were all right, I guess."

"Anyone stand out to you?"

Something about the way she asked the question brought his hackles up. "Nah, not really," he answered. "You?"

Candi twirled a pink curl around her finger. "I was impressed with the one that was playing when we arrived. Tanya? The one you followed out into the hall."

Seb could feel her eyes on the top of his head as he focused on the phone and fought to control his voice. "Who did I follow?"

"The Aaliyah look-alike. You left the room right after she did," Candi said, her tone far too even.

Seb pretended to search his memory. Under the table, he gripped his knee and dug in hard to cover the fact that he was freaking the fuck out. How could he have been so stupid? Of course people saw him chase after Toni. He hoped that was all they saw.

"Oh, I wasn't following her. I had to hit the head." He

shrugged one shoulder, hoping that sold the lie. "It was a bitch of a commute and I had to piss."

"Oh," she said after a beat.

"Anyway, you left before the second round. There were some talented people in that group. All in all, the day wasn't a total waste."

A smirk lifted the corner of her mouth. "I went to show my support, not actually sit through ten thousand renditions of 'Stairway to Heaven.'"

Seb laughed. "Oddly enough, I only remember one of those."

Candi's gaze sharpened. "Anyone I actually know come out to throw dirt on my proverbial grave?"

"Zeph, but that was before we got there."

Candi cursed under her breath and nodded. "Zeph would be great. You think they'd accept? If we made an offer?"

"Wait, you *want* us to find someone?"

Candi sighed dramatically. "You're pretty, but not very bright."

"Fuck you." Seb laughed again, despite himself. "Seriously, though. I thought you were going to talk to Lilly and smooth things over before it got to this point."

"And say what? *I'm sorry, Mommy?*" She exhaled a bitter laugh. "I'm not her fucking ward. If I want to party, I'm going to party."

"You blew off the showcase, Candi," Seb reminded her. "And you were the one harping on about how doing the festival circuit would break the band worldwide."

"Yeah, well." Candi scrolled through her phone. "I wasn't always alone in that. You were right there with me, for a time. Don't put it all on me."

Seb slumped in his chair and ran both hands through his hair. "That's fair."

"Damn right it is," she said, tossing her cell onto the table.

The waitress returned with their drinks and a bowl of snacks. Seb thanked her.

"You have to help me fix this mess," Candi argued suddenly, desperation creeping back into her voice. "I... Seb, I can't lose this. I don't want to go running back to Daddy with my tail between my legs and listen to him say *I told you so* for the rest of his life."

She dug into her purse and pulled out a bottle of pills. She popped the cap and tossed one in her mouth.

Seb looked around to see if anyone noticed, but they were all absorbed in their own conversations. The one Candi-obsessed photographer Seb had recognized from the hotel had moved from his spot across the street. Seb couldn't see him, but that didn't mean one of the others didn't get a shot of her indulging in her habit.

He leveled a glare at Candi.

"What?" She bristled. "They're prescribed."

"By whom? You haven't been to a doctor in all the time I've known you."

Candi grinned. "A girl has friends."

"Friends."

"Very good friends." She washed the pill down with her coffee, grinning at Seb over the lip of her cup.

"If you're serious about wanting to fix things, you have got to cut this shit out. Besides," he added, "it's not healthy. You're not... You need to take better care of yourself, Can."

"Listen to you. Pot." She pointed to him and then to herself. "Kettle. Since when did you go all *straight edge* on me? When we met, you were out of your head on who knows what."

Seb winced, remembering the sorry state he'd been in. It was the last time he'd spoken to his father, and it had been a blowout.

Those first few nights with Candi were a blur of liquor, parties, and more liquor. Plus a few other substances Seb hadn't bothered to identify before taking them.

Candi sighed and leaned forward, lowering her voice to a near-whisper. "Hey, I'm sorry. I didn't mean to bring up bad memories. I just... My family's been up my ass."

"This isn't the way to handle them," he said. "All you're doing is proving them right."

She blinked lazily. "Maybe they are."

"Stop." Seb kept his voice low. "Don't say that. You know it isn't true."

Candi opened her mouth, as if to protest, but snapped it shut. At that moment, she seemed so young.

"Can we go somewhere else? And talk?" he asked. "Somewhere with fewer cameras and cell phones, maybe?"

Candi eased back into her chair. She looked sad and a little lost. "You..." she began, the word catching on a breath. "You're going to write me off too."

Seb slid his hand across the table and held it open for her to take.

She hesitated before finally slipping her hand into his, and Seb gave it a squeeze.

"I care about you, Can, you know that. Right? Hell, you're one of my best friends. I'm not going to write you off," he said, choosing his words carefully. "But..."

Candi flinched and tried to retract her hand, but Seb held on.

"But," he said, softer this time, "something's got to change. You know that, right? Not only because, Jesus, it's not healthy, but also because you're pushing away everyone who cares about you. How can we all have one another's backs when you're all caught up in..."

Seb nodded toward her purse.

Candi's gaze slid to her purse and then to the table and their hands. She curled her fingers around his.

"I'm supposed to be looking out for you, and for Lilly and Tiff and Kayla—that's part of my job. I can't do that like this, stuck in the middle. I can't." He waited for her to meet his eyes again. "You feel me?"

"Yeah," she said and cleared her throat. "Yeah, sure." Her voice was stronger the second time, and she mustered up a smile that Seb was glad to see.

"I'm not abandoning you, I promise."

"M'kay." She gave him a nod and Seb let go of her hand. "But I need you to help me make sure they don't replace me. I want everything with the showcase to go well, I do. I want someone who can help carry the load while I'm...while I'm sidelined. But I wanna come back. Soon."

Seb sat back in his chair. "You do what Lilly asked you to do—"

"Told," Candi snapped, her voice low. "What she *told* me to do."

"Do what they've asked you to do and you'll be fine," Seb said calmly. "In the meantime, we need someone to step in. Someone who can shred almost as good as you, not that there are many who can."

He knew of one person but pushed any thoughts of Toni back into the vault.

Candi's smile was sweet, genuine. One he rarely saw lately. "And I want to help whoever that is." Sincerity rang in her words, much to Seb's relief. "I could...I dunno." She bit her lip, uncharacteristically unsure of herself. "I could help them learn my stuff so they don't fuck up completely."

Seb nodded, eager to encourage this line of thought. "Yeah? That's a fantastic idea."

A slow smile spread across her pink lips. "Can't have them

ruining the Lillys' reputation, now, can I? I have to protect my girls from amateurs."

Seb grinned, ready to have her on board. "Absolutely. You've worked too hard to let someone come in and wreck it all."

"So," she said brightly, more like her usual self, "you'll let me know when you choose someone? Where will the band rehearse? I wanna be there."

"Slow down," Seb cautioned. "Talk to the girls first. I mean *really* talk. You should come to Kayla's. We're gonna go through the pool of prospects."

Candi flinched a little. "I don't think I'm Kayla's favorite person right now," she said, almost contrite. "Maybe you could smooth the way?"

"Like I always do," Seb said.

"Like you do most of the time," Candi reminded him, her tone playful. "Please? I'm not good at making nice. I can get—"

"Obnoxious?" he offered, only half teasing.

"Defensive," she finished, narrowing her eyes. "You know I don't handle this shit very well."

"I know. I'll see what I can do," Seb said, knowing it wasn't really his fight but unable to say no. Candi may have grown up with enormous wealth and privilege, but she'd never really had anyone in her corner. He got that. He could be that for her. "Can't promise anything, since I'm in the shithouse myself, but I'll try."

"You always try," she said, giving him a warm smile. "You're the best, Sebastian Quick. I don't know what any of us would do without you."

He waved her off, a reluctant smile tugging at the corner of his mouth. It felt good to be needed, but it was a slippery slope. He'd already let them all down, let his own issues cloud his judgment and get in the way.

He'd made that mistake years ago and wasn't interested in

letting history repeat itself. Not when he'd finally found his place in the world.

"Toni!"

Seb's head snapped up, his heart suddenly in his throat. "What?"

"That was her name, the girl with the black and purple hair," Candi said, meeting his startled gaze. "She was good. Scary good."

He swallowed thickly. "Was she?"

"Yep. Hot too."

"I hadn't noticed." Seb needed to get out of there. Fast. He plopped some money on the table. "Anyway, I've got shit to do."

A knowing smile spread slowly across Candi's lips. "Sure, Seb. Whatever you say."

CHAPTER 13.

"I KNOW MY PICK," TIFF announced to the room. They had gathered in Kayla's loft to talk through their options for their temporary guitarist.

"Gary's too old for you." Kayla laughed when Tiff gave her the finger. "Or maybe you're into silver foxes now?"

Seb wasn't too surprised when he arrived and found Candi already there. She could talk her way in or out of almost any situation, and she'd never been one to rely on anyone else to do her talking for her. He chose to take it as a good sign that she'd been allowed to participate in the decision-making process without any go-betweening from him.

There were empty pizza boxes strewn across the hardwood floor of the living room and on top the steamer trunk that served as Kayla's coffee table.

Lilly, Jordan, and Tiff had taken the sofa, with Tiff's feet resting in Jordan's lap.

Seb chose a spot on the floor, resting his back against an ottoman. Candi had straddled one of Kayla's dining room chairs.

Kayla sat perched on a windowsill overlooking the park below. She was the only member of their gang that lived outside New York City, and they'd all given her shit about it until they saw what she got for her twenty-five hundred per month rent.

"Not him, you Dave Grohl wannabe." Tiff paused mid-insult to think. "I mean, sure. He was hot, but I meant the girl from Philly."

"She was good, but she was kinda... I dunno." Kayla tapped the tip of the drumstick she'd been twirling against her temple. "Sweet, maybe? Too innocent? I think Zeph's a better fit for us."

"Zeph is one of the best out there, but not a good fit for us," Lilly stated. "Zeph needs to be out front and center, not playing behind someone else. I've been telling them that forever."

"So we're back to Philly, 'cause May had some serious timing issues." Kayla scrunched up her nose in distaste.

"She's not that young, Philly...er...Toni," Jordan provided, thumbing through his notes. "Inexperienced, but she's been making a name for herself."

Seb wondered what sort of notes Jordan had written about her, but he knew what they all meant. Toni wasn't that young— they were only eighteen months apart—but she *was* sweet. Still, there was a fierceness to her that he hadn't seen in her before. *Then again, eight years is a long time.*

"She's at least twenty-one, right?" Tiff stood and moved to peer over Jordan's shoulder.

"Almost twenty-five, believe it or not."

"Christ," Kayla muttered. "I would have thought nineteen, if that."

"As long as she's legal, capable, and available, what difference does it make?" Jordan asked. "The real question is, is she the one?"

Seb glanced around at the others, surprised to find Kayla's gaze on him when he turned to her.

"What?"

"Nothing," she replied, after a beat. "You've been kinda quiet about all of this."

He loved Kayla, but she was far too perceptive for her own good. "Ultimately, it's about you, not me."

Candi jumped up and strolled over to where he sat. "Papa Quick here is wondering how *I'm* feeling about all this," she said, ruffling Seb's hair.

Seb leaned away from the contact. She knew damn well his hair was off-limits. He glared at her, though with no real heat behind it. Brat indeed.

Candi winked at him as she plopped down and stole his half-eaten slice.

Ah, so she was fun, playful Candi today. It was the best possible scenario.

Laughing begrudgingly, Seb ceded his spot to her. He got up and moved to the table where all of the candidates' profiles had been laid out. He pretended to scan them all, but his eyes were glued to Toni's photo.

The woman staring up at him, dressed in a black crop top, with glossy hair and a don't-doubt-my-greatness expression, was a stranger to him.

And yet somehow not.

SEBASTIAN, AGE 15—ANTONIA, AGE 14

"Hold still for one freaking second."

"No! I don't like taking pictures," Nia complained, hiding her face in the crook of her arm.

Seb sighed. "You realize when we're famous, people are going to want to take your picture all the time."

Nia made a face of disgust that had Seb rolling with laughter.

"*You* go be famous. I'll be the woman behind the scenes producing hit records and raking in all that money. That's where the real success is, you know."

"Where'd you hear that?"

"I read it in an old copy of *Billboard*, an interview with Frank DeLuna. He was an engineer at A&M Records." She pulled a dog-eared copy of the magazine out of her backpack. "See? He was an assistant engineer in some dinky studio, then he was a master engineer, and finally a producing engineer. He's worked with, like, everyone."

Seb took the magazine from her. "If he's so big, how come I've never heard of him?"

Nia snatched the magazine back. "That's the whole point, dumbass. He doesn't need to have his photo taken, except for maybe in interviews like this one. For the trade magazines."

"*Pfft.* Sounds boring."

"*DeLuna* doesn't need the spotlight," Nia continued loudly, hands on her hips. "*DeLuna* only wants to work and make a decent living. Be like DeLuna."

Seb snapped her picture anyway.

"You guys don't need to worry about me," Candi announced casually.

Seb tore his gaze from Toni's photo. He had to keep his head on straight and his thoughts away from Antonia fucking Bennette. Something that would prove impossible, thanks to the words that came out of Candi's mouth next.

"I think we should go with young Toni."

Seb held his breath as Lilly met Candi's eyes and the two women became locked in a silent exchange.

His mind spun. If they chose Toni, his life would become infinitely more complicated. Toni was his first real regret. She was his past. His shame. Having her around would remind him of all the ways he'd failed.

THE GIRL WITH STARS IN HER EYES   171

Not only that, he'd made a promise to Candi. Toni might pose a real threat to her position in the Lillys if she was as good as everyone seemed to think—which she was. He could easily picture her with them long term.

Christ.

"You really think she'd work out, though?" Seb heard himself say. All eyes turned to him. "Like you all said, she's green. Forget her real age, her emotional age seemed…younger. She might not be cut out for this. Not everyone can make it in this industry."

Seb swallowed the bile that crawled up his throat. He was covering his own ass, and he knew it. Part of him wanted to rewind the clock a few seconds and take it back. Toni deserved this chance more than anyone, and he all but owed it to her. If this was truly what she wanted, what right did he have to stand in her way?

"You must be psychic or something, 'cause I didn't get that from her at all," Kayla said, studying him too closely for his comfort.

"Neither did I," Tiff added. "I mean, I only talked to her for a few minutes, but she seemed pretty cool. A little shy, but also, like… I don't think she'd take shit from anyone, if that makes sense."

"Exactly," Kayla agreed. "She may not have a ton of experience, but neither did we."

"True. We've all had to get up to speed pretty fucking fast," Tiff chimed in.

"Some of us more than others," Candi muttered.

Tiff gave her the finger and Candi smirked, completely unapologetic.

"My point is," Kayla continued, her annoyance clear, "she'd catch on. We'd make sure of it."

"And it is *only* temporary," Candi stated. She looked at Lilly and, again, they were caught in a silent conversation. "I think she's perfect."

Seb didn't need words to understand the exchange between them.

Finally, Lilly nodded. "All right, Toni Bennette it is."

"Finally!" Tiff exclaimed, tossing the résumé in her hand to the floor.

Kayla tapped a drum fill against her thigh, nodding. "Cool, cool. This might work out after all."

"Right, so clear your schedules," Jordan said. "I'll make the offer. We nixed Zeph and May. Does that mean Aurora is our second choice?"

"Which one was that?" Tiff asked.

"The redhead from California that came in after we broke for lunch," Jordan supplied.

"She wasn't bad." Tiff tilted her head back and forth as if to say so-so. "Sure, but I'd want to bring her in for a callback."

Jordan surveyed the room. "Everyone on board with that?"

"Fine with me," Lilly replied. Her eyes kept landing on Candi, whose smile was wide.

Seb wasn't surprised by their decision. He knew in his gut it was the right call. Not for him—for him it might be a fucking nightmare. But for the Lillys and for Toni? It was the right decision.

"I guess the Lillys have a new guitarist," Jordan stated, relief clear in his voice.

"A *guest* guitarist," Candi clarified, eyeing him. A few cracks appeared in her cheerful facade.

Nonplussed, Jordan nodded. "Yep, *guest* guitarist. YMI will be happy. Andre's been ringing me daily."

"That's how we'll spin it to the press, right?" Candi asked, the first hint of insecurity creeping into her voice.

"For now," Lilly said, her expression devoid of emotion.

Seb had known Lilly could be ruthless, but everything about this—from Candi's dismissal to her replacement—had been downright clinical.

"And I'll be there to help her learn my parts," Candi supplied, her voice unnaturally bright. Seb heard genuine fear there.

"That's a relief," Tiff said, giving Candi a broad smile. "'Cause those time changes on 'Hurt U' are a bitch, girl. I ain't walking her through that spiderweb you and Seb created."

Candi grinned. "As if you could. Seb wrote it and even he has trouble playing it."

Seb couldn't argue. He wasn't on the same level as Candi. Or Toni, for that matter. He'd always had trouble translating what he heard in his head to his fingertips. It was one of the reasons he cherished the symbiotic relationship he had with Lilly and Candi. One reason why he was so desperate to hold on.

Sometimes, it was as if Lilly and Candi could read his thoughts, his ideas, before he could fully formulate them, breathing life into his melodies and taking them places he could only dream of going on his own.

Even beyond the music, Lilly especially got him. They understood each other on some deep, subatomic level that he didn't really understand but knew he couldn't live without.

Only one other person had ever known him in the same way.

"I'll reach out to Toni," Jordan said, as if plucking her straight out of Seb's thoughts. "Meanwhile, Seb will secure rehearsal space at SAGA and work out a schedule." Jordan looked at Seb to confirm.

Seb nodded and pulled out his phone. "Already on it."

This was his job, these were his people, and he was going to do whatever he could to help them. Even if it meant locking all his bullshit angst over Toni back inside the vault and swallowing the goddamn key.

CHAPTER 14.

ANTONIA, AGE 15—SEBASTIAN, AGE 16

"WE'LL BE STUCK IN BORDON like everyone else if we don't make some money."

"Summer's coming, things'll pick up at the shop. And I can make extra cash mowing lawns and shit," Seb assured her.

"I can babysit when Mo doesn't have me at the bar," Antonia offered. "Ten bucks an hour, easy. And they need a bagger at the supermarket."

"What's that pay?"

"Six dollars an hour."

"Isn't that below minimum wage?" he asked, doing the math.

She shrugged. "It's money. I'm not going to complain."

"Yeah, you got a point." Seb met her eyes. "So, we have a plan now."

Antonia nodded. "We have a plan."

———

The time stamp on Richie's email read three in the morning. Toni anticipated the days she'd be up until three, four, five in the morning, recording at a place like Phactory Sound. Maybe even the Phactory itself.

At least Richie had been patient while she weighed her options.

T,

I booked ten days with Ian Cross early next month. I'm sure you're familiar. He's worked with everyone. Needs lead guitar, keys, and drums for one of his artists, no doubt platinum already. I floated your name and he wants to meet you.

Best,
RM

P.S. You make any headway with the money thing? Please say yes. You're my only hope, Toni-Wan. 😊

Or not.

Toni's insides buzzed like someone had poked at a beehive inside her chest. The prospect of becoming Richie's business partner lit her all the way up, but to do it she'd have to liquidate.

Newly restored, Minx sat on a guitar stand in the corner. A single shaft of sunlight pierced the parted curtains and fell lazily across her neck like something out of a magazine ad. Pretty, perfect Minx, the seductress. Toni had only just gotten her back. How was she supposed to sell her?

Groaning, Toni rolled out of bed and shuffled into Yvette's room to moan about her shitty predicament before remembering her BFF was already at work. After brushing her teeth and splashing some cold water on her face, she slinked back into the living room, threw herself down onto the pullout's lumpy mattress, and grabbed her phone.

Maybe she'd get lucky and find an email from a Nigerian prince.

TONI: Give me $30,000 or the Tempur-Pedic gets it.

It took longer for Yvette to respond than Toni expected. She had an unhealthy obsession with that bed.

YVETTE: Aww, babe. If I could, I would.
TONI: I know. I do have some exciting news, though.
YVETTE: ZOMG! Ur going to be a Lilly?!

Ha! As if.

TONI: Nooooo, Richie emailed me. He wants me for an Ian Cross project next month. 10 days.
YVETTE: Am I supposed to know who that is?
TONI: Only that he has several Grammys to his name.
YVETTE: That's cool 2 then I guess
TONI: Sorry 2 disappoint U
YVETTE: As long as UR happy. 😊
TONI: It should at least put a dent in the 30k.
YVETTE: Yeah. I really wanted that Lillys deal for you, though. Sorry, babes. Their loss.

Toni found it hard to muster up anything like Yvette's confidence. It had been three days since her audition, and she'd heard nothing. It was just as well.

Sure, it would have been an interesting experience to be in a band like the Lillys for a while, get a taste of the life she'd always openly despised but that secretly fascinated her. The travel, the playing to sold-out crowds, performing on shows like the Grammy Awards. But there was never a real chance of that happening. Not even without a ghost from her past haunting her lately, and probably especially with him.

Toni had mostly succeeded in pushing thoughts of Seb aside over the last few days.

She hadn't thought about him when Elton requested she play some Caspian's Ghost. She hadn't thought about him when she returned to the Phactory for her next session. Toni definitely hadn't given him a single thought when she caught herself playing the opening chords of "Black Hole Sun" at the Unicorn Thursday night.

ANTONIA, AGE 14—SEBASTIAN, AGE 16

"You know who you look like?" Antonia asked as Seb tuned his guitar. It rested on his denim-clad knee, above the frayed edges of a hole forming over the joint.

"If you say Johnny Depp, I'm going to push you off this ledge."

Antonia giggled. "Ew, no. I mean, he's okay, but no."

Seb plucked at the D string as he twisted the peg on his old Gibson acoustic, listening for pitch. Antonia marveled at the fact that he could do that without a proper tuner.

"Dave Navarro?"

"Maybe if he had long hair and fewer tattoos," Antonia replied. "Or, like, none."

"I want some," Seb said, strumming a few chords. "Tattoos."

"I know, I know. You want a portrait of Amy Lee on your forearm, and the lyrics to 'Black Hole Sun' emblazoned—thank my SAT prep class for that word—across your scrawny chest."

Seb's head popped up. "I'm sorry, did you say 'scrawny'?" He squinted one eye at her. "I am *swole*, little girl. I've been working out."

Antonia looked around. "Working out where? Lifting boxes of lug nuts for your old man?"

Seb pressed his palm to his chest in mock indignation. "Did I or did I not carry your clumsy ass all the way the fuck home when you twisted your ankle?"

"Dude," Antonia said, rolling her eyes. "I was twelve and I weighed, like, eighty pounds. I'm almost as tall as you are now."

"Hardly," Seb bit back, clearly not liking that idea at all.

Antonia giggled. She knew she was full of shit. Seb had grown three inches in the last three months alone, and she was struggling to reach her mother's height of five foot six.

"Scrawny, my ass," he muttered to himself as he finished tuning. "Take it back!"

"Fine, fine," Antonia conceded, laughing. "You're a towering giant of a man."

"Thought so." His hair had grown long and draped his shoulders in shiny black waves that flashed bits of auburn in the sunlight. "Who is it you think I look like, anyway?"

Toni was struck with a sudden bout of shyness. Maybe she shouldn't have brought it up.

"Nobody."

Seb looked at her, one eyebrow arched and lips pursed.

Toni stared at them for a beat too long before dropping her gaze somewhere safer.

"Chris Cornell," she mumbled, picking at a piece of rubber sticking out from the molding on her Keds.

"Say what?" Seb leaned in close and Toni's stomach did a little flip.

"I said," she replied, voice loud enough to push Seb back, "you look like Chris Cornell."

The smile that stretched across Seb's mouth was almost worth the embarrassment. He knew Toni had a poster of the singer taped up inside her closet, out of sight of her father who'd tear it up if he saw it.

Toni waited for Seb to tease her, to call her out on her one celebrity crush, but he dropped his gaze back to the guitar.

"Yeah?"

"A bit. Probably just the hair," she said, looking away from his darn dimple.

They fell quiet and Seb strummed the opening chords of her favorite Soundgarden song. She stayed quiet as he sang, his voice deeper than even a year ago, and told the butterflies in her stomach to cut it the heck out. It was only Seb.

Shaking herself out of her thoughts, Toni rooted herself in the present. This session with Ian Cross was a great opportunity. He'd worked with some of the biggest names in the industry.

Toni would get a chance to show what she was really capable of, and hopefully Cross wouldn't be as much of an ass as Jerry Gant.

Having steady gigs at the Phactory was a step in the right direction, even if she couldn't buy in.

Toni might have enjoyed working with the Lillys for a little while, but she had no clue how to feel about the Seb component. The idea of working with him seemed far removed from the dream they'd shared so long ago. What would that even look like?

Needing to get out of her own head, Toni decided to treat herself to a meal out. She fished out some clean clothes and was heading to shower when her phone rang.

Very few people actually called her, so Toni checked the screen out of sheer curiosity. She frowned at the 212 area code, her finger hovering over the reject-call button before her brain caught up with the possibility that Seb might be at the other end of the New York number.

Toni took a breath and accepted the call, lifting the phone to her ear with a shaky hand.

"Hello?"

"Hi, is that Toni?"

"Yeah, uh." Her brain scrambled to place the voice. "Mr. Igwe?"

He chuckled. "People don't even call my dad that. Jordan is fine."

"Oh, okay." Toni sat on the arm of her sofa bed. "Jordan it is."

She closed her eyes, preparing herself for the disappointment of rejection. She'd already had one stroke of good fortune today. This shouldn't bring her down. She wouldn't let it. She didn't even want the job, Toni reminded herself. And at least he called to do it over the phone, rather than sending an assistant to do it. Or an impersonal email. Very classy.

"Listen, I'll cut right to the chase. We were all really impressed with you," he said.

"But?" Toni slapped her hand over her mouth. Let the man speak!

"Nah, no buts. Do you want to join the Lillys?"

Toni almost dropped the phone. "Do I... I'm sorry, *what*?"

"It's on contract, of course, but it'll be for at least six weeks."

"Six weeks," Toni echoed as she made a mental calculation. Six weeks would likely take her out of the running for the Ian Cross project.

"The compensation is generous," Jordan continued, perhaps sensing her hesitation. "We wanted to find the best, and YMI is willing to pay. I know you're a session player. What's your rate?"

"My rate?" Apparently, she couldn't stop parroting him.

"You know what, never mind," he said. Toni could hear typing in the background and the squeak of an office chair. "You're our first choice, and I really don't want to go through all of this again, so... How about five per week, and points if you end up on any recordings?"

"Five...?" Toni fought to catch up to the conversation. "Five hundred dollars?"

Jordan laughed, loud and hearty.

"Sorry, thousand. Five thousand per week. Five hundred dollars," he finished, still laughing. "You're a funny one."

Was it possible to choke on thin air?

"Could you hold for just a sec?"

"Uh, sure," Jordan said.

Before he could finish, Toni put him on mute as a coughing fit overtook her. She struggled to catch her breath and wrap her head around what was happening. Math was never her strong suit, but she knew that it was an obscene amount of money. And would put her firmly over the finish line.

Phactory Sound could be hers, at least in part, and she wouldn't have to sell Minx.

It was too easy. There had to be a catch.

"Sorry," she said when she resumed the call. "I, uh...thought I heard someone at the door."

"No problem. As I was saying, everyone is very excited to bring you in. You'd have to stay in New York for the duration, but we'd cover your hotel and transport," Jordan continued, oblivious to Toni's state. "Or we can help find you a short lease, if you want something less transient."

Toni swallowed. He was rattling off details, and her brain still hadn't caught up to the money thing. "I'm... Sorry, did you say five thousand dollars *a week*?"

"Yes."

"For six weeks?"

"Minimum, yes." Jordan's tone changed. "I think that's more than fair."

"Yeah," Toni replied quickly. "No, it's more than fair. I... Wow. I'm..." She broke into deranged laughter and had to clear her throat. "That's..."

It was a lot—the money, the job, the doors it would open for her. Could she do this? Could she step into the spotlight, albeit a borrowed one, and deal with all that came with it?

Did she really have a choice?

"Toni? Did I lose you?"

There was really no choice to make. "When would you need me?"

Jordan's chuckle was warm and tinged with relief. "I take that as a yes."

Toni opened her mouth to say hell yes, but hesitated.

"Can I sleep on it?"

There was a brief silence on the other end before Jordan said, "Sure, of course. But I'll need to know by lunch tomorrow. I'd need time to reach out to our second choice if you decide to break my heart, love."

Toni decided she liked Jordan. Then again, she did seem to have a soft spot for Brits. One thing niggled at her, though. "I do have a question."

"Fire away."

"You said the showcase is in three weeks, but the contract is for six?"

"Ah," Jordan replied but didn't elaborate. "Let's call it insurance," he said after an uncomfortable silence. Then, "Sorry, but I do have a meeting to get to. I look forward to your answer, Toni."

"You'll have it before lunch tomorrow," she promised. "And thanks for the opportunity."

"Perfect. Talk then."

The call ended, and Toni stared at her phone. She stared until the screen went to sleep. Until her fingers hurt from squeezing it, and her lungs burned from disuse. Sometime in the last few minutes, she'd forgotten how to breathe properly.

Holy.

Shit.

And why was Toni's first thought of Seb?

When they were younger, she'd worked so hard to gain his approval, especially when it came to her guitar skills. Her mother had taught her the basics, but it was Seb who had encouraged her to keep at it. To stretch. To find her limits and surpass them. Because of him, she'd sought the best instructors. Because of him, she'd never stopped learning. Growing. Improving.

And now, he might very well have had a hand in the band's decision to hire her. Toni couldn't help but recall all the times she'd sat with Seb, listening to him plan a future for them that looked very much like the one she had laid out in front of her.

Now, they would likely be working together, though maybe not the way they'd imagined back then.

Not particularly interested in trudging down memory lane again, Toni opened her text messages.

TONI: they want me
YVETTE: U told me 😄
TONI: not the studio THE LILLYS 😳

Less than a second later, Toni's phone rang. She had to hold it away from her ear to protect her delicate hearing from Yvette's enthusiastic screams.

CHAPTER 15.

WHEN TONI CALLED JORDAN TO tell him she was signing on, she hadn't expected to find herself in New York the very next afternoon. She made a note: when you said yes to Jordan Igwe, he gave you very little time to change your mind.

He'd sent a car service to Penn Station to bring her and her gear straight to his office.

"Toni. It's great to see you again," Jordan said when she arrived. "Come on in."

He led her through a small waiting area and into his private office. It was modest, considering the neighborhood, furnished with a walnut desk, a few leather high-backs, and a studded leather love seat. The degrees that lined the wall were impressive.

Toni hovered next to one of the chairs. She'd half expected Seb to be at the meeting. He'd said he worked with the band, though he hadn't said in what capacity. She knew he wasn't *in* the Lillys. Maybe he worked as a roadie or stage manager? She had stuck to her decision *not* to google him. One she was beginning to regret.

"Everything okay?"

Toni blinked.

Jordan smiled at her and gestured for her to have a seat.

"Yep, everything is great," she said, mentally kicking herself for letting her mind wander like that. "Uh, thanks for bringing me in. I'm grateful for the chance. I know I'm not well known, or known at all." She laughed, nervous.

Jordan waved a hand. "First of all, there's no need to walk on eggshells around me. You're here because the Lillys want you. All of them."

This was news to Toni. "Even Candi?"

"Especially Candi. She's going through some things, yeah? But she's going to be around to help you with the music."

That was actually a relief. After listening to their EP *Lick* with a more attentive ear, Toni realized she had her work cut out for her.

Candi Fair may have a boatload of issues, but the woman also had skill. Her style was layered and intricate.

Jordan slid a stack of papers across the desk. "This is a pretty standard contract, but you should look through it carefully. Phone a friend if you want, preferably another attorney. Unfortunately, I'm up against the clock, or I wouldn't do it this way."

"I'm sure it's fine." Toni reached for a nearby pen.

Jordan grabbed it off the desk before she could get there, and Toni snatched her hand back. Startled. Had he changed his mind already?

His expression dark, Jordan leveled Toni with a look that made her shrink a little in her chair. "Never do that again."

"Do...what? I thought..."

"This..." Jordan jabbed his index finger at the stack of papers. "This is not your contract. It's the contract for a lighting company I used for a tour last year."

Toni frowned. Was it some kind of test? "I don't understand."

Jordan Igwe, Esquire, offered her an enigmatic smile that confused her even further. "That's the smartest thing you've said today."

Toni adjusted her opinion about the man. He might be a sadist.

"Never sign a contract, any contract, without reading it," Jordan warned her. "I don't care if it's a recording contract, a utility hookup, or your mobile phone. Read. Everything."

Toni nodded. "Of course. You're right. I was excited and you're, well, you seem legit."

"The deadliest snakes are often the prettiest." Jordan winked. "You don't know me, love. I could be an asshole."

Toni grinned. "Are you an asshole?"

"Only on Wednesdays."

Of course, it was Wednesday. It was an old joke, a Seb joke, and Toni wondered how close the two men were.

Jordan slid a different document across the desk, this one a scant two pages long.

"I have to run some things by you," he said. "And if you want to change your mind, that's cool. No hard feelings. But I think you should know what you're getting into."

Ah, here was the catch. "Sure. Go ahead."

"Right, okay. First, as I said, this is not a permanent gig. You'll be filling in for Candi until she can...rejoin the band."

Toni nodded. "Perfect. No problem."

"Brilliant. The band has an important showcase at the end of the month. That gives us three weeks to get you up to speed and comfortable with the material," Jordan explained. "We'll also work with you to create a public image. I find it's best to give the press something to chew on or they go looking. Are you already a fan of the girls?"

No.

"Totally."

"Great, so you're no doubt familiar with their EP, *Lick*. We'll start rehearsals tomorrow, concentrating on those tunes."

Toni made a mental note to listen to it again on repeat tonight. "Um, I hate to ask but, any idea where I'll be staying?"

"We'll book you a room in a decent hotel," he replied.

"Okay, thanks."

"Don't get too excited," he added. "It'll come out of your five thousand per week. If you want five stars, you'll be paying for it."

"I think I can deal with two stars."

"Please, Miss Bennette," Jordan teased, adopting an accent even more posh than his own. "Don't settle for any less than three."

Toni laughed, some of the anxiety draining from her shoulders.

"Any meals during sessions, rehearsals, and the like will be on the band's account, but the rest is on you. So don't go too wild with room service."

"Damn, I was looking forward to finally trying beluga."

One corner of his mouth curved up. "You may order one serving of beluga on me," Jordan offered, tipping his head in a small bow. His phone rang and he straightened, all business again. "If you're still saying yes, that is."

While Jordan took the call, Toni read through the contract. It was pretty straightforward, written in plain English, and essentially laid out the terms he'd explained to her, with one exception.

"No fraternization?" she asked when he finished.

Something flashed across Jordan's face, gone before Toni could decipher it.

He tilted his head, regarding her closely. "You seeing anyone?"

"Beg your pardon?"

Jordan held up a hand. "I'm not on the pull, I swear."

Toni shifted in her seat. She was quickly losing the thread of this conversation. "On the what?"

Jordan muttered under his breath something about English-to-English translation. It reminded her of Elton. Maybe it was a Brit thing.

"What I mean to say is that I'm not trying to chat you up. The no-fraternization clause means you can't have a romantic or physical entanglement with anyone in the band or crew."

"No, I know what it means," she said. "I've never seen it written into a contract before." Not that she'd had many contracts set in front of her.

Toni had never been interested in celebrity gossip, but Yvette had filled her in on some of the rumors surrounding Seb and Candi before Toni could stop her.

She hadn't wanted to hear it. In retrospect, it was probably a good thing. It would help Toni keep things in perspective.

Her decision to pretend she didn't know Seb at the audition had been a spur-of-the-moment thing. At the time, she didn't understand why he'd played along. Now things were clicking into place.

"Happens a lot in corporate America," Jordan continued. "And, sorry to say, it's happening more and more in our industry."

Our industry. Toni loved the sound of that. "I have one request."

"I'd be surprised if you didn't," Jordan replied, narrowing his eyes at her. "Shoot."

"Can you refer to me as Toni B in any press you do? I—I don't want my last name out there."

His brows rose. "You running from the law?"

Toni exhaled a laugh. "No, nothing like that. I prefer to remain private, if I can."

"Hmmm," he said before nodding. "Well, I can't promise anything, but we will do our best. Toni B it is."

"Thanks." She reached for the pen, letting her hand hover over it as she looked up at Jordan. "Is it safe now?"

Grinning, Jordan picked it up and handed it to her. "I trust we've learned a valuable lesson today," he said in that same exaggerated accent.

It was official. Toni liked him a lot.

———————

If the last week of her life had been a video game, Toni felt like she'd been given a cheat code.

She'd gone from her tiny shared apartment in Fishtown to Jordan's hip New York office address, and now she was meeting with the band at Lilly's Brooklyn brownstone.

The motherforking Lillys.

Toni was part of the band. For a little while, anyway.

Richie had taken the news much better than she'd expected, wishing her luck and asking her to put in a word for the Phactory. As if she wouldn't. He also said the partnership was a done deal, even though she didn't have all of the cash yet.

Minx was safe and currently nestled in the trunk of Jordan's Audi A4.

When they arrived at Lilly's, Jordan strode into the kitchen like he'd done it a million times before. Toni stayed close behind him.

Lilly stood over the stove, stirring a large pot of something that smelled heavenly. It was only when the scents of garlic and rosemary hit her nostrils that Toni realized she hadn't eaten anything since eight in the morning.

"We're here!" he yelled through the open doorway.

The kitchen was bright and airy, modern but not industrial, despite the stainless-steel and white-lacquer finishes. Weathered driftwood had been repurposed to add warmth to the cabinet doors.

Toni instantly felt at home in the space. There was care in the details. "*Hei*, Jordan." Toni thought she saw a hint of a smile as Jordan hugged her from behind.

Lilly never turned her attention away from the stove but reached her arm back to pat him on the head as he continued into what looked like the dining room. It was awkward and told Toni a lot about the relationship between them.

"Hello, Toni." Her name sounded exotic in Lilly's lilting accent, and Toni paused mid-step.

"Uh, hi," Toni replied. "Your home is gorgeous."

"Ready to work?" Lilly's focus remained on the simmering pot.

"Yeah, thanks for having me."

Lilly made a quiet humming sound and lifted the spoon to taste. She reached for a small bowl of pink salt on the counter, tossing a few pinches into what looked like a light stew.

Toni waited, but Lilly didn't acknowledge her again.

Conversation over, then. Got it.

Toni found Jordan in a dining room that had been set up as an acoustic rehearsal space.

"There she is!"

Tiffany Kim jumped up from her spot on the floor and pulled Toni into a hug, a large pair of headphones around her neck. She'd been lounging on an ivory throw rug with a bag of Sun Chips, a tablet, and a notebook on the floor beside it.

The mountain of curls atop her head tickled Toni's face, and she laughed into the embrace. "Nice to see you again."

Tiffany leaned back and made a face. "Listen to her, *nice to see you again*. Cut that shit out, girl," she said, laughing. "The audition's over. You made it, let your hair down."

"Give the poor thing a chance to get acclimated. Geez." Mikayla Whitman walked over and stuck out her hand. She was petite—tiny, really—with pale, freckled skin, pin-straight red hair, and an assessing gaze. "We met last week. Kayla."

"I remember," Toni said, shaking the drummer's hand. She was amazed someone so tiny could play with such power. "I'm Toni."

"Uh, yeah," Kayla said. "We all know who you are. I gotta say, you've got chops, girl."

"Serious chops," Tiffany added, slapping her shoulder. "Welcome to the party."

Tiffany was about the same height as Toni. Dressed in a Cucinelli blouse and pin-striped pajama bottoms, she had an eclectic style about her. It was the wardrobe equivalent of a mullet—business up top, party down below. Toni liked her right away.

"Thanks," Toni said, looking around.

A small drum kit sat in front of the bay windows, a pair of steel brushes resting on the head of the snare drum. The dark hardwood floor had been covered with various area rugs, no doubt to protect it from the feet of the drum stands and the various amps strewn about the space.

Next to the kit, a five-string Ibanez bass leaned against the wall. It was stunning, with a burst of cerulean blue in the polished finish and probably cost more than Toni made in a month.

Mesmerized, she gravitated toward the instrument, her hand outstretched.

"You play bass too?" Tiffany walked over to her.

Toni dropped her hand to her side. "Not really. I only dabble."

"Take a closer look. It's a loaner."

The instrument felt a little foreign in her hands, the neck wider than Toni was used to, even for a bass. "It's gorgeous," she said.

"Isn't he? I think I'm going to keep him, but I haven't picked out a name for him yet."

"You name your instruments too?" Toni set the bass gently down.

Tiffany ran a finger down one of the strings. "I have five—some have clear personalities." She stroked over the polished body. "This one's definitely a dude. A Luke, maybe. Or a Chuck."

Toni laughed. "Chuck the bass?"

Tiffany's smile revealed a small dimple in her chin. She had a heart-shaped face and eyes so dark brown they were almost black. The off-white of her blouse set off the deep tan of her skin beautifully. "Sure, why not? Chuck is a good, beefy name."

"Why not," Toni agreed. She held out her hand. "I'm Toni."

Tiffany frowned, confused. "I know, we've met. Twice now."

Toni smiled. "Not officially."

Tiffany took her hand, her soft calluses grazing Toni's palm. There was strength there, the kind that only came from hours of playing.

"Tiffany Kim, but the fam calls me Tiff."

"Or PITA," Kayla said as she settled on the wide windowsill. She had a bottle of beer in one hand and a drumstick in the other, tapping the latter against her thigh in a familiar rhythm.

"This really is a beautiful house," Toni said, admiring the kind of crown molding she'd only seen on HGTV.

"Thanks," a voice behind her responded. Lilly walked into the room carrying a tray of steaming mugs. She set it down on the buffet against the wall.

Toni took in the instruments and setup again. She'd obviously missed a memo somewhere.

"Sorry, I didn't realize we were starting rehearsals today."

"We're not," Kayla supplied. "We're just hanging out."

"Ah. I thought…"

Kayla's gaze followed Toni's as it swept the room. "Oh, this stuff? It's always here 'cause we usually end up jamming," she said, running a fingertip across one of the cymbals. "I use this kit when it's late and Lilly wants to work on new arrangements but doesn't want to piss off her neighbors."

"I'm fairly sure they hate me on principle," Lilly deadpanned.

Toni kept stealing glances at her. She couldn't help it; there was something magnetic about the Norwegian. Like being in the presence of Thor.

"This is your first time working in New York, right?" Kayla asked Toni.

Toni nodded. "I've been to shows up here before, but never played one. SAGA was the first time I ever plugged in an instrument up here." Toni took a breath, the realization surprising her. "It was…something."

"New York can be intimidating, but there's a trick to winning over a NY audience," Kayla said.

"Yeah? What's that?" Toni asked, curious.

"Don't suck," Kayla and Tiff replied in unison.

"You needn't worry," Jordan interjected. "The showcase is in a controlled environment, closed to the public, though the house will be packed. And I doubt we'll do any public gigs while you're with us."

Toni's elation dipped at the reminder that this was all temporary. Which was ridiculous. It's what she'd signed up for.

"Who knows? It might be permanent," Kayla tossed out casually.

Judging by the look on her face, Lilly wasn't amused.

Tiff may have actually growled. *Yikes.*

An uncomfortable silence settled over the room before a shout from the kitchen split the air.

"Where my bitches at?" Candi strolled into the room, all smiles, and made a beeline straight for Toni. "Hey, lady! It's so nice to finally meet you for real."

Toni found herself wrapped in a perfume-scented hug that she did her best to return, quickly reaching her limit on physical contact for the day.

Candi's romper matched the cotton-candy pink of her hair, and Toni remembered she'd worn pink the day of the auditions. She guessed that was Candi's thing even when she wasn't onstage.

"Ready for your fifteen minutes?"

Toni was a bit taken aback by the flippant comment, but Candi's smile remained, as did her grip on Toni's forearm.

"Leave it, Candi," Jordan admonished. "You can head right back out the door if you're only here to stir the pot."

Candi's shocked expression would have been a little easier to believe if she weren't also laughing wildly. "I can't believe you think so little of me," she huffed, a hint of a southern twang emerging.

Everyone found a place to settle as Lilly reentered with a tray of soup bowls. Whatever was in them smelled incredible. As she went around the room, each person took a bowl and a spoon from a cup on the tray.

Kayla scooted over on the sill and patted the space next to her. Toni accepted the invitation with a smile.

"I've been waiting for this all day," Jordan said. "Don't know if I mentioned it, Toni, but Lilly likes to spoil us with her cooking."

"I only do it so you lot don't die on me," Lilly grumbled, the words softened on her tongue by the curl of her accent. Her expression was stern, a stark contrast to her delicate Scandinavian features and the love she'd obviously put into making whatever it was that smelled so good.

During the break in the conversation, Toni's stomach growled. She cringed.

"Jordan, did you not feed this woman?" Kayla shook her head in mock disgust.

Sheepish, he grimaced around a spoonful of what appeared to be chicken and dumplings. "Sorry, Toni love. I knew we were coming here and it's all I could think of." He held up his bowl. "Besides signing you on, of course."

Toni accepted the last serving and a spoon from Lilly, her mouth already watering. "It's fine."

"Have you done much work outside Philly?" Candi pursed her lips and blew on a spoonful of the stew. She'd claimed one of the club chairs that sat on the threshold between the living room and dining room.

"None," Toni answered before taking a bite. It was so good. The chicken practically melted in her mouth, the dumplings were light and fluffy, and the broth was savory, with chunks of carrot and bits of herbs. "Oh my God, this is amazing."

"Right?" Tiff said between bites.

"Lilly, you're from Norway?"

Lilly slowly turned to look at her, probably the first real acknowledgment she'd afforded her. "Yeah." Lilly's focus was intense, curious, and Toni felt like a strain of bacteria under a microscope. "My father is from Oslo, but my mother is from California."

"I, uh, think I read that somewhere."

Lilly's nod was slight, her face a perfect mask of boredom. Or was it disdain?

"You did your homework," Jordan said around a mouthful of stew. "Good start."

"Lilly's from Asgard," Candi supplied cheerfully. "Kayla's from Athens."

"Georgia, not Greece," Kayla added.

"Her parents are nerdy types. Professors or something," Candi informed her.

"When she isn't on the skins, she's got her nose buried in a book," Tiff added.

"And Tiff is from the glittering streets of LA. Right, Tiff?" Candi asked.

Her mouth otherwise engaged, Tiff gave her a thumbs-up.

"And you?"

Candi grinned, shrugging. "I'm from everywhere and nowhere."

"Otherwise known as Mississippi."

Candi scowled at Kayla. "Fuck off, I lived there when I was in the first grade." She turned back to Toni, her smile once again in place. "I was born in Jersey, but we moved around a lot for a while."

"How about you, Antonia Bennette?" Tiff asked. "You originally from Philly?"

"Uh, no." Toni shifted in her set. "But I've been there for a little over five years."

Toni pushed the food around in her bowl. She hated explaining her background and decided it was best to keep it simple, especially since she didn't know what Seb had told them.

"We moved around a lot too," she said to Candi. "But I went to junior high and high school in a small town in Pennsylvania. I doubt any of you would know of it."

"Well, you're in the Big Apple now," Kayla said, raising her bowl in a toast. "Welcome to the big leagues, Miss Bennette."

Toni grinned. "Thanks."

Kayla laughed, nudging their shoulders together. "Toni Bennette. Too freakin' awesome."

"I like that name. *Antonia*," Candi said, smiling in a way that softened her sharp features. "It's pretty. Named after anyone?"

"My grandfather's name was Anthony. He died before I was born. I don't really know much about him."

Another awkward silence descended upon the room and Toni could have kicked herself. Why had she decided to share that cheery tidbit? Ugh, she was blowing this already.

Chitchat had never been her strength. Put a guitar in her hand or stick her behind a microphone in a recording booth, and Toni knew what to do. This was new terrain and she was stumbling all over it. No wonder she only had two friends.

"Well, Toni," Tiff said, "welcome to the Lillys. You're in for the ride of your life."

"Yeah, it's going to be fun but it's a lot of work." Kayla worked a drumstick between her fingers like a baton. It was spellbinding. She wasn't even looking at her hand, and Toni marveled at the kind of muscle memory you'd need to do it so effortlessly. She couldn't wait to watch Kayla play live.

"It's a hard business," Lilly said, changing the entire tone of the conversation. "It's hard to be a woman in it."

"It is," Jordan reluctantly agreed. "But you're young. Enjoy it."

"It's like you're not allowed to grow," Lilly continued as if Jordan hadn't spoken.

"You are, as long as you stay in your lane," Tiff countered, a hint of bitterness creeping into her voice.

"That's the key," Candi agreed. "Get where you belong."

Toni had an inkling that comment was directed at her.

"On the cover of *AARP*, right, Lilliana?" Kayla said, grinning.

Lilly frowned. "Ugh, shut up. I've already got the gray hair."

"One," Tiff leaned in to whisper in Toni's ear. "She found one gray hair, and she won't shut up about it."

Toni laughed.

"Wait 'til you're about to wake up to thirty," Lilly said to Kayla. "Maybe you won't be so glib."

"I'm not glib. I'll be dying my hair next year, I'm sure. Red and gray aren't a good combo."

"Are you guys really worried about getting older?" Toni hadn't meant to ask that out loud. She glanced around the room. All eyes were on her. "Sorry, I... Your whole message is so empowering," she clarified. "You talk about living in your own skin and accepting everything that makes you *you*. I'm just surprised to hear you say that."

"We're not overly concerned. We just know how this game works," Lilly said, her tone matter-of-fact.

"It's a cutthroat business," Candi said, cutting her gaze to Lilly for the briefest of moments, but long enough for Toni to know she didn't want to get in the middle of whatever those two had going on. "Society rewards beauty, and it's not only in music."

"Fashion, art, film, you name it," Kayla supplied. "Though I hide behind a drum set, so no one really gives a shit what I look like."

"The grungier the better, right, Kayla?" Tiff grinned over at her.

Kayla pulled at the hem of her threadbare Sex Pistols tee. Her jeans were holes held together by a loose netting of denim. "Works for me," she said. "But you, Lilly, and Candi? Y'all better grab the Botox."

"No needles for me," Lilly said flatly.

Candi surprised Toni by grabbing her bicep and squeezing hard. "Don't let 'em stick me, Toni," she cried out in an exaggerated pout. "We have to protect each other!"

"Fuck that," Tiff said. "Brown don't frown, right, Toni?"

Toni's laugh caught even her by surprise. What a motley crew.

"There are...things we have to do to get to the top, and things we have to do to stay on top once we get there," Lilly said, effectively cutting the laughter short. "It's a job. It's got a lot of perks, of course, but the second word in music business is *business*. If you're not making money, making music is a hobby."

Ouch.

"Unless you're just starting out," Jordan said, evidently reading Toni's face.

Lilly looked at Jordan. Her brow creased for a moment, and then she turned to Toni and Candi.

"Let's get to it, then."

Toni was surprised when Candi grabbed the mahogany-topped Fender Telecaster and plugged it into an amp that sat under the bay windows. She stood frozen for a moment.

"What about your arm?" Toni had noticed the absence of the sling she'd seen in a recent photo.

Candi smiled at her with glossy pink lips and not a hint of teeth. "I'll be okay. You can mirror me for a while."

"Oh." Toni exhaled. Of course, she was there to learn. "That would be great, thanks."

"Where's your guitar?" Candi brushed her cotton-candy-pink hair out of her eyes and nodded toward Toni's case.

Toni had gone from the train station to Jordan's office and then to Lilly's, and she still had all of her gear with her. Jordan had been kind enough to bring it inside. Leaving Minx in his SUV wouldn't have been wise, even in Lilly's bucolic neighborhood.

A kernel of pride forming in her chest, Toni knelt and opened the locks to reveal Minx in all her restored glory. Part of her couldn't wait to see the look on Seb's face when he saw the guitar. He'd always said it belonged with her.

After an hour in the capable hands at Ninth Street Music, where Toni took the opportunity to try out several of Gibson's newest models, Minx was as good as new herself. The luthier's eyes had nearly popped out of his head when she'd pulled Minx out of her case.

Perching on the arm of a chair, Toni lifted her up and settled the guitar on her thigh. Grabbing a cord, she bent and plugged into the amp next to Candi's. It was smaller, but it would get the job done.

"Where did you get that beauty?" Candi asked, sounding almost breathless.

Toni looked up to find her admiring Minx. She dug a pick out of her pocket and began tuning it.

"It's...been in my family for a while," she replied, opting to keep things vague. The chances that any of them had heard of her mother were slim, but she didn't want to risk it.

"Nice," Kayla commented from behind her small drum set. She'd traded her ubiquitous drumsticks for a set of brushes.

From what Toni had heard, Kayla could hit hard. So it was probably a good idea to forego the sticks and avoid disturbing Lilly's neighbors. It did make Toni wonder why they were practicing in Lilly's dining room as opposed to the cellar.

"I live down there," Tiff replied when Toni asked. "Lilly rents me the basement apartment. It's small, but it's only me, so it works."

Toni smiled. "That's cool."

Tiff shrugged, her focus on the acoustic bass in her hands. "I'm not picky about where I sleep."

Candi snorted. "That's an understatement."

"Don't start," Kayla reproached her.

Candi held her hands up in surrender and then dropped them to strum a chord on her guitar. The rest of the chatter fell silent and Toni looked around the room.

There were no real signs of strife or hostility between the band members, outside of some snarky banter, and Candi's arm seemed perfectly fine. Toni wondered what was really behind Candi's temporary absence from their lineup.

Not that she was about to ask. Whatever it was, it was none of her business. They'd hired her to do a job, and they were paying her a hell of a lot of money to do it—more than she thought the job was worth. None of it made any sense, but Toni was going to roll with it.

"Let's start off with something we all know," Tiff suggested.

The four of them looked around the room at one another for a moment, and Toni recognized the silent conversation for what it was. It was the kind of communication she'd always read about in band interviews, when they talked about synergy and mind reading.

Toni had always chalked that up to PR nonsense, but she could see it with this group, and it made her feel like even more of an outsider.

Kayla nodded and began to tap the end of her brush against the rim of the snare drum, establishing a rhythm and a tempo for whatever they'd agreed to play.

Candi widened her stance, the guitar slung low on her hips, and started to strum out a familiar chord progression.

Toni knew that song. It was "I Burn."

According to an article she'd read, the band's impromptu cover of the early alternative rock tune had transformed the Lillys from an obscure act into a viral sensation and one of the most sought-after bands in New York. It was apparently the moment that led to all of it—the EP they'd sold ten thousand copies of out of the back of their van, and the bidding war over who got to sign them to a recording contract. All of it stemmed from one fiery delivery of an obscure cover.

When Tiff's bass joined Candi's guitar and Kayla's drumming, Candi nodded to Toni.

"Take over on rhythm," she shouted over the music.

For a split second, Toni's mind went blank. She looked down at Minx, at her shiny new strings and her tortoiseshell pick guard and positioned her left hand on the strings to form a C-sharp chord. With her right hand, she brought the pick down to match the staccato rhythm Candi played across the room, bouncing between the C-sharp and the straight C.

Candi played along with her until the top of the next measure, and then she broke off to improv a swooping lead guitar part. Using the pedals at her feet, Candi added a bit of distortion and reverb to her sound. It floated over the foundation the rest of them continued to lay down.

Toni watched her intently, her hands already on autopilot as she continued to play the simple rhythm. Her focus was on Candi and the intricacy with which she played.

Holy hell, was she good. Her phrasing danced in and around the rest of the band in a way that gave the song far more sophistication than the original.

Toni glanced at the others and noted that they were all tuned into Candi too.

Her pink hair hung into her face as she dropped her head to her chest and...*played*, lost in the music.

Out of the corner of her eye, Toni saw Lilly enter the room. She walked over to a barstool in the corner and picked up a microphone that had been resting there. Lilly sat down and drew the mic cord through her elegant fingers, leaning one fist on her jean-clad knee. In the other, she held the microphone and rested it on her thigh as she watched and listened, her gaze scanning the room, lingering on Candi longer than the others.

A wistful expression crossed her face, so swiftly it might have been imagined. Then she looked at Toni. Not her face, thank goodness—Toni was still ridiculously intimidated by the woman— but at Toni's hands.

Toni played as crisply as she could manage, proud to hold her own in such elite company. Seemingly satisfied, Lilly's gaze moved on.

"From the top of the first verse," she said, lifting the microphone to her lips.

Her long, white-blond hair was pulled up into a haphazard ponytail, leaving strands to float around her face like feathers. She wore a couple of layered tank tops and faded blue jeans. Nothing special, really, but Toni's gaze keep drifting over to her. There was something about Lilly that commanded attention. Elton had been right. She had *it*, whatever it was.

She began to sing, her voice smoky and a little teasing.

After the first verse, Kayla introduced the kick drum, giving the song a little more weight.

It drew Toni out of spectator mode. She made eye contact with Kayla and Tiff, and when the song shifted into the heavier section, she was right there with them.

Lilly's voice soared; Candi's layering guitar lent gravitas to the song, texture and light. Toni had locked into Kayla and Tiff, and the three of them built a solid wall of sound to support the two leads.

When the song ended, Toni's skin buzzed with the rush of playing with a unit, as a unit. She'd never experienced anything like it before.

She wanted more.

"Not bad," Candi said, turning to Toni and finally showing some teeth in her smile. "Let's see what you can do on lead, little starlet."

CHAPTER 16.

SEB USED HIS KEY TO open Lilly's front door and was greeted by the familiar sounds of the Lillys in rehearsal—with one exception.

He closed the door behind him and listened closely to the music coming from the dining room. There was something...off. No, not off, but definitely different.

Walking through the kitchen, he found Jordan at the stove dipping a ladle into a giant pot, spooning some of its contents directly into his mouth—the heathen. He nodded toward Seb, chewing.

"You made it," he mumbled around a mouthful.

"Hey," Seb replied, peeking into the pot. "Damn, did Lilly make chicken and dumplings again?"

Jordan nodded and stuck the ladle into the pot for more.

Seb snatched it from him. "That's unsanitary," he warned his friend before dipping it in himself. "Why didn't you text me?"

Jordan stepped back, laughing. "Figured you'd make it here eventually. You take the train?"

"Nah, I wish. I drove. Thought I'd save time, but I got stuck in traffic." Seb sighed at the pitiful amount that remained at the bottom of the pan. "Shit, there's barely anything left."

He managed to rescue a dumpling and a morsel of chicken. Flavor exploded across his tongue. "God," he said, closing his eyes to chew. "I don't know why this is always so good."

"Nordic magic," Jordan replied, chuckling. He thumped Seb's shoulder with his fist.

"No shit." Seb opened his eyes. "I didn't see a practice on the schedule tonight."

"Oh, no. There wasn't, but I thought we should get Toni together with the girls as soon as possible."

Seb froze.

"Toni?" He croaked out the name.

"Yeah, the guitarist filling in for Candi?"

"I remember who she is," Seb said, scrambling to cover. "I didn't know she was coming so soon. And she's...here? Already?"

Jordan frowned, clearly stumped by Seb's confusion. "I thought we agreed to get her started right away."

"Well, yeah, but..."

But what? He had no objections, none that he could voice. Seb still hadn't had a chance to talk to Toni. Not that he'd made any effort to reach out to her, or her to him.

He had no clue what he'd walked into. Had she told them she'd known Seb when they were kids? Had she told them how he'd abandoned her? How he'd left her behind to save his own skin? Had she revealed how wrong they were to place their trust in him?

"Mate..." Jordan tilted his head, frowning. "You all right? You look like you're gonna pass out."

Seb cleared his throat. "Yeah. Good, I'm good. How, uh... How is it going so far?"

Jordan opened the fridge and grabbed a bottle of water. "Want one?" Seb shook his head. "Well...so far so good, I think."

Jordan looked toward the dining room. The song had paused for a moment, and Seb could hear soft chatter.

"They seem to be clicking, and no one has frightened her off yet. Even Candi is behaving," he added.

Seb's gaze snapped to Jordan's. "Candi's here?"

Jordan spoke slowly. "She offered to show our newbie the ropes, didn't she?"

"She did," Seb said, hoping his shock and panic didn't show. "Right, sure. Man, this is… It's all happening so fast."

He clasped his hands atop his head.

Jordan took a long pull from the bottle. "Kinda has to, though, yeah? The suits are antsy, and Lilly is in a tight enough spot. We don't want to give YMI any more reasons to pull the plug."

"No kidding." Seb let his arms drop to his sides.

Jordan looked at his watch and cursed under his breath. "Hey, listen, since you drove, could you do a bloke a favor and see our young miss to her lodgings? I've got to get going."

"No worries." Seb silently thanked the powers that be. It might offer him the perfect opportunity to clear the air with Toni, or at least to get on the same page. "Where is she staying?"

"I got her a room at the Fairfield near Penn Station. Her stuff's over there." He pointed to the banquette in the corner of the kitchen where a small suitcase and a duffel bag were piled.

Seb groaned. "Why'd you put her there?"

"It's clean, cheap, and it's not too far from SAGA."

"Okay," Seb said. "No problem. I got it."

Jordan smiled, relief evident in his eyes. "Thanks, bruv. I'd planned to take her, but it doesn't sound like they're going to be done anytime soon." He hooked his thumb toward the dining room. "Sounds like they're making quick progress."

Seb recognized the opening chords to "Widows." He nodded, tuning in to the rehearsal once more. The band sounded good. Tight. He turned back to Jordan, who was searching his pockets for something.

"Where'd I leave my mobile?"

Seb spotted it on the counter by the stove and handed it over. "Big date?"

If he didn't know better, Seb would think Jordan was blushing.

"It's not a *date* so much as a hang-out type of situation," Jordan said not-so-convincingly. "I'm making my famous curry."

"I see," Seb said, knowing Jordan didn't cook for just anyone. "Well, I hope she likes it spicy."

"I hope *he* does too."

Seb grinned at him. "Ah, so it's not the food critic from last week, then?"

"Oh God, no," Jordan said, horrified. "She couldn't bloody well turn it off. Kept critiquing everything."

Seb arched a brow. "Everything?"

"Every damned thing." His mouth twisted into a grimace. "No, tonight's this hot-as-fuck hockey player I met on BA 789 on my way to London last month. He has a thing for accents and home cooking." Jordan winked as he pulled his keys from his pocket. "Thanks for taking over on babysitting duties."

"Anytime," Seb said, chuckling. "Have fun playing puck bunny."

Jordan gave him the finger but there was a definite bounce in his step as he strolled down the hallway.

After he left, Seb moved to the doorway separating the dining room from the kitchen. He was careful to stay in the shadows, eager to observe the dynamics in the room.

Kayla was behind the cocktail drum kit he'd procured for them several months back. It was odd for him to see her sitting behind such a tiny set of drums. Kayla herself was petite, but she somehow managed to dwarf the full-size kits she usually played with her larger-than-life presence and style.

To the front left of Kayla stood Tiff, with Candi off to the right. Seated next to her was Toni, her focus on the instrument in her hands and, goddamn. It was Minx!

Toni wielded her like a sword, her movements practiced.

Precise. Damn near perfect. She was every rock and roll fantasy he'd had for her come to life.

Seb had severed his relationship with Fate the night he snuck out of Bordon, but perhaps Fate wasn't quite finished with him. With either of them. Toni had been returned to him. He had to find a way to make things right between them.

"I didn't think you were coming," Lilly said from beside him, where she sat on a stool by the door. Watching.

"I had a meeting with Carlos about the timeline for the show-case. Jordan forgot to clue me in."

Lilly hummed in response, her gaze bouncing from Toni to Candi and back.

Seb tilted his head toward the pair of guitarists. "Early predictions?"

Lilly's gaze slanted to his. "Our Candace is wearing her good-girl mask today."

"That's not necessarily a bad thing, is it?"

"Perhaps not," Lilly agreed. "But it's more likely to be the calm before the storm with her, *sant*?"

Seb couldn't argue. He noticed Candi watching Toni's hands. Her expression was blank as she stared at Toni's fingers as they moved.

Toni looked up and caught her gaze, hers a little apprehensive from what Seb could see.

It took a second or two for Candi to plaster on a smile, but she managed. Seb had to give her points for that. It wasn't an easy situation, and everyone seemed to have set aside their grievances for the sake of the band.

Maybe Candi's plan would work out after all, for everyone.

The song ended and Tiff took off her bass and set it down on the stand at her side. She stretched her arms above her head, twisting her torso left and then right.

"Fuck, y'all. I'm tired."

"My hands are numb," Kayla said, grinning at her reddened fingers. "That was a good sesh."

"Impressive," Candi said, looking at Toni with something like admiration.

Toni smiled, her relief written all over her face.

Seb bit back his own smile, pleased for her. He'd always said hers was a rare talent.

Her sleek black-and-purple hair had been pulled back into a bun at her nape. It looked good straight, but Seb kind of missed her curls. He caught himself studying her, the way her body had changed over the years. His gaze drifted over the apples of her cheeks, the slight upturn at the end of her nose, and her long, elegant limbs. The way her jeans hugged the curve of her ass as she stood and stretched.

Whoa.

He banished that thought real quick.

"Hey there, Seb!"

He blinked and found Kayla grinning at him.

Shit.

Seb offered the redhead a small wave. When his gaze returned to Toni, she was packing up her gear with quick, jerky movements.

"If you guys don't mind," Toni said, her back to the room, "I'm gonna head to my hotel."

"I'll drive you," Seb offered too quickly.

Toni's head whipped around. "What? No, th-that's okay. Jordan said he'd take me."

"He had to split," Seb said, not missing the hint of panic in her eyes.

"Don't worry," Tiff said. "Sebby doesn't bite."

"It's okay, I can take the train," Toni replied.

"He asked me to take you," Seb added, trying to telegraph his need to speak with her alone. "And it's late. You don't wanna deal with the train and all your gear."

"I'd say ride with me, but we're going in opposite directions," Kayla supplied.

Several emotions crossed Toni's face, too fast for Seb to decipher them all, but the one that stood out the most was resignation. Not a good sign, but he'd take it.

"Okay," she said, giving him the barest of glances. "That's nice of you, thanks."

"Could I bum a ride with you too, sugar?" Candi's smile was artificially sweet. *Great.*

Beside him, Seb felt Lilly stiffen before she stood and walked out of the room.

Seb shot a glare at Candi who shrugged, unperturbed.

"Where's Masturini?"

"I gave Eric the night off," Candi replied, not meeting his gaze.

"Meaning you ditched him."

Candi didn't bother to hide her gloating grin. "Anyway," she said, dragging out the word, "I figured you could take me home."

Seb hardened his gaze.

She blinked and her eyes slid to Toni. "I meant, you know, you could drop me off after you drop off little Toni, here."

"I can manage the train, o-o-or grab a Lyft," Toni said.

"I'll drop you both off," Seb said. "It's no big deal."

Candi make a little sound of disapproval, but Toni silently nodded when Seb met her eyes.

They really needed to talk. Alone. Toni, however, didn't seem to feel the need.

After they stored her gear, she climbed into the back without a word.

"I don't know why you're taking this route," Candi complained while Seb drove them toward her Upper East Side apartment. "It would have made more sense to drop Toni off first and then me."

"Not really," Seb said for the dozenth time since they'd gotten into his car. "Toni's hotel is closer to me. I don't want to double back."

Out of his periphery, Seb saw Candi turn to him, her eyes practically boring a hole into the side of his face. He knew what she was trying to do, and he wasn't interested in engaging. Besides, he was anxious to get a moment with Toni. Toni, who sat quietly in the back seat, her face virtually pressed to the window, as if the closer she got to the outside of his SUV, the better.

Every once in a while, he'd catch her staring at him in the rearview mirror. He couldn't begin to guess what was going through her mind.

By the time they pulled in front of Candi's apartment building on East 80th, the car had gone completely silent. Seb stopped in a no-loading zone.

Candi turned to him, incredulous.

"Here you go." He gestured toward her building. "Sleep tight."

Her doorman, Jakub, walked over to the car, and Seb unlocked the door so the man could open it.

There was no mistaking the resentment in Candi's eyes, but she plastered on a smile and turned to Toni.

"See you tomorrow, babes."

"Good night," Toni said. "And thanks for earlier. It really helped to play along with you."

Seb caught the tail end of her smile in the rearview.

"Hey there, Seb," Jakub said as he helped Candi out of the car.

Seb lifted a few fingers from the steering wheel in salute. "How's it going, J?"

"I can't complain," the other man replied.

Candi grabbed her bag from the footwell and jumped out, Jakub hot on her heels as she power walked to the front door.

In the lobby, Seb recognized a member of her family's security detail sitting by the desk. The man straightened in his chair when he saw Candi enter and touched the com at his ear.

With her safely tucked away, Seb exhaled, a little of the stress and anxiety leaving his chest. He quickly checked his phone for messages and waited.

And waited.

He checked the rearview again, perplexed. "Aren't you going to move up here?"

Toni met his eyes in the mirror. "Wasn't planning on it."

Seb sighed and turned around to face her. "Really?"

She pointedly looked out the window. "I'm comfortable here."

"Nia. We need to talk."

She turned back to him, her expression glacial. "Do we really?"

Seb held her gaze. After a brief standoff, Toni sighed and rolled her eyes. It was a move so familiar, it caused a twinge in Seb's heart.

She slid out of the back seat and slammed the door behind her with enough force to rock the car. A second later, the passenger door opened, and she climbed inside, shutting the door with a resounding bang that plunged his SUV into silence.

Seb stared out the front window. It was late, but plenty of people still strolled the tree-lined sidewalks.

Now that Toni was there next to him, now that they were alone, the words wouldn't come. He'd had years to agonize over what he could say to her, how he could explain why he'd left the way he did. Why he stayed away.

"I'm tired," Toni said, her tone flat and unyielding. "Can you say what you need to say and drive at the same time?"

"No," Seb said, keeping his eyes forward. He felt hers on him, though.

"What do you want, Seb? Why am I here? In New York, with this band... With you. Why?"

He did turn to her then. "I had nothing to do with you being here, Nia."

Her eyes squeezed shut, her face pinched. "Don't call me that."

"Sorry. Old habit."

"Break it." It was a quiet demand. As if for emphasis, Toni turned back to the window.

A black car pulled in front of them, one of those shiny executive sedans that frequented neighborhoods like this one.

The driver got out and walked around the car to open the door for his client, a woman in a sleek black cocktail dress. She was pale, tall, thin, and could have been anywhere between twenty-five and seventy years old. Money, Seb had discovered, was its own fountain of youth.

"Hurry up," the woman snapped as the driver pulled several designer suitcases from the trunk and handed them to Jakub, who had jogged out to greet her.

"Evening, Ms. Bolton."

"Take those up," she replied coolly as she walked toward Candi's building.

Jakub followed her, pausing briefly when he saw that Seb was still there. He raised a curious brow.

Seb gave him a thumbs-up, and Jakub smiled before returning to his task. Beside him, Toni snorted.

"What a life," she said, shaking her head.

"Which one?"

"The doorman is doing his job, and he seems all right. Probably pretty good at it." Toni turned to watch Jakub and the woman through the glass doors. "I couldn't do it, though—be nice to people who treated me like shit."

"You're jumping to a big conclusion, there," Seb said. "You don't know what that woman is like."

"Yeah, I do, and so do you," Toni replied, turning to look at him. "She doesn't see her driver or that doorman as people. They're things. They're tools, there to do her bidding and make her life easier."

Despite juggling her suitcases, Jakub gestured for the woman to go in first and she made no move to hold anything herself. The driver sped off as Seb and Toni both watched Jakub and the woman disappear into the elevator.

"Why do people like that always end up on top?"

"There's a kind of ruthlessness you need to be successful, really successful, I think," Seb answered.

Toni turned to him. "I hope I don't have that in me."

"You don't," he replied automatically.

Toni gave him a wan smile. "You don't know that." She turned her attention back to the window. "You don't know anything about me."

"So tell me."

"Drive."

He held a hand up in surrender before starting the car and putting both hands on the wheel, making a show of placing them at ten and two. "Driving."

Seb pulled away from the curb. He decided to take an indirect route, wanting time to get on some semblance of solid ground with her. Having Toni reappear in his life at such a pivotal moment had to mean something. At the very least, it was a chance to set some things straight. Again, though, the words didn't come.

Several silent stoplights later, Toni sighed loudly. "You wanted to talk, so talk." She leaned her head against the passenger window. The light from passing cars and streetlamps made a kaleidoscope of her features.

Seb had a hard time keeping his eyes on the road and was grateful when they ran into a bit of traffic on Fifth Avenue. Everything about her was the same and nothing was.

As a teenager, Antonia had been a ball of frenetic energy. Always talking. Always moving. Always eager to share her opinion and her mood. This quiet, resolute version of her unnerved Seb a bit.

"I don't know where to start," he admitted. "I'm glad you stuck with it. The music, I mean."

"I never thought I'd see you again," Toni said quietly.

"Same." It was an easy admission.

Toni rolled her head along the headrest to look at him.

Seb thought she'd say something, but she just stared. He squirmed under the inspection and fought to keep his eyes on the traffic. After several uncomfortable minutes of silence, he couldn't take it anymore. "What?"

"You went out of your way to get me alone, and you're not saying much."

Seb sighed. "Can I kidnap you for a bit?"

She shifted in the seat. "Umm…"

"I can't do this and drive," he said, not above begging.

As if the universe were trying to give him a break, Seb spied a car pulling out next to the park and pulled into the open spot. He shut off the engine.

"Want to take a walk?"

"Not really," Toni answered. "Say what you want to say. I'm tired and tomorrow's probably going to be a long day."

Seb unbuckled his seat belt and turned to her, steeling himself.

He owed this to her on her terms, not his. "I'm sorry. I'm so fucking sorry. You have no idea."

Toni stared through the windshield. "What are you sorry for, Seb?"

His thoughts whirred like helicopter blades. Where did he even start?

"For leaving Bordon the way I did, to start. Taking money out of our stash and leaving you in the lurch," he said in a rush.

"Yeah." Toni blew out a breath. She did sound tired, and Seb wondered if it was the right time for this. "That...was a shitty thing to do."

"I know," he agreed, almost relieved for having gotten it out. "I needed to get out fast, and...and I knew you'd be okay."

"You didn't know that," she bit back, turning her head. Her eyes flashed hot with emotion for a moment, and then it was gone. Like someone had turned out a light. "But you were a kid. We were kids. We didn't know much of anything back then."

"Still," Seb said, not knowing what else to say. "I want to apologize and explain, maybe. The way things went down back in Bordon, it wasn't... I didn't—"

"Seb." Toni held up her hand. "I don't have the energy to rehash the past. And I really don't need a lengthy explanation. It was a lifetime ago. I moved on. You obviously did, so...let it go."

What if I don't want to, he thought but he had to respect her wishes. Forcing his guilt onto her wouldn't do either of them any good. Seb needed to get them to a place where they could work together for these six weeks and not tear each other apart at the seams.

"How did you end up with this crew?"

Seb was surprised by her question, but hopeful she had the same goal in mind.

"It's a long story," he said, shifting to match her pose. A

late-night jogger crossed at the light and disappeared into the park. "I met Lilly in a club one night. We hit it off."

"She's hard to read," Toni said.

Seb nodded. "She can be, especially at first, but she's a good person. Talented, driven... Sometimes a hard-ass."

Toni snorted. "I saw a bit of that tonight. Makes me even more nervous for when the real rehearsals start tomorrow."

"Nah, don't be nervous," he said, wanting to reassure her. "I caught the tail end of what you guys were doing tonight. You'll be fine."

Toni lowered her eyes. "We'll see."

"The important question is, are you going to be okay working around me?" Seb needed to know. He didn't want to cause her any more pain than he already had.

Toni turned in her seat to face him. "What is it you do for them, exactly?"

"Mostly, I try to keep the band from running off the rails." Bang-up job he'd been doing of that lately. "I arrange for them. With them. With Lilly and Candi," he replied, noticing the way her gaze sharpened when he said Candi's name. No doubt she'd seen all the stuff in the press. *Great.* "We're working on some originals for them. And I sit in on the gigs sometimes, when they need a second guitar."

Seb struggled to voice his role in the Lillys. He turned Toni's question over and over in his mind. The answer was hard to put into words.

"Officially, I'm their manager, but...I'm not in charge."

"Didn't think you were," Toni said, her tone matter-of-fact. "Neither is Jordan, though he seems to have a strong handle on the business stuff."

"Yeah, Jordan's saved our asses a couple of times already," Seb confessed, giving her a soft smile, which she merely blinked at. He dropped it. "I should have brought him in sooner. I've never managed anyone before. I'm a songwriter, primarily. But no one would take them seriously. Four women, you know?"

Toni nodded. "Boys' club. I get it."

"Yeah."

"It's weird," she said.

"Is it?"

"Not that." She waved him off. "I mean...this." Toni made a sweeping gesture between them. "You working with them behind the scenes and me stepping into the spotlight, albeit temporarily." She paused. "I'd be happier in your position."

"Still afraid of the whole fame thing?"

Toni shook her head. "I was never afraid of it. I'm more... repulsed by it."

Seb frowned at that. "Then why are you doing this?"

Toni turned away. "I need the money."

He scrambled to think of reasons why Toni would be desperate enough to subject herself to something she despised. Nope. None of his business.

"Ah." Seb figured she'd tell him if she wanted him to know. There was one question he did need to ask. "Why did you pretend not to know me?"

Toni looked at him. "Why did you play along?"

"I–I don't know," he answered, realizing it was the truth. "Shock, I guess." *Not to mention the no-fraternization clause.*

Toni seemed to accept his answer, even if she didn't seem to buy it. "I didn't want knowing you to be the reason why I was called up. I was pissed."

"And now?"

"Well." She shrugged and turned away again. "We've sort of lied to the others. How do we tell them the truth without it sounding...I dunno, like a deliberate deception?"

Seb had reason enough to keep their past quiet. No need to put his every interaction with Toni over the next month under a goddamned microscope. He had enough of that with the whole Candi situation.

"Agreed," he said. "No need to bring it up."

"None at all," Toni said. "I'll be gone soon, and things will go back to normal. Right?"

Whatever normal was. "Yeah."

"Good."

Seb chose to ignore the part about her presence being temporary. That was a later problem. They sat in silence for a while, and he wanted to hold onto the moment. Being with her again, even like this, it was...

Toni yawned.

Checking the clock, Seb realized it was almost 2:00 a.m. He started the car and pointed it in the direction of her hotel. They were quiet for the rest of the drive, but Seb's thoughts buzzed inside his head.

There was more, so much more, that he wanted to say to her—to know about her. But he didn't need to be a genius to decipher Toni's body language.

She wasn't going to open up to him. She wasn't going to give him any information about her life, and she didn't seem particularly interested in his. There wasn't going to be a heartfelt reconciliation, no warm reunion. Definitely no going back to where they were before. Like she said, they weren't kids anymore. Too much time had passed. Too much hurt inflicted, all by him.

"Thanks for the ride," Toni said as they pulled up in front of the Fairfield.

There was no doorman to greet them, and Toni jumped out and grabbed her stuff before Seb could make a move himself. He lowered the passenger window when she closed the door.

Toni folded her arms against the car door but turned her head to watch the traffic behind him. Despite the late hour, it was only marginally lighter than midday.

"I am curious about one thing," she said. "Why did you only take half of the money? You could have taken everything you put in. Only a third of it was mine, if that much. Shit, you could have taken it all."

Seb frowned. "I didn't... I couldn't leave you with nothing, Nia."

Toni tilted her head to the side, confused. "But, Seb, you did," she said. "That's exactly what you left me with."

Before he could answer, she turned and walked away.

CHAPTER 17.

"ARE WE ALL SET, THEN?"

"Yes, Seb. You're all set. The bill's been paid, and the girls are good to go."

Hands on his hips, Seb nodded. "Cool, cool."

He stood in a corner window on the fourth floor of SAGA and watched the city go by below. Down the hall from the room where the band rehearsed for the third day, Seb felt settled. Settled enough, which was a welcome relief after the last couple of weeks.

His conversation with Toni the other night still had him rattled, but he saw it as an opening. He didn't want to accept that he'd burned that bridge entirely. There had to be a way back to some kind of friendship. He hoped. And he knew he had a lot of work to do to get there. Toni deserved that, and more.

In his pocket, his cell phone vibrated. Seb fished it out and checked the number, smiling at the caller ID.

"Hey, Carlos."

"Seb, yo." Carlos sounded out of breath, and there was a lot of ambient noise behind him. "I've been trying to reach Jordan."

"He's on his way back from LA." Seb checked the time. "Should be landing soon, though. What's up?"

On the street below, Seb watched two businessmen argue over

a taxicab, one gesturing to his watch and the other to his stack of luggage on the curb.

"Listen," Carlos said in a tone that made Seb sit up straighter. "I thought you should know."

"Know what?"

"I'm out."

"Out of what?"

"I got called upstairs this morning and handed a severance check," Carlos spat. "A fucking check. For nine thousand dollars."

"Wait, what are you saying?" Seb dropped into the nearest chair.

Carlos Venegas had been the Lillys' champion at YMI. He'd brought them to the label's attention and had advocated for a second chance when Candi had missed the showcase. He'd fought for them as much as Seb and Jordan had.

"I'm sorry, man," Carlos said. "But you're on your own with these people now."

"Shit," Seb breathed. "But, no… I mean, don't worry about us. We'll figure something out, but you, what are you going to do now?"

"I honestly don't know, man." He sounded so dejected.

Seb wished he could do something for him. "Does Jordan know?"

"Not yet," Carlos answered. "Got through to you first."

"You need to talk to him, or I can. He knows everyone in LA, London…" Seb said, his mind already racing through his mental address book. "Between the two of us, we can put in a word for you somewhere."

Carlos chuckled, but the sound was devoid of mirth. "Thanks, but people like me are obsolete. Mine is a dying art, my friend. I feel like a fucking dinosaur."

"Dude, you're forty."

"That's my point," Carlos said. "Who's going to want a

forty-year-old artists-and-rep guy on their payroll? Face it, the dream is over. A&R is officially dead."

"Nah, man," Seb countered. "With your experience and your track record? Someone's gonna call."

"Well, we'll see," Carlos replied, sounding less than convinced. "In the meantime, I'm going to take a vacation. I haven't had one in, like, ten years."

"See? It's time. De-stress yourself and then look at your options."

"Thanks. But, anyway, listen…"

"I know," Seb cut him off. "Without you there, we've got no one on the inside in our corner."

"They know what they have, what your band could do if the stars align properly. They're stupid about everything but the money." Carlos huffed out a laugh. "The twins may not know shit about music, but they know numbers. Don't let them bully you too much."

"What about our current situation?"

"How is that going, by the way?" Carlos asked. "I heard the auditions were successful. You found someone to fill in for Candi?"

Carlos sounded eager. It was clear how invested he was in the band.

Seb's thoughts turned to Toni. He swallowed.

"Yeah," he said, his voice suddenly thick. He cleared his throat. "Yeah, she's good. Rehearsing with them as we speak."

"That's fantastic," Carlos said, genuinely pleased. "And Candi is handling all this okay?"

"She's even helping Toni learn her parts."

"Who?"

"The guitarist. She's from Philly," Seb said, hoping to keep anything out of his voice that would give him away.

"Ah, cool. Well, I can't wait to hear her play." Carlos paused. "And...how's Lilly handling all of this?"

Seb thought of the way she'd been looked at him lately. Thought about the distance he still felt between them now.

"She's Lilly" was all he could say.

Carlos made a humming sound of agreement. "Well, I know we aren't technically working together anymore, but keep me posted, will ya?"

"Of course," Seb agreed without giving it a second thought.

"And if there's anything I can do..." Carlos offered.

"Likewise," Seb said. "Anything at all."

"Thanks," Carlos said. "Hey, before I let you go, you should tell Jordan to check and see if there's a key man clause in the band's contract."

"A what?"

"It's like a get-out-of-jail-free card," Carlos explained. "I was your point of contact at the label. Sometimes, attorneys will put a clause in the contract that says if the key contact for the artist leaves"—he paused—"or, you know, gets fired for no good goddamn reason, the artist can choose to terminate the contract."

"Really?" Seb was shocked he'd never heard of such a thing.

"Yeah, it's old school, but that first guy you brought in to represent the girls wasn't the brightest star in the firmament," Carlos said, clearly disgusted.

Seb would never forgive himself for hiring the first entertainment attorney that showed interest in the band without vetting him. He should have reached out to Jordan right away, but he'd been too stubborn and all too eager to do it himself.

"Have Jordan check," Carlos continued. "And even if it isn't there, you might be able to negotiate it into your next deal or even renegotiate this one. You never know. Worth a try, especially with the new management."

"Wow, man. Thanks."

"Sure," Carlos said, a smile in his voice. Seb was glad to hear it. "We'll catch up when I get back from my vacay."

Seb grinned. "You already know where you're going?"

"Wherever the fuck nine grand will take me."

CHAPTER 18.

THIS WAS HELL. AFTER THREE days, Toni had thought she'd figured out how the band worked. Everything had gone pretty smoothly thus far.

Too smoothly, as it turned out. The honeymoon phase was definitely over.

"Fuck you, it's not me," Kayla shouted from behind a gleaming set of Ludwig drums. "I counted it off. You come in on one-and-two-AND."

Tiff shook her head. "No, I don't. I come in on the *second* one-and."

"Um, she's right. The intro is all drums," Toni agreed. "I don't think the bass drops in until right before the backing vocals."

"You're both wrong," Kayla grumbled. "Am I the only one in the room with ears?"

"Back at Lilly's, didn't you say you liked having a drum intro?" Toni asked. "Maybe if you listened to it—"

"Who's got the track?" Kayla demanded, cutting Toni off. "Can someone pull up the goddamned track so we can hear the goddamned thing? I'm sick of this shit."

Kayla's face was so red, Toni worried she might burst a blood vessel.

Toni had zero experience playing in a band, outside of impromptu jams at the Unicorn. She wondered if these sorts of outbursts were common.

Lilly appeared nonplussed and merely sat in a chair, tipping her head over the back with her eyes closed. Her waist-length blond hair nearly brushed the floor.

They'd been at SAGA for hours and hadn't gotten through more than two songs. It was coming up on three o'clock, and they hadn't shown any signs of stopping for lunch. Toni made a mental note to pack some granola bars or something for next time—she was starving.

Kayla used her phone to pull up the song in question. The tiny speakers were no match for the size of the room, which could have fit a full orchestra.

The bleached hardwood and bright floor-to-ceiling windows made the space seem suited to something more tranquil than the scene currently unfolding.

"See?" Kayla pointed a finger at Tiff. "I told you, one-and-two-AND."

"How the hell am I supposed to hear anything from over here? Point your phone at a mic or something."

"Who do I look like, a friggin' sound guy?" Kayla scoffed. "Pull it up on your own damn phone if you're too lazy to haul your ass five feet and listen to mine."

Tiff turned to Toni. "You hear it, don't you? I come in later than she thinks."

"I…"

"Don't kowtow to her, Toni. She knows I'm right and doesn't want to admit it."

"Fuck you, Emily Dickinson," Tiff snapped.

"Jesus, enough!" Lilly's voice cracked the air like a whip, silencing everyone.

Toni stood gaping as the others slinked back to their figurative corners.

"We have less than three weeks to sound like a real unit," Lilly stated more calmly than Toni thought she would after that outburst. "And you two are sitting here wasting my time with your petty bickering."

"*Your* time?" Tiff countered.

Lilly leveled her with a glare. "*Our* time, then. Happy?"

"Just making sure you didn't kick me out too when I wasn't looking," Tiff mumbled loudly as she turned away.

Toni recoiled from the low blow, but Lilly only nodded, smiling. It was anything but friendly. "Take ten. I need some air."

Toni stood frozen to the spot, as did the others, until Lilly left the room.

"Way to go, Tiff," Kayla hissed.

To her credit, Tiff looked guilty as hell. "Fuck all of this." She sighed and tossed an apologetic look Toni's way. "Nothing against you."

Toni nodded. "No worries."

"Shit." Tiff set her bass in its stand. "I better go appease Mother."

"Uh, you think?" Kayla sniped back.

Tiff glared at her. "Fuck off."

After she too was gone, Kayla took over the chair Lilly had occupied and buried her nose in her phone, leaving Toni essentially by herself.

She needed to shake it off, all of it. The Lillys fought as hard as they played, and it would take some getting used to, but she could handle it. "I'm gonna…uh…see if I can find a vending machine. You want anything?"

Kayla made a sound that sounded close to the word *no*, so Toni left the room.

She followed the signs to where several vending machines offered different types of snacks, almost all of them unhealthy.

Toni eyed the sugar-packed, salt-laden goodies with something akin to lust. Her gaze landed on a pack of Junior Mints, their chocolate-covered, minty yumminess taunting her from behind the glass. She'd been obsessed with them as a kid, and Seb would get some for her every time they went to the movies. Toni's mouth began to water.

She agreed with her taste buds. It was the perfect snack for the kind of day she was having. Toni reached for her wallet only to realize she'd left it, and her bag, in the rehearsal room.

"Shit, Antonia," she complained to her reflection in the glass. "You really came out here with no cash?"

A crisp one-dollar bill appeared over her shoulder, and Toni almost jumped out of her skin.

Seb held up his hands. "Sorry, didn't mean to spook you."

"I'm fine," she huffed, annoyed and jittery.

Intellectually, she knew she'd see Seb today. He'd been trying to continue their conversation from the other night, and she'd successfully avoided being alone with him until now. Toni certainly hadn't expected him to sneak up on her.

"You sure?" He withdrew his hand, a bit sheepish.

"I said I'm fine." She turned her back to him. In front of her was a doorway that she knew led to a long corridor. Since she couldn't get a snack, she'd settle for stretching her legs. She walked through the door and turned left, relieved when Seb didn't follow her.

Toni paced the corridor, feeling like an interloper.

She knew these songs. She'd absorbed them into her bloodstream. But as with Jerry Gant, she'd opened her big fucking mouth. They hadn't needed her to voice her opinion on anything.

Those first few days had been so casual. They'd eased into

the material, and Toni had apparently eased herself right into a false sense of security. Candi had showed Toni the fingering for a couple of the chords she'd had trouble hearing on the recordings. Once she had it, though, she had it.

She'd slipped right into the pocket when they jammed through the first two rehearsals and had broken out into her solos with ease. Everyone had been impressed, and Toni's trepidation about taking the gig had begun to melt away.

She should have known it was only a matter of time before she went and stuck her foot in it. Mo was right about one thing—she didn't know when to shut up.

And now, to add insult to injury, Seb was still hovering in front of the vending machine as she made her way back. He looked at her like he expected her to cry or something. "Sorry again about before." Seb trailed behind Toni as she headed back to the rehearsal room. "Hey, weren't you going to get something to eat?"

"Changed my mind."

Seb caught up and lightly cupped her shoulder before retreating from her space.

Normally, Toni would keep on walking, but something made her stop. It was the brief touch, there and gone again before she even felt a need to flinch away.

He remembered.

She turned to face him.

The corner of his mouth tipped up into a smile, and she was again struck by how incredibly good-looking he was. Time hadn't only been kind to Seb, it had evidently fallen in love with him and wanted to have his babies. So unfair.

She was pretty sure she'd wanted that, too, once upon a teenager.

Seb searched her face, his dimple receding.

"Hey," he said, reaching into his back pocket. "I've got more ones, if there's something you want from the machines back there."

"I'm not really hungry, but thanks." Toni bit the inside of her cheek. It was an unnecessary lie, but the idea of being in any way vulnerable in front of him bothered her.

Seb's mouth twisted into a smirk like he could see straight through her. "Is that why you were staring so longingly at the trail mix? C'mon, you gotta eat. Who knows when you'll get another break?"

Toni bristled. They weren't friends, and he had no right to talk to her like he knew her anymore. "I don't need you to babysit me."

"Not babysitting, only trying to help," Seb promised. "I'd do no less for any of the girls. Part of my job, remember? Besides, you look like you've been through hell."

She offered him a slow blink. "Gee. Thanks."

Seb laughed. "No, that's not... Sorry, that came out wrong. I meant to say it sounds like things are getting serious in there today."

Toni conceded with a nod. "I look that rough?"

"Nah, you look good. Great, even," he added, his gaze tracking down her body before he seemed to catch himself. "But that little vein is pulsing under your right eye."

Toni frowned. "My what is what?"

He pointed in the vicinity of her right eye, and Toni's hand moved up without her permission before she dropped it.

"I can handle it," she said, hearing the pout in her own voice. "I think..." She let out a breath, sagging a little under the pressure of the situation. "I dunno, Seb. I think I screwed up back there."

Seb ducked his head. "I seriously doubt that, Nia. What's got you spooked?"

How had they fallen into such easy banter? The first time Toni saw him, she'd wanted to rip his balls off. The second time, she'd thought she'd humiliated herself in front of him. And the last time they'd really spoken, she'd felt more indifferent toward him.

Now? She didn't know what to make of their predicament.

Though he continued to deny it, Seb had more than likely landed her this opportunity of a lifetime. She was one step closer to her dream.

Toni had to admit, as apologies went it was a pretty damn good one. Still, she couldn't let him back into her life that easily.

He'd burned her once, and she wasn't about to let him do it again, no matter how pretty he was with his thick black waves and sparkling green eyes and…

Focus, Bennette.

Toni exhaled and walked a few steps away, putting some much-needed distance between them. Her thoughts were going haywire, something she hadn't experienced in forever.

"It was like friggin' *Game of Thrones* in there," she said, seizing on what was actually important. "And I'm pretty sure I'm the Ned Stark in the room."

Seb laughed. To his credit, he tried to hide it this time.

Toni spun on her heel to level him with what she was sure was the meanest stink-eye he'd ever seen.

Seb only laughed harder. "Sorry, I forgot what a nerd you are."

"Hey!" She pointed a finger at him. "You're the one that made me watch every damn episode of *Farscape*. Twice."

"John and Aeryn forever, baby," Seb declared triumphantly. His open, unguarded expression was so damned familiar, it stole Toni's quip.

It struck her that this was Seb, the angsty, ill-tempered, secretly-a-teddy-bear guy that had stolen her heart without him even knowing it.

His laughter faded, leaving behind the echo of a smile Toni hadn't thought she'd ever see again.

She looked away, unwilling to get caught up in the nostalgia.

"Is it always like that between them?" she asked to get them back on safer ground.

Seb scratched at his stubble. "Yeah, but it's not as bad as it looks. This is part of their process," he said, turning more serious. "Really, though. How are you holding up?"

"You make it sound like I have a terminal illness."

"Sorry." Seb's smile brightened again. His eyes were always so soft for her, but it surprised her to see that now.

Toni ignored the warm feeling in her chest. She was there to work, not reminisce. But the opportunity to get to know what had become of the boy who had shaped so much of who she was today was almost too tempting to resist.

He also knew these women well, and Toni needed his help to understand them, or at least her role while she was there.

"Lilly hates me" was what came out of her mouth. Like they were back in high school and she was complaining about their physics teacher, Mrs. Morten.

"She doesn't," Seb protested. "Well, she might, but she hates everyone right now. It's a new dynamic, and Lilly doesn't handle change well."

"I get that, I really do, but I have to wonder if this wasn't a bad idea altogether. If they can't even get along with one another, I have a less-than-zero chance of making this work."

And I need this to work. The thought of going through all of this only to fail...

Toni flattened her back against the wall and tried hard to keep her eye on the prize, on the thirty thousand dollars that would change her life.

Seb stepped closer. "I don't think you believe that," he said, shoving his hands into the pockets of his jeans. They were worn and looked soft yet somehow rugged at the same time. Kinda like Seb. "You know you belong here as much as anyone. You're good, Nia. Really fucking good."

"*God*," Toni breathed, smiling despite herself. "Until we ran into each other at Phactory Sound, I had completely forgotten that you used to call me that."

Seb's mouth twisted into a grin. "You hated it."

"Not entirely."

His eyebrows rose and Seb shifted, flattening against the wall beside her, close but not too close.

Her seventeen-year-old heart would have sped up regardless, but Toni wasn't a kid anymore.

"You used to punch me on the arm," he said, his tone teasing.

"Like this?" Toni punched his bicep and pulled her hand back when her knuckles met solid muscle. "Shit! You hiding granite under that tee? Ow."

"You know it." Seb's grin brought back the dimple Toni used to fixate on.

She looked away, her attention drawn by the sound of a bass run Toni recognized as the intro to the song they'd been working on.

Seb nodded toward the doors. "Sounds like they're done butting heads for now. You want me to make a snack run? Bring 'em in to the horde?"

He looked so hopeful, so ready for things to be okay between them that Toni felt herself nod. She'd said she didn't need explanations or apologies. Maybe it was time for her to act like it and cut the guy a break.

"That'd be great." Toni exhaled at last, feeling lighter already. "Some trail mix will do for me."

"Oh, sure," Seb said, smirking. "No Junior Mints?"

Toni laughed with delighted surprise. "You remember?"

"I remember everything," Seb replied, his eyes searching hers. "You could never resist them. It was the only way I could coax you into doing anything without you complaining."

"Yeah? Like what?"

"Like the first time you let me play Minx."

Toni couldn't hide her shock. "Oh my God, I'd forgotten that too."

They'd been fourteen and fifteen, respectively, and Seb had begged her to let him sneak it out to the alley while her dad was passed out on the sofa upstairs. It had only taken a family-size bag of Junior Mints to convince her. Well, that and Seb's adorable pleading.

He'd called upon every weapon at his disposal, running his hand through his hair, smirking in the way that always deepened his dimple the most, and lowering his manly, postpuberty voice to a purr.

Not that Toni had realized it at the time, but it had been a seduction of sorts.

Seb turned to lean a shoulder on the wall, facing her. The move brought them within inches of each other.

Long lashes brushed the tops of his cheeks, and a slow smile spread across his lips. His jaw was covered in a light stubble, and one dark curl kissed his forehead.

"How could you forget?" Seb chuckled softly. "I was an idiot. Almost got you grounded for life."

"Mo wouldn't have grounded me. He would have had us both arrested for burglary."

Seb's laugh was a low rumble. "You're probably right." He studied her for a bit. "You weren't thinking straight or you never would have let me grab her. You were too excited to get that candy."

Toni swallowed because, no. That was not the reason. At all.

"I didn't think they sold Junior Mints outside of, uh, movie theaters." Geez, could she sound any more breathless?

Seb's gaze dropped to her lips. His parted and he blinked slowly, then quickly as if clearing his vision. He took a deep breath.

"I'll be sure to keep some on hand," he said as he pushed off the wall. "Never know when I'll need to bribe you again."

CHAPTER 19.

PEOPLE GAVE SEB A WIDE arc as he paced back and forth along the sidewalk, muttering insults under their breath as they passed. Seb couldn't care less.

But when he clipped the shoulder of a passing pedestrian, he realized he was being an asshole.

Especially when the guy yelled, "Watch it, asshole!"

Seb mumbled an apology and ducked into the alley where he pressed his forehead into the unforgiving brick wall.

The alley smelled sour, like day-old garbage juice, and Seb figured that's what lay pooled at his feet. Fitting.

He needed to take a hard look at his life choices.

Had he flirted with Toni? He wasn't sure. He'd checked on her, offered her some advice about the band, promised to keep her favorite snack available.

That was all copacetic, right? So why did he feel like he'd crossed a line?

It was Antonia. He'd known her since they were kids.

Only, the thing was…

Toni was kind of…well, she wasn't a kid anymore.

Even dressed in her Eagles tee and cutoff jean shorts, Toni was cute.

Seb mentally checked himself. Toni wasn't cute. Kittens were cute. Toni Bennette was sexy as hell. But she was also sweet and vulnerable and *comfortable* in a way Seb hadn't experienced in a long time. Not since, well, her.

When he'd seen her staring at the vending machine like she wanted to crawl inside and eat everything in sight, he couldn't help but want to talk to her. Hear her thoughts. Watch her eat.

Okay, that part was creepy, but Seb hadn't been able to help himself.

It kept hitting him over the head how much he'd missed her. And now he had a slim chance to have her in his life again. Maybe for no longer than a few weeks, but it was better than nothing. It was a hell of a lot better than the last eight years without her.

She'd always been good for him, so why should now be any different? They could be friends again, and he might even be able to help her career.

Friends.

Surely he could manage that.

He pushed off the wall and tried the door. Of course, it was locked. This was Seb. He hadn't bothered to check before he let it close behind him.

Resigned to walk around to the front, Seb stopped in his tracks when he saw the circus parked outside the glass doors.

It was SAGA, and the media could have been there for anyone, but Seb had a bad feeling. It was far too early to expose Toni to this type of scrutiny. The tabloids would dissect every morsel of her life until there was nothing left.

Seb couldn't let that happen to her.

Which was why they'd all agreed Candi would have to be ultra discreet if she did join the rehearsals at SAGA. Come in through the back entrance, at least.

So he didn't understand why her big black Escalade was pulling up to the front curb. It certainly wasn't part of the fucking plan.

Seb marched toward the SUV, pulling out his cell to text Jordan. He was cut off on the sidewalk by the swell of photographers outside the entrance. Luckily, none of them had spotted him yet, and he realized marching into the middle of that wasn't his best idea.

He ducked back around the corner and peered around it to monitor the situation.

SEB: Paps outside the studio
JORDAN IGWE: Fuck. R U kidding me?
JORDAN IGWE: Where's Candi?
SEB: Guess.

Seb's jaw clenched. He thought he'd crack a tooth as he watched Eric help Candi out of the SUV. She strolled through SAGA's front doors like she didn't have a care in the world, while the reporters hovered like buzzards waiting for scraps.

Great. Fucking great.

What the hell was she doing? Seb was tired of course-correcting. The press would be all over her appearance there, and all over the rest of the band, which meant they'd have to find another place to set up shop. Preferably outside the city where no one cared about them yet, or at least cared less about Candi.

Fuck. Why couldn't one thing run smoothly? One damn thing. He'd thought Candi was fully on board. Why would she pull a stunt like this?

Seb slipped back down the alley, prepared to bang on the door until someone heard him. Luckily, a guy had stepped out for a cigarette. Seb took a deep breath as he passed by, thanking the heavens as that sweet, sweet secondhand smoke teased his senses. He'd officially quit, but the craving hadn't really gone away.

He took the stairs two at a time, and rehearsal was back in full swing when he got up to their room. He pushed inside, stood by the door, and listened for a while, amazed by how incredibly Toni had slotted into the band.

They sounded like they'd been playing together for three years instead of just three days.

After a moment, Seb signaled to Lilly that they needed to stop. Kayla waved one stick in greeting.

"Seb!" Tiff called. "I heard you were bringing snacks." She frowned at his empty hands. "I don't see any snacks. Why do I not see snacks, Sebby?"

"Why Sebby no bring snacks?" Kayla echoed, mimicking Tiff's baby voice.

What followed was a chorus of *no snacks, no snacks* that brought a reluctant grin to his face.

"Do I look like fucking Hospitality?" he quipped.

Seb turned and caught Toni's eyes, hers dancing as she joined the refrain, and he temporarily forgot why he was in the room.

Friends.

"Did you grab any Evian?" Candi asked, sounding annoyed as she entered behind him.

Seb turned to her, biting back some choice words. "Didn't know you were coming today. Could have used a heads-up."

She removed her glasses but didn't meet his eyes. "I couldn't leave Toni to these wolves all by her lonesome."

How magnanimous.

"We have a problem," he said to the room, though he kept his eyes on Candi.

She looked up, seemingly pleased with herself, but her eyes were glassy and unfocused. *Shit.*

"What sort of problem?" Lilly asked, eyeing Candi warily.

"The press are here," he informed them. "It's a fucking zoo downstairs."

"Fuck," Tiff hissed, throwing a furtive glance Candi's way.

"Shit on a stick," Kayla said, groaning.

"They may not be here for you," Seb hoped aloud. "But I texted Jordan. He's going to send a van around back."

Candi made a sound of disgust. "Why can't we walk out the front door like normal people?"

As if she hadn't just strolled through the gauntlet of cameras.

"Because nothing about what we're doing here is supposed to be for public consumption," Lilly said before Seb could respond. "Let's pack it up."

"Damn, just when we found our groove," Tiff complained. "Nowhere in the city is going to be private enough if they know what we're up to."

"I didn't confirm anything," Candi said, adjusting the sling on her arm.

Seb folded his hands on the top of his head. "I'll find another location, don't worry about that. Right now, we need to get you guys out of here as quickly and quietly as possible."

"Should we head over to Jersey?" Kayla asked. "There's a studio not far from me. It's small, and there's no common room, but…"

There was a collective moan. "No offense, Kay, but it's Jersey," Seb said. "Also, it's too close. Nothing's stopping them from crossing the GW."

"What about SAGA's studio in Connecticut?" Lilly suggested. "It's quiet up there."

"Jordan and I will ask around," Seb said. "The trick is to find someplace discreet. Most decent places, at least in the city, are well known and make it too easy to find you. There's always a leak. A fan spots you on the street, or a pap pays off a delivery guy for info."

"The price of fame," Candi said. "Welcome to my world."

"We've been living in your world for almost a year, girl," Tiff said, her tone playful.

"Yeah, but this is a whole new level," Kayla stated bitterly. "They're like vultures lately."

"Everyone say *Thank you, Candi*," Tiff snarked, bowing to her with a flourish.

"Thank you, Candi," Candi replied, grinning. Sobering, she sighed. "Look, I didn't think... I'll leave via the front. They'll follow me if I chat with them for a while."

And just like that, Seb figured out her angle. "That's quite generous of you, Can."

She blinked at him. "Merely doing what I can to help."

Seb shook his head. He'd underestimated how calculating she could be. It was more than wanting to be seen at SAGA—she *wanted* the press to speculate about her future with the band. But why?

As if she'd read his mind, Candi smiled and patted the sling on her arm. It was a pink leopard print with her name spelled out in some sort of crystals or rhinestones. Loud, like her entrance.

"It might work," Lilly said. She turned to Candi. "If you can keep them busy, we'll slip out the back."

Seb's phone pinged.

JORDAN IGWE: Van will be there in 12 minutes. U ready?

"Van's on the way," he informed the room.

"When it gets here, Eric can take me down through the front," Candi said. "I'll keep the masses entertained while you all make your getaway."

"You sure you're okay with that?" Tiff asked, concern etched across her features.

Candi waved her off. "Honey, I'll eat those guys like buttered popcorn. Num-num-num!"

"You're a piece of work," Tiff said, laughing.

Candi laughed with her.

"Welcome to our new normal, I guess," Kayla said, sounding less than enthused.

"We have to get used to it," Lilly agreed. "Thanks for...the diversion, Can."

Candi seemed surprised.

Seb was too. Lilly had to have seen it for the power play it was meant to be.

"Oh, it's not a problem. I'll meet up with you all at Lilly's, after we lead them on a little goose chase." She and Lilly shared a look, and Lilly nodded. "I'm going to freshen up and then grab Eric. He's in the common room. Reading." Candi scrunched her nose up like that was the dumbest thing she'd ever heard.

"Wouldn't hurt you to crack open a book every once in a while," Kayla said, her tone harsh.

Candi scoffed. "I read."

"Googling yourself doesn't count," Tiff said, breaking into the familiar bass line from Bowie's "Fame."

Candi gave her the finger as she walked out the door.

Grinning, Tiff gave her a two-finger salute and flipped the switch on her amp.

"*Faen*, I'm surrounded by adolescents," Lilly said.

Seb chanced a look at Toni. Between whatever the hell that was between them in the hallway earlier and the current crisis, he'd been avoiding eye contact with her. But he looked at her now and he didn't like what he saw.

Eyes wide, lips thin, and apprehension written all over her face, Toni appeared poised to bolt. Not that Seb could blame her.

She caught his gaze and he mouthed the words *You okay?*

Her nod was nearly imperceptible but Seb thought he saw a

little of the tension ease from her shoulders. Toni closed her eyes and took a deep breath, then bent to put Minx in her case.

While the women packed their gear, Seb kept an eye on the scene below.

The chaos ratcheted up several notches once Candi stepped out the front doors. Eric had evidently called for backup, because three exceptionally large men surrounded the SUV when it pulled up.

Candi was a neon-pink dot in a sea of dark suits and black camera lenses, holding court like the princess she was. Seb was low-key impressed with her taking one for the team, even though he didn't think her motives were pure. They wouldn't be in this mess, after all, if she hadn't broken protocol.

He texted Jordan.

SEB: Now or never.
JORDAN IGWE: They're pulling around now. FYI, it's a white passenger van.
SEB: Tell me it at least has tinted windows.
JORDAN IGWE: Sorry. Best I could do on such short notice.

"Shit," Seb muttered. "You guys ready?"

He looked at Toni and she nodded, firmer this time. Lilly was already holding the door open for the others.

"Let's make a break for it," Tiff said, hoisting her bass bag up onto her shoulder.

"I'll get the rest." Seb grabbed the remaining bags, and the group headed to the back elevators.

Seb ushered the trio to the back door, which led out to the alley. He popped it open and glanced outside. A white van turned into the narrow passage, and it looked like Candi had done her job because there was no one there.

"We're good, come on." He waved the van down and the driver stopped right outside.

Seb walked quickly to open the back doors so they could all stash their gear.

"We might need to bring on some freaking roadies for these rehearsals," Tiff complained. "Lugging all of this stuff around is gonna get old."

"No one told you to bring three bass guitars," Kayla said, hoisting her two cymbal bags into the van.

Seb took Toni's case from her, grinning as she shook her head. "Second thoughts?"

"You say this is normal for them?" Her eyes followed Tiff and Kayla as they continued to bicker even while climbing into the van. She looked back at him and lowered her voice. "I honestly thought they were about to throw down earlier. Reminds me of those two guys that used to work at the auto shop with you. The Johnson boys?"

"Chris and Paulie, yeah. Heh." He chuckled. "I forgot about those guys."

"They were always sniping at each other," Toni said, helping him secure the gear so it wouldn't bounce around during the drive. "Thought they were going to kill each other at some point."

"They still at the shop?"

"As far as I know," she said before turning from him and heading toward the van's sliding door.

Seb turned to find Herbie jogging toward him, camera clicking away.

"Heya, Seb! What's going on?"

Shit.

Seb shoved at the pile of instruments, hoping they were secure enough, and slammed the door shut. He rounded the back of the van, only to find Toni standing there, one foot on the step, frozen as a cameraman he recognized from *CelebWatch* stood at the mouth of the alley, his camera trained on her.

"Fuck!" Seb closed the distance between them. "Get in."

Toni didn't seem to hear him, so Seb took her shoulders in his hands.

"Toni," he said in her ear and he felt her tense under his fingers. Something smoky and sweet hit his nose, and he inhaled before he could stop himself. Toni shivered, bringing Seb back to his senses. "Get in the van."

She didn't move.

"Seb! Who's that? Is that a new band member? Is Candi out permanently? How bad is her arm?" The reporter was closing in, and Seb cursed under his breath.

Finally, he felt Toni inhale sharply.

"Oh God," she said.

"Go on, get in," he told her, giving her a gentle push. "And duck down. I'll handle this."

Toni climbed in, throwing a terrified look over her shoulder. Seb closed the door behind her and rapped the window.

"Go!" he ordered the driver. "I'll follow later."

The engine revved, rocking the van on its wheels, but the alley was quickly filling with photographers. Another minute and they'd have to mow people down to get through.

The way they were swarming, Seb didn't have much of a problem with the thought of doing just that.

"Who is that?"

Seb spun around at the sound of Herbie's voice. He was pointing his Nikon through the windows of the van. It gave Seb an idea. It was a bad one, but it was an idea.

"Herbie," he said, adopting as friendly a tone as he could manage. "How would you like some exclusives?"

Herbie's eyes widened. He eyed the van and then looked back at Seb. "Are you going to tell me who that new girl is?"

Seb threw his arm around the shorter man's shoulder and tried to steer him away from the van. "Even better—I'll get you a press pass for an event the band's doing in a couple of weeks." The words rushed out of him, the urgency of the situation making him impatient.

Herbie narrowed his eyes with suspicion. "Exclusive?"

Seb nodded, whipping his head around when he heard shouting from the driver.

"Yeah, promise," he said, turning back to Herbie.

"What do you need from me?" the veteran reporter asked, after a slight hesitation. Seb could almost count the dollar signs hovering above the man's head.

"Can you create some sort of diversion?" Seb said, leaning in conspiratorially. "I want to get the rest of the press out of the way so the van can get clear."

Herbie seemed to think a moment, then nodded. "You're gonna have to yell at me," he said. "And pretend to punch me. Shouldn't be that much of a stretch for you."

"Hit you?" Seb asked, not following.

Herbie recoiled. "Not *actually* hit me, no. You'd break my goddamned jaw." Herbie grabbed Seb's arm and spun him around to face the other end of the alley where the crowd of paparazzi had clogged up their exit. One lone SAGA security guard was trying to keep them back and failing spectacularly. Another had caught up with the *CelebWatch* unit and was escorting them back toward the others.

"Tell the driver to back up and leave the way he came in," Herbie suggested. "Meanwhile you kick up a scene with me. I'll chase you down toward the others and it'll give them something to focus on while the ladies get away."

Seb narrowed his eyes at him. "You come up with that on the fly?"

"I may have used a similar tactic before," Herbie said with a gleam in his eye. "We have to hurry, though."

Seb nodded and strode to the front passenger door. He banged twice and the driver lowered the window.

"Back up and head out the way you came in," he said.

The driver seemed to get it and put the van in reverse.

Lilly pressed her palm to the window, worry etched on her face. Seb gave her a thumbs-up. She bit her lip, an uncharacteristically vulnerable gesture, but nodded.

Herbie moved quickly out of the way and then turned on Seb. "You *asshole*!" he yelled, winking at Seb.

Seb rolled his eyes and cleared his throat. "Yeah, well…fuck you!" he said, then took a wide swing at him. It was all he could do not to laugh at the absurdity of the situation.

Turning, he strode purposefully in the direction of the other photographers. Seb could hear Herbie's footsteps chasing behind him.

"Your driver tried to kill me! I'm going to sue the hell out of you!"

As threats went, it was a good one. Seb scowled appropriately, and the rapid fire of camera shutters greeted him when he got to the end of the alley.

Seb could almost predict the headline.

Rock star's boy toy assaults respected journalist.

He snorted to himself and turned to face Herbie, who was charging up fast. Herbie stopped and shoved his finger in Seb's face menacingly.

"You wait until I'm done with you," Herbie said theatrically. An actor he was not. "You won't have a pot to piss in, Quick."

"Herbie, what happened?" one of the other paps asked, scowling at Seb as he did but still snapping away with his camera. A scoop was a scoop.

Herbie shook his head and made a show of brushing imaginary dirt off his shirt. "You'll be hearing from my lawyers," he said before storming off.

"Hey, Seb!" someone shouted. "Why are you attacking the press?"

"Seb, are you and Candi fighting? We haven't seen you two together in a while."

"Candi still in the band, Seb? How bad is her wrist? Will she play again?"

"Who was that other chick, Seb?"

This was from the same *Celeb Watch* reporter that tossed the nastiest questions at them the night of Kurt's party.

"You plan on sleeping with her too?" he asked, squeezing through the mob, arm extended to shove a digital recorder in Seb's face.

The flashes were blinding, even in daylight, and Seb tried to shield his eyes. He'd been around Candi for a while now and thought he was used to this—the noise, the pushing, the claustrophobic nature of being at the center of the storm.

But this? This was something else. Something uglier.

"Are you hooking up with all the girls, Seb?" the guy yelled over the others. "How did Candi hurt her arm, anyway? Things get a little rough between you?"

Seb realized three things in the moment of silence that followed as the rest of the press pool held their collective breath. The van, thankfully, was gone.

So was Candi.

And he had to find a way out of this shitstorm without punching one of these motherfuckers in the face. For real this time.

As if someone had suddenly turned up the volume, the shouting started again.

"Did you guys officially split?"

"How *did* Candi get hurt?"

Even Herbie seemed taken aback by this line of questioning, but he kept shooting.

Seb's hands balled into fists.

"I got you, man," a voice said behind him as a hand curled around his bicep.

Seb didn't know the security guard's name, but he had never been so grateful to see a man in uniform.

"Thanks," Seb said, jogging backwards as the guy, joined by several other members of the SAGA staff, formed a wall between Seb and the media. "I owe you one."

"They're parked outside my fucking house," Lilly said, peeking out the window.

Seb had taken the scenic route to Brooklyn but it hadn't seemed to matter. Either someone had followed the van, or they'd already guessed its destination. Lilly's address wasn't the best kept secret in New York, something they would need to address down the road if she planned to keep the brownstone. She was too fond of the shops and restaurants in her neighborhood, and her statuesque Nordic beauty was too easily recognizable.

"This is a whole-ass mess," Tiff said, stretched out on the sofa hugging a pillow to her chest. Her braided black hair hung over the arm of the sofa like a thick naval rope.

"Thanks, Captain Obvious," Kayla grumbled as she sat cross-legged on the floor of the living room. She had apparently raided Lilly's kitchen and was halfway through a bag of chocolate-covered almonds.

"Well, it is!" Tiff stated mournfully. "What are we supposed to do now? We can't rehearse here. Even if Lilly's neighbors hadn't threatened to set the place on fire the last time you brought in a full drum kit, the longer we stay here, the more press are going to show up outside." She turned to look at Seb. "And what was that back there in the alley with poor Herbie?"

Seb waved her off. "Herbie's fine."

"Did you *actually* punch him in the face?" Kayla asked. "Not that I haven't wanted to deck a few of those assholes myself, but Herbie's not the worst of them."

"No, of course I didn't." Seb felt the beginnings of a headache coming on. "We faked the whole fight to get you out of there."

Lilly turned to him. "Why would he agree to do that?"

"I promised him an exclusive."

"What kind of exclusive?" Toni had been quiet during the exchange, and Seb turned to find her curled up in an armchair, gnawing on her bottom lip.

"I told him I'd get him into the showcase."

"You told him about the showcase?" Lilly gawked at him.

"No, I kept it vague," he replied. "I told him it was an event and promised him exclusive access."

"Not that any of it matters. We won't be ready for it," Tiff lamented. "I just wanna play. When did this stop being fun?"

"When Candi decided to fuck up our very good plan." Kayla grabbed a pair of drumsticks from her bag and began to tap rapidly against her thigh. Hard enough to make Seb's muscles tense up in sympathy.

"Obviously, it wasn't that great a plan. We haven't even had our first world tour. Don't even have a proper entourage." Tiff shifted onto her side and closed her eyes. Seb knew she'd be asleep in minutes. It was how she dealt with stress. Tiff could sleep through anything. He envied her.

Lilly got up and left the room, no doubt heading toward the kitchen. Baking was her coping mechanism.

"I need some air. I'm going out back," Kayla announced before she jumped up and left.

Well, then. Didn't he feel even *more* like shit? He'd had one job—to keep Candi in line and the media at bay. Okay, two jobs. Three if you included not letting Toni's face get splashed all over the tabloid media.

He'd checked Twitter, but there was nothing about her that he could find. Not yet, anyway. Small miracles.

Seb put his hands on his hips and dropped his chin to his chest.

Behind him, Toni sighed. "Remind me again what I signed up for?"

He turned to her, wishing he had the words to reassure her. It was, indeed, a whole-ass mess. He was quickly losing confidence in their ability to pull this off. In his abilities to take care of these people and do right by them. By her. "C'mon. Let's get you back to your hotel."

CHAPTER 20.

THEY MANAGED TO LOSE THE pair of photographers that followed them from Lilly's house and doubled back to Seb's car. Today had been...a lot.

He'd insisted on seeing Toni all the way up to her room, and she realized she wanted the company—his company—for a little while longer. Being around him again after so long should have felt awkward, and it did, at times. But she also found it easy. Familiar. Disturbingly so.

"Hey," he said as they rode up in the elevator. "You okay?"

Toni nodded, but her shoulders felt tight and she couldn't meet his eyes. "I might have a place for us to rehearse. If I call in a favor."

"Where?"

"The Phactory," she replied, hoping she wasn't overstepping some boundary.

"You might need to call in that favor." He sounded...tired.

Toni looked up at him, biting her lip.

"What's wrong?"

"Nothing, I'm fine," she answered too quickly. Seb had a way of looking at her, even now, that made her feel exposed. Toni took a deep breath and tried again. "I'm fine."

Seb tilted his head, studying her the way he used to when they were teens. Like he had a personal Antonia-meter and could suss out when she wasn't being completely honest.

"You're not fine," he said softly. "Talk to me."

Toni searched his face. He knew something was eating at her and he wanted to fix it, whatever it was. That's how Seb was built. See a problem, fix the problem. That much hadn't changed either.

She knew he wouldn't let it go.

"That." Toni hooked a thumb over her shoulder. "What happened back there, that's exactly why I didn't want to be a part of anything like this."

Seb's face fell. "I know. And it wasn't supposed to go down like that. I'm sorry."

Toni felt a grin pulling at the corner of her mouth. This time, she didn't fight it. "You're getting really good at using that word."

The elevator doors opened, and Toni walked the short distance to her room, swiping the key card to let them in. Behind her, Seb let out a soft laugh. "Practice makes perfect, I guess."

Toni smiled at him as he walked past her and into the room, his expression as soft as she'd seen it since they stumbled back into each other's lives.

"That was…" She searched for the words. "Ugly, back there."

Seb nodded, his hair falling into his eyes. "Yeah, it's never been this bad."

She sat on the edge of the bed. "It's only going to get worse as the band gets bigger. You know that, right? It's not like you guys are going to be able to walk around unnoticed, not even you. Even if they weren't a kick-ass band, there's…"

"Candi," Seb finished for her, his shoulders sagging. He crossed his arms and leaned against the wall by the door. "I'm doing everything I can to shield them—and you—from the worst of it."

"So you're the tool that makes everyone else's lives easier?"

"I have to be." It sounded like a promise.

His expression was so open, so earnest, Toni wondered what had happened to him in the years they'd been apart. This version of Sebastian Quigley was still new to her, and even harder to read.

"I've been meaning to ask," Toni began cautiously, unprepared for the way his focus shifted.

Seb squared his shoulders and pierced her with his gaze. "Anything. Ask me anything."

For a second, Toni's tongue wouldn't work. To buy time, and remove herself from Seb's particular brand of intensity, she made a show of putting her gear away. "Why Quick?"

Behind her, Seb chuckled. "What, you don't like it?"

Toni smiled to herself because she did like it. A lot. It was sexy. A total rock-star name. "I just wondered if there was a story behind it."

"Nah," he said, but Toni didn't buy it. "I mean, not really." Seb rubbed a hand over his face and plopped down into the room's only chair. He looked around, probably taking in the generic decor. He laughed softly to himself.

"What?" With nothing left to futz over, Toni took a seat on the bed and faced him as he continued to laugh. "What's so funny?"

"Nothing."

Seb flexed his fingers, studying them. He glanced up at her and back down at his hands. "The only thing I ever liked about the name Quigley was that it started with a Q."

Toni smiled.

He returned it. "Okay, did I ever tell you about the time I tried out for the track team?"

"At Bordon High?" she asked, frowning. "You?"

"Yeah."

"But...you never... I mean, how did I miss that?"

"I was twelve."

Toni's frown deepened. "You...tried out for the high school track team...when you were twelve."

Seb nodded, a smirk on his lips. He had amazing lips.

Toni forced her gaze back up to his eyes, but they were sparkling and gorgeous and...

"I'd read, or maybe heard somewhere, that schools—colleges—gave out sports scholarships," Seb continued. "I didn't play any sports, but I was pretty good at running. From Sheriff Williams, at least."

Toni started to laugh and covered her mouth.

"No, don't worry." Seb made a go-on gesture. "Laugh it up, it's freaking hilarious." He joined her.

Soon they were both doubled over. Seb's laugh was beautifully full-throated and reminded Toni of all the moments they'd shared all those years ago. God, how she'd missed this.

"B-but how did they let you try out?" Stretching out across the foot of the bed, Toni rubbed at the cramp in her stomach and tried to calm down. She rolled to her side and propped her head on her hand.

After a bit, Seb caught his breath. His mirth faded as he looked at her, and something moved behind his eyes before he blinked it away.

"You know I was kinda tall for my age."

Toni remembered the day they met. She'd thought he could have been a high-school boy and had been surprised to find he was close to her in age.

"I dunno," he continued, looking over her head as if he could somehow see the memories in the abstract print on the wall behind her. "I wanted to get out of that town *so* bad. I thought...I thought if I got good at track, I could get a scholarship somewhere."

"You knew you had to actually *be* in high school to graduate from it, didn't you?"

Seb dropped his gaze back to hers. "I was twelve. I didn't know much about anything," he said, his smirk bringing out that damned dimple. He leaned forward and rested his elbows on his knees. "But yeah, I knew that. I wanted to impress the coach so when I *did* get to high school, I'd have a place. A path."

"That's actually kinda smart," Toni agreed.

Seb tapped his temple. "I have my moments. Anyway, it almost worked. The coach was impressed. Called me Sebastian Quick. Said he'd keep an eye out for me in a couple of years when I started there."

"Wow. Impressive. What happened?"

Seb made a long-suffering sound. "By the time I started my freshman year, he was gone. Retired and moved to Florida."

"Oh, damn."

"Yeah," Seb agreed, groaning. "I even went to the new coach and asked if some word had been left about me, about Sebastian Quick."

"I'm guessing not?" Toni's heart went out to young Seb.

Seb sat back and folded his hands across his stomach. "Hey, at least I got a cool new name."

Toni wanted to reach out and squeeze his knee, something. He was close. All she needed to do was stretch out her arm. He looked like he needed it, and Toni wondered if there was anyone in his life he could go to for comfort. Reassurance. From what she'd seen of him and Candi, that wasn't a source of solace. His relationship with the others, while close, didn't appear to be intimate.

"You can't do it all alone, you know," she told him. Seb frowned, confused. "You need help with all of this, with the band stuff. Shouldn't there be, I don't know, a posse or something? Handlers, drivers, all that?"

"Yeah, I..." Seb seemed to bristle at the idea of bringing more people into their circle. "I don't trust the label to bring in the right people, and we don't have the capital to hire our own. Not yet."

Toni got it. It was a trust issue, and he'd always had those. She supposed some things never changed. But she also knew she was right. He knew it too. She could tell by the way he didn't argue with her.

"At the very least, the band needs its own security."

Seb nodded, wheels turning. "I can ask Masturini for security references."

"Masturini?"

"Head of Candi's detail," Seb provided.

Oh. It sounded like a completely different world. "Good idea."

Their eyes locked and something shifted between them. Toni could practically see the wall between them crumbling down.

Much of the anger she'd been holding onto for the last eight years had mellowed into a distant disappointment. Maybe they could make it through this project without issue. Maybe they could even try to be friends again.

Toni was surprised to find she wanted that. She'd missed him, this.

"Thank you," he said, his voice almost a whisper as he held her in his gaze.

"For what?"

Seb's smile was soft. "I forgot how good you are at that."

"At what?"

"Being rational. Thinking outside yourself, your needs."

"I have my moments too," she said. Seb's smile widened, and something else loosened in Toni's chest. Like a spring coiled too tight for too long had finally sprung.

They held each other's gaze for a long moment, and Toni felt words bubbling up into her throat. Questions she'd been wanting to ask him for eight years, the ones she hadn't wanted to broach in the car the other night.

Why didn't you tell me you were leaving?

What drove you away?

What kept you away?

She opened her mouth. "Should I make the call?"

Seb frowned with confusion.

"Phactory Sound, in Philly," she reminded him.

"Oh." He blinked as if to clear his head. "Yeah. And I'll try Jordan, see if he's come up with any ideas."

Seb stood and walked over to the window.

Toni found it hard *not* to notice the way his ass looked in those jeans. He always did wear them well. Standing in front of the window, he offered her a view of his broad back and the lean muscles that moved under his long-sleeved tee.

She forcibly pulled her gaze away. The truth was she didn't know what to think about Seb. She sure as hell had no idea how to feel about him. Was he a friend? Was he a stranger? Something in between?

This wasn't anything like how she'd thought their reunion would go. She'd imagined more yelling—mostly from her—and lots of tears—preferably his. Not this subtle ease back into familiarity.

Maybe it was because she was away from home. Away from the people who knew her and would tell her she was being too easy on him, giving him a pass. Because she was, wasn't she? It couldn't, *shouldn't* be this comfortable to be around him again.

She shouldn't feel needed by him, and she shouldn't want that either.

Toni unlocked her phone. Richie picked up on the third ring.

"Hey, I was just talking about you."

"Good things, I hope."

"Of course," he said. "Ian asked if you were still interested in working with him. He's got another project booked here. A big one."

"Really?" She thought she'd completely missed that opportunity. "For when?"

"End of December," Richie replied. "I told him you were tied up at the moment."

"That's actually what I called about."

"Coming home early?" He sounded hopeful.

"Yes and no."

She filled him in on everything that had happened, leaving out the part about her and Seb and their past together. Richie had questions about the setup they'd need, the length of time, and other logistics she hadn't a clue about. But when she turned to ask Seb, she found him asleep in the chair.

"I'll make sure you get all the info," she told Richie quietly.

"Awesome. Thanks, partner!"

Toni disconnected, liking the sound of that.

She approached Seb.

He looked so uncomfortable, having so completely failed to fold his six-foot-plus frame into the tiny desk chair that she had to stifle a laugh. Poor guy. She'd known he was tired.

Toni whispered his name. When he didn't respond, she lifted her hand, hesitating a second before cupping his arm. The warmth of his body and the power she could feel in the muscle beneath her fingertips made her heart beat a little faster.

Leaning closer, she took in his face, the long lashes fanning his cheeks. Her gaze danced over the waves of his hair, the pout of his lips. It had been years since she'd been this close to him, and her heart all but unfurled in her chest.

Fuck.

He shifted in the chair and Toni jumped back.

"Idiot," she whispered, chastising herself. A little louder, she called him again. "Seb?"

His brow crinkled. "Hunnnh. Five mnnn."

She guessed he meant five more minutes. Toni was happy to let him sleep as long as he liked, but not in that torture device. "Seb." She nudged his thigh with her knee.

When his eyes opened, he looked up at her. Before he had a chance to throw his guards up, Toni saw what he'd been trying to hide all this time. Need. Hope. Something else she was afraid to contemplate. Then he ran a rough hand over his face. When he looked at her again, his shields were back.

"Sorry, didn't mean to pass out on you." He sat up, groaning. "This chair is awful. Any luck with the Phactory?"

"Yeah, we're good to go." Before she could think better of it, Toni grabbed his arm. "Get up."

Seb looked at her, amused. "I'm going, I'm going."

"No, you're not." At his bewildered expression, Toni pulled until he got the hint and stood. She ushered him toward the bed. "Take a nap. I don't want you falling asleep behind the wheel."

Seb shook his head. "I'm fine to drive."

"This isn't a discussion." She snatched his keys from the desk and pocketed them.

"Like that'll stop me from getting them." Seb's grin was positively feral, but then his mouth fell open and his eyes went comically wide. "I-I... I didn't mean..."

Toni laughed softly and swept his leg out from under him.

Seb went crashing onto his back and bounced on the mattress, air rushing out in a half laugh, half cough.

"Where'd you learn that move, Bennette?" He looked awestruck. Or turned on.

"Took a self-defense class when I moved to the city," Toni replied, untying his Doc Martens.

"You don't have to do this," he mumbled, already half-asleep again. "I should go."

Toni paused in the middle of loosening the second shoe. "I know I don't have to, but I'd never forgive myself if...if something happened. You're tired. Sleep. I'll wake you in an hour."

Propping himself up on his elbows, Seb tilted his head to regard her. "One hour. Then I'll get out of your hair."

Toni smiled. The old Seb never would have given in so easily. Point, Antonia.

He flopped back and closed his eyes as Toni dropped his foot. She sat in the chair and pulled out her phone, grinning at the light snore already coming from the bed. Her bed. The one Seb was currently on.

When the hour was up, Toni stood and walked over to him. Holy Christ, the man was too pretty for words. He was also down for the count.

She yawned. It was getting late, but he obviously needed rest more than she'd thought. She eyed the space next to him and made a decision.

Setting an alarm on her phone to wake her in an hour, Toni slipped off her Chucks. She twisted her hair into one long braid so she wouldn't look like an electrified squirrel when she woke up, and then eased down onto the mattress. The king-size bed left plenty of space between them. Plenty. A more than appropriate amount of space, she decided, between her and the long, lean, *hot* Sebastian Quick.

Toni was an adult. Adults could sleep in...*on*...the same bed without it meaning anything, without it conjuring up all sorts of memories of teenage fantasies and all the scenarios she'd imagined of what it would be like to be with him like this. Well, not like *this*. There had been far less space between them and many fewer articles of clothing.

She stared at the ceiling, suddenly not so tired anymore. Which was ridiculous. This was nothing. It meant nothing.

It didn't stop Toni from rolling to her side to face him. She studied his profile, her fingers itching to trace the slope of his nose and around the parted lips of his sinful mouth. Even in sleep, there was a crease of worry on his forehead, and Toni fought hard against her desire to smooth it. To soothe him.

It wasn't her place. Was it anyone's? Seb was a caretaker; he always had been. Who took care of him? The question plagued her more than it should.

Still, it wasn't long before the soft cotton of the bedding proved too much to resist and she drifted off to sleep.

Startled awake minutes later by the alarm, Toni's heart sank when she saw the empty space next to her, but the note on the pillow gave it wings.

Nia,

> *You always did look out for me.*
> *You're an angel.*

> *Seb x*

CHAPTER 21.

SEB WAS SURPRISED WHEN THE buzzer rang. He rarely had visitors at his fourth-floor Hell's Kitchen walk-up. Even Candi stayed away. He could count on two fingers the number of times she'd been at his place.

Somewhere in the recesses of his stupid, delusional heart, he hoped it was Toni. Not that she even knew where he lived.

After he woke up next to her in the wee hours of the morning and watched her sleep for longer than he'd admit to himself, Seb's head had been full of all sorts of impossibilities and realizations.

One, no one knew him like she did. It didn't matter that years had passed, Antonia could read Seb like the menu in a diner. Two, she still cared about him. That was a goddamned miracle all by itself, but the way she'd looked after him... It fucking *floored* him.

The last thing he'd realized was that the pull he'd had toward her when they were teens hadn't been imaginary, and it was even stronger now. She was a beautiful, vibrant, supremely talented, fiercely independent woman. A woman he was very much attracted to. And it scared the living daylights out of him.

Even scarier, he thought she might be feeling a little of it too.

So.

Yeah.

There was that.

The buzzer sounded again and Seb's pulse jumped. He pushed the button on the intercom. "Yeah?"

"It's Kayla. Let me up."

Huh. That was the last person he'd expected. Seb buzzed her inside the building. He opened the door, leaving it ajar so she could enter while he went back to packing.

It had taken no convincing at all once he told Jordan about the Phactory. A quick conference call with the rest of the band, and approval from the label, cemented their plans. Jordan had reached out to a travel agent he knew to secure hotel rooms for them while they were in Philly. They would all drive down before lunch tomorrow—everyone except Candi.

Everyone agreed it would be better for her to stay in New York, at least for now. Surprisingly, she didn't seem too bothered by it.

Seb grabbed a few pairs of jeans. He wouldn't need much in Philly, and anything he left behind he could sneak back up 95 to grab. He was debating the merits of taking his guitar when Kayla called out from the front room.

"Yo!"

"Back here," he replied, pulling a pile of underwear and socks out of their drawer.

"Geez," Kayla said, leaning in the doorway. She wore a vintage Stetson that Seb had last seen hanging in Lilly's closet. "Are you taking two pair for each day?"

"I hate doing laundry on the road. Takes up too much time."

"Can't argue with the logic," Kayla agreed as she wandered through his bedroom, inspecting things and being generally nosy. Normal for her.

Seb had learned not to get too bent out of shape about it. After a prolonged silence, he looked up from packing his duffel. Kayla had folded her arms and stood watching him.

"Uh, you're being a little creepy."

"Am not," she huffed.

"I assume you didn't come here to watch me pack," Seb said, straightening up. "Got all your stuff together?"

Kayla nodded. "All set."

"Cool. Then, uh…"

"Who is she to you?"

Seb stilled and met Kayla's eyes. Her hazel gaze was shrewd, her lips pulled into a knowing smirk.

He resumed folding the T-shirts on his bed. "I assume you're not talking about Candi."

Kayla laughed. "I know all about *that* train wreck. Which is over, right?"

"Yeah. It's been over."

"Not sure why you thought that was a good idea in the first place," Kayla said, stepping over to him. She picked up a shirt and folded it. "Can's got more than baggage—she's got a whole set of Louis Vuitton luggage, custom made, to carry around all her issues."

"Yeah, well… I'm not traveling too light myself," Seb said. "And Can and I, we weren't… Look, I know what it looked like, but it was never real. Most of it was for the cameras."

"You invested a lot of your time, not to mention your *nights*, into something that wasn't real," Kayla countered. "But that doesn't answer my question. Who is Antonia Bennette to you?"

Seb fisted the shirt in his hand and dropped it to his side. He wasn't surprised, not really. Mikayla Whitman was their resident genius, with an IQ that hovered somewhere around Neil deGrasse Tyson-levels. Seb guessed it was a by-product of having two world-renowned academics as parents, a fact she'd insisted they keep out of the band's bio. That didn't stop Tiff from ribbing her for it.

Kayla had a way of seeing through people—through him—that

he could never explain. It reminded him of Antonia more than he would've admitted before now. Seb turned to face her. There was no use lying.

"Remember that tiny town I grew up in? The one in PA?"

Seb could see the light bulb flicker on over Kayla's head.

"No fucking way!" Kayla's eyes widened over a shit-eating grin. "I *knew* you knew her from before the auditions but, damn. I thought maybe she was a former hookup. Instead, she's the one that got away!"

"No." Yes. "It...it wasn't ever like that with us."

"Uh, those heart eyes you stare at her with say otherwise," Kayla said, calling him out in the worst way possible.

Heart eyes? Seb made a mental note to cut that shit out. "She was like a little sister to me. We were friends. Best friends. I mean, she was probably my only friend growing up."

"Aww, poor thing." Kayla sat on the edge of the bed, clearly settling in for the long version of his sob story.

Seb didn't bleed for just anyone, but Kayla was family. And it felt good to be able to confide in someone he could trust implicitly. He knew she wouldn't betray his confidence, not even to Lilly and the others.

He sat on the edge of the bed. "Our town wasn't an easy place to grow up in, and our parents didn't make it any easier. We... Antonia and I were each other's support systems. For years, all throughout our teens until I..." *Abandoned her.* "Moved away. She was...kinda all I had."

"I get it," Kayla said, sympathy and understanding in her voice. "I'm glad you at least had each other. And now?"

"Shit." Seb leaned his elbows on his thighs. "I hadn't seen or heard anything from her in almost eight years. Not until a week or so before she showed up to audition, and I didn't even know she'd be there. Hadn't heard anything about her since I left Bordon."

"Really?"

"I mean," Seb hedged, "I'd asked around about her a few years back, but other than that, no. Then Jerry Gant's people call me about him throwing a shit fit at a session down in Philly. I show up with my guitar, and there she is."

"Wow."

Seb ran a hand through his hair. "Yeah. Wild, right?"

"Wild as hell. You'd seen her play, and you didn't think to bring her up to audition? That's fucking short-sighted." Kayla frowned at him. "Or did you?"

Seb shook his head. "Nah. It crossed my mind, but nah. I keep meaning to ask Jordan how he found her."

"Huh," Kayla said, grabbing another T-shirt to fold. She was so tiny, the thing would have been a dress on her. "Well, that sure explains the deer-in-headlights look the two of you exchanged," Kayla concluded. "And then she looked pissed. Seems better between you now, though." She grinned up at him. "You two kiss and make up?"

"No kissing. No-frat clause," Seb reminded her, not that he had any intention of going there. "And she has every right to be pissed. I was young and dumb."

"So, not much different from now," Kayla said, winking. "Except for the young part."

Seb laughed. "Fuck you."

Kayla's laughter quieted. "You didn't have to lie about knowing her," she said, serious now. "Unless you plan to—"

"No, no plans to, uh… Yeah, no," Seb interjected before she could finish that thought.

Of course, if anything *were* to happen between them, it would have to wait until after Toni's contract was up.

"The lie wasn't intentional, believe me. For either of us. And I–I didn't know how to come clean without looking like a complete douchebag. As for Toni, she just wants to play, to get some experience."

"And get paid."

"And that," Seb agreed. He took the last of the shirts from Kayla and put it in the bag. "There's nothing going on between us. I mean, I hope we can be friends again but that's up to her."

Kayla perched on the corner of his bed. "Have you said you're sorry for whatever dickish thing you did?"

"Hey! How do you know it was dickish?"

Kayla grinned. "It's you."

Seb snatched up a pair of his boxer briefs and threw it at her head.

Catching the underwear easily in one hand, she laughed but Seb felt the guilt creeping back in. If she only knew.

Antonia Bennette had every right to feel however she needed to feel toward him, and he had no right whatsoever to even be in her orbit, but here they were. For a time. He planned to make the most of it.

"You…" He dropped his gaze. "You gonna tell the others?"

"Nah," Kayla said, tossing the underwear into his duffel. Seb met her gaze, grateful until she said, "I'll leave that distinct pleasure to you and *Antonia*."

Kayla sang her name as if Toni were a Broadway song, and Seb chuckled.

He zipped up his bag, shaking his head. "You ain't right."

Kayla grinned. "I like to think I'm just the right kind of wrong."

Seb couldn't argue with that, and he wouldn't change a thing.

CHAPTER 22.

REHEARSALS HAD GONE SURPRISINGLY WELL since they'd moved operations down I-95. The Phactory had turned out to be the perfect choice, and Toni couldn't have been happier. Even though she hadn't yet completed her buy into the partnership, Richie treated her like an equal and she found she was developing a sense of ownership. It was addictive, and she was proud of the space she would soon call her own. If only in part.

"I think this might be my favorite studio ever," Kayla sighed as she perused the day's lunch selections.

"They don't cater," Seb said, shaking his head at her. "I had to order in and haul all this stuff back here from reception."

Kayla bit into a cheesesteak egg roll from a restaurant in nearby Chinatown. They were a favorite of Toni's too.

"My God, this is good." Kayla made moon eyes at Seb. "I think you might be my favorite person ever."

"I'm pretty sure he's the only one who could put up with your weird ass," Tiff said, stealing a piece of the egg roll from Kayla's plate, which was piled high with local goodies that Toni had recommended. She figured one way to get to know a city was via your stomach, and that was especially true of Philly.

"Not worried I'm going to rage out and throw your bass to the floor?" Seb said, laughing. "Threaten to break your fingers?"

"Can't we sue for defamation or something?" Tiff asked,

shaking her head. "I can't believe that rag *CelebWatch* posted all that bullshit about you."

"Herbie didn't even corroborate any of it," Kayla added. "He told them it was a misunderstanding."

"That only made it sound like I paid him off," Seb said.

"With what money?" Toni asked. Seb shot her a look and she stuck out her tongue.

He laughed.

Toni loved watching him with the others. There was such an easy rapport between the group, minus Candi. And it was obvious they all cared deeply for each other, even if they did tease one another relentlessly.

Seb had found himself a family.

"What I still don't understand is what the heck a *Krimpet* is," Tiff said, inspecting one of the snack cakes between her fingers with obvious skepticism.

"Suppose it sounds more appetizing than *sponge cake*," Seb answered, swiping one from her package. "I loved Tastykakes as a kid, especially the pies."

"I remember," Toni blurted out before she caught herself.

Seb stiffened but was smart enough not to look at her.

Toni wasn't sure she could cover with him looking at her.

She glanced at Kayla, who barely concealed a worrying smirk. Toni coughed to clear her throat. "I, uh, I remember loving the peanut butter ones."

"Peanut butter cake?" Kayla's mouth went slack.

"Sort of," Toni clarified. "They're these little, round, flat pieces of cake with a layer of peanut butter on top. Then the whole thing is dipped in chocolate."

"Oh, my heart," Kayla said, flattening her palm on her chest. "High-end sushi, stupidly good sandwiches, *and* supersugary local junk food?"

"Don't forget the breweries," Seb chimed in.

"This town is, like, what Kayla would build if she could build a town," Tiff finished. "Jordan's missing out."

"I hear no lies," Kayla agreed, reaching for another egg roll.

Jordan, who had been keeping tabs on the New York press, had relayed how the NYC tabloids were baffled as to where in the city the band was holed up.

Seb had driven up yesterday to see Candi, he said to keep up appearances. Be seen around her place as usual.

Toni resolved not to have an opinion on that.

After the SAGA fiasco, it had been decided that Candi would stay in New York and be photographed in strategic places to throw the press off their scent. She was also supposed to be recuperating from the injury Toni had learned was completely fake.

Toni chose not to have an opinion on that either. Not her business.

Some members of the press were speculating the band was in Jersey, while others had initially been convinced they were in Lilly's brownstone. A number of photographers had parked outside for two days straight while she used an app on her phone to turn the lights on and off at random. That had been a great source of entertainment at dinner the first night.

Lilly scrunched her nose up at today's lunch selection. "Isn't there anything here that won't clog my arteries and kill me before we even make it to the showcase?"

"Kale salads and falafel wraps should be here soon, Lil," Seb told her.

Lilly nodded at him, a fond look in her eyes. Toni didn't quite understand the dynamic between them, but there was something there. A familiarity that would have given her pause if she didn't know about Seb and Candi. Surely he hadn't slept with both women. Right?

Not my business.

"Could you wonderful, talented angels possibly play and eat?" Seb asked the room. "We're on the clock, remember. And I'm sure Richie here has better things to do than watch you all stuff your faces, yeah?"

"Nope." Richie leaned back in his console chair, one ankle propped on the opposite knee and his fingers laced behind his head. Despite the unusually cool temperatures outside, he was dressed in his usual uniform of a T-shirt and cargo shorts. "I'm good."

"Let's run through 'Hurt U,'" Tiff suggested, nodding to Toni as the band returned to the live room. "See if our little Toni can match Candi's tone."

Toni had spent more time listening to the Lillys than she had any other band in a long time. Not all of it was about work; she genuinely enjoyed the arrangements. Lilly had a way of delivering lyrics, finding ways to make them more poignant, more challenging. Sometimes even finding humor where Toni had missed it. Hers was a unique style reminiscent of earlier decades without her sounding like an imitation, much like what Toni tried to do when she dabbled.

Seb had said they were working on original material for the band's debut album, and "Hurt U" was the first one Toni had heard. It was more indie pop than she'd expected from them, but catchy. Very radio-friendly.

"It's less about copying her note for note and more about getting the feel. The sound," Seb said, following them inside.

"Let her figure it out for herself, Sebastian," Lilly warned him. "She'll either get it or she won't. You playing stage mom isn't going to help."

Toni frowned at Lilly, who turned away to adjust the volume in her headphones. Had she said something to piss Lilly off?

"Rude much?" Kayla mouthed silently to Toni as she settled behind her kit.

Toni smiled, appreciating the support.

"Not sure what's up with her today, but don't take it personally," Seb leaned in to whisper near Toni's ear as he passed on his way to rejoin Richie in the other room.

She had to close her eyes for a moment to control her reaction to him. She hadn't expected him to suddenly be so close. She couldn't let her reemerging crush become a problem. Because let's face it, it was inevitable.

Seb was kind and generous, selfless to a fault. The angry, brooding young boy had grown into a thoughtful though maybe still haunted man. Toni liked him.

After wiping her mouth and hands, Tiff strapped on her bass and counted off the intro.

Toni closed her eyes and let muscle memory pull her out of the Seb-shaped thoughts swirling in her head—thoughts that had no business occupying time that wasn't her own. She was on the Lillys' dime.

Lilly began to sing, and Toni opened her eyes, transfixed. Lilly's voice was pained. Haunted.

If you never mend your broken heart,
You will always live your life in parts.
Open your eyes.
The truth is, it was all a lie.

Toni felt the lyrics in her bones. The song was about regrets and sacrifice. About hurting someone without realizing it, and not knowing what to do to make it right.

Without thinking, her gaze slid to the glass, to where Seb sat bent over his laptop in the control room. Had he written this?

Though you never meant to hurt,
The one you love hurt you.

It was… Yeah.

After the first run-through, Lilly held up a hand. "Something's missing, some…I don't know…"

"Do you still like what I'm doing on the bass?" Tiff asked.

Lilly nodded. "I do…"

"But?" Tiff asked. Lilly tapped her chin with one finger.

"What if I doubled up on the hi-hat in the choruses?" Kayla asked, demonstrating.

"Nah," Tiff shook her head. "Too disco-y."

Toni opened her mouth. Closed it. When she realized Lilly was staring at her, she flushed hot.

"What?" Lilly asked. "You have an idea?"

The denial was on the tip of Toni's tongue, because this wasn't her band. Not her song. She was a hired gun, albeit a very well-paid one. The situation reminded her of the last time she had a session at Phactory Sound, and she wasn't about to make the same mistake twice.

Except that Lilly had an expectant look on her face. And now the other two women were looking at her. And Seb was standing behind the glass—watching her—and…

Screw it.

"I was wondering… I mean, I thought maybe…" she began before chickening out. "You know what? Never mind."

"What?" Lilly asked again, more insistently this time. God, she was a formidable woman for someone so slight.

"The…intro," Toni started. She straightened her shoulders. "I think it would go really well if we…if *you*…staggered it." She glanced around at the members of the band. Was she even explaining this well? Was it a silly idea?

Kayla nodded. "Show us."

"Well, first the bass," Toni said, mimicking Tiff's bassline for a measure and a half. "And then I'd, er, the *guitar* would come in here, playing harmony on the fifth." She played as she explained and Tiff took over on her instrument, nodding.

"I like it," she said.

"Do you want me to stay on the cyms for that intro?" Kayla asked, playing a light staccato rhythm on the bell of one cymbal.

"I... Yeah, that's pretty cool," Toni agreed. "Don't you think? That way, your guitar can layer through the chords and build to the beginning of the first verse."

"Dramatic," Lilly said.

Toni turned back to her, unable to decipher her expression. Was she annoyed? Impressed? Bored? Hungry?

"Do it that way," Lilly said, or rather ordered, and the other two women nodded. Lilly closed her eyes, and they started the song again.

This time, Tiff started. She added a bit of syncopation to her line that Toni latched onto immediately, and they exchanged a smile.

Toni floated her guitar over the groove, locking into the feel that Tiff and Kayla set down and adding layer upon layer until Lilly started the verse.

They sailed through the song and Toni caught Tiff's eye. The bassist gave her one of the best stank faces she'd ever seen, and Toni laughed. Tiff broke into a grin.

Kayla was grinning from ear to ear, her hands flying with a precision that astounded Toni every time.

By the time the chorus came around again, Toni was singing along. She locked eyes with Lilly, who gave her a slight nod as she sang. It was as good as a blessing.

This was happening.

Toni had this. Had *it*.

Fuck the Jerry Gants of the world.

CHAPTER 23.

THEY WERE DEEP IN IT again today.

Kayla was a beast on drums.

Richie had half-jokingly asked her to go easy on his brand-new kit a few times before he gave up. She promised him she'd buy the studio another one when she left.

"A real one," she'd insisted.

She had quick hands and two lead feet. Her kick drumming could be fast and precise, or deliberate and moody. Whatever the song called for.

They ran through their cover of "I Burn" from the Toadies, and Toni got chills watching Kayla play. The woman was a machine.

Tiff was, hands down, the best bassist Toni had ever heard. There were shades of old funk in her choices, and she'd clearly been influenced by post-alternative musicians like Interpol's Carlos D. Tiff played her instrument as if it were a wild animal and used every muscle in her body to wrestle it into submission.

The fact that she played a six-string was impressive enough, but when she broke out a resin bow for the solo in the middle of one song, Toni almost forgot to play her own instrument. So much for yesterday's breakthrough.

Then there was Lilly.

Lilly who rarely spoke to her but could bring her close to

tears with the power of her voice. The first few rehearsals Toni had with the band, Lilly barely sang. She'd mouthed through the songs, probably listening for any little mistake Toni would make, she thought.

Okay, that probably wasn't fair, but Toni felt like she'd stuck her fingers in a friggin' meat grinder whenever she took one of the solos Candi had perfected and tried to make it her own.

Lilly never said anything, not out loud, but her face had spoken volumes. *Not good enough.*

Again, fair. Toni had fallen into the habit of mimicking Candi's style, something Tiff had called her out on more than once.

"She's not here. You are," she'd said. "Fucking act like it. Damn."

Playing Candi's parts had been the safe bet. Not today, though.

Today, those solos belonged to Toni. She'd murdered each one and gave as good as she got from Tiff and Kayla.

And maybe—maybe—because of that, Lilly let loose.

When Lilly announced that she wanted to add an old Alice in Chains song to the set list for the showcase, Toni did an internal fist pump. That was right up Toni's alley, and she relished the thought of rocking out on one of their songs with this band.

All throughout, Toni could feel Seb's eyes on her. Sometimes, she'd look up and find him staring at her hands, a proud expression on his face as she played. Other times, she caught him staring at *her.* She didn't know what to make of that, especially when he quickly looked away. Most especially when he didn't, and their eyes met.

It was a dangerous game they were playing.

When Seb left to arrange for lunch, Lilly called for a fifteen-minute break. Toni ran to the bathroom, then headed toward the lounge to grab a Coke from the vending machine.

She needed a hit of caffeine and sugar to get her through to the next meal. While Tiff and Kayla seemed like they could play through the night and it wouldn't bother them, practicing nonstop for hours had sapped all of Toni's energy.

If the stakes weren't so high, she'd compare it to the all-day practices Seb used to insist upon when they were teens.

Memories of Seb's arms around her, his hands on her hands as he showed her which chords to play. His palms hot and a little rough against her skin as she held her breath and pretended not to understand, making him demonstrate over and over.

"Toni." The sound of her name in Lilly's accented voice was so foreign to her ears that it didn't immediately register. "Toni?"

She turned to find Lilly standing behind her. "Sorry, my brain is a little fried." She offered a smile, expecting Lilly's usual indifference in response.

Instead, Lilly grinned. It was an odd sight to see but did nothing to alter Toni's perception of her as slightly removed from the world around her.

"Understandable." Lilly walked over to the machine and scanned the choices. "I'd kill for a Dr Pepper."

Toni blinked, surprised. "You like Dr Pepper?"

"Yeah, I developed a weakness for it when I moved to the States."

Toni pointed at the colorful button displaying a bottle of Dr Pepper resting in a pile of ice. "Looks like you're in luck."

Lilly shook her head. "No, I can't get one."

"Why not?"

Lilly sighed and rested her fair head against the machine. Even slouched over, she was still half a head taller than Toni—long and lithe and lean.

Toni stifled a laugh because Lilly appeared as forlorn as a woman mourning the absence of her mate.

"I can't get one *today*."

"Oh. Because of your throat?"

Lilly frowned down at her. "My throat?"

Toni gestured to her own throat. "I thought maybe it wasn't good for singing or something."

Lilly's brow relaxed. "No, not that. I know if I have one today, I'll want one tomorrow. And every day after, while we're here, anyway. There's a reason I don't keep any in my house."

"Wow, okay. You don't just *like* DP, you're actually addicted."

Lilly's gaze snapped to Toni's, her expression inscrutable but not unfriendly.

Panic clogged Toni's throat. Had she said something to offend her? Was it already time for another episode of *Toni and Her Big Fat Mouth?*

After a beat, Lilly barked out a laugh, startling Toni enough for her to take a step back.

The blond laughed until tears sprang from her eyes. She wheezed, bracing one hand on the vending machine as she bent over.

Toni's smile grew gradually. She had no idea what she'd said, but if it got Lilly to laugh it was worth the embarrassment.

"*Faen*, I can't believe you said that." Lilly looked at her, still amused and fighting to recover from her laughing fit.

Toni didn't know whether she should be offended or not. "Uh, what did I say?"

At that, Lilly fell into another bout of laughter.

Toni's face heated. She replayed her last words in her mind and, *ohhh*. She rolled her eyes.

"Get your mind out of the gutter. I meant Dr Pepper, you perv." Toni opened the cap on her bottle and took a sip. "I know the others love bathroom humor, but I thought you were better than that."

Lilly smiled warmly at her. "Oh, *kjæreste*, you don't know me at all."

Toni smiled back. It was all she could do because no, she didn't know Lilly. She hadn't really been given the opportunity to know her.

To save some money, Toni had decided to stay at home, so she wasn't at the hotel with the rest of the band. Or Seb, who was the best reason for turning down a room. They rehearsed, they ate most meals in the studio's common room, they all went their separate ways to sleep, and then started it all over the next day. In her haste to put some much-needed distance between herself and Seb, Toni hadn't given herself a chance to know Lilly at all, or any of them. Not really.

"I suppose that's my fault," Lilly said, as if she'd been eavesdropping on Toni's thoughts. "I'm not as touchy-feely as Kayla and Tiff."

"Don't let Kayla hear you call her touchy-feely," Toni warned her, hoping it was okay to tease.

"Uh, no." Lilly slashed one elegant hand through the air. "I'd wake up in the morning with one of her sticks in some uncomfortable place."

Toni grinned.

Lilly studied her for a moment. "You sound good with us."

Toni let the unexpected praise wash over her before she cleared her throat. "Thanks. I'm sorry it took me a while to lock in, but I think I've got it now."

"You do," Lilly agreed, turning back to stare at the bright Dr Pepper button. "Better every day, but you need to believe in yourself more. Don't wait for other people to tell you you're doing good. Or me." She looked at Toni. "You knew when you weren't cutting it, right?"

Toni nodded, dumbfounded. Lilly had said more words in the last ten seconds than she had in the last ten days, at least around Toni.

Lilly glanced over Toni's shoulder and down the hall. Her gaze was unfocused, her thoughts somewhere else for a moment before she seemed to return to their conversation.

"I know I can be...cold. Don't take it personally. I don't get close to people very easily."

Toni understood that. "Neither do I."

"I see that," Lilly said. "But once you do, it's hard for you to exorcise them, isn't it?"

"Yeah. I guess," Toni conceded. "To be honest, there haven't been that many people like that in my life. My best friend, Yvette..."

Lilly held her gaze, her expression neutral. "Sebastian."

This time, Toni's fear was warranted. She and Seb still had a silent agreement not to disclose their shared past. Fuck, this wasn't good.

Toni opened her mouth to say something, anything, but her mind went blank. She didn't want to lie. "We grew up together."

Lilly nodded.

"But we were only ever friends," Toni rushed to add, hoping to ease any concerns. "I... We...haven't violated the terms of my contract." Lilly's eyebrows lifted but Toni barreled on. "Don't be too hard on Seb for keeping it from you. I think he brought me in to, I dunno, make up for...how he left things with me from before. I hope I've proven myself enough to justify the cloak-and-dagger."

Lilly frowned. "Brought you into what?"

"To the audition."

Lilly laughed, the sound bright and clear as a bell. "That wasn't Seb. I was the one who had them call you."

Toni understood the individual words, but strung together, they made no sense. "I thought... How?"

Lilly propped one shoulder against the vending machine. She crossed her ankles and leaned her head on the bright, shiny surface. Even in a faded tank top, lumberjack flannel, and low-slung skinny jeans, Lilly could have passed for a supermodel. She was thin but not frail, with long, elegant limbs and delicate features.

"I come down to Philly every now and then, when I need to get out of New York," Lilly informed her casually. "Even before the band, I found the city a little…oppressive at times. Claustrophobic."

Toni nodded. Often the sheer size of New York terrified her.

"No one knows me down here, so I can chill out. I take the train, check into a hotel, and try out different restaurants. Clubs."

"You won't be able to do that for much longer."

Lilly nodded slowly. "That's the…goal, I guess."

"I don't envy you that. Wait, you've been to the Unicorn," Toni concluded, finally putting the pieces together.

"Ah! That's what it was called. Yes, I was in there a few months ago," Lilly confirmed. "Didn't know anything about it, just followed the music. You were playing an Arctic Monkeys song, I think. I remember being impressed enough by your skill." She looked at Toni. "But when you did 'Man in the Box,' I wrote your name down on a napkin. Anyone can master the technical, but what you did… It moved me."

It was a light-bulb moment. "That's why you wanted to throw an Alice in Chains song into the set," Toni said, her head spinning. "Because of me?"

Lilly straightened to her full height and regarded her thoughtfully.

"Listen, you've got something special. You definitely have the talent to make it in this business." Her gaze drifted back to the vending machine, this time lingering on a button featuring a bottle of water.

Lilly sighed and fed her dollar into the machine. She waited for the water to drop and scooped it up before straightening and turning back to Toni.

"There's a good chance someone will make you an offer when you leave us, once they hear what you can do."

She sounded...sad? Disappointed?

Toni ignored the weird twinge in her own chest at the thought of giving up the band. This was only a stepping-stone, not a whole new path.

"*If* you leave us, that is." Lilly pursed her lips, playing at mind reading again. "Who knows where Candi's head is?"

"She was a real help," Toni said hurriedly, uncomfortable with the trajectory of this conversation. And with the narrow possibility it offered.

"Don't let your guard down with Candi," Lilly warned, her eyes narrowing.

It was Toni's turn to frown. "I thought you two were close."

"We are," Lilly confirmed, her gaze drifting. "I–I care for her, but I don't trust her. Can't trust someone who can't trust themselves."

"You think she'll be a part of the band going forward?" Toni had to ask. Her curiosity had been driving her to distraction.

"We've told her to keep her ass in NYC before she fucks everything up completely," Lilly said with more venom than Toni expected. "Hopefully she'll listen."

As if she remembered who she was talking to, Lilly straightened and smiled, but it didn't reach her eyes.

"I hope things work out... It wouldn't be the same without her." She met Toni's gaze, searching it. "But I'm beginning to think it wouldn't be the end of the world if she didn't come back."

And, okay. She really said that.

Lilly gave one last, forlorn glance at the vending machine and turned to go.

"You sure you don't want a Dr Pepper?" Toni called after her. "I'll split it with you. Less guilt," she teased.

Lilly glanced over her shoulder. "I'll share one with you on your last day. Deal?"

"Deal."

"And remember, it's about the journey, Antonia. Not the destination," Lilly declared. "Enjoy this part."

CHAPTER 24.

PHILLY WAS THE FIRST PLACE Toni had ever been proud to call home, and she wanted the city to leave the same kind of impression on the others as it had on her. New York was fantastic—capital of the world, blah, blah, blah—but Philly was Philly. She was excited to finally take the crew to the Electric Unicorn.

She'd been avoiding it, the collision of her two worlds. Yvette had given her shit for not introducing her to the band—and even more shit for not bringing Seb around. Toni had tried to explain that everyone was too exhausted to socialize at the end of a long day. That they were keeping a low profile. She had run out of excuses.

And she found she wanted to see how they'd react to each other, if the oil and water would mix. She wanted—needed—a second and third opinion about Seb, because her defenses were falling fast around him. Not that he'd made a move and not that she expected him to. There was the no fraternization clause in her contract. And there was Candi and whatever the situation was with her. And there was...their history, such as it was.

He cared. Everything he did, everything he said showed Toni how much he cared about these people. He still cared about her, too, and that was an intoxicating thought, but he'd definitely been keeping his distance. Toni had decidedly mixed feelings about that.

"It's like taking respite in the country," Tiff quipped in the worst PBS-special-style English accent Toni had ever heard.

Fishtown had developed a strong personality in the five years that Toni had been coming there. She couldn't afford to live in nearby NoLibs. Hell, back then, she could barely afford a cup of coffee in its trendy cafés, but one night she'd stumbled into the Unicorn—at the juncture between the two neighborhoods, a throwback from when the area was dark and shabby—and she hadn't ever left.

"You talk like you aren't a desert transplant," Kayla said, nudging Tiff with her shoulder as they approached the entrance.

"Shhh," Tiff replied. "Stop spilling my California secrets all over these Philly streets."

The Unicorn was hopping, especially for a weeknight. Toni was glad for that. The four of them, plus Seb and Richie, took up spots at the end of the long bar.

Toni introduced everyone to Elton, who regaled them with endless stories of his misspent youth on the streets of London.

He and Lilly seemed to bond quickly over their expat status and were soon huddled together, deep in conversation. Toni was sure Elton and Jordan would have some Union Jack-related reminiscing to do once he came down from New York.

Kayla and Tiff had discovered the ancient jukebox in the corner and were already arguing over what song to play first.

"This place is different," Seb said, taking the stool next to Toni's.

He set a pint of amber liquid in front of her, the head thick and creamy. Whatever he had in his glass was darker. Probably one of Elton's stouts he was always trying to get her to try.

"You like playing here?"

"Yeah," Toni said. "It's chill."

"It's got an interesting vibe. I didn't really catch it...on your videos." He smiled sheepishly and looked around, no doubt taking in the eclectic decor.

Elton had old license plates nailed to the walls, framed concert posters from defunct venues, and various midcentury thrift-store finds. It was random. Toni fit right in.

"Kinda suits you, though," Seb said, turning back to her.

"In what way?"

One corner of his mouth tipped up. "Hard to figure out what's going on, but you can't stop staring."

Toni blinked slowly. "You come up with that line all on your own?"

Seb grinned. "All by my lonesome. Songwriter, remember?"

Despite herself, Toni returned it, but this thing with this—this lack of resolution—was getting to her.

Despite his denials, she'd half convinced herself that being called up for the Lillys was indeed part of some grand apology, a way for Seb to make right the wrongs he felt he'd done to her. To learn it was all happenstance was almost a letdown, even though she kept telling herself it didn't matter. She could no longer fool herself into thinking *he* didn't matter.

It was a lie. Of course he mattered. He always had, and Toni needed to accept that he probably always would, whatever they ended up being to each other.

"What's got you thinking so hard?" Seb searched her eyes. Even now, after all these years, she was evidently still an open book to him.

Smiling to herself, Toni shook her head.

"And now she's smiling." Seb's dimple magically appeared. He was giving her flirty Seb tonight. Cool, cool.

"I was just thinking that I haven't heard you play in a really long time."

Seb's gaze dropped to the bar top. "Don't much anymore, not

unless I'm writing or sitting in with these guys. I double on tracks with the gang sometimes, when Lilly's looking for some resonator or slide guitar."

"You have a resonator?"

Seb nodded. "Yep. Vintage. 1938. Picked it up when I was down in New Orleans. Sweet little thing."

Toni gaped at him. "You do realize you'll have to show me."

Seb's grin unfurled into a smile that made the temperature in the room rise a few degrees.

Toni realized she'd been trailing her fingers across her collarbones in a blatant invitation. *Oh, hell.* She straightened up and rested her elbows on the bar top.

Seb did the same, and his attention drifted elsewhere.

It stung more than it should have, but that clause in her contract probably hung like a banner over her head.

"Hey." She poked his arm.

Seb turned back to her. "S'up?"

"You haven't told me how you hooked Lilly up with the gang."

Seb's smile was different this time, wistful.

"Lilly and the Gang, I like that. Maybe we should use it." He finished his beer and signaled for another. "Let's see, I'd recently moved back to the East Coast."

"I thought you were in Miami."

He thought for a moment. "Right. Miami, via LA."

"Wow." Toni hadn't done much traveling. Or any.

"Ever been?"

"To Miami?"

Seb thanked the bartender when she set a fresh pint in front of him. "Either."

"No." Toni toyed with the coaster under her glass, determined not to ask the questions that tickled the back of her throat. "When I moved to Philly, I didn't have much."

Seb frowned, perhaps thinking about the same broken promises she was. "How long you been here?"

"Five years, give or take," she said. "Took me longer than I'd
hoped to get out of Bordon."

"Shit," Seb muttered, his face darkening. His eyes filled with
sadness and regret. "Nia, I…"

She shook her head. "Water. Bridge."

After a moment, Seb nodded.

"So," Toni prompted him. "Lilly?"

"Lilly, right." He took a sip of his beer. "Uh, she was at this
pub down in SoHo."

"Singing?"

"Yeah." There was a burst of loud voices, and he glanced down
to where Lilly appeared to be introducing Elton to Jordan.

The two men embraced, loud cries of "Hey, mate!" carrying
down to where Toni sat. She smiled, knowing how much Elton
missed the UK.

"Old friends?"

"I don't think they know each other," Toni replied. "But
they're both Brits. It's rare for Elton to meet his people."

Seb laughed.

"So, Lilly was singing in a pub in SoHo, and you walked up
and said *Hey, baby, I'm gonna make you a star*?"

He chuckled. "No, nothing like that. She was doing her thing,
twists on familiar songs, the sort of thing she does now. The sort
of thing you do," he added. "Blew me away."

"She certainly has a sound," Toni agreed.

"She does. I met Candi a bit after that and introduced
them. And I'd met Tiff while I was in LA, so I brought them all
together."

"And the rest, as they say, is history."

"Herstory," Seb said with a grin. "It's really Lilly's vision that keeps it all together. She met Kayla at a lecture on the works of Octavia Butler, or so the story goes."

"What about you? Do you only write for other people?"

Seb nodded. "Yeah, pretty much. I fell in with a newly signed act while I was in LA, wrote a couple of songs for them," he said. "One of them was top 40 on the rock chart a couple of years ago."

"Whoa, really?" Toni couldn't contain her smile. "That's... that's amazing, Seb. Why didn't you tell me?"

"When?" Seb said, spinning his stool to face her. "That first time I walked into the Phactory, I thought I was seeing things. I'm surprised you didn't haul off and punch me in the face."

"I wanted to," Toni admitted. She'd also wanted to kiss him, which was the scarier revelation of the two. So she kept that to herself.

"I would have deserved it. Worse, even," he replied, then lowered his eyes, giving his head a shake before he looked up at her again. "I'm torn, you see. I want you back in my life, but I haven't earned you."

"Earned me?" Toni was all too aware of how breathy that sounded.

"I haven't..." Seb's voice faltered. "There's no way I could ever make up for what I did."

"I thought we established that we were both kids." Toni put a hand on his arm where it rested on the bar. Seb smiled, gratitude in his eyes. "I need to understand, though. Why did you leave?"

Toni had been living with the question for too long. She wanted, *needed*, an answer.

"I left," Seb began, swallowing hard. "That night, I–I thought I'd..."

Whatever it was, Seb was struggling through it. The pain on his face was unbearable, and Toni instinctively slipped her hand into his.

They locked eyes and Toni felt an old familiar pull. She opened her mouth to say…something, she didn't know what.

Another voice beat hers to the punch.

"Well, look at you, all grown up!" an all-too-familiar alto sang.

The world, such as it was, tilted, everything shifting out of phase. Seb was still there. The rest of the band chatted away at the other end of the bar. Elton was smiling. He looked so damn happy.

But for Toni, the air was too thin. She tried to meet Seb's eyes, to ground herself in them.

But Seb was looking past her shoulder, and the look on his face confirmed everything.

Toni slowly turned in her seat. It took a moment for the sum of the details to register in her mind.

The same eyes as hers, set in a similarly shaped face, peered back at her.

Toni's breath left her in a rush as she stood to face a woman she hadn't seen in more than fifteen years.

"Hey, Toni-tone?" It was Kayla's voice coming from somewhere to her right. "Who's this?"

"It's…" Toni took a shaky breath and stood on shaky legs. "Mommy. Hi."

CHAPTER 25.

ANTONIA, AGE 8

"YOU LOOK PRETTY, MOMMY."

"Thank you, Sweet Potato." Mary adjusted the flower in her hair and smiled into the mirror.

Antonia wrapped her arms around her mother's waist.

"Don't get me all wrinkled."

"Sorry."

Antonia moved to her mother's side and looked at all the shiny, sparkly things on the dresser. She reached for a giant pearl pendant on a necklace that hung from the mirror's frame but snatched her hand back when her mother rapped her fingers with the back of her hairbrush.

Tears stung the backs of Antonia's eyes as she looked up at her mother's face, which was twisted with anger. "What have I told you 'bout touching my things?"

Antonia stepped away from her mother. She knew that tone of voice, knew she'd done something really wrong. "I–I'm s-sorry," she hiccupped, fat tears falling from her eyes now.

Mary sucked her teeth, annoyed, and turned back to her reflection in the mirror. "Your auntie Dot is watching you tonight. You be good."

"Can't I go with you?"

"No," Mary said, the weight of the word leaving no room for discussion. She turned and looked at Antonia. "Fix your face. Dot don't want no crying babies around her."

———————

"Antonia, girl. Look at you!" Toni's mother smiled wide as she stepped forward to wrap frail arms around her. "When I saw you on TV, I couldn't believe my baby girl was all grown up."

"Mommy…" Toni had no words, save that one. She clutched the back of her barstool until her hand went numb.

Mary Bennette stood there looking at her as if there was absolutely nothing wrong with this scenario. Like she hadn't shipped her daughter off to live with a total stranger, father or not, in a place not fit for a kid, and not checked in on her once in over half her life.

"You've done good for yourself, baby girl." Mary's gaze scanned the people in the bar.

Kayla stepped forward, offering her hand. "Nice to meet you, Toni's mom. I'm Kayla." Her voice was a bit more polished than Toni was used to.

"And I'm Tiff."

Mary shook both of their hands, looking expectantly at Seb, her eyes twinkling.

Toni knew exactly what her mother was thinking; with his bad boy facade, Seb was exactly the kind of guy she would have gone for. Probably still did.

Seb made no move to introduce himself, something that seemed to dim the wattage on Mary's smile.

Her gaze bounced back and forth between Toni and Seb before finally landing on Toni.

"And who is this? Antonia, did you go out and snag a boyfriend?"

"Toni," Seb said. At Mary's confused expression, he rolled his shoulders and spun on his stool to face her. "Her name is Toni."

Mary shook her head, her nose wrinkling. "No, it sure ain't. I wouldn't name my daughter Tony. That's a boy's name."

Kayla threw an arm around Toni's waist and pulled her in to her side. "Well, this is our Toni. I don't even know this Antonia person you're talking about." She winked at Toni, and Toni felt a wave of relief at the show of solidarity. She wished Yvette were there already, although her best friend would probably have shown Mary the door by now.

Her mother looked around the group, her gaze assessing them one by one.

Toni realized she hadn't said more than one word to her. She cleared her throat. "What... What are you doing here? And how did you even know where to find me?"

Mary's smile returned. "Like I said, I saw you on TV. I called your father and—"

"TV?" Kayla said.

"You called *Mo*?" Toni asked at the same time.

"Sure. Used to call him all the time before he told me you left town."

Toni's jaw dropped. In all the years she had lived under her father's roof, he'd never once told her that her mother had called.

Mary looked at Kayla and Tiff. "There was a story about how my daughter was joining a famous band. I assume that's you all. It was all over *CelebWatch*—I love that show, by the way—though they don't know it's my Antonia. All they had was a video of her getting into a van or something with you all up in New York."

She turned back to Toni, her smile blinding and full of pride.

Toni felt sick.

"I knew it was my baby girl the *second* I saw her. Got her mama's looks, don't she?" She reached for her, but Toni stepped back. "Sweet Potato, could we talk somewhere?" Mary glanced at the others. "Somewhere private?"

Beside her, Toni felt Seb stiffen.

Toni gave his hand, which she'd still been holding, a subtle squeeze before letting go. "Sure…Mom."

Toni led her mother to the back room. Thankfully, it was empty, though the thought of being alone with Mary after all this time filled Toni with a sickening dread.

She had loved her mother as a girl. Worshipped her.

Mary had named her Antonia after her own father, or so she'd said. With Mary, nothing was ever to be taken at face value.

Toni's wasn't a bad childhood, but it sure wasn't a good one. Mary made sure Toni had the basics—clothes on her back, even though they often came from various lost-and-founds. She'd had food in her belly, though often of the canned and jarred variety. And Mary had kept a roof over her head, though most nights it was the kind of room you rented by the hour, and always near whatever club her mother was playing for or gambling in. Often one and the same.

When Toni was really little, Mary would take her along to her gigs. She was the adorable little blues woman's daughter, sitting at her mommy's feet while she worked her magic on the crowd.

Toni still had Minx with her from the day's session, and had stashed it in the back room. She knew the moment her mother recognized her.

Mary's gaze landed on the case on the floor. Her eyes widened and a smile spread across her plum-stained lips. "Is that my Gibson?" Mary walked over and bent down to open the latches.

Toni wanted to protest when her mother picked Minx up and held her as if she were made of spun glass.

Propping her foot up on a chair, Mary set the guitar on her

knee and tested the tuning before breaking into a straight four-chord blues similar to the one Mo had played. Identical, actually.

She looked at Toni and smiled. "You took good care of her, baby girl. She looks as good as new! I forgot how good she feels in your hands. I'm glad you didn't sell it."

"I wouldn't," Toni heard herself say, despite having come so close to doing just that.

Mary looked back down at the guitar. "I'm surprised Maurice didn't. It's worth a bit of change. Would've thought he'd cash in as soon as he got his hands on it."

"I think he kept it to keep me there," Toni said. "A hostage to keep me in line, I guess. He knew how much I loved it."

"Keep you in line?" Her mother frowned. "You always were a good girl. And a joy to me."

Toni couldn't believe what she was hearing. It was like her mother had lived in an alternate reality.

Mary had palmed her off whenever she could. Little Antonia had a host of "aunts" and "uncles" at the clubs in both Baltimore and Chester, people who agreed to watch over Mary's kid while she went off to gig. Or whatever.

"Is that why you sent me away?" Toni asked, cursing the familiar ache in her chest.

Mary gasped. Her breath actually left her in a whoosh, and she looked as if Toni had slapped her. She set the guitar gently down and smoothed her hair back. Jet black with streaks of silver, it was beautifully complementary to her mahogany skin.

She was stunning in her prim cotton dress, button-down sweater, and little twill loafers. Some perverted version of a modern-day Stepford wife.

"You think I *wanted* to send you to Maurice?" Mary shook her head again and again. "No. No, I never did. I *had* to, Antonia. Jesus, don't you remember?"

Toni remembered. She'd spent the whole day in school waiting for the bell to ring so she could get to her mommy. Had waited all day to hear her mommy sing Stevie Wonder's "Happy Birthday," hug her silly, pepper her cheeks with lipstick-covered kisses, and call her *Sweet Potato*.

"Maybe you forget." Mary sighed. "You were only ten."

"I was twelve," Toni reminded her. "It was my birthday."

She had come home to their one-room efficiency above Bubba's Crab Shack expecting a birthday surprise. But all Mary had cared about that day was the gig.

The gig, the gig, always the gig. Or the next poker game.

But there had been a birthday surprise. Toni had gotten to go to the gig with her that night. She had been *so* excited because she'd never been allowed out on a school night.

Mary's eyes widened. "Well, I'll be. You're right. It was."

She frowned, perhaps remembering what happened that fateful night. Mary rolled her lips into her mouth as if biting back words. Her gaze darted to Toni and then away.

"Such a long time ago," she said. As if that changed anything.

"I didn't mind it, you know. The way we lived," Toni offered.

"So dramatic. Listen to you, 'the way we lived.'" Mary waved her off. "We did fine, didn't we?"

"Mom, the only hot meals I got were when you were in residence at that upscale BBQ restaurant in Fell's Point. Most of the time, I ate cold cereal for dinner—if we even had milk—I had the discounted day-old sandwiches at school because you only gave me a dollar for lunch. Hell, I saw myself to and from school from the time I was six," Toni rattled off, poking at old wounds.

"At least I kept you in the same school," Mary bit back. "Wasn't easy keeping us in one area like that."

"No small feat," Toni agreed. "We moved around more times

than I can remember. If anyone had bothered to call social services, I bet they would have placed me in foster care."

"Lucky for you, your father took you in." Mary sniffed, clearly annoyed by the implication.

"Some days, I wished for it. I even thought about calling CPS myself." At Mary's stunned expression, Toni shrugged. "I was lonely. Sad. When you weren't playing somewhere, you were hanging out in a back room gambling, or handing the little money you made over to a bookie."

Mary turned away. She wrapped her arms around herself and sank down onto one of the colorful sectional pieces.

It was no secret that Mary had a problem. Most of the time, they'd barely had two coins to rub together. When they did, Mary would splurge, making big bets on unwinnable races or buying dresses for her gigs. Mary loved to look the part and gave little thought to the future.

Every once in a while, she would fall deep into debt with one of her bookies and they'd have to go into hiding, or on a "vacation" to nowhere. More often than not, she'd leave Toni with Miss Dot, or Miss Lenora, or whomever was convenient.

Toni looked at her mother. It all made sense now, her surprise visit.

"You need money. That's why you're here."

Mary's eyes snapped up to meet her gaze. To her credit, she didn't try to deny the assumption.

Toni found her own seat on one of the poufs that often doubled as footrests when musicians hung out there. "I don't have any money, Mom."

Mary's gaze flicked to Minx, and rage flooded Toni so fast she thought she might drown in it.

Her mother flinched when she saw Toni's expression, whatever it was.

Toni had to take a couple of deep breaths before she could control her voice. "Didn't you ever wonder?"

"Wonder what?"

"Why Mo never put me on the phone when you called."

Mary blinked. She seemed to think it over before answering. "I figured you were busy in your new life."

"It didn't bother you that your own daughter never seemed to want to talk to you?"

"Look, Antonia," Mary said, straightening up, "it was a long time ago."

"Not for me it wasn't."

Mary pursed her lips, unmoved by Toni's pain. "You were a kid. Staying with me was… It wasn't healthy. Wasn't proper."

"And sending me to live above a shithole bar in the middle of nowhere with Mo—who you kept telling me, over and over, was the worst man on earth—that was your solution?"

"You were a club rat, Antonia," Mary snapped. "Living over a bar was nothing new to you."

"Mo's place isn't a club," Toni shot back. "Mo isn't some kindly venue owner with a soft spot for good music, pretty faces, and cute kids. He's an asshole."

Mary sniffed, indignant. "Well, you sure sound like your father. I guess something of him is in you after all."

She stood and smoothed her hands down her skirt. It was then that Toni noticed the set of diamond rings on her hand.

She shot to her feet. "You… You're *married*?"

Mary startled. She wrung her hands in a futile attempt to hide her ring finger. "He's real nice," Mary said, recovering quickly and trying her best to keep her smile steady. "You'd like him."

"When?"

Her mother hesitated.

Toni was going to be sick.

"It wasn't something I ever planned on doing," Mary explained. "You know me, I ain't made for being tied down."

Ouch.

"But Carl's a simple man. Doesn't put pressure on me to be anything but what I am."

Mary's smile would have been sweet were it not for the tears stinging the backs of Toni's eyes.

"Why do you need money?"

Mary held out her hands. "I got into a bit of trouble, nothing serious."

Tony took a stuttering breath. She glanced at the door, cursing herself because she didn't think she could deal with this alone. She silently begged for someone to walk in. Yvette, Elton... Seb. Even as the thought solidified, Toni grabbed onto it.

Seb was the only one who knew about Mary, knew everything she'd been through with her and because of her. Toni wanted him there. Wanted his hand on her shoulder, wanted his strength and support. She shouldn't need him like this, not after all this time, but there it was.

"You don't need this old thing," Mary said, as if Toni didn't know what Minx was worth. "You can afford a new guitar, with you being in a signed band and all. Those girls look like they're going places." Mary reached for Toni but seemed to think better of it and withdrew her outstretched hand. "I'm proud of you, Sweet Potato."

"It's only temporary," Toni said.

"What is?"

"The Lillys. I'm only going to be with them for a couple more weeks at the most."

Mary's face fell. "But I thought... On *CelebWatch*, they said—"

"It's all speculation. I'm only filling in until their real guitarist... comes back from medical leave."

Her mother squinted. "What's wrong with her?"

"The same thing that's wrong with you, Mary. She doesn't know when to stop." And, shit. Mary was not the person to share inside info with.

Mary crossed her arms and leveled her with a look. "We on a first-name basis, now? You never used to talk to me like that," she huffed. "You really are Mo's daughter."

"Well," Toni said, shrugging, "if I wasn't before you sent me there, I guess I am now. You can't have my guitar."

"It's *mine* by rights," Mary protested.

"Whose rights? What about my right to grow up with a mom who cared more about her daughter than a fucking guitar?"

Mary's lower lip wobbled as if she were about to cry. "I–I really need the money, baby girl."

Toni stood her ground. "For what?"

"That ain't none of your business." Mary scowled, her entire demeanor changing so fast it gave Toni whiplash. "Damn, you got mouthy growing up around that man."

Toni bent down and snapped the guitar case shut. She stood it upright, resting it on one edge, and wrapped her arms around it. "You've got a husband," she said. "I'm sure he can lend you some money. And you've got that sparkly ring. Borrow against that."

"I planned to," Mary admitted. "But it won't be enough. I'll be short twenty grand, even with the ring. Five, if I had the Gibson."

"Which you don't," Toni stated, unmoved by her mother's once-again-quivering voice. "How did you get so far in over your head, anyway?"

"I ran into a streak of bad luck." Mary moved forward. "Let me take it. I'll get you something even better. By the end of the month!"

Her fear was palpable, and Toni wondered how she planned to hock the ring without her new husband noticing it was gone.

"Please, Sweet Potato," Mary pleaded. This time there were genuine tears in her eyes. Genuine terror.

Toni's conviction wavered. Her grip on the guitar eased as her mind supplied one horrible scenario after another.

"I need your help, Antonia," Mary said, her gaze watery but direct. "I wouldn't have bothered you, but…I can't figure a way out of this one."

Toni's mind raced. She couldn't finish her contract with her pawn-shop guitar. Maybe she could borrow one from Seb or one of the others? Candi, maybe? Or she could ask Jordan to give her an advance on her pay so she wouldn't have to part with the guitar at all.

She might have to walk away from the Phactory deal, but…

"My husband won't understand," Mary added, probably sensing the crack in Toni's resolve. "He thinks I walk on water, you see. And my son, he's only—"

Toni reeled back as the floor seemed to drop out from under her. "Your *what*?"

Mary's mouth closed with an audible snap. At least she had the grace not to look Toni in the eye.

If the remorse Toni saw in her mother's face was real, Toni couldn't find it in herself to care.

My son.

She had a brother out there somewhere.

Toni couldn't even speak. A razor-sharp stone had formed and firmly lodged itself in her throat.

My son. A son that Mary Bennette had somehow found a way to be a mother to. A son she hadn't chosen to leave behind.

"You need to go now," Toni managed to croak.

Mary opened her mouth. Closed it. Pressed her lips together, her nostrils flaring. Finally, she inhaled a deep breath and let it out slowly.

"Whatever my faults," she said, her chin held high, "I did my best by you."

"*God*, just go." Toni wanted to scream, but her throat was closing.

After collecting herself, Mary walked to the door and stopped, shoulders dipping before she turned around to face her.

"I'll see you again soon, Sweet Potato."

CHAPTER 26.

THE SECOND HE SAW TONI'S mother lighting out of the Electric Unicorn like it was on fire, Seb knew things had gone sideways.

He looked at Kayla and her concern mirrored his.

"Go to her," she said, her voice laced with it.

A hand on Seb's forearm drew his attention. "Go on," Elton said. "I'll make sure no one bothers you."

Seb nodded, grateful to the weird little man for his perceptiveness. He obviously cared a great deal for Toni, and Seb was happy about it.

Tiff and Jordan had charmed free drinks out of Elton and drawn a few admirers, so Seb slipped away easily.

The back room was up a narrow half flight of steps behind the stage. When Seb stepped inside the room, he found Toni standing in the middle of it staring into space. The tears that streaked her cheeks propelled him to her.

As soon as she registered his presence, Toni let go of the guitar case. It fell, partially landing on a little ottoman, just as Seb pulled her into his arms.

Toni wept. Great hiccupping sobs that Seb felt in his own chest. He'd only seen her like this once before, and it scared the shit out of him now as it had then.

After several long minutes, she quieted down and sagged against him. Seb led her to one of the longer pieces of the mismatched sectional strewn about the room. While she settled, he closed and locked the door.

"Stay," she said, her voice strong.

"Not going anywhere."

Toni nodded, as if reassuring herself.

Seb grabbed another small stool and dragged it over, sitting across from her. He got as close as he dared. Spying a stack of takeout napkins on the plastic coffee table, he snagged a couple and handed them to her.

"Ugh, thanks." She offered him a watery smile. "Sorry about that."

"No need to apologize." He offered her another napkin, but she declined.

"Don't go around thinking I'm a crier. I'm not," she said. "I never cry."

Seb nodded. "I only remember you crying once when we were kids."

"Twice," Toni corrected him. She gave him a pointed look. "I cried when I got my ears pierced, remember?"

"Oh, God. Right," he said, glad to see a hint of a smile on her face.

Toni surprised him by covering one of his hands with hers. "I don't mean to keep bringing up the past. It's just…" She sighed heavily. "I can't seem to get away from it."

"Maybe Yvette would be better for this kind of thing?" he offered.

"No, no. I didn't mean I wanted to get away from *you*. Not now. I–I keep comparing you—*us*—to the people we were before. We're not," she said. "Mo's not. Mary's not. You're not," she repeated, holding his gaze.

"You definitely aren't little Antonia Bennette anymore. You

don't let anyone rattle you." Seb knew he needed to tread carefully, but she needed to talk about it. That much was clear. "What did she want?"

Toni huffed out a laugh. "Money. And when I told her I wasn't a big rock star rolling in cash, she asked for the Gibson so she could pawn her for the cash."

He drew back. "Minx?"

Toni smiled, even if it was a little wobbly. "You remember."

"How could I forget?" Seb said truthfully, just as the case finally slipped off the ottoman and crashed to the floor.

Toni jumped up with alarm.

"It's fine," Seb reassured her. He did a quick check to be sure, and the guitar looked no worse for wear. "Don't worry. These old cases were made to be thrown around in airports. A two-foot drop ain't gonna break Minx."

Toni eyed the case dubiously, but her shoulders relaxed. "You're right, I know."

"Trust me."

Toni laughed. "Maybe someday, when I figure out you and your games."

Seb frowned. "What games? I don't play games."

She met his steady gaze with one of her own. "Everyone does, at least everyone from before."

"I don't," he protested. "Never did."

Toni's laugh wasn't sharp, but it cut him deep.

"Why should I believe that?" She was serious. He knew this wasn't really about him, not entirely, but he still felt the need to set things straight once and for all.

Seb moved into her space and took her hand, tightening his fingers around hers. "Why would I lie to you?"

"You don't lie, you withhold truth," she said, her voice small. "You dance around it. Why you left, this whole Lilly situation…"

"I can't dance, remember?" Seb joked, needing to lighten the mood. They'd been in a good place lately, or so he'd thought.

Uncertainty filled her brown eyes as she looked up at him. "Why did you leave? Bordon. Why did you leave...?"

Me.

That was the unspoken word that hovered between them.

"I couldn't stay," he said, opting for the simplest truth. "Mitch would have killed me. Or I would have killed him."

Flashes of their last fight often haunted Seb's dreams. The loathing Mitchell Quigley had directed at him. The hatred Seb had felt from his own father. For him.

The pain of his own split lip, and the crunch of his fist against his pop's jaw.

"We were supposed to get out together," Toni said. This time, there was no heat in her words. No accusations. Plenty of regret, and a lot of pain that twisted Seb's gut. "We had a plan."

Looking in her eyes, Seb couldn't hide how he felt, all of the remorse and shame and fucking *longing* for her. It had killed him to leave her, had killed him to stay away. She'd been all he had.

Toni nodded as if she'd heard his thoughts. "What really happened that night? Why did you leave, Seb?"

"Because..." He exhaled a shaky breath. "You have to understand, I wanted to take you with me. I wanted to grab you and run."

"I would have," Toni said, not a trace of uncertainty in her voice. "I would have gone *anywhere* with you. Didn't you know that? God, Seb, we talked about it all the time, us getting out of there together."

"Yeah, but we were going to be smart about it," he said. "We were saving up, doing research, and figuring out where and when and how. You weren't ready to get up and go with a couple thousand dollars and no landing place."

"Oh, and you were?" Toni dropped his hand. "What difference would it have made?"

"You weren't even seventeen," he reminded her.

"And?"

Seb let out a bitter laugh. "Mo hated me even before you came to town. Imagine how he would have felt, what he would have done, if you had run off with me."

Toni's brow furrowed. "You were worried about what *Mo* would think?"

"I was worried about what he'd *do*, Nia," Seb said, trying to keep his voice calm and failing. He grabbed her other hand, needing to make her understand. "He could have called the cops. You do realize that, don't you? He loathed me. Who knows what he would have told them?"

She closed her eyes, shaking her head as if it hadn't been a possibility. "I honestly don't think he would have even blinked," she said. "Maybe if I had taken Minx, he would have called the cops on both of us."

At that, Seb had to laugh. "Yeah, probably. Still..." He dropped her hands and paced a few steps away. He had to make her see. He'd had no choice.

"All I'm hearing are excuses, Seb," Toni said. "All I'm hearing is that you left, took your money, and didn't look back. Didn't think twice about me."

Seb turned to face her.

"I had *nothing* to offer you, Nia. Less than nothing. A life on the run, living who knows where? You'd already been there and done that with your mother. You had a whole goddamned drawer full of T-shirts to show for it," he said, willing her to understand. "And me, I'm... Well, I learned the hard way I'm not that much different than Mitch."

Toni's mouth dropped open. "That's... That's... Seb, why

would you think that, just because you got into a fight with him?"

Seb ran both hands through his hair. No use dancing anymore. The music had stopped.

"The night I left," Seb started, then paused. "No, I need to back up."

He turned and walked to the other side of the room, searching for words that would make sense. Leaning against the wall, he let his head thump back and stared at the flickering fluorescents behind the yellowing ceiling panels.

Toni had moved to sit on the back of a chair across from him. When he dropped his head, she was watching him expectantly.

Seb blew out a breath. "Mitch blamed...blames...me for my mom's death."

Toni frowned. "What?"

"She had cancer, that's what took her from us, and my pop, he thinks it's 'cause she had me."

Toni gasped. "That's..."

"I know." Seb nodded. "But he's convinced."

"Jesus," she whispered. "Seb, I'm... I had no idea. Why didn't you ever say anything?"

"I wasn't big into heart-to-hearts, if you recall."

She hummed in response.

"Anyway, we fought a lot about it, especially after high school," Seb continued. "He wanted me gone. And I wanted to *be* gone, but..."

Toni's eyes widened. "You were waiting for me to turn eighteen. Graduate."

Seb nodded.

"So what changed that night?" Fear laced her words.

"We got into it." Seb pushed off the wall and shoved his hands through his hair. He couldn't stay still. "I mean, we were always getting into it, but this was different. *He* was different. Angrier, more...cruel, I guess. He was drunk. I came in from wherever I'd been. Probably with you." He looked at her.

She stared up at him with rapt attention, worry knitting her brow. He had the overwhelming urge to smooth it away, but she wanted to hear this. And he owed it to her to tell her, no matter the consequences.

"He came at me," Seb said, letting the memories come. "He started yelling almost as soon as I came in the door. I knew he was drunk, but... He had something in his hand. A wrench or something, I don't know exactly, but he swung it at my head."

"Oh my God!" Toni shot to her feet.

"It wasn't the first time he hit me with something." Seb touched the scar on his eyebrow.

"You told me you got that playing football," Toni said, narrowing her eyes as she approached him. Carefully, she reached up and traced a fingertip over the ancient wound. It was like an electric shock and Seb drew in a sharp breath.

"He threw an ashtray at me," he said, barely able to speak. She was so close, so tender. It was breaking his heart to tell her this now.

Toni went very still, watching him. "How old were you?"

"Wasn't long before we met. Eleven, maybe?"

Toni blinked at him as if seeing him through new eyes. She slid her hand into his hair and pulled until his forehead rested against hers.

Seb closed his eyes and let out a shuddering breath.

"A-anyway, he...he lunged for me and I grabbed the arm that had the thing in it. We wrestled a while before I tripped on something and fell over. He hit his head on the edge of that old trunk we had in the living room. Remember it?" His voice had fallen to just above a whisper as he recounted the details but, fuck. This was hard with her so close, but Seb wasn't about to move an inch. Not one.

He placed a hand on her waist. Lightly, because she didn't always like to be touched.

"Yeah, I remember." Her tone matched his and she inched forward. Toni brought her other hand up and cupped his cheek. It nearly tore a sob from his throat.

"Caught him under the eye," Seb continued. His throat felt like he'd been gargling with sand. "He really lost it then."

"He hadn't lost it before then? Sheesh, Seb. You're lucky he didn't kill you." Her thumb swept back and forth across his cheek, and Seb brought his hand up to cover hers. It was almost too much.

Seb opened his eyes.

Toni was watching him, her expression so tender, so full of... But that wasn't possible.

"I'd never seen him like that." He blinked, nearly forgetting his train of thought as he stared into her eyes.

Toni seemed oblivious to his free fall.

"I'm not talking about that one night," Toni said. "I'm talking about all the other times he hurt you. He's a sick man. I had no idea."

Seb's hand tightened on her waist. "I didn't want you to know."

"Why not?" Anger flashed in her eyes, but it was tempered. "Wasn't I always there for you?"

Seb brought his hand up to her face. "Always."

"Then why?" She seemed so genuinely confused.

"When I was small, when my mom first got sick, I asked her what I could do, you know?" Seb searched Toni's eyes. She nodded. "I wanted to help. I didn't understand what it all meant. And my pop, he was angry all the time. I can't ever remember him *not* being angry.

"Anyway, I asked her what I could do. And she told me to take care of my dad."

Toni bit her lip, her eyes filling with sympathy and understanding.

Seb shook off the dull ache the memory always brought.

"He was all I had left, but he didn't see me that way. He blamed me for losing her. Blamed me for ever being born. It made me angry, living around all that...hate. By the time I met you, I was already ruined."

"Ruined?"

"Incapable of connecting, of...being *not* pissed all the time. And that night, when he came at me—pushed me into the floor after I had fallen, pressing that cold metal against my throat, I... snapped."

Toni released him and stepped back. "What happened?"

He fought the urge to reach for her. It felt wrong, not having her closer. All wrong. But he pressed on.

"I pushed him off me. Kicked him, really. Right here." Seb pointed to the center of his chest where his boot had landed on his father. "He went flying. And for a minute, it felt so good, Nia. *So fucking good.*"

He looked at her, waited for the horror in her face to appear. When it didn't, he frowned. Didn't she get it?

"I stood over him. I laid into him, everything I'd ever wanted to say, I said. How he never loved me, never loved my mom. How he wasn't capable of loving anyone." Needing to move, he began to pace, the rage and pain from that night surfacing from a long-buried hole in his chest.

Toni slowly approached him again.

She wasn't getting it. Wasn't seeing what he'd laid out before her. He was twelve different kinds of fucked up, and he'd inherited it honestly. The only reason he hadn't run away sooner was...her.

Seb let Toni see him, all the broken pieces.

"I told him he was a drunk and a deadbeat and the shittiest father that ever lived. That I was going to leave and never come back. And you know what he said?"

Toni gave the barest shake of her head.

"He said the day I died would be the happiest day of his life."

"Holy fuck," she murmured, her expression pained. "How...? How could he say that to his only child?"

Seb laughed bitterly. "Because it's true. Why would that make any difference?"

Toni flattened her hands against his chest, and it was more than he could bear. His heart tried to beat itself out of his rib cage and into her hands.

Seb put his hands over hers and held them there. Held her gaze. "I picked up the tool he had dropped," he said, barely able to get the words out because he knew this would change everything between them. "I raised it above my head and held it there while I looked him in the eye," Seb continued, watching her pupils dilate. "I waited. I waited for...for-for-for a *plea*, an apology, some fucking remorse, *anything*. But there was nothing."

Seb shook his head as she looked up at him, wide-eyed. "He gave me nothing. It was like he *wanted* to die. And I..." He swallowed hard. "Nia...I wanted to kill him. He'd broken me."

"You weren't broken, Seb." Shaking her head, Toni curled her fingers into his shirt, gripping it as if he were about to run. "You were hurting, and he was a monster, but you...you were good. You *are* good."

A tear slipped down Toni's cheek, which made Seb both irrationally angry and irrevocably hers.

Fuck.

Antonia Bennette was more than family to him, she was home. And he'd been in a self-imposed exile for eight years.

A hell of a realization when he knew his next words would likely sever her from him forever. Seb dropped her hands and stepped farther away from her. "Good? The hell are you talking about, good? Mitchell Quigley made me in his image, and if I did what every cell in my body was screaming for me to do that night, I'd have proven it to him. *That's* what stopped me. Not any goodness, not any sense of right, or respect for life and fucking death. I just didn't want to show him he was right."

"He wasn't right."

Seb let out a short, bitter laugh. She was so goddamned stubborn.

"Do you know what I did those first few months after I left Bordon?" he asked, determined to make her see. "Know how I survived? Drugs. I sold drugs for a gang in Pittsburgh. That's how I earned the money to head out west."

That got her attention. Toni crossed her arms and cocked her head, every inch of her a challenge.

It made him want to kiss her. A ridiculous, irrational thought that made him take a few steps back.

"So you left Bordon to, what, to save me from you?"

Fucking finally.

Seb exhaled. "Mo was a bastard but with him, at least, you were safe. You had a place to live, food."

Toni snorted. "Now I know your memory is shot if you're calling what they serve at Mo's *food*."

Seb smiled before he could stop himself, but it fell away quickly. "I'm sorry I hurt you. I didn't…" Without thinking, he reached out and ghosted his fingers over Toni's hair. She'd left it curly today and it was soft. So soft. "I think I convinced myself, eventually, that you'd forget me. It's not like we were…"

Toni shivered under his touch and Seb swallowed hard, swaying into her as if pulled by gravity. He leaned back before he did something irresponsible, like give in to his growing need to kiss her. Not a good idea, even if she was looking up at him like she wouldn't mind if he did, thick black lashes fanning her cheeks in slow sweeps.

Her hands went to his waist.

"Toni?"

Her lashes fluttered as she searched his eyes. Hers were soft, and there was no mistaking the longing in them.

"Nia?" A whisper.

Toni carded her fingers into his hair and pulled, this time guiding him straight down to her mouth.

Seb only had a chance to take in her closed eyes and furrowed brow before her lips pressed gently against his. It was as sweet and gentle a kiss as he'd ever had, and exactly what he'd been afraid of. Because it was her, his Nia.

Somewhere in the back of his mind, Seb had always known it would be dangerous to be this close to her. It was just a press of lips, but there was so much in the kiss. The period at the end of a run-on sentence. A promised fulfilled.

Toni sighed in the back of her throat, her lips parting slightly, inviting him in.

Seb groaned and cupped her face in his hands, cradling it as gently as he could manage because, like that, he was on fucking fire.

Every nerve ending in his body went on high alert, fueled by the soft sounds she made. Sexy, and needy, and *fuck*.

This was Nia. His Nia.

Her arms went around his neck and she pulled herself flush against his body.

Seb thought he might lose his mind. She tasted like salt and sugar and lime, and he wondered why it had taken him nearly ten years to realize no one else would ever do. No one else would ever be her.

Toni broke the kiss. She pressed her forehead to his collar-bone, her breaths fast and heavy.

Seb could feel the wild beating of her heart in the palm of his hand where it was pressed against her back. He held her tight to him, unable—unwilling—to let her go just yet. He rested his chin atop her head and fought to get his own breathing under control. To quiet his mind because it was racing ahead of him, conjuring up thoughts of long nights and early mornings. Of waking up next to her the way he did the other night and not leaving. Maybe *never* leaving.

"So..." Toni began after a long moment of silence, peppered only by their breaths. "That happened."

She lowered her heels to the floor and leaned back, looking up at him through her lashes.

"It did," he agreed, regarding her carefully.

Toni smoothed her hands down the front of his shirt. "And how do we feel about that?"

Was she kidding?

"We...feel...good about it?" Seb didn't know what she wanted to hear, and saying *I think I fucking love you and I think I always have* wasn't an option.

She giggled. She actually giggled. And it was like someone had removed a 50-ton weight from Seb's shoulders. He couldn't have stopped the broad smile that stole across his face if he'd tried.

"Was that a question?"

Seb pulled her in again, pleased when her eyelids fell to half-mast. No doubt she felt the evidence of just how good he felt pressing against her belly.

"I feel...good."

Toni hummed. "Indeed."

"And you?" he chanced, already seeing the answer in her eyes.

"I'm..." She glanced down. And if Seb didn't know any better, he'd think she was blushing. "I've been wanting to do that since I was about thirteen." She looked up at him again and smiled. "So, yeah. I'm good. Better than good, only…I can't believe you spent all these years believing that bullshit about you and Mitch."

Seb let her go, an echo of the guilt and shame he'd felt a few minutes ago pinging through him. He shoved his hands into his back pockets.

"Tell me you don't actually think you're anything like that asshole."

Seb studied her. The conviction with which she said it made him want to believe. "Maybe, maybe not," he said. "It's in me, though. You get that, right?"

"No more than Mary and Mo are in me," Toni said plainly, and the truth of that stole across Seb's brain like a thunderclap. She was nothing like either of them, except in only the barest of ways.

She'd obviously inherited her mother's talent, and maybe some of her father's stubbornness.

"What did Mary say that upset you? Can't only have been about the money or the guitar."

Toni sighed and Seb knew she wasn't happy with the swift subject change, but he was raw in a way he hadn't been in forever. He couldn't take much more.

"She got married," Toni answered, her voice flattening. "And apparently I have a brother out there somewhere."

Whatever he'd been expecting her to say, it wasn't that. "The fuck?"

"I know." She pursed her lips. "Guess she figured out a way to settle down in…" Her eyes went wide. "Shit, I don't even know where she's living now."

"Not to be a dick, but do you care? I assume you turned her down, since Minx is still here."

"Hell yes, she's not getting Minx." Toni sucked her teeth in disgust. "I came so close to falling for her bullshit, but then she slipped up."

Seb grinned. "You always were able to see through people."

"I'm having a hard time seeing through you, though."

"Me? I'm an open book."

She shook her head. "Nah, you're not."

"How am I not? I shared shit with you I've never told anyone else. Ever. Christ, Nia, I'll answer any damn question you want," he promised. "But don't be disappointed when the answer turns out to be I was hungry, I was tired, or I was bored."

Toni laughed, her smile lighting up her whole face. Seb's overwhelming need for her happiness was like a punch to the gut.

"I can ask anything?"

Seb nodded.

"Good to know," she said but turned away, surprising him. He'd been ready to confess anything and everything to her. "I'll make a list and get back to you."

Toni picked up her guitar and checked the latches before folding her arms on top of it.

Seb brushed a loose wave back from his forehead and sucked in a breath to settle himself. "Feeling up to heading back out there?"

"Yeah, I'm okay." Toni reached for the door, then stopped. She looked at him, her brow furrowed. "Do you think the press can identify me from those pictures from SAGA?"

"It's possible," Seb conceded. "But I don't think they know your name, or they'd be down here staking this place out."

"How hard is it for them to find me, though? My mother did."

"She had your pop to confirm her suspicions. The press have no idea who you are. If they had a clear shot of your face, they would have found your social media."

Toni grimaced. "I don't really do social media."

Seb smiled. That didn't surprise him. "You and Tiff, man. What do you have against the twenty-first century?"

"Nothing," Toni said, shrugging. "Never found the need for it. I only really hang out with Yvette and Elton. They know where to find me."

"You kinda need it to market your music, don't you?"

"Nah." She shook her head. "I'm not out here trying to be a star."

"Nia," Seb said, and watched her melt a little. He filed that away for later. "Whether you know it or not, your star's already rising. You might want to check YouTube."

"Ugh" was her only response. Then she sobered. "We... Whatever this is between us, we have to cool it until..."

"Until you finish out your contract?"

"Yeah. I can't afford to blow this gig. And violating the no-fraternization clause, of all things, wouldn't be a good look. You know?"

Seb frowned because, no. He hadn't known she had one in her contract, too, though he should have. "Don't worry. I can be good."

Toni pouted, her full bottom lip poking out in a way that made Seb's stomach tighten.

"What?"

"Are you saying I'm not irresistible, Quick?"

Seb slowly closed the distance between them. "I can show you just how irresistible you are," he said, not bothering to suppress the growl in his voice. "Say the word."

The knock on the door startled them both, and Seb took a giant step back.

Toni opened it and Elton stood on the other side.

"There you are, love." He looked from Toni to Seb and back. "Everything okay?"

Toni cleared her throat and lifted her chin in that way she used to do when they were kids, whenever someone doubted her. "All good. What's up?"

Elton glanced at Seb and he nodded.

"If you're feeling up to it, a few of the regulars are asking if you're going to play tonight," Elton said. "They saw you sitting at the bar."

Toni blanched a little. "Uh, I don't know."

Elton's smile was indulgent. He clearly cared a great deal for her. Seb smiled to himself.

"We haven't heard your dulcet tones for weeks, my darlin'."

Toni rolled her eyes, but grinned. "Dulcet tones?" She looked at Seb and hooked a thumb toward Elton. "This dude."

Seb shrugged. "He's not wrong. But are you sure you're..." Seb searched for the right words. "Are you up for it after...?"

Toni seemed to think it over, but she was still grinning.

"It's just us chickens out there, my girl," Elton said, affection in his voice. He clearly knew her well. "And I've already said no cameras, to protect everyone's privacy."

Seb liked that Elton wasn't trying to bully her into performing, simply letting her know that it was a safe space. He suddenly understood why he'd only seen videos of her playing at the Unicorn. This place was a haven.

"I do have a new cover I was working on," she said, looking at Seb as she bit her lip. Freaking adorable.

"Show us what you got." Seb winked her.

Her mouth twisted to the side as she fought the smile he could see in her eyes. "Is that a challenge, Quick?"

Seb smiled wide. "Of course it is, Bennette."

CHAPTER 27.

ELTON HAD BEEN TELLING THE truth. The Unicorn was relatively empty, thanks to a food and music festival on the waterfront. Aside from Seb and the band, only Yvette, Elton, a few regulars, and a couple of the waitstaff were in attendance.

It would be the perfect setup for her normal gig, but this audience was loaded with people she wanted to impress. Toni liked Jordan. In an industry she knew was filled with sharks, he seemed to have the band's best interest at heart. She had also come to admire the women in the Lillys. And then there was Seb…

Toni plugged Minx into the DI box and signaled to Luca. They turned up the volume on the PA system, and the speakers hummed to life around her. She strummed a ringing chord to test the volume and then gave the guitar a quick tuning. It didn't need much, since they'd been in the studio all day.

"Play a little bit for me," Luca said, adjusting the knobs on their sound board.

Toni launched into the opening chords of Metric's "Sick Muse."

"Fuck yeah!" someone yelled beyond the lights. It sounded like Kayla, and Toni chuckled to herself.

Before she could get to the bridge of the song, Luca cut in. "That's good, now give me some vocals."

Toni hesitantly reached for the mic stand, using both hands to adjust the height. Whoever had been on last was tall, and she had to lower it quite a bit.

"She is small but mighty!" Definitely Tiff this time.

"Elton doesn't tolerate hecklers," Toni quipped. "Do you, Elton?"

"Toss 'em right out on their arses," he said, not missing a beat. "Unless, of course, they're as lovely as you, miss."

"Ooo," Tiff said. "I like this one."

"Really, Elton?" Toni laughed.

"I still need to get your levels. Sing something," Luca reminded her.

Toni picked up the song where she'd left off, channeling her best Emily Haines as she sang about how everybody wants to fall in love.

Her cheeks heated and she decided it was due to the lights beaming down on her and not because she'd finally had a breakthrough moment with Seb.

He had revealed so much. And she knew there was more that he wanted to say but hadn't been able to.

Toni understood that. There was a lot she wanted to say to him too. And now that they'd opened that door, she knew it was only a matter of time. It was as if a dam had burst and they were both holding back the flood with their fingers.

"I'm good if you are." Luca gave her a thumbs-up and tucked himself in the corner, out of sight.

Toni silenced the strings. "Any requests?"

"Freebird!" Kayla yelled, predictably.

"Elton, please commence with the tossing out on her *arse*," Toni joked.

"Hey!" Kayla protested, dragging out the word. Toni could hear the humor in her voice. "This is me getting into the spirit of open mic night."

"It's not open mic night, Kayla," Jordan said, laughing.

"Don't spoil my fun."

"Play some Prince," Yvette called out. It wasn't a bad suggestion, but Toni had something else in mind.

Toni flipped through her mental songbook as she pulled a stool over to the mic. She hopped onto it and settled Minx on her thigh. *Ah,* she thought as the perfect song came to her.

It only took a few chords before she got a reaction from the small crowd.

"No...fucking...*way*!" Kayla's voice cut into the silence between the breaks in the music.

Life moves through you
Like ripples moving through still waters.
No one can touch you;
They never cared too much for you.

Toni sang the lyrics for what must have been the thousandth time. The song was as much a part of her as the calluses on her fingertips.

Kayla appeared in front of the stage. She waved her arms in the air as she danced and looked up at Toni, her face full of joy.

"I fucking love this tune!"

Tiff joined her and soon they were entangled in some sort of impromptu jig.

Slowly, the others moved from the bar to the tables near the stage. Toni saw Jordan pull out a chair for Yvette and sit beside her. He looked up at Toni, a huge grin on his face.

She forced herself not to seek out Seb in the small crowd, though she could feel all of his attention on her.

Butterflies are free

Until they reach the shore of the sea,
Trapped by a siren sound,
And then they spiral

"Down and down and down and down!" Tiff and Kayla joined Toni as she sang the line. She grinned down at them.

Out of the corner of her eye, Toni saw someone enter the stage. She turned to find Seb walking toward her.

He picked up an acoustic guitar that had been resting on a stand and held it up to show Luca as he strummed. Luca hopped up from their seat and pointed at another DI box, gesturing for Seb to plug in. A moment later, Seb had fallen into rhythm with Toni.

She stood wide-eyed as he joined her center stage, her hands continuing to play on muscle memory alone as her mind blanked out.

When Seb reached her side, Toni came back to herself. She moved over to give him room at the microphone.

And when you say go, you mean go, not baby, come
back.
And when you say stay, you mean stay, baby, never go
away again.

So many memories flooded her in that moment that it took everything in Toni to keep going. Their voices together, the way Seb's rhythm guitar perfectly complemented her lead—it was almost as if no time had passed. They were both light years better as players than they had been all those years ago, but the connection was as strong as ever. God…she loved this. Had missed it. Missed him.

Toni wanted to grab Seb's hand and drag him into a dark corner.

As if reading her mind, Seb held her gaze, his focus laser

sharp. They finished the song that way, locked together in a chorus of possibilities.

When the song ended, the room exploded with applause.

"Oh my *God*!" Tiff jumped onto the stage, surprising Toni. "That was amazing! It's like you guys rehearsed it."

Kayla climbed up too. "I haven't heard that song in years. Really great arrangement, Toni."

"It was a good arrangement," Jordan agreed from his seat near the stage.

"Glad you liked it," Toni replied. She looked at Seb as she continued. "We used to play that a lot when we were kids."

Toni felt Seb stiffen beside her and her eyes snapped to his. *Fuck. Talk about a record-scratch moment.*

Seb closed his eyes and gave the tiniest shake of his head, but there was a hint of a smile on his mouth.

"Wait." Tiff held up a hand. "What did I miss?"

Seb opened his eyes and looked at Toni as if to say *Cat's out of the bag now*. Then he turned to Kayla.

"From what I can tell," the redhead began, "our Little Miss Toni and Big Brother Seb grew up together and…may have had a thing in high school?" At Seb and Toni's simultaneous protests, she put up both palms. "Or not."

"We were *friends*," Toni rushed to clarify.

"Best friends," he said, holding her gaze. "We lost touch."

She nodded.

"Does she know you stalked her online?" Jordan sat back, arms crossed, and shot Seb an evil grin.

"What?" Shocked, Toni looked at Seb who was quickly turning red.

"No, I… It's not like… It was after…" He laughed nervously, running a hand through his thick hair. "Shit. I told you to check YouTube."

"I think I better," Toni agreed, poking him on the arm. His gaze softened.

"Since when are you on YouTube, Toni?" Yvette asked.

"Found it!" Kayla held up her phone, triumphant.

"You didn't need to see us home," Toni said after Yvette jogged up the steps to their front door, leaving them *some privacy to hash out their shit.*

"Wanted to," Seb replied simply.

It was a little cool for late August, but that's not why Toni shivered as she stood facing Seb in the quiet night.

He looked up at the early-twentieth-century rowhome. "Yours?"

Toni snorted. "Yvette rents the one-bedroom on the third floor. I rent her sofa bed."

Seb's brow lifted. "You *rent* a sofa bed?"

"Sort of. Long story."

"I want to hear it sometime," he said, looking down at her with a focus that make her toes curl.

"We have a lot to catch up on, I guess."

The space between them gave birth to a loaded silence, and Toni wasn't sure where to go from there. How was she supposed to resume a friendship that had been at rest for so long? Where was the tablature that showed how to navigate a love interrupted?

"I had fun tonight." Seb shifted on his feet, which brought them closer. "You sure know how to show a guy a good time."

"Was it the part where my mom tried to shake me down?"

"Yeah, definitely," Seb replied, his eyes twinkling in the light of the streetlamps. "Familial extortion always makes for a fun night."

Toni laughed at the absurdity of the entire situation. "Glad we could entertain you."

"Yeah, well," Seb began, rocking back and forth on his heels. "Got to find *something* to do in this dinky little town."

"Don't start in on Philly," Toni warned, pointing a finger at him.

Seb smirked at her. "So defensive."

"You were the one born in the backwater," she reminded him.

"Low blow, Bennette." He smiled and pulled his bottom lip between his teeth. Toni caught a glimpse of the tongue that had melted her knees to goo a few short hours ago. Her teenage fantasies didn't hold a candle to a real kiss from Seb.

"I had fun too," Toni admitted when they'd fallen silent again. "I–I missed playing with you."

She could see the effect of her confession in the way his gaze softened. In the way he inhaled a breath that shuddered on the way out. In the way he looked at her like she'd granted him a wish.

"Nia…"

"Seb, I…"

He laughed softly. "I feel like we're in the middle of one of your rom-coms."

Toni rolled her eyes, but her face threatened to split in two, her smile was so wide. He hadn't been kidding when he said he remembered everything.

"One," she protested, giggling like she hadn't since she was a kid. "I made you watch *one* and you still won't let it go. It's been, like, ten years, Sebastian."

"Yeah, but now I get stuck watching it every time it comes on TV 'cause it reminds me of you."

Seb's eyes widened as he seemed to realize what he'd said, but Toni lit up inside.

"What else reminded you of me?"

"Everything," he whispered, moving closer again. They were

two magnets fighting a universal pull. "I know I don't have the right to ask, but... I mean, I know we have, *I have*, a long way to go before you can forgive me."

"I forgive you," she assured him more quickly than she'd ever thought she could have. "You are forgiven every slight, real or imagined, Sebastian Quick."

Seb looked at her like she was a miracle. "Trust, then. I have to earn that from you...from everyone, really."

He was right. "Tonight was a good start, I think."

Seb nodded before he looked back up at the house to where Yvette had turned on the lights. "I should let you get some rest."

"Yeah." Toni tried and failed to hide her disappointment. She didn't want him to go. Toni didn't know what else there was to say but she knew she wasn't ready for the night to end.

Certain parts of her really, really weren't ready.

Judging by the way Seb kept swaying toward her, something told her a big—*ahem*—part of him wanted to stay.

But.

It wasn't smart, so Toni clung to reason. She cupped his shoulders and turned him around, giving him a little push.

He groaned, laughing. "I'm going, I'm going."

"See you in the morning?"

Seb turned back to her. "Jordan and I need to run up to meet with the suits at the label, but then I'll be right back down here."

"Okay." Toni hesitated, hoping for...something. After a few heartbeats, realizing she was being utterly ridiculous, she took out her keys and picked up Minx's case. "So..."

"Good night." Seb's voice was a caress.

"G'night." She started up the steps but a gentle touch on her elbow made her stop and turn back.

Seb leaned in, and for an endless second, Toni thought *This is it*. Her eyelids fluttered shut as she waited for the electric shock of his lips against hers. She had to swallow down more disappointment when Seb kissed her cheek before moving his lips to her ear.

"I just wanted you to know," he whispered, his breath hot against her skin, "I am practicing some *Herculean* restraint right now."

Seb pulled back but kept his hand on her elbow, his thumb brushing back and forth and sending little jolts of pleasure throughout her body.

"Impressive," she managed, sounding not at all breathy and needy and pathetic. If he made the slightest move to kiss her, Toni knew she'd be climbing him like the old oak tree in the field at the edge of Bordon.

The corner of Seb's mouth lifted like he knew it too.

"Thank you for listening," he said, releasing her. "For giving me a second chance I *know* I don't deserve."

Toni turned to face him when he pulled away. With her standing on the steps, they were nearly at eye level. "That's the thing, Seb. You *do* deserve it. And more."

CHAPTER 28.

SEBASTIAN, AGE 17—ANTONIA, AGE 15

"I HONESTLY DON'T KNOW WHAT you see in her," Antonia griped. "She's...she's got no personality. Nothing."

"She's the most popular girl in school," Seb said, confused.

"So? She's still not your type."

He blinked, the smile slipping from his mouth. "You saying I'm not good enough for her?"

"No, *butthead.*" Antonia slapped him on his chest. Such an annoying little shit. "That's not what I'm saying." She huffed out a breath. "I'm saaaaying she's... Well, she doesn't seem like your type, that's all."

He crossed his arms. *This ought to be good.* "What's my type, then?"

Antonia opened her mouth but seemed to catch herself. She chewed on her bottom lip and cast her gaze everywhere but at him. It made heat rise to Seb's face. Did she really think he wasn't good enough for the likes of Heather Johansson?

"I dunno," she muttered. "Someone with a brain, for one thing."

Seb laughed, an odd relief washing over him. "You don't think Heather has a brain? She's president of the A/V club. Supersmart."

Antonia cast her eyes skyward, but another expression crossed her face. Seb really didn't know what to make of it.

"Whatever." She shoved her hands into her back pockets. "We were supposed to hang out Saturday night and listen to the new Mutemath album, that's all."

"We can still do that," Seb assured her.

"Nah." Antonia pouted like the child she was. "Not if you're gonna smell like Heather What's-her-face."

Seb grinned. "What's the matter, you jealous?"

Antonia looked at him, and Seb thought he saw panic in her eyes before she looked away again. He wondered if there was a reason she didn't want to be alone Saturday night, something to do with her asshole dad.

"Maybe you're right," he said, straightening. "She's not really my type."

He didn't miss the smile Antonia tried to hide behind the *Spin* magazine she grabbed from their stash.

Seb knocked the magazine out of her hand, stretched out on the platform of the abandoned train station that served as their hideaway, and put his head on her lap. As expected, her fingers found their way into his hair. It had become a thing.

"New Mutemath, huh?" Seb stared out at the blue sky.

"Yep," she replied, popping the P.

Peering up at her, he winked. "Sounds a lot better than what I had planned, anyway."

Seb could have watched them all day. More precisely, he could have watched *Toni* all day.

It was still so surreal, having her in the same room as Lilly, Kayla, and Tiff, all working together to create a wall of sound so fucking gorgeous he wanted to weep.

"Shiiit," Jordan muttered beside him as they stood in the

Phactory's control room and watched the magic unfold in the live room. "Toni is bloody amazing."

"Right?" Seb's chest filled with pride. "I've never heard the band sound this good before. It's kinda scary."

Toni had taken everything that Candi had done for the songs and elevated it to an entirely new level. Seb didn't even think she realized how good she was, she was so humble about it. Confident, but somehow still unaware.

Whether she knew it or not, Toni was slowly becoming a part of this band, a part of the Lillys family. His family. All of them together, at last.

"Is there room for both of them, Candi and Toni?" Jordan folded his arms across his chest, his head nodding to the beat of the song. "She brings something entirely new to the table. I mean… I hate to say it. You know how much I love Candi."

Seb snorted. "It's me, Iggy. You and Candi get along about as well as the Gallagher brothers."

Jordan grinned. "Which one of us is Liam and which of us is Noel?"

"That's up for debate."

"If only we had that Oasis money," Jordan said, chuckling. His eyes were glued to the scene in the other room. "After the *CelebWatch* stuff, the label is even more dead set on keeping Candi in the mix, but if they hear this…"

Toni and Lilly were harmonizing over the breakdown of one of the new songs Lilly had added to the set. The way their voices blended made the hair on Seb's arms stand up, it was that good.

"That's bloody otherworldly," Jordan whispered, mirroring Seb's thoughts.

"Lilly likes her," Seb offered. "Shouldn't matter what the label thinks. I know it does, but it shouldn't."

Jordan hummed in agreement. "It's the way the business

works. Did you know she had my assistant calling all over Philly looking for a female guitarist that liked to cover Alice in Chains?"

Seb turned his head. "Lilly did? I had no idea how you found her. Kept meaning to ask."

"Yeah." Jordan turned back to the window. "Lilly had seen her play. Couldn't remember her name or the name of the bar."

Seb tried to wrap his head around that new tidbit. The universe had been conspiring against him. Or in his favor.

The jury was still out on whether his reunion with Toni was for the best or not. Sure, he was damn glad to have her back in his life, but what did the new Seb and Toni look like?

Ever since they left New York, he'd spent several sleepless nights staring at the ceiling of his hotel room and replaying moments from their past.

All the times he'd caught himself staring at her. The way he'd found any and every excuse to touch her. The white-hot anger he had when she started dating, well, anyone—and the way he'd pretty much sabotaged every relationship he had.

Seb never understood why he'd done those things, but he saw it now. Plain as day. He fucking loved her then, and he loved her now.

How had he not realized it before when it was so damned obvious? Not that Seb had known anything of love before Toni came into his life. No wonder he hadn't recognized it.

But now, all those confusing feelings, ones he'd long thought dormant, were wide-fucking-awake, crystal-fucking-clear, and screaming for him to do something about them.

Which, of course, he couldn't. Or shouldn't. At least, not while she was working for the band.

And if she becomes a permanent member…?

How great would that be for her, though?

It would kill him to be near her every day and not get as close to her as his heart demanded. Not tell her what he hadn't known to tell her all those years ago.

Seb took a breath and shoved those thoughts to the back of his mind. It was all theoretical, and it wasn't about him anyway. It was about Toni and what *she* wanted. Whatever that was, he'd do what he could to make it happen. Seb would lay the world at her feet, even if it meant losing her all over again.

The thought was enough to make his chest burn, but he was getting ahead of himself.

Candi was back on her best behavior, toeing the line at least. She and Lilly would work out whatever was going on with them; they always did. Things would go back to normal, whatever that was. And Toni would probably be offered a deal of her own, once the label got a look at her and heard what she could do.

Maybe then he and Toni could… "No," Seb muttered.

"No what?" Jordan asked, looking at him quizzically.

"Nothing."

The song came to an end, and Kayla stood to stretch. That was Seb's cue to check in with them. He pushed through the doors and walked into the room, stepping over cords and weaving his way around microphone stands.

He stopped when he got to Lilly.

"Taking a break? You've been at it for hours."

She practically buzzed with excitement, her eyes bright and her cheeks flushed rose-pink. Seb hadn't seen her like that in months. She flashed him an ivory smile, and it was dazzling.

"*Faen*, have we?" Lilly swiped at the damp strands stuck to her forehead. "I don't want to, but okay. We should maybe stop and refuel."

Lilly rarely got this worked up at a rehearsal. Seb turned to find the rest of them in a similar state, all exhausted and damp but apparently happy.

"Food!" Kayla yelled, climbing out from behind the drum kit and tossing her sticks to the mat. She turned to Seb, clasping her hands in front of her. "'Feed me, Seymour.'"

Seb chuckled. "I'll feed you, hold your horses."

"You been watching old musicals again?" Tiff asked Kayla as she wiped down her bass and set it in the stand.

"Hey, there are some great rhythms in those old songs," Kayla replied. "Some of the tap sequences in those Gene Kelly films? They were something else. I have a mad crush on Cyd Charisse."

"I'm not ragging on you. My favorite is *West Side Story*," Tiff said, grinning.

"*Spring Awakening*," Lilly added.

"Of course you'd say that," Kayla teased. "It's dark as fuck."

"It's not dark, it's just not...peppy."

"I'd hardly call *West Side Story* peppy." Tiff raised her arms above her head, stretching what must have been tired muscles.

Toni hadn't looked in Seb's direction during the exchange. He tried to catch her eye, but she'd turned to wipe down her guitar. Still, something about it seemed deliberate.

Seb frowned, hoping it was exhaustion and nothing he'd done. She'd seemed so happy a few minutes ago.

Okay, he was reading way too much into her body language. She was probably just tired. The band had been at it for hours and it was barely lunchtime. Which reminded him.

"So, food?"

"Can we get out of this place for an hour or two?" Kayla asked. "I love it here, but I don't even remember sunlight at this point."

"No kidding," Tiff agreed.

"I feel like a vampire. Am I sparkly yet?" Kayla pretended to inspect her arms. "Let me out of this dump. No offense, Richie!"

"None taken," came the engineer's reply through the monitor. "By the way, there's someone here for you."

Seb turned in time to see Candi standing in the outer doorway. Or, at least, he thought it was her. The pin-straight dark hair threw him off for a moment, but then she waved at him through the glass. He glanced at Toni and, sure enough, she was looking right at her.

"Fuck," he muttered and pushed through the door into the control room.

"Hey!" Candi jogged over to him. "Where my girls at?"

She was on something, Seb could tell right away. He was used to seeing her in various altered states. He couldn't be sure the others wouldn't notice.

"What are you doing here?" Jordan asked, his voice clipped.

"I missed you guys," Candi whined, trying to peer around him and into the other room. "I got bored in the city all by myself."

Her eyes were glassy and unfocused.

"Where's Masturini?" Seb curled his fingers around her bicep to steady her when she wobbled on her feet.

Candi pouted. "Tara is parking the car."

"Who the hell is Tara?"

"She's the shiny new bodyguard I got," Candi replied, looking at him like he should have known this already.

Seb didn't know any fucking thing except that, for someone who professed she wanted to help set things right for the band again, Candi seemed hell-bent on self-destruction.

"What happened to Eric?" Jordan pulled out his phone.

Candi made a sour face. "He wouldn't bring me down here, so I grabbed someone who would."

Fucktastic. Eric could be a pain in the ass, but he was good at his job. He knew how to handle Candi's antics. Seb glared at her.

"Oh, come on," she said, running a hand up his chest to curl around the back of his neck. "Don't be such a miserable bastard."

Seb eased out of her grip. "You do remember why we agreed you should stay in New York, right? Were you followed?"

"No" came the response from a voice to their right.

The woman who had answered was around six feet tall. She had sharp features, and her black hair had been pulled back into a sleek bun at her nape. The crisp white linen of her tunic stood in stark contrast to her dark-brown skin. In relaxed tan khakis, she looked more like she was on vacation than on the job, but Seb recognized the shrewd look in her dark eyes, as well as the familiar bulge at her hip and the earpiece she wore.

"Cobb. Tara Cobb," she said, extending her hand. Former military, he'd guess. Or FBI.

"Sebastian Quick." Her handshake was firm. Reassuring. "Does Masturini know you're here?"

Cobb gave him a sharp nod. "I informed him en route. I know he's against it, but he doesn't sign my paychecks."

"I get that, but…"

"But," Cobb said before he could finish, "I've also been apprised of the situation." She nodded toward Candi, who was digging in her purse.

Seb exhaled a slow breath when she only took out her phone and started taking selfies in the studio.

"I figured it was better to bring her here than to leave her to her own devices," Cobb said, moving close so only Seb could hear her. "The wig was her idea, but I rented a minivan so we'd be less conspicuous."

"Good thinking." Seb ran a rough hand through his hair as Candi opened a social media app. "Please don't post any of those."

Candi stopped and rolled her eyes at him, sighing heavily, but put the phone away.

Cobb pulled out hers. "I'm going to let Eric know we've

arrived. He made arrangements for her hotel, unless…uh…" She looked at Seb, the first hint of uncertainty in her expression.

"No, that's good," he rushed to clarify. "If she's staying tonight, she'll need a place to sleep. After we get some food in her."

"Whatever you need," Cobb said, typing rapidly with her thumbs. She slipped her cell into her pocket. "Eric's up-to-date and on standby."

Seb liked her already.

"Did someone say food?" Candi smiled up at Seb and pulled her sunglasses out of her hair to slip them on. "I'm fucking *starving*."

For lunch, Richie suggested a hole-in-the-wall taco joint around the corner from the studio, and they'd invited him along. Seb hadn't had a chance to get to know the guy, but Toni seemed to trust him and he was a total pro. There were no snide comments, no leering looks, only professionalism and courtesy. Richie had gone out of his way to accommodate their needs.

Seb hadn't missed all the gold and platinum records lining Richie's office. Phactory Sound would be an ideal place to record, if they were able to keep the location under wraps. He made a note to bring it up with Jordan.

When they arrived at Segundos Taqueria, Richie led them to a long row of tables the servers had pulled together for them. He took an end seat and Toni sat beside him, with Lilly on her other side, Tiff and Kayla across from them, and Jordan in between. Cobb took a small table by the door, which left Seb to sit with Candi. Great.

Throughout the appetizers, he kept trying to get Toni's attention, if only for a moment. Just to check in. Every time he caught her looking his way, she turned quickly away.

Next to him, Candi pressed in close, making a show of leaning her chest against his arm to look at his menu, as if they needed to share.

Seb sat back, picked up her menu from the table, and gave it to her, ignoring her pout.

"I could eat this guacamole all day every day," Kayla said, licking a bit off the heel of her palm.

"You say that about all food," Tiff replied. "I honestly don't know where you fit everything you consume. You must weigh, like, ninety pounds dripping wet."

"My dad calls me the runt of the litter," Kayla said, nonplussed.

"Flattering," Lilly chimed in.

Kayla shoved a chip loaded with guacamole into her mouth and spoke as she chewed. "I was a preemie, but I had a big appetite. My mom says I was always eating, so I wasn't in the NICU long."

"I was a preemie too," Toni said.

Seb cut his gaze to her, surprised. He hadn't known that. As if she felt his eyes on her, Toni pointedly did not look anywhere near his direction.

This time, there was no mistaking the sudden chill. Candi's presence certainly wouldn't help to thaw it.

Despite the things he and Toni had shared, Seb hadn't really had the chance to explain his relationship...friendship...whatever it was with Candi. Thinking back, Seb realized Toni hadn't really asked. He guessed they weren't there yet, but he itched to tell her.

The truth was, he *wanted* her to ask. Wanted the chance to confirm that there was nothing that would prevent them from figuring out what they could be to each other. And he knew what he wanted, even if he wasn't sure if it were possible.

"We're survivors, you and I," Kayla said to Toni. "Life tried to snuff us out early, but we gave it the finger and kept on going."

"Damn right," Tiff said.

"Were you a preemie too?" Toni grabbed a chip and stuck it into a bowl of black bean salsa.

"I don't think so, no," Tiff replied, her voice tapering off. She shoved a piece of quesadilla in her mouth. "So, Ms. Fairmount, what brings you down to the country? Run out of playthings in NYC?"

Tiff cut her eyes to Seb, and he frowned. *What the hell?* Tiff knew there was nothing going on between them.

Candi jumped on the opportunity. She wrapped her hands around Seb's bicep and put her head on his shoulder. "I couldn't stay away anymore. I, uh…" She turned so her lips were right by his cheek. Seb stiffened. "I missed you so much."

Toni stood abruptly and excused herself to go to the restroom.

Seb wanted to follow her but knew he shouldn't. Candi seemed to take that as a victory. She relaxed in her chair and picked up the menu again.

"I want something hot and spicy," she said.

"I thought the plan was for you to stay in Manhattan and"— Kayla held up air quotes—"recover. Where's your sling, anyway?"

Candi tossed the laminated menu onto the table. "This place is a dump. Don't they have any decent restaurants in Philly?"

"Nope," Kayla said, giving her a pointed look. "They're all in New York. You should head back. If you call now, I'm sure you can get your usual table at Sardi's."

Beside her, Tiff snorted.

Candi's gaze snapped to them. "You act like you aren't happy to see me."

"We don't understand why you would risk coming here," Lilly said. Her words were measured, but Seb could see the vein fluttering at the base of her throat. She was angry. Livid, if the daggers in her eyes were any indication.

Candi pulled out her phone and thumbed through it before holding it out to Seb. "Since the ruse is up anyway, I figured I didn't need to hide anymore."

Frowning, Seb took it from her. He cursed aloud when he saw the screen. The article was only hours old.

CelebWatch: BREAKING NEWS
Rock and Roll Dream Dies for the Oil Princess

"What the shit is this?" Seb asked her.

Jordan leaned over and took the phone, scrolling down as he read aloud. "'Socialite-cum-would-be-rocker Candace Fairmount was caught on video—sans sling—partying at the blowout birthday bash for her bestie, Naya Broward.'" He frowned. "I didn't get an alert for this."

"Christ." Seb ran both hands through his hair. This was *exactly* the kind of press they didn't want.

"Jesus, Candi," Tiff said, massaging her temples.

"Oh, joy. It gets better," Jordan said, reading on. "'Seems the heiress's injury, the one that allegedly prompted the band to bring in the mystery woman we told you about two weeks ago, isn't as serious as reported. We called it! Candi and Lilly are on the outs. Sources say it's a tug of war over manager Seb Quick.'"

Seb glanced at Lilly, who glared at Candi.

"Can someone explain why when the artists are women, they always make it about who's sleeping with whom?" Tiff asked. "Boy bands break up and it's all *creative differences*. We're reduced to catfights and hair-pulling."

"I don't see why we can't end this charade and get back to work," Candi said, completely nonplussed. "It would totally shut down the rumors. The showcase is in ten days. We can be ready by then if we buckle down."

"We're ready now," Kayla shot back.

Hurt flashed across Candi's face before she schooled her features into her usual expression. "It's my band too," she said, taking her phone back from Jordan. "The label wants me back in."

"What did they say?" Tiff sat up in her chair as she looked from Candi to Jordan.

"They *do* want you, Candi," Jordan replied. "But they also want an act that's reliable. One that won't pull a no-show if they're booked to headline a festival, for instance. It's not good for ticket sales. Fuck, we really need to hire our own bloody PR people."

Candi slammed herself back into the chair. "You do realize, *Jordan*, that Lilly and I are the reason we got signed to begin with. They want the Lilly and Candi show, not the...whatever this is now."

"You mean a better band?"

Candi leveled Kayla with a look that was meant to wither her. Kayla gave it right back.

"Before someone says something they might regret," Seb cut in, "could you all take a breath?" He turned to Candi, hoping she'd read the damned room for once.

"I'm not going to sit here and let them push me out of my own goddamned band." She crossed her arms and looked around the table. "This little situation is temporary, remember?"

"No one is pushing you out," Seb countered.

"As I told you before," Lilly said, her voice laced with profound disappointment, "it's up to you whether you want to be a part of us. Entirely up to you."

Candi relaxed. "Exactly, and I'm not going anywhere."

"Showing up here when you're supposed to be in New York," Lilly continued as if Candi hadn't spoken. "Showing up here *high* on whatever you're on," she all but hissed, standing to loom over the table. "Showing up here and throwing your weight around as if you have any at the moment… None of that tells us that you want what's best for *us*. The band."

Candi opened her mouth. Closed it. Looked at Seb for backup, but he had none to give. After all, what could he say? It was all true.

"I see what this is," Candi said, her eyes narrowing to slits. "This was never about giving me a second chance."

"A *second* chance?" Kayla interjected.

Candi shot to her feet. "This was only ever about cutting me out. Replacing me, as if you could with someone like—"

"Watch it," Seb warned Candi.

She barked out a laugh. "Or what, *Sebby*?"

Seb's jaw clenched so tight, he worried he'd break it.

The entire restaurant had grown eerily quiet. Thank God they were the only patrons, or this whole thing would have been on Twitter.

Toni chose that moment to return, her steps slowing as she got to the table. She glanced around the scene, then met Seb's eyes, frowning.

"Fuck this. I need to pee," Candi announced before tossing her napkin on the table and stalking toward the restrooms.

All eyes turned to Seb.

"You made her your problem," Kayla said. "Deal with it or we will. I'm sick of this shit."

Toni resumed her seat at the other end of the table. This time, she looked right at Seb. He saw confusion, but he could also see the hurt before she dropped her gaze.

Fuck.

"Scylla and Charybdis," Kayla muttered as she resumed her assault on the guac.

She wasn't wrong. Seb was indeed caught between a rock and a hard place. This pattern of chasing Candi and convincing her to do the right thing only to have her circumvent everything they were working toward was getting old. Seb was tired. But he'd signed up for it. All of it. Because, in the end, it came down to the family and keeping them together. Whether Toni was to be part of it was a conversation for later.

Judging by the look on her face, it would be a short one.

Resigned, he stood and went after Candi.

By the time he coaxed her back to the table, dinner had been served. The conversation was stilted, but they somehow managed to avoid another confrontation.

To her credit, Candi ate her food and said very little. She was also much more lucid. Seb was grateful for that. When the group got up to leave, he waited for Toni and touched her elbow, silently asking for a moment.

"Hey."

Toni turned her head, frowning. "What?"

"Everything okay?" Seb tried to keep his tone light.

She folded her arms across her body. "I'm fine."

"You don't seem fine. I mean, *we* don't." Seb waited for her to put him out of his misery, but Toni shifted her gaze to the flyers taped to the weathered wooden telephone pole beside them. "Really, Nia? The silent treatment? C'mon. Scream at me or something."

She looked at him. "And say what?"

"You've been...off all day. Did something happen before...? Did I do something?" *Please don't let Candi get to you.*

Toni rolled her lips between her teeth.

Seb waited, watching the debate play out behind her eyes. Finally, she let out a sharp exhale.

"You should go to Candi. I need to make a quick trip home."

It felt like a physical blow, and Seb struggled to maintain eye contact. He didn't want to lose the ground they'd gained, not over something like this. "We're still friends. Right?"

If there was to be nothing else between them, he hoped like hell he hadn't lost her friendship too. Hadn't lost his chance to be a part of her life.

"Friends," Toni said, her voice flat. She looked over Seb's shoulder toward their group. To where Candi stood waiting for him, no doubt. "Sure, Seb. We can be friends."

Toni jogged to catch up with Richie as he walked toward the studio. Seb could do nothing but stare after her.

A dude approaching the restaurant smirked as he reached for the door. "That looked harsh."

"What did you say?" Seb asked, frustration eating at him. "You have a problem?"

The guy held up his hands, eyes wide. "No, dude."

Good for him, because Seb was seriously fucked.

"Seb, are you coming?" Standing by the minivan, Candi held out her hand, so certain he would take it.

"What are you doing, Can?" He was beyond fed up. "What are you doing here? In Philly? We had a game plan, one you agreed to. One you helped orchestrate."

Candi pouted. "I know, but—"

"All you had to do was stay in New York and stay out of trouble," Seb continued, struggling to keep his voice low. "So what was all that bullshit? Do you *want* to lose everything? Everyone?"

"It already feels like I've lost everything." She was looking for reassurance.

Seb had none to give, but he tried. "No one is trying to push you out," he reminded her, hoping she would hear him this time. "You're doing a pretty good job of that on your own."

She looked up at him, her eyes accusing. "You certainly didn't waste any time replacing me."

"What are you talking about?"

"I'm not blind, Seb," Candi snapped. "You fucking her yet?"

Seb's jaw clenched. He held it shut, opting for silence rather than the alternative where he said something they would both regret. He took a deep breath and let it out slowly.

"Candi," he said with as much calm as he could maintain. "Go. Home. Stick with the plan or you *will* lose everything."

A slow smile spread across her lips. "Stick to the plan," she said with more emphasis than necessary. "Got it, loud and clear."

She climbed into the van and slammed the door shut.

Cobb, who had been standing a discreet distance away, frowned at him as if to say *What's going on?*

Seb shook his head. Fuck if he knew.

CHAPTER 29.

"WHAT DID YOU EXPECT?" YVETTE was anything but under-standing. For a hopeless romantic, she was surprisingly bitter. "The man isn't a saint. He hasn't been secretly pining for you for eight years and saving himself for your inevitable reunion. So he's fucking the heiress. So what?"

"Jesus, Yvette."

She used her spoon to crack the chocolate shell on her pint of Franklin ice cream. "He's young, he's hot, and she's…well…"

"Young, hot, rich, and famous," Toni supplied. "And you're right, I shouldn't be upset. Except that it sure hasn't stopped him from kissing me."

"And you're certain they're *together*-together? From what I've read, they split up a while back." Yvette eyed her knowingly. "If he was all up on you and then he went back to Blondie, then I'd be pissed. Don't sit there and stew, ask him what's going on. Because, from the little I've seen, Seb seems like a genuinely decent guy, even if I still haven't completely forgiven him for what he did to you."

"We were kids." Toni dipped her own spoon into the pint, avoiding the chocolate coating because she didn't want to die at Yvette's chocoholic hands. "And he had…reasons."

"For leaving or for staying away?"

Toni thought about everything Seb had said, about the guilt he'd carried for all those years. "Both, I guess, a lot of them misguided."

"He seems like someone with a lot of shadows following him."

"You could say that," Toni agreed. "But this thing with Candi, I really don't get it. He doesn't even seem to *like* her."

"What makes you think they're still sleeping together?"

"I…" Toni thought about it. "She just seems so possessive of him. You should have seen her at dinner. I thought she was going to hump him at the table."

"Maybe he broke it off and she doesn't want to take no for an answer. Didn't you say there's a no hookups clause in your contract?"

"Yeah."

Yvette picked a piece of chocolate out of the ice cream and popped it into her mouth. "Maybe they *had* to break it off."

"Huh." Toni hadn't considered that.

"Isn't that why he doesn't want to start anything with you?" Yvette asked. "For now, anyway."

"Yeah," Toni agreed. "We kinda agreed to wait until my contract's up."

"Which is soon," Yvette reminded her. "Assuming you want to explore something with him, which I'm pretty confident in saying you sure as hell do, it would probably be wise to clear the air. Find out, once and for all, if Candi is still in the picture."

Yvette's eyes narrowed at whatever expression Toni had on her face. She didn't know what she looked like, but she knew what she felt, and it wasn't what she'd expected. The thought of leaving the Lillys… It hurt more than it should.

The bell rang, startling her out of this revelation.

"You expecting someone?"

Toni shook her head as she got up. "No, you?"

"Who would I be expecting? I'm firmly in the no-drama zone, now that Sana and I are done."

Toni pressed the intercom. "Hello?"

"Uh, hey," came the scratchy voice. "It's Seb, can I come up?"

Toni's head whipped around to her roommate.

Yvette had frozen with the spoon halfway to her mouth. She got up. "Let the adventure begin. I'll be in my room listening to Massive Attack. Loudly."

Toni turned back to the intercom. "Sure, come on up." She pressed the buzzer.

Then she looked around the living room. She'd taken a shower after dinner, to clear her thoughts, and had left her clothes where they'd landed. She had a few seconds to run around, scoop things up, and shove them into her dresser before there was a knock on the door. Thank goodness her bed was at least made. She rarely folded the sofa bed, since they didn't often entertain company.

Seb was the picture of contrition when she opened the door, hands shoved into his pockets and head bowed as he looked up at her through his thick lashes. He was gnawing ruthlessly on his bottom lip, and she realized it was a nervous tic.

"What are you doing here?"

"Is it okay?" He peeked behind her, probably checking to see if the coast was clear. "I–I wanted to let you know we've called it for tonight. Everyone's in a food coma back at the hotel, so you don't need to come back in."

"You could have just called me. Or texted."

Seb nodded. "I could have done that, yeah. I, uh... Look, could we talk for a sec?"

"Yeah, of course. We're friends, right?"

Toni stepped back to let him inside and kicked herself for how snide that must have sounded. She'd been a little cruel to him earlier. Yvette was right; it hadn't been fair to jump to conclusions, despite Candi's behavior.

"You're always welcome," she added belatedly, hoping it softened the blow.

Seb turned to face her and her step faltered. His smile was so full of relief.

She returned it and they stared at each other.

Seb seemed to be giving her silent permission to look her fill, and she took him in, head to toe, and he did the same. Toni wondered what was on his mind. Recognized the fact that she desperately wanted to know.

"You want to sit down?"

Seb turned toward the sofa bed but spun around again. "I don't want to keep you up—I know you're probably tired. I–I need you to know something."

"Okay." Toni leaned back against the door.

"Right...so..." Seb laced his fingers together atop his head. It made the hem of his Henley ride up.

Toni found an interesting spot to look at on the floor.

"I swear, I had it all worked out on the way over here." He sighed heavily and Toni looked up to meet his gaze. "Nia..."

"I'm sorry about earlier," she heard herself say. "I was..." *Jealous.* "...a little surprised to see Candi. Things have been going so well. With the band, I mean."

Seb's arms dropped to his sides. "You guys sound fucking phenomenal," he breathed, awe in his voice. "God, it's been amazing to watch."

Toni smiled. "Yeah?"

"Yes, you *have* to know how much they love working with you." His voice was warm and filled with pride. Toni felt it in her solar plexus. "Lilly has really opened up. It's... Yeah."

"I didn't expect to love it so much, being in a band. Being in *this* band. I have a map, you know. Of what I want to do with my life. This wasn't on it," she admitted quietly.

Seb nodded as she spoke. "I get that, but... Things don't always work out the way we plan them. Sometimes the unexpected happens. The very last thing you ever thought would happen happens, and it leads to something better. Something more than what you ever thought you could have."

Toni met Seb's gaze.

He swallowed hard. "Candi and I aren't together."

Toni stopped breathing when he inched forward. "Okay," she croaked.

"I wanted you to know that."

"Why?" Her voice barely existed anymore. She looked up at his face, at the intensity in his eyes. The unspoken plea there.

"Jesus, Nia..." He leaned forward and pressed his forehead to hers. "I can't believe we're here like this."

"Neither can I." Toni closed her eyes and waited.

She didn't have to wait long.

Seb brushed his nose against hers. Long, warm fingers cupped her nape as he tilted her head back with just a hint of pressure. When their lips met, it was a whisper of a kiss, but it was enough to sap the strength out of her knees. They buckled and Seb caught her with a strong arm around her waist.

He kissed her as if he'd been holding his breath since the last time. He kissed her as if he'd been as starved for her as she'd been for him. He kissed her as if his sanity were on the line too. As if he were just as hungry, hopeful, and heartsick over all the time they'd lost.

Groaning, he stumbled forward and pressed her into the door, dipping his knees as he deepened the kiss with a groan that vibrated through her entire body.

And, Jesus Christ. If Toni thought their stolen kisses in the back room of the Unicorn were something, they were nothing compared to the way he was devouring her now.

Every sweep of his tongue against hers sent her reeling. Toni grabbed greedy handfuls of his shirt, desperate to feel the warmth of his skin beneath it. But as feral as Toni felt, Seb was a slow-moving storm.

He cradled the back of her head so tenderly, she wanted to cry. The kiss was soft and so freaking slow, making her drunk and setting her blood to boiling. Seb kissed like they had all the time in the world, but Toni knew she would die soon if he didn't put his hands on her. Anywhere. Everywhere. Now.

When breathing finally became an issue, Toni turned her head, gasping. "God…"

Seb moved his mouth to her neck, slipped his muscular thigh between her legs, slid one hand down to her ass as he pulled her in to his body, and rocked her against him. Want hit her so hard and fast that it knocked whatever breath she'd managed to collect right out of her lungs.

She was seriously about to combust.

"Goddamn," Seb breathed against her skin, hot and wet. "God, I… The things I want to do to you."

Do them, her body screamed, even as reason warned her to throw on the brakes. She had way too much on the line.

Seb appeared to be engulfed in a similar war within himself. He dropped his head to her shoulder, panting.

After a minute, he took a deep breath and let it out slowly. "Well, that was worth the wait."

A laugh bubbled up Toni's throat and burst from between her tingling lips. "Beats my high school daydreams."

Seb eased back and slid his hands up to her waist. He grinned down at her. "High school, eh?"

"Mmmm," she replied. Dazed. "As if you didn't know."

"I didn't," he said.

Seb's pupils were blown wide but rimmed in her favorite shade of green, and Toni couldn't look away. They stayed that way for a long minute until the corner of Seb's mouth tilted upward.

"This is getting awkward," she said slowly.

"No, it's not," Seb countered, looking every bit like a cat who'd just discovered the last bit of cream.

Toni wanted so badly to kiss him again, but memories of playing this little game of theirs, countless times before, tickled her competitive bone. Plus she loved rediscovering their common history.

"Do you remember the score?"

She blinked but kept her gaze steadily on his. "144 to 132, me."

Seb lowered his chin, his eyes still hot on her, and released his grip on her waist. "Dream on, pint size. You were never ahead of me."

"I so was," she shot back playfully, ignoring the urge to launch herself at him. "You lost, like, four games of Chicken in a row."

His jaw dropped open in exaggeration. "I call bullshit."

"Not bullshit," she countered, laughing.

They quieted, both grinning like fools, neither willing to lose their old game.

Toni ran a hand around to her nape and brought it forward, slowly, through her hair, over her shoulder, down into the V of her tee, between her breasts. Slowly caressing herself the way she hoped Seb wanted to do.

"Damn you," he growled, his eyes going half-lidded.

This was proving way too easy. When she licked her lips and let out a breathy sound, Seb rolled his eyes and turned away.

"Yes!" Toni exclaimed, laughing.

Shaking his head, Seb turned back to her, his eyes twinkling. He looked...happy. "That was fucking unfair, and you know it."

"You think I'd pass up a chance to use a new weapon in my arsenal?"

His grin was wicked.

"You want me," she said, loving the way his nostrils flared. "I'm going to use that against you."

Seb threw his head back and laughed. "When did you get to be so evil?"

Toni's smile softened as everything fell quiet between them again.

"Yes, I want you, and for more than...fulfilling a fantasy," he said, lifting a hand to brush it over her hair.

"Same," she admitted. "But—"

"There's no rush," he said, anticipating her protest. "I don't want this...me...to get in the way of what you want for your life."

Toni nodded. "Same."

Seb pressed his lips to her forehead. "Sleep well, Bennette," he said quietly against her skin.

"Sweet dreams, Quick." When he stepped back, Toni opened the door for him.

"Oh, trust me. They will be," he said as he started down the steps.

Toni closed the door, pressed her back to it, and slid to the floor in a puddle of goo.

"That sounded like a lot of fun. Why'd you stop?"

Yvette's voice made Toni jump. She made a noise of surprise and then she dissolved into giggles. "Timing. Besides, I wasn't about to sex him up with you five feet away," Toni quipped. "And what happened to you blasting music?"

Yvette looked at her as if she were the most naive person on the planet.

"Whatever," Toni said, too blissed out to care. "It was, though. A lot of fun."

"I can see that." Yvette slid down next to her and offered her the pitiful amount of melted ice cream that was left in the pint.

Toni shook her head. She didn't want to erase the taste of him so soon.

"You're awfully casual about this."

"About what?"

Yvette shrugged one shoulder. "I wonder... Well..."

"Spit it out, Yvette."

"While you were out here *clarifying things* with Sebastian, I got to thinking. I mean... What are you doing?"

Toni frowned. "I'm sitting on the floor with my nosy best friend."

Yvette gave her a look. "That's not what I asked, and you know it."

"What do you mean, what am I doing? You're the one that told me to, and I quote, 'let the adventure begin.'"

Yvette nodded. "I did, and you did, and I'm still so proud of you. But I didn't expect this little twist."

Toni turned to face her. "No one is twisting. There's no twist. Shonda Rhimes is not writing my life story, though I know you wish she were."

"Oh, that would be juicy." Yvette grinned. "But no, I don't mean it like that. I mean...I guess after you got a little ego boost from this gig, I thought you'd see yourself in a different light."

"What's wrong with my light?"

"Not a damn thing, girl, I keep telling you," Yvette said. "Except when's the last time you went on a date? A real date?"

"I—" Toni's mouth remained open around the elongated vowel. She couldn't really call any of her recent interactions with Seb a date, though her insides tingled just thinking about him. The truth smacked her right between the eyes. "I don't know."

"Which proves my point. You have a goal in mind, your

career. And that's fine. But do you want more? A relationship? A family? All that jazz? Not that you need that to be complete," she hastened to add. "But have you thought about any of that stuff?"

"Honestly, I haven't," Toni answered. "Would it be nice? Yeah. But it's not like I feel like I'm missing anything in my life right now."

"And that's cool, babe. I wasn't telling you to throw yourself at Seb, or anyone. I'm only suggesting that you not put your plans in jeopardy for something that may not last. I want you to be happy."

Happy.

What did that even mean? Toni was happy playing music. Recording made her happy. Performing made her happy, too, though she didn't always want to admit it.

Toni had never, ever thought she'd see Seb again. She hadn't fantasized about being with him since before he skipped out of Bordon. Was this thing between them just that? A fantasy?

As far as relationships went, she liked some of the trappings, the doing things together, the getting to know someone, and the sex.

Okay, she really liked the sex. Really, really.

But could she, *should she* have any of that with Seb? Didn't she owe it to herself to figure that out? After.

After she fulfilled her contract. After she did what she'd signed on to do for the Lillys. After she got paid. And after she signed her name on the dotted line and Phactory Sound was hers and the Lillys were in her rearview mirror. Then she'd be free to explore. Right?

"I'm not happy, but I'm not unhappy either," Toni finally answered. "And I'm not waiting or settling—I'm doing my thing. Eye on the prize."

Yvette nodded. "Just be careful, okay? This guy has a place

in your heart that's been there for a long time. It may have been sealed tight for the last eight years, but seals have a way of getting broken."

As if Toni needed any more proof that Yvette knew her better than anyone.

In the end, it really only came down to one thing. Was there a place for Seb in her life anymore, or for her in his? It was too early to tell, sizzling kisses aside, what a Seb-and-Toni might look like. Whether it would be a solid friendship or something infinitely more. And what if they tried for the more and ended up estranged again?

She'd just gotten him back. She wasn't ready to lose him.

"I want to know him, *this* Seb," she admitted quietly. "I want him in my life. I know that much."

"Well, then, ignore me. Think about what you want, what you really want out of a friend, or even a partner, and decide whether he can give it to you."

"Guess I have a few days to figure it out."

Yvette stood and reached for her. "He'd better not screw up again, or I'm coming for him."

Toni adored how protective Yvette was of her. She gave great advice for someone whose own love life was perpetually in flux.

Toni smiled, taking Yvette's hand and letting her pull her to her feet. "I love you."

"Awww." Yvette gave her a squeeze before pulling her into a half hug. "I love you, too, chickadee, but I need to go hose myself down. Why didn't you tell me I eat ice cream like a two-year-old? This shit's everywhere."

CHAPTER 30.

THE BAND WAS DOWN TO its last rehearsal before the planned move back to New York. They needed to be there a few days before the showcase to meet with the stylist. Seb had to admit he was curious about what they had in mind for Toni.

She had an eclectic sense of style. Some days she was nineties rocker grunge, others she was sleek and sophisticated, and yet other days she dressed as if she wanted to disappear.

The *CelebWatch* thing blew over quickly, thanks to the latest Hollywood sex tape. Seb was relieved. He watched the tension drain from Toni little by little as the days went on. He also didn't miss the way Lilly and the others had fallen in love with her.

He couldn't blame them.

One week removed from the kiss in her apartment, and he hadn't been able to think of much else. He woke up hard as granite every morning, and not even an indulgent jerk in the shower had done anything to abate the bone-deep ache he had for her now.

"I'm going to miss this," Richie said.

Seb's head snapped up. He'd been sitting on the sofa in the control room, his head in his hands, lost in thought. He'd nearly forgotten where he was.

Richie nodded his head toward the live room where the band was wrapping up one of the tracks from the set list.

"I don't think I've ever enjoyed a project this much," Richie continued. "I haven't even had to do much, but it's been kinda cool to watch that come together in there."

Seb looked past him and through the glass. There was a break in the music and the girls were laughing at something Toni had said. The mics hadn't caught it, but the laughter was loud and clear.

"They've got something special, don't they," Seb said. It wasn't really a question.

Richie nodded. "I hate to admit it, but yeah."

Seb looked at him. "Why hate?"

The other man sighed and swiveled to face him. "It's rare to come across someone like Toni. A natural musician. She's got an ear for production, too, in addition to her mad guitar skills. And did you know she could play the violin?"

Seb shook his head. "No, I didn't know that."

"She didn't either." Richie leaned back in his chair.

It was a high-back leather office chair that often seemed like an extension of the man. He zipped back and forth on the hardwood every day like a Roomba.

"Her first session here, she came in with this local singer-songwriter who'd found her in a Craigslist ad."

Seb raised his eyebrows.

"Yeah," Richie agreed. "I know. Anyway, the guy said he might want some strings on one of the songs. They couldn't find anyone available, and it was holding up the session. Finally, out of frustration, I guess, Toni walked into the instrument room and came out with a violin. That woman sat down, picked out the notes, took a second to tighten the bow, and recorded the damn part. It was a simple line, but still. When I asked her about it, Toni stared at her hands in disbelief. 'I haven't touched a violin since the ninth grade,' she admitted to me."

"Shit." As far as Seb remembered, she'd only taken a few lessons after school before giving it up.

Richie looked him in the eye. "I want her to stay in Philly, but...I'd be a liar and an asshole if I didn't recognize what's going on in there."

Seb nodded. "I hear you. And I was thinking, Jordan and I are going to tell the label the girls want to record here."

"Do they?" Richie's eyes widened.

"Lilly loves it here, and everyone else has been so relaxed," Seb told him. "It's such a different vibe than they're used to."

"Dude," Richie said, leaning forward. "I would clear the books to have them record here. Best of both worlds, as far as I'm concerned. I'd get to engineer?"

"Man, of course," Seb assured him.

"And I'd get to ease Toni into being here on a regular basis, though..." He paused as the band started up again. "If things keep going the way they are, I don't see her being here full-time. Do you?"

Seb frowned. "Full-time?"

"Yeah, well, as full as she'd want," Richie said. "Once she finishes with this contract, she's coming on as my partner. Didn't she tell you?" Richie frowned. "Shit, I hope she hasn't changed her mind already."

Seb stood and walked over to the glass separating the two rooms. So that's why she needed the money. Made sense. Toni was never one for life on the road. In the spotlight. He wondered why she hadn't mentioned this to him.

The band was in full swing, and Lilly stepped up to the mic, her voice soaring over the instruments. Her eyes were closed, and she swayed to the music.

Across the room, Toni's eyes were fixed on the blond, a satisfied smile on her kissable lips. She looked so happy, so completely engaged. Maybe she had made up her mind after all.

"I think you're right," he said at last, feeling both elated at the prospect of Toni finding a home with the Lillys and devastated at what that might mean for the two of them. Contract clause or not, he knew all too well the pitfalls that arose from getting involved with someone you worked with.

"Scylla and Charybdis," Richie said, echoing what Kayla had said days ago. When Seb turned around, Richie chuckled. "Rock, meet hard place."

"We're gonna take a break," Lilly's voice came through the monitors.

Richie turned and gave them an "okay" sign. The women shed their instruments and stretched.

Seb watched as Toni was pulled into a hug by Tiff and Kayla. Lilly begrudgingly joined in, and then the quartet dissolved into laughter. Scylla and Charybdis indeed.

Seb found her sitting on a piano stool in one of the isolation booths, hunched over a blond acoustic with her back to the door. The earbuds she wore were plugged into her phone.

Toni plucked lightly but intently at the strings. The sound of the music was faint, and he could only make out the occasional chord, but the progression seemed familiar.

She played for a moment longer before popping the earphones out to dangle from her neck. Her shoulders sagged with a heavy breath, and the sight of it pinched Seb's already guilty conscience.

"What are you working on?"

Toni tapped her phone to stop the track. "I'm only noodling."

Seb stepped farther into the room and let the door shut behind him. The sudden silence was deafening, and Seb wondered if she could hear his racing thoughts. There was so much he wanted to say. To ask.

"Sounded familiar."

Toni turned to look at him over her shoulder. The light in the room was sparse, but Seb could still make out the challenging glint in her eye. "Does it?"

"Yeah."

She pursed her lips and slid her gaze to the side as if deciding what and how much to share. Shrugging, she returned her focus to the instrument in her hands. As she played, the origin of the music crystalized in Seb's mind and he stepped back from it and from her, from thoughts he'd tried very hard to suppress since their last kiss.

Toni hummed as she played, the same melody he'd heard when he walked in, but now he could hear the marriage between the old and the new.

Seb folded his arms and leaned a shoulder against the wall. "When did you finish it?"

"I haven't," she replied, still strumming. "Hadn't even thought about it in forever."

"Why now, then?"

That challenging gaze flicked to his again. "Just came to me, I guess."

Seb cocked his head. "You guess?"

A stray curl had fallen over Toni's eyes, and she blew it away with a quick breath before a tiny smile touched her lips. "What else could it possibly be, Sebastian?"

Seb's chest tightened at the way her voice curled around his name, and he felt his lips tug up in a matching grin. He wanted to eat her alive.

Fortunately, she had turned her attention back to the guitar.

He moved to the piano and rested his elbows on the top so he could see her hands. He'd always loved to watch her play.

"I'm surprised you remember it," she said. There was something in the tone of her voice. An unspoken dare.

Seb accepted it. "I told you, I remember everything," he said.

Toni's fingers faltered for a millisecond. No one else would have noticed, but Seb still knew her. Somehow, despite the miles and years that had separated them, he still knew Antonia Bennette. She was still...her.

Toni strummed with purpose, striking each chord as if it meant something to her. She hummed louder, hints of unsung lyrics behind the rhythm in the melody.

Seb didn't believe it had *just come to her*. He hoped she'd been as affected by the other night, by all the time they'd spent around each other, as he'd been. Maybe there was more than a crack in the door.

"You okay?" Her voice startled him out of his straying thoughts.

"Yeah." Seb cleared his throat. "I came to check on you, actually."

"Check on me?"

Seb nodded.

"I'm good. Needed a minute to myself. Got a text from Mo. Mary's been trying to get him to take Minx back so she can come get it from him, since I'm being an ungrateful little witch."

Seb's brow rose.

"Her words," Toni clarified.

"I can't see Mo doing anything she'd ask him to do," Seb said. "Your mom may have inadvertently brought you and your pop closer together."

"Ha, yeah." Toni made a face. "Anyway, I needed a minute. I'm okay, though."

"You sure?"

"Yep." She popped the P on the single word, turning one

syllable into two. It was one of the many little tics that he had missed. "I have nothing more to say to or about my mother."

"Gotcha. I, uh, I also wanted to say again, good call on using the Phactory for rehearsal. Everyone loves it here." Seb gave himself props for having the good sense not to pry. There was no use trying to force her to open up, especially given their history. "You, uh… You do a lot of work here?"

There. He'd given her a door. It was totally up to her whether to open it or keep it closed.

Toni placed a hand on the strings to stop their ringing. She looked up at him, and he could see her working through how much she wanted to share.

"Richie told you," she stated. Seb nodded and she mirrored him. "It took me a long time to get my foot in the door in this scene."

Seb held her gaze. He was afraid to say a single word, afraid she'd stop there when he wanted to hear more. He wanted to know everything. There was only so much he'd been able to glean of her burgeoning career from Google. He still knew next to nothing about her life.

Toni set the guitar on the floor, resting it between her knees.

"You were right, you know."

"About what?" Seb leaned closer. Toni kept her eyes down. He wished like hell she'd look at him.

"No one took me seriously at first. It didn't matter how good I was, I couldn't get anywhere. Couldn't even get paid for the work I did manage to get. Plenty of those 'play for free and you'll get experience' gigs but no real jobs. It was…" She let out a bitter huff of a laugh. "It was demoralizing."

"Shit, sorry." Seb wanted to go back in time and punch every asshole who had mistreated her. Of course, he'd have to start with himself. "How did you finally break through?"

"I kept coming back, kept showing up. People would get sick or stuck or injured and I'd fill in." There was pride in her voice and Seb was glad to hear it.

"You made yourself unforgettable."

Toni looked up at him and her smile reached her eyes. He lost his power of speech for a moment.

"Well, I *am* pretty good."

Seb returned her smile. "You're fucking incandescent, Nia."

Her own smile dipped at the nickname and Seb straightened, an apology on the tip of his tongue for crossing their invisible line. Again.

"No one else has ever called me that, you know." The words were softly spoken. Intimate.

He let out a slow breath. "I should hope not."

One delicate eyebrow flicked up. "You think you're so special?"

"No," Seb answered, going for honesty. "No, I'm not special. But...maybe...someday I can become someone special."

Her lips parted slightly, all traces of amusement gone and replaced with something Seb was afraid to put a name to. Surprise? Hope? Definitely desire.

Whatever it was, he didn't want her to stop looking at him like that. Ever.

Seb leaned back against the door. It was probably the only thing holding him up.

Toni's eyes glittered in the low light of the booth, a million thoughts blinking behind them like stars. He wanted to know each one intimately.

A wistful smile stretched her lips and she shook her head ever so slightly. Toni returned her attention to the guitar, and Seb blinked for the first time in minutes.

She was so fucking beautiful, he ached.

She'd tied her hair into a ponytail, a cloud of curls that dangled from the crown of her head exposing her long neck. His gaze caught on the curve where her neck met her shoulder, a spot he'd once caught himself fantasizing about as a teen before he'd dismissed it. What an idiot that guy had been.

Toni resumed playing. It was the same song, only now she played with purpose. Her fingers flowed over the strings, a sight he had always loved. And then she opened her perfect, cupid's-bow lips and sang.

I am under you.
How could I be so wrong?
The years have not scrubbed you from my veins.
I am under you
Though it's been too long
Since you almost kissed me in the rain.
I am under you.
Strange to ever think that I was free.
I am under you, and I hope that you're not over me.

Seb's heart pounded in his chest as the words registered in his brain. Jesus Christ, he was trying to be good. Trying to do right by her for once in his miserable life.

Toni kept playing, though she hummed the melody. Perhaps she'd run out of words.

Seb sure had.

She looked up at him and gave him a shy smile.

Seb pushed off the door and took the two steps to her at the same time Toni put the guitar down and stood.

He pulled her into his arms, and they crashed together, all lips and teeth and tongues.

Toni wrapped her arms around his neck and hooked one knee

up over his thigh. Molded herself to him as Seb cradled her head in one hand, the other hand cupped around her thigh to hitch her up higher.

She was desperate, making hungry little noises that made him positively feral.

Seb groaned and turned until her back hit the carpet-covered soundproofing panel on the wall. Toni's legs went around his waist like they belonged there.

Fumbling for the door, he flipped the lock, grateful that the glass on the window was slim enough that they wouldn't be seen from this angle because Seb had no intention of letting her go.

"Seb." Toni broke away, breathless. "I need…"

"I've got you," he said, dropping his mouth to her neck, to nip at the soft skin there. She smelled faintly of coconut, a scent he now realized he'd long associated with her. Seb pressed kisses into her skin, and she angled her head away to give him more access. She practically vibrated in his arms.

Her legs bracketed his waist and Seb dropped one hand to cup her ass. His already hardening cock filled fast as she began to undulate against him.

Oh. Hell.

He wanted to do *everything* to her but some tiny part of his brain, at least, registered where they were. But they were alone.

Seb rocked into her, making sure she felt the evidence of his arousal right where he knew she needed it.

Toni moaned softly and Seb's blood roared. He growled low in his throat and returned his attention to her skin, grazing along the column of her throat with lips and tongue and a hint of teeth that seemed to unravel her.

He wanted her to come undone. He wanted that more than he wanted his next breath.

"Nia," he breathed in her ear. "Tell me."

"I…" She panted against him, her hips moving with increasing urgency. "Fuck, you're so… I need…"

Seb lifted his head and she leaned back to look at him, eyes heavy-lidded and soft. He'd never thought he'd get this. Never thought he'd be allowed to have this with her. Damn well knew he didn't deserve it, but he wasn't strong enough to pull away. Not right now.

He lowered her to her feet. Keeping her gaze in his, he slipped a hand between them and found the button of her jeans. He ran a finger along her waistband as he searched her eyes.

She gave one jerky nod and sighed with relief when Seb flicked open the button. Her eyes slid closed as he lowered the zipper and slipped his hand between her flesh and the elastic of her underwear.

Heat. Slick, wet heat met his touch and Seb had to bite back another growl. The way her mouth went slack made him want to rip every stitch of clothing from her delectable frame, lay her out on the piano, and devour her.

But time. And location. Thank God for the little sense he retained.

Seb found the spot where she throbbed, pressed it gently, and she shivered. Circled it with the tip of his finger, and she moaned so loudly he was grateful they were in a soundproof room because he wanted to hear her.

"Fuck, Nia… You're so beautiful like this."

Her eyes fluttered open into slits, but it was enough for him to see the hunger in them. She bit her lip and rocked against his hand.

Gazes locked, Seb let her find her pleasure. Loved that she felt free enough to use him to chase it.

"Seb," she whispered. "I'm… I'm gonna…"

"Let go," he told her, eyes drinking in the way desire made her skin glow. When she began to flutter around his fingers, Seb wrapped an arm around her waist.

She shivered and let out the tiniest squeak before her entire body shuddered in his arms. Seb almost lost it right fucking there. He throbbed painfully against the zipper of his jeans, but he wasn't about to look away.

"God…Seb…" After a minute of what looked like trembling bliss, she sagged against him.

"Holy shit," he whispered. "Holy fuck. Nia…"

Seb withdrew his fingers when she rested her forehead against his chest. They were sticky, wet, and he had the overwhelming urge to lick them clean…so he did.

Toni straightened and watched him, her lips slightly parted and her eyes wide with disbelief. "Oh my God," she said, breathless and panting.

Seb's cock pulsed dangerously as the taste of her exploded on his tongue. He was close to ruining his pants.

Toni watched, rapt, and then her gaze dropped to his groin. She looked up at him from under her lashes, and before he could protest, she had his zipper open and had taken him in hand.

It was a shock to the system, the feel of her fingers around him. And perhaps the purest relief he had ever known.

"Wait," he groaned, shuddering. "You don't…"

A squeeze of her hand cut his words off and he grabbed her shoulder to keep from falling as she began to stroke, hard and fast.

It was quick and dirty, the only way it could be with him so worked up. He was going to come, and it was going to be a mess.

As if sensing it, Toni cupped her other hand over him as the first wave hit.

Seb's knees threatened to buckle as white-hot pleasure shot up his spine. He had to bite down hard to contain the scream that tried to crawl up his throat. Images of her on her knees, on her back, of him on his knees looking up at her, all of the things he wanted to do with her his mind supplied as he tumbled down and down and down.

He rested his head against the wall as the last slivers of ecstasy sliced through him.

She raised her hand toward her mouth, eyes riveted to his release on her palm.

"Don't," he managed to say.

She stopped and looked at him, confusion all over her face.

"Better to be safe."

A dawning understanding filled her eyes and she nodded. Toni gave him one more soft stroke before she let him go and turned her face into his neck. After a moment, she moved away, leaving a sudden burst of cool air in her wake.

Seb was able to turn his head enough to watch her pull a cloth from her bag and wipe her hand. She returned as he sagged against the wall, his lungs still working hard to reroute the oxygen back to his brain.

Toni smirked up at him as she cleaned him up.

"How bad is it?" His voice was like sandpaper.

"Not very," she rasped, a grin tugging at her lips as she tucked him in and zipped him up. She tossed the cloth into a wastebasket by the door, then fixed her own clothing.

Toni studied him for a long minute. "That was unexpected."

"I kinda think it was inevitable." Seb dared a grin.

She seemed to think it over before she nodded. "Maybe, but the timing could have been better."

"I know," he conceded, sobering.

She nodded again and cut her gaze away as she stepped back.

Seb wanted her close. Wanted to reach for her, but now that the haze of desire had cleared, he wondered if he hadn't fucked everything up.

"Are you okay?" *Are we?*

Toni waved a hand, dismissing his concern. "Yeah." She walked over to the guitar. "Don't overthink this. It was...probably inevitable, like you said, but it doesn't have to change anything."

Ah. Right.

He cleared his throat and levered himself off the wall. "So, that thing you were playing..."

Toni turned to look at him and he was relieved to see her smiling. "Did I seduce you with my siren song?"

He grinned. "Something like that. It's one of ours, isn't it? From before."

"Yeah. You like what I've done with it?" She picked up Minx. Only then did he notice the braided leather strap attached to her, and a different kind of warmth bloomed in his chest. "It's not finished, obviously, but..."

Seb stared. He couldn't help it. That she'd kept his gift all this time...

"I love it," Seb confessed because he couldn't say the words he really wanted to say. He was falling, had fallen.

The way her smile softened when she looked at him, he thought maybe she understood.

CHAPTER 31.

BACKSTAGE AT JOHN'S PUB, THE New York crowd was restless and animated. The room was packed with industry people, promoters and event organizers and venue owners alike. And, of course, YMI execs.

Toni was nervous, though she didn't know why. This wasn't her gig, not really. She was meant to be a prop. A stand-in. But somehow over the course of the last month, she'd been a part of something. And it had felt good.

These last few weeks with the Lillys, rehearsing and relaxing, Toni had felt like one of them. Her imagination had been quick to supply what it would be like to really be in a band like this. To travel with them and create songs with them, to laugh and bond and do all of the things she'd always professed to never want. And would likely never have done.

She shouldn't want it but... If Candi wasn't invited back, would she stay? Could she?

Would they want her to? Would Seb? Could she and Candi both be part of the band?

"Stop frowning," Kayla said, nudging her with the toe of her strappy sandals. The stylist had put the redhead in a sleek, off-white romper. It was elegant, and Kayla looked amazing in it, but it wasn't *her*.

Kayla gave Toni a one-armed hug and Toni smiled with gratitude.

"Sorry, this whole live-gigging thing is kinda new to me, at least in front of an audience this big."

"Get used to it," Tiff said. "This is nothing. After tonight, everyone's going to be after you. I still don't get why you haven't been playing out more, making a name for yourself."

She tugged at the hem of the pleated mini they'd put her in. Tiff, normally so comfortable in her own skin, seemed anything but. Again, she looked all right—cute, even—but it wasn't her style at all.

"Not everyone wants to be a rock star," Seb chimed in as he entered the back room.

It was a spacious green room, at least three times the size of the one at the Electric Unicorn, brightly lit and well furnished with the kind of amenities Toni had only read about in magazines. Catered food and drink, enough to feed an army, fluffy towels, and vases filled with fresh flowers, all courtesy of YMI.

Tiff and Kayla both took seats in front of the enormous vanity, touching up their makeup and fixing their hair.

Toni wondered if she should have made more of an effort. She'd thrown on a little mascara and some lip gloss before she left her hotel, but she hadn't blown out her hair. She left her natural curls to do whatever they wanted, adding only a little product in them to moisturize. At least she'd worn the outfit that had been chosen for her.

She'd expected to be poked and plucked, greased up and stuffed into some god-awful leather contraption, but Lea, the stylist, had shown up to her hotel room, taken one look at her, asked what her favorite color was, and left.

Toni looked down at her designer black jeans and leather biker boots and wondered if she'd be allowed to keep them. The jeans fit like a second skin and were the most comfortable pair she'd ever worn. The same went for the boots.

Both, undoubtedly, cost more than her entire wardrobe. In fact, the only thing on her person that she could probably afford was the vintage Runaways tee Lea had fashionably distressed and the purple tank she wore underneath.

The look was edgy and stylish but more her than what Tiff and Kayla wore.

Tiff caught her eye in the mirror. "What's with the frown?"

"Just wondering if I should put on more makeup or, I dunno…" Toni shifted on her feet.

"You look fine," Kayla assured her. "At least you don't have to worry about spilling anything on your bright-white jumpsuit thingy. I'm afraid to even have a slice." She cast a longing glance at the enormous New York–style pizza on the buffet table. "It's cruel."

"You'll live," Tiff said, laughing.

The band had left Philly two days ago. Seb and Jordan had insisted they take some time off after the grueling schedule they'd had.

Toni had spent the time at Phactory Sound, learning a bit about the running of the place. She didn't have all of the money in hand yet, but Richie was excited to get her up to speed.

There were moments when Toni caught herself looking for the girls in the live room or expecting to find Lilly in an iso booth plucking at the piano, Seb at her shoulder helping her to craft a new song.

She caught herself missing them, and missing Seb most of all.

The time off was probably for the best, especially after their encounter in the iso booth. It had been incredibly hot, but also premature. The chemistry between them was bound to be explosive, but Toni wasn't sure what else they could or should have. When he told her he was needed in New York, she didn't ask him to stay.

She also hadn't missed the disappointment in his eyes.

Now that she was here, it all came flooding back, how right it felt. The band. Him.

Toni couldn't lie to herself anymore. The idea of belonging to something bigger than her was intoxicating, and the idea that she and Seb could make something out of the rubble of their past so very tempting. Could the universe finally do her a solid and grant her both impossible things?

"You all look amazing," Seb said. His gaze swept the room before landing on Toni, and the smile he gave her was private. Her skin heated from the look in his eyes. He held her gaze as he walked over. "You ready for this?"

She nodded. "As I ever will be."

"She's going to rock," Kayla said, winking at her.

"I'm so fucking anxious," Tiff exclaimed. She jumped up from her seat and shook out her arms, rocking her head back and forth as if to expel the excess energy.

"Where is Jordan?" Lilly had claimed a quiet corner and had sat there with her eyes closed for the better part of an hour. Toni figured it was part of her pregame ritual.

"Jordan's sitting with the twins," Seb replied.

"The twins?"

Seb turned to Toni. "The brothers that acquired the label."

"Ah, the Silicon Valley money," she recalled.

"Assholes," Tiff said. "I still can't believe they fired Carlos." She turned to Toni. "He was the one who signed us."

"He fought hard to get them to take all of us," Kayla added.

At Toni's confusion, Seb spoke up. "They originally wanted Lilly as a solo act."

"But I thought..." Toni stopped there, afraid she'd overstep. "Why did they fire him?"

"Cleaned house," Seb replied. "It's common when someone

new takes over. They fill the staff with people they know. In this case, they didn't know anyone in the music business, so they went after the people with the best rosters."

"Poached, I believe, is the correct word," Lilly added.

"Yep," Tiff said. "Clueless vultures."

"Just what the industry needs," Kayla grumbled. "More people who care more about the bottom line than the music."

"Shhh," Lilly hissed. "Save that for later, when suits and reporters aren't sitting less than a meter away."

"You're on in five," Seb informed them, checking his watch.

The butterflies in Toni's stomach morphed into velociraptors.

Toni hit the final chord of the first song and let out the breath she'd been holding. Her fingers tingled with the buzz of playing live, or maybe a lack of oxygen. She turned to Tiff, whose grin showed all of her straight white teeth.

She'd pulled her braids up into a high ponytail and they swung over her shoulder, shiny and black, as she plucked the closing notes on her bass.

Behind them, Kayla put her hand on a cymbal to silence it, signaling the end of the song.

In addition to the festival organizers, there were tour promoters, MTV execs, and various other movers and shakers in the crowd. Toni recognized one of the reporters as the man from the alley behind SAGA, the one that helped them dodge his colleagues.

Everyone was there to hear good music, and so far, they didn't seem disappointed.

"Thank you for being here, New York City! We hope you're ready to rock," Lilly purred into the mic and the crowd went wild, screaming and whooping like they were the Beatles.

Toni had never seen anything like it, much less been on the receiving end.

She turned back to Tiff, amazed.

Tiff winked at her. "Welcome to the big leagues."

They launched into the next song, and Toni immediately locked into Kayla's groove. Tiff's bass had more of a prominent role in this tune, and Toni was more than happy to lay back and let her have the spotlight. It gave her a chance to be more of a spectator.

She'd known it already, from the short time she'd spent working with her, but Lilly was a star.

Tall and angelic, she wasn't afraid to get dirty. Lilly was surprisingly acrobatic as she performed, often squatting low to make eye contact with the crowd or jumping up and down to get them to follow along.

During the third song, she actually stretched out on the floor and sang the first verse, back flat and long legs crossed. Toni had seen her do that before in a YouTube video.

She remembered it because Candi had stood over her and played, staring down at her like she wanted to eat her. It had been incredibly erotic.

Toni wasn't Candi, but she felt weird just standing still. She wandered over toward Lilly, who moved to her knees and smiled.

She beckoned Toni over with a seductive wave of her fingers.

Toni locked her gaze with Lilly's and launched into her solo while Lilly conducted her like an orchestra. It was such a rush, Toni couldn't stop smiling.

As the song came around to the closing verse, Lilly stood and hooked an arm around Toni. Pulling her to her side, she held the microphone between them.

Toni lifted a questioning brow.

Lilly pointed with the mic. "Sing the next bit."

Toni hesitated but did as she'd asked, taking over on lead vocals.

A small portion of the tickets had been sold to the public. From all reports, many of them had been scalped for twice as much as they were worth, the demand was so high.

People sang along, a choir of voices surrounding hers as she dug deep, past her fear of being front and center. Behind the curtain she'd kept closed all her life, the one that had kept the spotlight from shining down upon her.

Lilly's hand tightened on her shoulder, and Toni glanced at her when she picked up the harmony, locking into Toni's lead.

They'd sung together many times in rehearsal, but it felt nothing like this. Nothing like this rush of driving the song forward to its climactic finish. It was exhilarating. It was overwhelming.

It was too much.

When they got to the final chorus, Toni flubbed the guitar part which made her miss a vocal cue. Tiff and Kayla compensated, playing through another measure of the instrumental. "Toni B, everybody!" Lilly was quick to jump in, but it was as if the spell had been broken. "Let's give her some love!"

There was a smattering of applause, and a girl in front of the stage whooped. "Yeah, Toni!"

"Where's Candi?" another yelled, and others echoed the demand.

Toni made the mistake of looking out in the direction of the heckler. While a few people wore sympathetic and encouraging expressions, others were openly hostile. A few middle fingers were tossed her way and she flinched.

A half-empty cup came flying through the air toward Toni. It was batted down by one of the security guards, while two others grabbed the apparent offender and hustled him out.

Shaken, Toni backed away from the front of the stage.

"Ignore them," Tiff leaned in to say in her ear when she returned to her spot. Tiff hadn't been in any way hostile toward Toni, but it had been clear her allegiance lay with Candi. Or, at the very least, torn between her and Lilly.

"We want Candi!" came another shout.

Behind the drums, Kayla shook her head and seemed to hit the skins even harder.

Lilly tossed an apologetic look to Toni before launching into the final verse.

Toni's fingers continued to play but her mind was on the crowd. It was as if she could feel their growing hostility crawling across her skin. She hadn't felt like this much of an outsider since the first time she stepped on a stage.

The noise died down during the next number, and Toni began to enjoy herself again. Then they launched into the new song, "Hurt U."

Lilly and Toni had worked out the harmonies during rehearsals, and Toni knew they sounded good together. She also realized this song didn't belong to Candi. It was one their fans had never heard.

She caught Lilly's eye, wondering if she planned to do it the way they'd practiced, or if she should just stay in her lane and let Lilly go solo.

One look in the singer's eyes and Toni had her answer.

The blond strolled toward her, a red vinyl catsuit hugging her lithe body like it was made just for her, and it might have been. Her makeup was eighties vamp, the dark shadow on her eyelids making her ice-blue eyes pop. She was like a creature from another planet, beautiful and mysterious.

Lilly stopped next to her and Toni moved to give her room on her microphone, reenergized by the way Lilly held her eyes.

"Take the lead on the last chorus," Lilly yelled into her ear. Toni's eyes nearly popped out of her head. Hadn't they just tried that? This crowd had zero interest in hearing Toni lead. Lilly smiled. "Go on."

Lilly held her gaze, hers intense and focused. It was a challenge, and Toni wanted to rise and meet it.

Don't let them defeat you, her blue eyes seemed to say.

Toni sang to her—with her—as Lilly once again took over the harmony. Once again, they locked into each other, their voices perfectly complementing each other.

It was...incredible. Toni felt strong, powerful. She wanted to live in the moment forever.

She wanted it.

She *wanted* this.

Minx felt like a living entity in her hands, and Toni soloed through the outro like a woman possessed, dipping and weaving around the foundation before dropping back into the groove with Tiff and Kayla, matching Lilly's energy all the while.

When the song ended, there was a beat of silence and then a deafening roar. The audience went berserk, screaming and clapping.

"C'mon, give it up for Toni B!" Tiff shouted.

The crowd began to chant her name.

"Toni! Toni! Toni!"

She burst into giggles. What was happening?

Lilly bent her mouth to Toni's ear. "See? They love you. Love them right back."

She leaned back and winked before returning to the other side of the stage.

"Toni! Toni!" they continued.

Toni didn't know what to do. How to respond. But her entire body fizzed under the focus of hundreds of eyes.

"Toni!" Tiff called out, pointing at her guitar. "Play something!" Tiff's kohl-rimmed eyes danced with amusement, her lips curving in an encouraging smile.

Toni had a moment of panic. She racked her brain for something to play when she heard a voice from offstage. Turning, she saw Seb.

"*Butterflies*," he mouthed, smiling at her and then joining the chant.

"Toni! Toni! Toni!"

She hit the first three-chord progression, and the noise ratcheted up even higher as recognition filtered through the audience.

Toni shut off the part of her brain that told her she didn't want this adoration, didn't need it. In that moment, everything that her mother had been chasing all these years made sense to her. She understood how it could become addictive, the rush. The adoration. It was frightening how right it felt to be on this stage with these women.

She launched into the first verse and nearly the entire audience sang along with her this time.

When she got to the chorus, Tiff and Kayla jumped in. It wasn't clean, since they hadn't rehearsed it, but it was real and raw and everything Toni loved about the tune.

She peered into the wings during the instrumental, searching for Seb, and spotted him and Jordan. They were locked in conversation, arms flailing animatedly. It didn't look friendly.

There were flanked by two men, both dressed in dark bespoke suits, but that wasn't what clued her in to who they were. With their olive skin, stylishly trimmed chestnut-brown hair, and identical heights, the men were nearly impossible to tell apart. The twins.

They didn't seem too thrilled either.

Seb turned and caught her eye, and he looked...off.

"Toni! Last verse!" Tiff called.

Toni was grateful that she knew this song well enough to lose focus and still keep playing. She stepped up to the mic and tried to get lost in the music, in the crowd, but her mind was stuck on the look in Seb's eyes. Something was wrong.

A commotion caught her attention and she turned in time to see a flash of pink hair before Candi came stumbling onto the stage. Seb had a hand on her arm, and Candi snatched it away, causing her to knock into one of Kayla's drums.

Kayla had to stop playing and grab it before it fell over, which broke the rhythm of the song.

Tiff lost her place, which made Toni flub. She stopped playing and the whole thing came to a screeching halt.

Candi struggled to straighten her clothes and smooth her hair back. She was a wreck, clearly drunk or high or both.

At the side of the stage, Seb and Jordan both had horrified expressions on their faces.

"What's up, bitches?" Candi yelled.

Parts of the audience roared its approval, while the rest seemed confused.

Candi waved both arms in the air before strolling over to Toni, looking at her expectantly. "Thanks for holding my place," she slurred, her breath scented with alcohol. Her eyes were black saucers, no hint of blue in them.

Toni looked over her shoulder at Seb. *What do I do?* she mouthed.

Seb gave her a helpless shake of his head. She could tell he wanted to storm the stage, but that wouldn't have gone down well.

"Candi...Candi...Candi..." a few began to chant. Others booed. Some yelled Toni's name.

Tiff scowled at the audience and turned to Candi. She looked confused and hurt. "This isn't cool. Why are you doing this?"

"I'm giving them what they want," she sneered, pointing off-stage to where the twins stood watching.

The one on the right—Andre?—made a motion for them to hurry up.

"You've got to be fucking kidding me," Tiff murmured to Toni. "I'm so sorry, girl."

"It's okay," Toni said, relinquishing her spot. She unplugged Minx when Candi reached for it. There was no way in *hell* she was going to let her use her guitar.

Candi pursed her lips and randomly stuck out her hand, fingers beckoning with impatience.

As Toni made her way off, a roadie rushed by her en route to giving Candi a guitar to play.

After a brief struggle finding the correct jack, Candi plugged in, creating some ear-splitting feedback in the process. The crowd ate it up. She struck a hard chord and let it ring out while she pumped her hips and waggled her tongue at them.

Toni rolled her eyes. Time to go.

"Nia." Seb stepped in front of her. His jaw was tight and his eyes full of regret, compassion, and something else she dared not name. "You don't need to stick around for this. Let me take you somewhere."

"And leave the girls to fend for themselves?" she said with a nonchalance she didn't feel.

"Jordan is here," he countered. "And if I stay, I'll probably only make things worse." He ran a rough hand through his hair. "Christ, what a clusterfuck."

Toni didn't have the energy to deal with his self-loathing, not tonight, but she tried. "Seb, they need you. I don't."

Oops. Wrong thing to say. He looked stricken.

Toni exhaled. "I mean, I... I'm okay. I'll go wait in the dressing room. They need you. Candi needs you too. Do whatever you can to mitigate the disaster. That's kinda your superpower, isn't it?"

Seb winced when Candi struck a particularly dissonant chord. "Fucking Candi," he muttered before meeting Toni's gaze again. "I'll make this right, I swear." Seb put a hand on her arm.

She shook it off and nodded, relieved when he stepped aside. She continued past him but ran into Jordan on the way to the dressing room.

"Toni—" he started.

"Don't sweat it," Toni said, cutting off any apologies. "I assume I'm getting paid for the time I put in?"

"You'll get the full six weeks, Toni. I promise. And then some."

Hearing it out loud stung more than it should. She was done. She wouldn't be in the studio with the Lillys again, wouldn't work on new music with them. There would be no late-night tacos while they compared musical influences.

It was never meant to be permanent. And this wasn't what she wanted anyway. It wasn't.

"Thanks."

"Look, Toni, we didn't know they were going to do this." He was obviously pissed and that helped. A bit.

"Jordan, it's fine. Really."

He scrubbed his hand over the fine waves in his close-cropped hair. "If you ever need representation, call me. Yeah? I have a feeling you'll be in demand after this."

Toni managed a smile. "I will, thanks."

After she made it back to the dressing room, Toni plopped down onto a small love seat and closed her eyes. The band had launched into one of the new covers, the Police's "Next to You."

She heard Tiff's intro and anticipated Kayla's fill, which would be followed by...

The guitar didn't come in. Of course it wouldn't come in on

time because Candi didn't know this arrangement. She might not even know the song. The band continued to play and, finally, Toni heard Candi strum some errant chords.

Toni opened her eyes. Above the vanity, three flat-screen TVs were tuned into the closed-circuit feed of the stage.

Candi looked confused and angry.

Toni caught the look Kayla gave Tiff and they snapped into the groove a bit harder, trying to give Candi something to latch onto.

For her part, Lilly began to improvise the melody, clearly trying to follow Candi's lead. The whole thing devolved into a disjointed jam with no real structure or foundation. And Candi continued to flail, almost out of tune.

The crowd quieted down. They were losing them.

By the time they managed to end that song and go into the next one, people were starting to boo.

A man appeared in the doorway and Toni recognized him immediately. It was one of the twins, the new owners of YMI.

"Toni, is it?" He stepped into the dressing room, immaculately dressed in his tailored suit. He was taller than he'd seemed before, and there was something birdlike about him, with his sharp angles and lifeless eyes.

"Yeah," she finally replied as she sat up and began to wipe Minx down.

"You need to get back out there," he ordered. *Ordered.*

Toni looked up at him, certain she'd misheard. "Excuse me?"

"Get back onstage," he said, pointing at the monitor. "We need to salvage this shit."

Why the fuck he thought she would *ever* go back on that stage was beyond her.

"Aren't you the reason I got pulled off and Candi went on?"

He rolled his eyes. "Yes, but she's in no condition to actually play. We needed her out there for the visual. Look, I don't have time to sit here and explain how this works to you. Get up. Grab that"—he pointed to Minx—"and get your ass back out there."

Toni blinked. "I'm going to have to decline your oh-so-polite request."

"It's not a request," he barked.

She stood and faced him. "I'm sorry, you seem to be under the impression that I work for you. I don't. I was hired to do a job, I did it, and now I am going home."

"Who do you think signed your paychecks?" A sly grin appeared when he realized Toni hadn't thought of that. "Finally, a language she understands."

Shit.

He stepped to the side and gestured to the door. "If you don't want to breach your contract, and thereby forfeit the balance of the obscene amount of money you demanded to even *take* this job, I suggest you move your pretty little ass."

Toni's jaw clenched so hard, she worried she might pop a filling. Of all the unmitigated gall...

He arched an eyebrow and glanced down at his watch.

Toni wanted to tell this asshole to fuck all the way off, but she couldn't. Not unless she wanted to lose everything. She did the only thing she could do—took a deep breath, grabbed Minx, and rushed back to the stage with the guy hot on her heels.

Seb's eyes widened when he saw her, but she shook her head.

"What are you doing?" he asked, but then his gaze must have landed on the guy in the suit because his eyes narrowed dangerously. "Andre, what the fuck is going on?"

"I'm fixing your mess," Andre said. "That's what."

"*My* mess?" Seb's voice boomed. "You're the one..."

"Seb." Toni placed a palm against his cheek and turned his face to hers. His eyes stayed on Andre. "We should do something," she said, dropping her hand.

He finally met her eyes, his filled with rage. "Do you want to go back out there?"

"She isn't going onstage," Andre said.

Seb and Toni turned to him.

"What the fuck do you want her to do?" Seb demanded.

"She can play back here. Stick her in between the speakers or whatever." Andre waved it off as if it were nothing.

Toni's heart lurched into her throat.

"The hell she will," Jordan said.

"That's bullshit," Seb yelled at the same time, a dangerous scowl on his face. Toni knew he was seconds away from decking the guy.

Andre turned to her. "You're a session musician, is that right? Think of this as a live session. No one cares who's actually playing, they came for the spectacle."

He pointed to Candi, who had launched into a dissonant guitar solo. Lilly stood with her arms folded above her head. She seemed lost. Tiff and Kayla stood back and watched as if their dream was circling the drain.

"Do you want your payday or don't you?" Andre snapped his fingers at her. "Come on, we haven't got all day."

What a dick.

Still, Lilly, Tiff, and Kayla had worked too hard for everything to fall apart now. If Toni could help salvage this night for them, she damn well would. Later, she could slink back to Philly and lick her wounds. "Fine," Toni heard herself say. "Fine, I'll do it."

She may have come into this for selfish reasons, but Toni had come to care for these people. She wasn't family, but they'd treated her like she was…family adjacent. She would do this for them, regardless of how it made her feel like a spare part.

Seb searched her face. He sighed when Candi's solo came to

a screeching halt and laughter pierced the air. Seb waved over the sound man.

"Kyle, can you give Toni a DL to plug in and then toss her into the mix?"

Kyle bobbed his head. "Yeah. I assume you want Candi as low in the mix as possible?"

"Long in her monitor, short in the house," Seb said.

Candi would hear herself, but the rest of the band and the audience would hear Toni.

Seb cupped Toni's shoulders. "You sure you're okay with this?"

She wasn't, but she sighed and glanced over at the girls. "If it helps them, yeah."

Seb's eyes searched hers, and Toni could tell there was much more he wanted to say, but what difference could it make? He walked to the edge of the stage and gestured for Kayla's attention.

She frowned at him.

"'I Burn,'" he yelled to her.

Toni walked up beside him, Minx in hand.

Kayla looked at her, then down at the guitar as Kyle plugged her in. Her eyes lit up, and she gave them a firm nod before turning to catch Tiff's attention.

Tiffany's gaze snapped over to Toni, and she grinned as Candi's solo ended to tepid applause.

Seb stepped onstage long enough to whisper to Lilly, who walked up to the mic.

"This is our last song tonight, my lovelies. Thank you for coming out."

She turned and looked at Toni.

Toni nodded, catching the eyes of Tiff and Kayla, and then began the intro.

On the other side of the stage, Candi started playing. She didn't seem to notice or realize that it was another guitar guiding her.

Kayla came in on her cue, and Lilly began to sing.

The song tightened into an edge as sharp as a knife as the four women rallied to perform at their best, carrying Candi on their backs all the way.

Toni stood in the shadows, the others in the light.

The irony wasn't lost on her. She'd always dreamed of finding a way to perform while somehow retaining her anonymity, but not like this. Not stuck in the corner with the extra cables and the cooler full of beer and water bottles like a piece of equipment.

But Toni played. She gave the Lillys everything she had left in her. When it ended, she asked Kyle to unplug her.

He gave her a sympathetic smile. "You were great."

Toni couldn't muster enough energy to return it but thanked him anyway.

Beside her, Seb practically vibrated with rage. She could almost see smoke coming out of his flared nostrils.

"I'm so fucking sorry, Nia. You want to get out of here?"

"I…" She had to swallow past the lump forming in her throat. "Can you give me a few minutes? I need—"

"Of course," Seb promised immediately, reaching up to cup her shoulder. He gave it a gentle squeeze and Toni stopped herself from leaning into his warmth. "I need to have words with Andre, but I'll come find you in a little bit, okay?" Seb's eyes pleaded with hers.

"Sure," she lied. "I'll wait for you."

As soon as he stepped away, Toni darted to the dressing room, packed her gear, and left. She needed to get out of New York and as far away from all of this as possible. She needed to get back to what she knew, what she could trust.

It wasn't her world. They weren't her people. So why did it hurt so damn bad to leave them behind?

CHAPTER 32.

"YOU FUCKING ASSHOLE." AFTER SEARCHING everywhere, Seb found Andre in the hall.

He was on the phone and he looked at Seb, first with surprise and then thinly disguised amusement when Seb stopped in front of him.

Seb wanted to rip that fancy smartphone out of his hand and shove it up his ass.

"I'll call you back," Andre said. He put the cell in his pocket and turned to face Seb. "Well, it all worked out for the best, no thanks to you."

"Who the fuck do you think you are?" Seb took a step but stopped himself.

"I'm the one who bankrolls your little rock 'n' roll fantasies," Andre sneered. "Look, I get you're upset. That could have gone better, but the press coverage tomorrow will be epic. We'll put up preorders on Tuesday—I'm told Tuesdays are typical for new releases, et cetera."

He sounded like he was making a grocery list. Like he hadn't used Toni to clean up their mess. Like she was a roll of fucking paper towels.

"You don't treat people the way you treated her," Seb said, struggling to keep his voice calm when all he wanted to do was strangle the douchebag with his own necktie. "These women are not chess pieces to be moved around and manipulated to benefit your bottom line."

Andre's brow lifted. "But...that's *exactly* what they are. And so are you." He chuckled, his expression one of disbelief. "You do realize it's all business, right? God, you're just like my brother. Look, this is a company. It's not about art or music or *feelings*, it's about money. I didn't buy this label to feel good, I bought it..."

He stopped to think. Then laughed to himself.

"Actually, I guess I did buy it to feel good. It makes me look cool. My brother is the romantic. He actually loves this shit. Me? I could have just as easily bought a gaming outfit or a racing team. It's all about my personal brand."

"Screw your personal brand," Seb snarled. "And screw you."

Andre laughed, utterly unperturbed. "Man, you're awfully worked up. Are you fucking the new guitarist too?"

He winked.

Seb's jaw dropped.

As if sensing he'd hit upon the truth, Andre laughed again. "You *are*! Not that I blame you. She's very fuckable."

Seb saw red. The feel of his fist meeting the smug bastard's nose was almost as satisfying as the crunchy sound it made.

"Fuck!" Andre stumbled back, his hands on his face and a generous amount of red oozing through his fingers.

"Seb!" Jordan was suddenly between him and Andre. "Stop!"

The pain took a moment to register in Seb's hand, and when it hit, he shook it out. Yep. There was Mitchell Quigley's son.

"Contract or no contract, you are *done*!" Andre hissed, spittle flying from his twisted mouth.

Jordan put a hand on Seb's shoulder. "You okay?"

Seb nodded, matching Andre glare for glare.

"Go. I've got this." Jordan gave him a push and Seb finally turned away, disgusted with himself for losing it like that. He didn't even bother protesting when Jordan apologized to Andre.

Seb had fucked up. Again. Always.

His hand throbbing, Seb found a corner in the dressing room. Defeated and at a loss as to what to do next, he slumped to the floor. He hadn't been surprised that Toni was nowhere to be found.

Why would she stick around? Tonight had been a shitshow, and he hadn't done a thing to stop it. He and Jordan both should have put their feet down harder when the twins demanded that Candi take the stage.

Andre in particular had hated the new lineup, and Seb didn't have to be a genius to guess why. Toni had outshone YMI's investment. Andre had been convinced there could be no Lillys without the Candi-Lilly dynamic. Had banked on it, so much so that he'd been willing to put up with Candi's antics. Worse, he'd probably been banking on that too. Almost like he'd wanted all the drama.

Toni presented a real problem. Without even trying, she was a star.

Seb had no idea where the other twin Daniel stood on things. He seemed to let Andre make all the decisions, but Seb didn't have it in him to care about the dynamic between the brothers. Pretty soon, he'd be out on his ass and he couldn't say he didn't deserve it.

"That was a right mess," Jordan said as he walked through the door. "Except when it wasn't. Lilly, Tiff, and Kayla are out schmoozing the promoters. Where's Toni?"

"Gone."

Seb hated the pity he saw in his best friend's eyes.

"Shit, I'm sorry. I can fix this." Jordan whipped out his phone. It was just like him to think he could fix everything, but it *was* Seb's problem. His failure. He should have seen this coming.

"Don't." Seb reached up and covered Jordan's hand, stopping him. Jordan sighed but complied. "Why did we let him bully us into putting Candi onstage?"

"That's my question to both of you," Lilly said as she walked into the room.

Kayla and Tiff were hot on her heels.

"Where's my girl?" Tiff said, glancing around. She looked at Seb, eyes narrowed. "Where's Toni? And what happened to your hand?"

Seb and Jordan exchanged a look.

"What the ever-loving *fuck* was Candi doing here?" Kayla wiped some sweat from her neck and arms with a towel and tossed it in a corner. "We were rocking and then she showed up out of nowhere. Whose bright idea was that?"

"The twins insisted," Jordan said. "Well, Andre did."

"Whose fucking band is this, ours or theirs?" Kayla asked, her face almost as red as her hair.

"Legally, it's YMI's, thanks to that shitty contract," Jordan said, side-eyeing Seb. "Not even I could get you out of everything your previous attorney allowed them to put in there. Most especially the say they have over your lineup. It's draconian. I'm half convinced they paid him off."

This was all Seb's fucking fault. All of it.

"What do you mean?" Tiff asked.

"He means I fucked up bringing that first lawyer in, and he screwed us over with the legalese." The least he could do was own up to it.

"They *own* us?"

"No," Lilly said to Tiff, her arms folded. "No, they don't. We'll be okay."

Jordan frowned at her. "What are you thinking?"

She straightened, chin high. "Take me to them."

"Uh, sure." Jordan moved to her side.

A look passed between them that Seb couldn't decode. He opened his mouth to say something, but a scream cut him off.

"Oh my God, that was amazing!" Candi crashed into the room, a bottle of champagne clutched in one hand. "It feels so good to be back."

Her smile fell when no one greeted her.

"Why so gloomy? Somebody die?"

"Jesus fuck, Can," Kayla said, disgusted. "Can't you read a goddamned room? That was a disaster."

Candi frowned. "It was not—they *loved* me."

"God, you're a fucking nightmare," Tiff muttered, turning around to pack her things.

"What'd you say?" Candi zeroed in on the bassist, her eyes cold. "If you have a problem, tell me to my face."

Tiff whipped around so fast, her long braids swung out wildly and Seb inched forward, afraid things might get physical. There had already been one too many punches thrown tonight.

But Tiff only eyed her for a moment, and when she spoke her voice was calmer than he'd expected. "I'm not sure if you'll even understand what I'm saying, given your...state, but you disappointed me, Candi." Tiff's arms hung at her sides, her shoulders slumped with fatigue or sadness or perhaps a combination of both.

Around them, the room seemed to hold its collective breath. Kayla leaned against the vanity, watching the exchange.

Behind him, Seb could feel Lilly and Jordan looking on as well.

"You grew up with a lot more than most people get in a lifetime," Tiff continued. "You've never known what it's like to...to be alone, really alone, with no one to rely on. No one to stand in your corner. No one to pick you up when you fall. You've *always* had someone there. So I get why you think you deserve support, no matter what you do."

Candi's eyes were unfocused, but at least she was listening. Seb watched as she tried to process Tiff's words.

"Everyone deserves support," she said, her words blurring together.

Tiff shook her head, her dark eyes flashing. "No, not everyone. Not the woman who strolled out onstage tonight, drunk off her ass, and played like shit in front of an audience that gets to decide how big and how far we go as a band. She doesn't deserve support. Not mine. Not anymore."

"Hold up, the label—" Candi started.

"She doesn't deserve to be a part of something as...as fucking *awesome* as this family if she doesn't appreciate it, if she hasn't earned it, if she *expects* it like it's her due," Tiff continued, her voice wavering as she pushed a few stray strands of hair from her face. It was damp with sweat. The cotton of her Blondie tee was soaked through from a hard night's work. "Someone like that doesn't deserve what we have."

Seb knew Tiff worked as hard as anyone, cared as much as anyone, but he had never seen this kind of emotion from her. She shook with it.

"I think what Tiff's trying to say," Kayla said, perhaps sensing how much this was getting to the bassist, "is that you've been taking us for granted. You've been walking around with this expectation that we're going to roll over and accept your shit. And Lilly..." She glanced over at Lilly, who stood frozen in the doorway, Jordan by her side. "Lilly loves you too much to do what really needs to be done."

"Lilly loves me?" Candi said, incredulous. "She tried to kick me out of my own goddamned band!"

"No, she didn't. We voted you out. *She's* the one who gave

you a second chance, which was really your third. Fourth. Fifth? Who the fuck knows, I've stopped counting," Kayla said, exhaling with obvious exhaustion.

Candi looked around the room, her entire demeanor shifting into one Seb knew well. Victim mode.

"Guys, I..." Candi began, struggling not to wobble on her feet. "I know I was hitting the scene a bit too hard, but it was all in good fun. I've brought us a lot of buzz."

"It's not the kind of buzz we want," Kayla said. "We don't need to be known for the booze and the parties and the drugs any more than we want to parade around in the dental floss that Andre tried to make us wear. That's such a fucking Hollywood cliché, and we're above it. We want people talking about our music, and about how much we fucking rock because we fucking do."

"We used to," Tiff said. "And we did again, with...well, with Toni."

Candi reeled back as if she'd been slapped.

"You want *her*?" She looked at each face in the room before landing on Lilly. "You think *she* could actually replace *me*?"

"Were you ever serious about cleaning up your act?" Lilly asked her, no anger in her voice.

Candi narrowed her eyes. "I thought you liked me dirty."

Lilly sighed.

"We want someone we can count on," Tiff said, her voice trembling. "And that clearly isn't you."

"Seb!" Candi exclaimed, spinning around to face him. "Please, talk some sense into these idiots."

"They sound pretty sensible to me, Can. What you did? Going to the label? Insisting on going on tonight? It wasn't cool."

"I won't let you tear us down with you, Candi," Lilly said coolly.

"*We* have a contract with YMI, not just you, Snow Queen,"

Candi retorted with derision. "Like it or not, I'm a part of this band. I'm here because the twins *want* me here. Andre knows what I'm worth, unlike you ingrates."

Lilly's gaze swept up from Candi's feet, taking in all five feet seven inches of her. "We'll see."

Lilly left the room and Jordan followed.

Candi snorted. "Such a fucking drama queen. My daddy could buy and sell her in his sleep." She took a long pull from the bottle in her hand.

Kayla shook her head and started packing up her stuff. Tiff finished packing as well and they both left the room.

Seb watched Candi pace about before she threw herself down on a love seat against the wall. "What happened to your big plan?"

Candi grinned up at him. "Worked perfectly, didn't it?"

Seb frowned. "What do you mean?"

"Right now, Lilly's probably talking to the twins and they're telling her that without me—without Lilly and Candi—there's no deal."

Seb huffed out an incredulous laugh. "Do you really think they'll back you after that out there?"

Candi looked confused. "Andre will, and he's the one with the power. I gave them what they wanted, and I sounded fucking awesome too."

"Can." Seb spoke slowly because she must have been more messed up than he thought. "You were...not good. You blew it and would have ruined the whole show if Toni hadn't saved our asses."

"Fuck Toni," she huffed. "She had her little minute in the sun. This is my gig."

"It was hers!" Seb yelled before reining it in. "She closed out the show, not you."

"But I—"

"We killed your feed, Candi. We replaced it with hers. She played offstage," he said, enunciating every word as clearly as he could. "You think that was you? Christ! How much shit have you taken tonight?"

Candi's mouth hung open, confusion clouding her eyes. She seemed smaller, all of a sudden. Younger. "No, I... It was me... I..."

Seb walked over and crouched down in front of her.

"I'm worried about you, Can."

"I'm fine," she muttered as if out of habit. There was no real fight behind the words.

"You're not. You're really not, and I should have done something. Helped you. Something."

Candi's expression hardened. "I don't need rescuing, Seb. Not by anyone, and certainly not by a nobody like you." She stood abruptly and Seb had to jump up and steady her before she fell over.

Candi pushed him away. "Leave me alone. Go to your new fuckbuddy."

"Jesus, Can."

"You think I missed the way you look at her?"

"I've known her since we were kids," he said.

Her jaw dropped open. "So you *planned* this?"

"What? No."

Candi stepped back from him. "Holy shit, you planned all of this, didn't you?"

"All of what?"

"Getting me kicked out, bringing in your high-school sweetheart," Candi spat. "Damn, when you get bored, you burn it all down, don't you? No one is safe."

Seb rubbed his eyes. He didn't have the energy or the patience to deal with this. He needed to get out of there and find Toni.

"Nothing I say is going to convince you what complete and total horseshit that is, so I won't even try," he said. "You need help, Can. You fucked up, and one day you're going to realize what you threw away. You did this. Not me, you."

"Fuck you, Seb." Candi shook her head, backing away toward the door. "You watch. One of these days, Lilly will decide you're not worth the effort either." With that, she left.

Then he was alone.

The weight of everything that transpired took his legs out from under him, and he collapsed heavily into the nearest chair.

He trusted Jordan and Lilly to sort out the label stuff for the band. If there was anything in the contract they could use, he knew Jordan would find it. It couldn't end like this.

Not like this.

He'd happily walk away if it meant the Lillys could get what they wanted.

As for Toni…

Seb couldn't let her walk away without knowing how sorry he was, or how much she was wanted, and not only by him.

———————

He breathed a sigh of relief when Toni opened the door to her hotel room.

"I figured you'd show up," she said, walking to the bureau. Its drawers were open and half-empty.

The room itself had a modest, nondescript decor and mass-produced prints on the beige walls. It was a step up from the Fairfield, but the label could have afforded better. He should have seen to it.

Toni's small suitcase was open on the bed.

"Anxious to get back down to Philly?"

Her back to him, Toni shrugged. "There's nothing for me here."

"That's not true," he said. She turned to look at him over her shoulder. "The band wants you."

She snorted. "Candi can't be on board with that."

"No one really cares what Candi wants anymore."

Toni resumed packing. "Didn't seem that way tonight."

"Tonight was a clusterfuck. The twins insisted on having Candi there… Well, one of them did." He sighed. "I didn't mean for this to happen, Nia."

"I know, but you could have handled it better," she said, turning to sit on the edge of the bed. "Letting her come onstage like that, in the middle of a song. It looked bad for everyone, not just her."

Seb nodded. "You're right. I should have stopped it."

Toni studied him. "Then why didn't you?"

Seb dropped his gaze to the floor. "Habit, I guess. Since the beginning, it's been Candi and Lilly, Lilly and Candi. And it fell upon me to keep things running smoothly. I was the only one she ever seemed to listen to, and I thought… Well, I don't know what I thought. I wasn't thinking. Andre was furious, threatening to pull the plug…"

"I get it," she said. "You love the band."

"Other than you, they're the only family I've ever had." He met her eyes.

Toni gave him a soft smile. "I'm glad you found them, and they found you. But Candi… She's toxic."

"I know," Seb said, sighing. "I thought maybe she was sincere when she said she wanted to change. Can't believe I bought her bullshit. *Kept* buying her bullshit."

"I don't think you did," Toni countered. "I think you *wanted* to—you and Lilly both—but I don't think you actually did. But it was probably easy to tell yourself that so you didn't feel guilty. I admit, I don't get why."

"Why what?"

"Why you let her get away with so much," Toni replied, watching him. She had a way of looking at him that made him feel seen. Sometimes too much. "Why did you let her pull your strings like that?"

Seb ran his uninjured hand over his face. "I guess... She reminds me of me," he said, shrugging. "For all their wealth, her family is bad news. And they treat her like an inconvenience, an embarrassment, and she leans into it. I don't know how to explain it."

"She sounds a lot like a young hothead I grew up with," Toni said, her eyes warm. "And I get you wanting to help her, but you almost lost everything. Good or bad, Candi has her family to fall back on. You don't. You never stopped to ask yourself if it was worth it? Because I have to say, I can't see her taking the same risk for you."

"How do you do that?"

"What?"

"Read me for filth and still be so gentle about it."

Toni cracked a smile. "Practice."

Seb returned her smile. "I've really missed you these last couple of days."

"I missed you too."

"Then don't go," Seb said, ready to beg.

Toni shook her head slightly. "I meant it when I said there's nothing for me here. They're not my band. As for you? The jury's still out on whether we'll be friends...or more. Or nothing at all. Nothing more than memories to each other."

A sharp pain sliced through Seb at the thought of losing her again.

"You'll never be nothing to me," he said, sounding like he'd swallowed shards of glass and his voice was the shredded aftermath. "And I hope you'll give me a chance to be something to you again."

Toni exhaled a soft breath and nodded. "We'll see how it goes."

It was better than nothing, and Seb grabbed onto the kernel of hope as if it were a lifeline.

Her phone rang on the bed, and Toni peered at it. Her brows shot up with surprise, and she picked it up to answer. "Hello?"

Seb watched her, taking in every detail of her features. The line of her brow, the mole underneath her left eye, the cute little button on the end of her nose. If he hadn't already figured out that he'd been half in love with her for over a decade, he sure knew it now. He loved her. He always had, and he always would.

"Slow down," she said. "What happened?"

Seb frowned but she shook her head and held up a finger. Then she put her phone on speaker and set it back down on the bed.

"Heck if I know, but she wanted me to loan her some money when I told her she wasn't getting that Gibson," Mo replied. "Shouldn't have ever bought her the damn thing."

"What?" Toni breathed the word, turning to Seb with a shocked expression. "You...? *You* bought Minx for my mother? I didn't know," she finished quietly.

Mo made a sound that was halfway between a laugh and a grunt. "Please, what you don't know about me and your mama could fill a church," he said, sounding both bored and amused.

A fond smile curved Toni's mouth.

"Anyway," Mo continued, "I thought I'd call and warn you, in case your mother tracks you down again. Don't you fall for her bullshit."

"Where is she, exactly?" Toni said, folding her arms. She seemed doubly tired all of a sudden.

"A motel outside Wilmington. That man of hers must've come to his senses. She said he kicked her out with nothing but the clothes on her back."

Toni met Seb's eyes and shook her head again. He could see the events of the night beginning to weigh her down. It was all so much.

"Now you listen," Mo continued. "Don't you even think about going down there. Ain't nothing you can do for her, except for throw your money down the drain. Mary Bennette knows how to take care of herself."

"Apparently not," Toni said, but there was no emotion in her voice.

"That's her business," Mo said. "Not yours. And ain't you got a gig tonight?"

Toni froze. "I–I did, yeah. How did you…?"

"I know you think I don't keep tabs on you, but I do," Mo said, sounding more like a father than he had in their whole brittle relationship, as far as Seb knew. "I may not…I may not have coddled you like you wanted, but I made sure you was looked after. You had a roof over your head, had food in your belly, clothing. Right?"

"And you made me work to earn all of it." A little anger flared in her expression.

"Just teaching you responsibility," Mo argued.

Seb wanted to reach through the phone and grab him by the throat. Which was such a Mitchell Quigley instinct that Seb's stomach soured. His hand still stung from him losing his temper, and the knuckles had begun to really swell up. He flexed his fingers and winced.

Toni's eyes snapped to his hand and she frowned.

Seb shook his head.

"Didn't want you growing up thinking the world was just

gonna roll out the red carpet for you because you're a pretty brown-skinned girl with some talent in her," Mo rambled on.

Toni's gaze flicked back to the phone. As backhanded as they were, these were likely the most complimentary things her pop had ever said to her. Seb couldn't imagine hearing anything so supportive coming out of Mitch's mouth.

"Are you having a stroke or something?" she asked.

Mo actually chuckled, the sound utterly foreign. "Don't sass me, girl."

"I'm just...I'm having a hard time believing you're Maurice Robb," Toni rebutted. "That guy never had a nice word for me, like, ever."

"Well, he's an old bastard," Mo said. "But he, you know...he looks out for his daughter. In his own way."

Toni was apparently shocked into silence.

Seb didn't know what to think himself.

Mo cleared his throat. "Anyway, thought I should warn you 'bout Mary and all. You have a good show and...and stay in touch. Don't let nobody run rough over you. Y'hear?"

"Uh... Yeah. Okay, I won't," Toni stuttered. "And thanks... Pop."

Mo grunted and the call disconnected.

Toni stared at her phone for a few seconds and then seemed to shake off the shock. She peered up at Seb. "That was..."

"Yeah," he said.

Toni gestured toward his hand. "You assault some unsuspecting wall somewhere?"

Seb looked down at his hand. "Oh, this? Nah, Andre's nose accidentally ran into my fist."

She gasped as she moved forward to crouch down in front of him. "Seb!"

He tried not to make a sound as she gingerly took his hand

in hers and inspected the wounds. His knuckles were raw, swollen, and pulsed with pain. He hissed when she tried to stretch out his fingers.

"Shit, Seb. You need ice." She tried to stand but Seb put his other hand on her cheek and she stopped and looked up at him.

"Nia..." Seb let his fingers ghost over her hair, following the journey before he met her eyes. "I'm so sorry for what went down back there."

"I know," she said.

Silence descended between them, and the tension in the air morphed into something else entirely.

Memories of their stolen moments played on a loop in Seb's head. The way Toni's gaze kept dropping to his lips told him he wasn't the only one wondering what would have happened if they hadn't stopped themselves at the Phactory that night.

Seb wasn't sure who moved first, but suddenly she was there in his arms. The sweetest sigh blew across his lips just before their mouths connected.

CHAPTER 33.

TONI DIDN'T KNOW IF THIS was a mistake or not, and she didn't care. It had been fourteen years since she first laid eyes on Sebastian Quigley, and for a good portion of those years, she had wanted him to be hers.

Whether it was for an hour, a night, or something longer, Toni wanted this. She needed it. And she deserved something good after the hell of the evening.

"Tell me what you want," Seb said as he pulled back. He smoothed a hand over her hair. "Fuck…"

"What?"

"You are so fucking beautiful."

Toni smiled into another kiss. And another. And then she was on her feet, pulling him to his and guiding him over to her bed.

He flinched when she grabbed his hand.

"Oh! Dammit, I'm sorry, I forgot." She lifted his injured hand up to her mouth and kissed around the redness there.

Seb pulled her hand back down to the front of his jeans and pressed her palm against the rock-hard evidence of his need.

"If you think I feel much of anything other than *this*," he said in a voice she hadn't heard from him before, "you know nothing about my priorities at the moment."

"Is that so?" Toni curled her fingers around him as much as

she could through the denim and was rewarded with a moan from Seb's sinful mouth.

He grabbed the back of her head and pulled her into a bruising kiss that burned any witty comeback she might have had right out of her head.

The kiss was different from the ones they'd shared before, laced with a desperation that made her head spin. Seb ate at her mouth as if he'd been denied food for far too long and was compelled to consume as much as he could before it was gone.

Before she was gone.

Toni banished any thoughts of later from her mind and concentrated on the now. She shoved his jacket off his shoulders and Seb shook it off, tossing it to the floor as she went up onto her toes and wound her arms around his neck. Closer. She needed to be closer.

Seb groaned into her mouth and dropped his hands to her thighs. He picked her up as if she weighed nothing and wrapped her legs around his waist. He walked her backward and lowered her carefully on the bed, as if she were something precious.

When he released her, she spread her arms and one hit her suitcase. She shoved weakly at it.

Seb took over and pushed it to the floor, sweeping everything else behind it before he returned his attention to her. His eyes were dark and wild, pupils blown wide with lust.

Toni reached for him and he melted over her, immediately going for her mouth. Starved. The kisses made her delirious, made her want to spill her deepest secrets, him at the center of every one of them. That she'd loved him. That she'd mourned him. That she carried him in her heart still.

Every part of him covered every part of her, and she luxuriated in the feel of him, of his weight pressing her into the mattress.

There were way too many clothes between them.

Seb's hands went to the hem of her tee and her tank. "Can I...?"

"Yes," she answered before he finished asking. "Please."

He peeled it off and made quick work of her jeans, stopping to kiss each bit of flesh as he laid her bare, until she squirmed under him.

"You," she demanded breathlessly.

Seb went to his knees and pulled his shirt over his head.

Impatient, Toni sat up and opened his belt. She popped the button on his jeans and looked up into his face as she pulled the zipper down.

Seb gazed down at her like he'd never seen anything like her before.

Toni opened his jeans and pulled them down his hips as far as she could.

Seb stood and took them off the rest of the way, his eyes hot on hers.

She slid back on the queen-size bed and shivered when he reached in the pocket and pulled out his wallet to retrieve a condom. This. Was. Happening!

He tossed the foil packet on the bed and knelt on the edge of the mattress, the front of his boxer briefs bulging with promise.

Toni took a moment to appreciate the beauty of him, from his sinewy muscles to the visible strength of his thighs. He hid a lot under the jeans and T-shirts she'd come to think of as his uniform.

Seb remained still, watching her. And Toni let him see; it was only fair. She had an idea of what he was thinking. She was think-ing it too.

We're here, finally.

Toni thought he'd dive right in, quench the thirst that had been building up between them for weeks.

Instead, Seb stretched out beside her and brought his hand up to trace lines on her skin. He drew a fingertip across her collarbone, down her neck, trailed it from her forehead, down the slope of her nose, and over her lips. She nipped at the digit and he pulled back, a soft smile on his lips.

"I don't think I've ever wanted anyone as much as I've wanted you, Nia," he said, his eyes following the unhurried path of his fingers.

Beneath his touch, Toni quivered like a leaf on a tree.

"It used to scare the shit out of me."

"When?" she said, amazed that her voice still worked.

"All the time, though I didn't know it." Seb lowered his lips to her stomach and placed a kiss there. He took a deep breath that she felt against her skin, and then he resumed his slow, torturous exploration. "I remember prom night."

"Prom?"

He nodded, humming with assent. "You looked like a goddamned angel. I didn't know what to do with myself. Or with you. You short-circuited my brain."

"I thought you were bored." Toni arched into his touch when he cupped a hand over her breast.

Her nipple pebbled against the cotton of her bra. She wanted to feel the touch against her skin but loved that Seb was taking his time. Was opening up to her. Sharing.

He chuckled softly. "Bored? I must have jerked off three times that night, hating myself for it every time."

"You did that…thinking about me?" Her voice squeaked as he pinched her nipple. "God, Seb…you're driving me out of my head."

"Welcome to the club," he replied, apparently content to just play. "It felt wrong. I mean, I thought… You were…like a sister. And I'd convinced myself you only thought of me like a brother."

Toni couldn't help it; she laughed. Her stomach shook with it.

"Like a *brother*? Jesus Christ, Seb. I had a crush on you from the moment we met."

"Yeah?" He didn't seem too surprised. She guessed he'd figured it out by now. "You hid it well."

"Too well, I guess."

He frowned and a shadow crossed his face. "Maybe, but so did I. So well I even fooled myself."

Seb met her eyes.

Toni let him see everything she was feeling. The lust, the love, the uncertainty.

He leaned down and kissed her. It started sweet, full of pent-up longing and maybe a little nostalgia, but quickly caught fire. Seb's tongue invaded her mouth, laid siege to her senses. He slipped his thumb inside the cup of her bra and brushed it across her nipple, catching her sharp squeal of surprise in his mouth before he pulled back to look down at her again.

"Seb…"

"Yeah?" he said, agreeing before he lowered his head, slid the fabric of her bra out of the way, and sucked the nipple into his mouth.

"I…" Toni twisted and squirmed as pleasure rippled through her, nerve endings firing in the most delicious way. *Holy hell.* Her hands flew into his hair and she pulled him in, silently demanding more.

Seb came easily, rolling on top of her as he settled himself between her thighs. He slipped the straps of her bra from her shoulders and fumbled behind her for the clasp.

"In the front," she panted.

"Thank God," he said, flicking it open and whisking the garment away. Seb worshipped her breasts, lavishing each one with exquisite attention before his kissed his way down her stomach. "So sweet."

Toni's legs fell open around his broad shoulders. When he licked a line across her skin, along the waistband of her underwear, she fisted a hand in his curls.

"Seb!"

"I know, babe." He hooked his thumbs in the strings at her hips and pulled them down her legs. "Holy Christ, I love your body."

With anyone else, Toni would worry about the swell of her tummy or the width of her thighs, but Seb had never looked at her as if she were anything but beautiful and perfect. Even when they were kids, he'd made her feel that way. She hadn't realized it until now, until he was staring down at her—naked and vulnerable beneath him—with wonder.

Seb's breath ghosted over the crease of her inner thigh as he brought his hand between her legs, his thumb tickling over her folds, pushing through to the throbbing pulse at her center.

"You're killing me," Toni whimpered.

"Can't have that" came his reply before he nosed his way into her. Then she felt his tongue on her and everything went hazy. "I knew it," he said.

"Knew...?" Toni could barely find words.

"Knew you'd be sweet."

Seb shifted, pushing her legs wider with his shoulders as he descended upon her with determined focus.

Toni's back arched off the bed as he devoured her, one hand in his hair, the other grappling for something to hold onto. She eventually found a notch in the headboard and gripped it hard.

He was relentless, spearing her deep with his tongue before pulling back to circle her clit with the tip or to take wide swipes with the flat of it.

Her body moved in a continuous wave, independent of her brain. She was one enormous nerve ending that started between her legs and ran throughout her body, while thoughts of *What are you doing?* and *How are you doing that?* and *Oh, shit, please do that again* raced through her mind. Some words even made it past her lips.

Seb hummed between her thighs like she was the best meal he'd ever had, and stars began to form behind her eyelids.

"Seb, I..." She forced her eyes open to look down at him.

"Hmmm?"

He raised his head to look at her with a hooded gaze, leaving her dizzy and conflicted. She wanted his mouth back on her, but she also needed more.

Toni tugged on his hair. "Come here."

He grinned. "Don't you know it's not polite to interrupt someone when they're eating?"

She threw her arm across her face because, really. "You did *not* just say that."

"What, not sexy?"

She grinned down at him. "Not in the least."

"Well, shit," he said as he crawled up her body. "Now I know what I've been doing wrong all this time."

"No wonder you're single," Toni teased, giddy because she already knew sex with Seb would be hot. What she didn't expect was for it to be fun.

Seb rested an elbow on either side of her head as he settled along the length of her body. "Luckily, I have other skills."

Toni opened her mouth to respond but could only moan wantonly as he slid his hard length across her apex. He rocked his hips, and Toni felt every ridge and bump as they dragged across her aching flesh.

"Hurry..."

"Hang on."

He reached for the condom and lifted off her long enough to

sheath himself. Toni was fairly sure he broke land speed records putting the thing on.

And then he was back, staring down into her eyes, hot and hard between her legs, his lips hovering over hers, and she was so ready. So ready to surrender.

"Let me in, Nia," he whispered as she lifted her knees and wrapped her thighs around his sides. Warm skin against warm skin.

She nodded and he pushed forward in a slow glide that had her bursting at the seams. Her eyes slammed shut as he filled her, her mouth dropping open on a silent moan.

"Jesus…" His breath was hot and quick across her lips, his voice rough. He buried a hand in her hair and fisted it, making her scalp tingle.

It was thrilling. The hard and the soft of him, the war between patience and impatience.

"I have been dreaming about this for years, about being this close to you, watching your face while you come apart."

"Me too," she managed to say.

Seb dropped his forehead to her shoulder as if it were all too much for him too. He sucked at a spot on her neck that sent a rivulet of pleasure straight to the juncture between her legs. She hadn't even known her neck was one of her erogenous zones.

Toni ran her hands down Seb's back, up into his hair, everywhere she could reach. He melted into her, his hips circling slowly as he fucked her deep.

It was so good. He smelled so good. Everything…was so, so good. Seb trailed his fingers down her leg. He cupped a hand behind her knee and hooked her leg over his thigh with determined purpose, driving in hard and setting her on fire.

His hips stuttered and he picked up the pace, lifting his head to look at her. It was unnerving the way he seemed to know what she needed before she could ask.

Toni's breath came in shallow hitches. She raised a palm to his cheek, held it there.

Seb's hips slowly stilled. He dropped his head and gently took her mouth, kissing her as if he needed the air from her lungs to breathe. Then he took up a punishing pace that shook the bed and her along with it.

All Toni could say was "more."

"Fuck," he whispered. "Fuck," he swore, again and again, as Toni felt her core tightening around him. Every stroke drove her higher and higher. Seb rocked into her, rubbed against her, touched every spot that she had—and some she didn't know she had—and it pushed her closer and closer to the edge.

"Yes," she hissed when he adjusted his angle.

He responded immediately, repeating the motion with a focused precision.

She grabbed his shoulders, keening, and Seb growled in her ear and flipped them until she was straddling his hips. The new position was too much. She rocked over him once. Twice.

Seb reached between her legs and pressed his fingers into her slick folds, sending Toni hurtling into outer damn space.

"Fuck, yes. Nia… God…" He took her waist in both hands and pumped up into her, slow and easy. In and out, teasing her quivering entrance before he pushed himself back inside.

Then hard and fast, relentless and insistent, and Toni erupted around him. Every muscle caught up in a full-body shiver.

Seb went wild. "Oh, Jesus. Nia…"

His fingers tightened on her hips, on just the right side of pain, and then he stiffened beneath her, every muscle taut.

Toni grabbed his head with both hands and dragged her lips over his. She licked into his mouth, uncaring of whether or not she could breathe. Fuck air, she needed this man. She needed this.

Seb shuddered one last time and then collapsed under her.

Toni followed him down, pressing her cheek over his thundering heart.

He rolled to his side, taking Toni with him and keeping her within the circle of his arms. When he slipped from her body, Toni immediately lamented the loss. Even though most of his skin still covered most of hers, she missed him already as their reality came crashing in around her.

"God…" He ran his hands up and down her back. "That… You…"

She smiled and fell onto her back.

Seb got up and went to the bathroom to dispose of the condom. When he returned, Toni pulled down the bedding and Seb climbed in next to her. He wrapped his arms around her, gathering her close.

Toni allowed herself a few more moments to bask in the mellow warmth of him. The alluring scent of him. His quiet strength.

Seb resumed his gentle exploration of her skin, her hair, touching her as if she were precious. Fragile.

Whatever became of them, Toni would cherish this moment between them.

"What will you do?"

Toni kissed a smooth patch of skin that had drawn her attention, maybe the remnants of an old wound, before she looked up into his eyes.

"I'm going home."

Seb nodded but he made no attempt to hide his disappointment. "And what will you do about Mary?"

"Not a damn thing," Toni said. She'd already put the matter in her rearview mirror. Mo wasn't right about much, but he was right about this. There was nothing Toni could do for her.

"A wise decision." Seb nodded again. "But you know she's not going to let it go if she thinks she can get something out of you."

"She can try," Toni said. "What about you?"

"Jordan and I told YMI the band wants to record at Phactory Sound."

"Really?" Toni cursed the hopeful flutter in her chest. "You think they'll agree?"

"It would be petty of them not to," he said, running a hand back through his hair. He tucked his hand behind his head and made a sound of disgust. "Probably depends on whether or not Andre has a broken nose."

Toni propped her head on one hand to see him more clearly. "You didn't."

He averted his eyes. "I'm a Quigley. It's what we do."

It was time he put a stop to this line of thinking.

Toni sat up and faced him. "Seb, you are *not* your father. What will it take to convince you? You're nothing like him."

Seb brought his battered hand up between them. "Evidence says otherwise."

She took his hand between hers. "He's cruel, vindictive, incapable of caring for anyone but himself. You're a good man, Sebastian Quick."

His smile and his eyes were soft for her. "I'm glad you think so. God knows I've given you enough cause to feel differently."

"You made a mistake," she said. "That makes you human."

Seb's smile melted away and his eyes filled with an unnamed emotion.

"What?"

"You," he said, reaching up to cup her cheek as his eyes took in her face and hair. "Just you."

Toni swallowed past the lump in her throat and wrapped her fingers around his wrist, holding him there. His pulse beat hard and strong beneath the pad of her index finger.

"Yeah, well... You too."

CHAPTER 34.

"SO, YOU MIC EACH PART of the drum kit?" It had been three weeks since Toni returned to Philly. She'd allowed herself a few days to veg out on the couch and lick her wounds before Richie called and told her to get her butt down to the Phactory.

"Exactly," Richie answered, pointing at each track on the screen as he listed them off. "Kick, snare, hi-hat, tom one, tom two, crash…"

Toni slid her brand-new chair closer to the mixing board. On her first official day, Richie had surprised her with the deluxe leather monstrosity, nearly identical to his. It later occurred to her this was the first piece of furniture she could ever call her own.

"Why not stick the drummer in a room and record them on their own, if you're worried about bleeding into the other instruments' mics?"

"There's bleed between drums, too, and cymbals," he replied with more patience than Toni deserved.

She'd been peppering him with questions since her first day. Toni half expected him to throw up his hands in exasperation and declare she wasn't worth the trouble after all, but he'd been nothing but patient. As it turned out, Richie was as eager to teach her as she was to learn.

"You can record them in a live room, of course, but then

you're limited in what you can do in postproduction. Mixing a live drum kit comes down to small modifications in the highs, mids, and lows, and that's about it."

"Oh, I get it," Toni said, the information clicking into place. "On individual tracks, you can fine-tune everything."

"Exactly," Richie said, spinning in his console chair, giddy as a two-year-old. "Told ya you were a natural!"

Three days after leaving New York, Toni had received an email from Jordan telling her he'd messengered a cashier's check for thirty-five thousand dollars. It sat on the coffee table for a week before she could even bring herself to deposit it. It had been the last tie she had to the band and, damn, but she missed them.

The amount was way more than agreed upon in her contract, but Jordan called the excess a bonus "for putting up with all the drama."

Toni had never written a check as large as the one she'd given Richie for her share in the Phactory, and she'd never been so proud to sign her name as she was when she signed the partnership agreement. After reading it thoroughly and having Jordan look it over, of course. He'd offered.

Since then, she'd spent most of her days, and some nights, at the studio learning the ins and out of what Richie did.

Everything that she'd wanted had come to fruition but somehow the studio felt too empty. Too quiet. The artists who had come through to record or to rehearse were good. Competent. But none of them had the fire and energy that the Lillys possessed.

Toni had been able to sit in on some very cool sessions with a few out-of-town acts. One of them recognized her as a member of the Lillys, and Toni had to take a moment alone before she could continue.

She missed them, often half expecting to walk into one of the iso booths and find Kayla or Tiff. Or Seb.

She hadn't seen him since the night of the showcase. Despite those incredible final hours together, and their promises to stay in each other's lives, they hadn't spoken outside a few innocent text messages about work or the weather.

Toni didn't read too much into it. She was sure Seb had his hands full with Candi and the band, and she was busy with Phactory Sound. They seemed to have an unspoken agreement not to complicate things any further.

She actively avoided any news about the band and wouldn't let Elton or Yvette keep her apprised of whatever they were saying in the tabloids, which was evidently a lot. It was no longer her business. Toni didn't think she'd see any of them for a while.

She certainly didn't expect Seb to turn up at the Phactory, yet there he was.

Toni rubbed her eyes. She'd been at the studio late the night before. Maybe he was a hallucination brought on by sleep deprivation.

Nope.

Seb was indeed standing in the doorway, his hands shoved in his pockets. He gave her a sheepish smile.

"Hey."

"Yo, Seb!" Richie stood and greeted him with a back-thumping half hug, half handshake. "Good to see you, man."

"You too, dude. How are things?" Seb's gaze slid to Toni's.

"Not bad," Richie replied, turning back to the sound board. "Busy, so I can't complain."

"Glad to hear it," Seb said, but his eyes were all for Toni. "Hey, you."

His soft greeting sent an unexpected wave of relief through her. "Hey, yourself."

"Got a minute?"

She smiled. "Yeah, I think I can spare a minute."

Richie laughed and shook his head. "Toni, take all the time you want." He turned to Seb. "She's been plastered to my side. I think she's trying to learn everything all at once."

Seb chuckled. "Sounds about right. Patience was never a virtue with her."

Toni stood and stretched surprisingly tight muscles. Maybe she had been in that chair too long.

"Stop talking about me like I'm not here," she chided them both.

Seb held his hands up in surrender and pushed the door open with his fine ass when she walked toward him.

Toni led him to the piano room. It was one of her favorite spaces in the studio. As soon as they stepped inside and closed the door, the rest of the world disappeared.

In the center of the space stood a Yamaha baby grand, its surface polished to a mirror shine. They'd just had the instrument tuned for a classical session taking place that night.

Seb walked over to the piano and ran a gentle hand over the keys before lightly pressing one down.

"You play?"

"A little." He shrugged. "Never took lessons or anything, but I picked some up when I was down in Louisiana."

"Play something."

Seb glanced up with a half grin before he pulled out the padded leather bench and sat down. He rested his fingers on the keys and took a breath, perhaps mulling over a few selections in his mind.

Toni thought he'd go for some New Orleans–style jazz, or some old piano rock. What he played, though…

"Is that Chopin?" Toni walked over, amazed.

Seb nodded as his fingers moved languidly over the keyboard. "There was a café in the French Quarter. They had an old piano and would let anyone play. This woman, Monica, she was about seventy, I think. She used to come in every afternoon and play the Études. Every day, the same time, the same pieces. This is Op. 10, No. 3. My favorite."

"Why always the same pieces?" Toni eased herself down on the stool next to him.

He shook his head, his black curls falling into his eyes as he transitioned into the next part.

"No one knew."

"Nobody thought to ask?"

"She didn't talk to anyone," Seb said quietly. He flubbed a few of the notes and cursed under his breath. After another false start, he stopped playing and lightly slapped his thighs. "I always get stuck there."

"I'm impressed anyway," Toni admitted.

"Yeah?" A smile played over his lips.

"Yeah," Toni said, keeping her face as devoid of expression as she could. "Who knew you could get those fat fingers of yours to move so gracefully?"

Seb shoved her shoulder playfully. "Fuck off, Bennette."

They both laughed until it faded into the silence of the room. Toni ran a fingertip across the keys, gliding it over each bump.

"So," she said, unable to handle the combination of the quiet and Seb's presence so close to her. She played an E-major chord, the same key as the piece Seb had played. "What brings you to Philly?"

Seb nudged her shoulder again and she looked up at him. "I told you I wanted us to be in each other's lives."

"You did." Toni released the keys.

"And I meant that."

"I'm glad."

"Are you?" His gaze dipped to her mouth and back up.

Toni rolled her eyes. He was so damned dramatic. "Idiot. Of *course* I am."

"Cool, cool." Seb's attention returned to the piano, but Toni didn't miss the grin tugging at the corners of his wickedly talented mouth. "Oh, yeah, I was also wondering if I could tempt you into playing with the girls again."

Toni gasped, delighted. "Recording here?"

Seb turned to her. "Let's say, hypothetically, that Lilly, Kayla, and Tiff made you an offer... Would you work with them again?"

Toni's heart thumped hard in her chest. Something about the look in his eye made her think he was talking about more than a couple of sessions at Phactory.

"What kind of offer?"

Seb stood abruptly and wrung his hands together as if he were psyching himself up for something. He bit his lip as he looked at her and seemed to be holding his breath. "Okay, look, there's an opening, right? In the group," he blurted on an exhalation.

Toni swiveled on the stool. "An opening."

"They need a guitarist," he said, standing in front of her with hope in his eyes.

"What about Candi?"

"After what happened, after you left, Lilly, Jordan, and I met with Andre and Daniel. And their lawyers."

He paused and looked at her.

Toni waited, her patience beginning to fray. "And? Come on, spill in complete thoughts, please."

Seb grinned. "Nah, I think I'll let them tell you."

"Who?"

Seb opened the door and stuck out his hand. "Come on, they should be here by now. I left New York a little before them. Wanted to see you first."

Toni let him pull her up from the stool and lead her back. She knew the others had indeed arrived because the noise level had ramped up from zero to eleven as soon as he opened the door.

"There she is!" Tiffany bounded over to Toni and pulled her into a bear hug.

"Oh my God, Tiff, don't break her," Kayla teased.

When Tiff released her, Toni inhaled a ragged breath in time for Kayla to come in for her hug. Thankfully, she was a lot gentler.

"Hey, girl."

"What the hell, you guys?" Toni grinned as Kayla released her. "What are you doing here? Ready to record already?"

Lilly walked over to her. "We missed you," she said plainly. "It's not been the same without you."

"We gave Candi her walking papers," Kayla added.

Toni glanced at her and then back to Lilly, whose blue gaze only belied a hint of sadness. The woman was a glacier.

"I can't imagine she was too pleased about that," Richie said, leaning against the console.

"No," Lilly said to him before turning back to Toni. "But it was the right thing to do. She didn't care about the band, not really. She didn't care..."

About Lilly.

She didn't say it, but Toni could finally see it. See what perhaps Seb had missed all this time.

Lilly's feelings for Candi were complicated, she knew that. And deep—she'd suspected that too. But they were apparently deeper than perhaps any of the others knew, judging by the way they treated Lilly. Like she was the ice queen she pretended to be, maybe even needed to be. For them.

As if sensing Toni's ability to read her a little more than probably most, Lilly blinked down at her. She gave Toni a slow once-over, as if seeing her for the first time, before meeting her gaze. She smiled. It was small, tiny really, but it was there.

Then the blond shrugged. "At the end of the day, this is a

business. We want to be the best, and that means convincing you to join us."

"For real this time," Tiff added.

Toni shook her head. "I–I can't. I'm flattered, but I just bought into this place."

"What's that got to do with anything?" Richie said. "Phactory Sound's not going anywhere. You *can* have both, you know."

"Both is good," Kayla agreed.

Toni's heart took off in a sprint. "The fans—"

"The ones who love the music will love you too," Tiff said. "The ones who only came for Candi's antics can fuck right off."

"Amen," Kayla agreed. "Besides, girl, you got some chops! Candi *wishes* she could play like that."

Toni appreciated the compliment, because every single one of them knew how irreplaceable Candi was when she was sober.

"Say yes, Toni," Kayla said, clapping as she began to chant, "Toni, Toni, Toni."

"Toni, Toni, Toni," Tiff chanted with her, smiling.

Leaning against the wall, his arms folded, Seb shook his head, amused.

"Don't do that," Lilly admonished, her tone brooking no nonsense.

The pair quieted down but tittered like naughty children.

"Don't pressure her." Lilly turned back to Toni, her eyes warmer than Toni had ever seen them. "They're not exaggerating— you're that good. And we do want you to join us. As a full member of the Lillys, not a hired gun. If that's something you want. It's your decision, Antonia, so do what's best for you. And if you don't want it, that's okay too. We'll figure it out."

"I–I don't know what to say." Toni couldn't fathom the idea.

"Take whatever time you need." Lilly lightly squeezed her

arm and stepped around her. "Let's go find a place to eat, give her some space."

Kayla touched Toni's shoulder as she followed Lilly out the door.

Tiffany pouted, but eventually gave in, hugging Toni fiercely before she left.

Toni turned to Richie. "What do I do?"

"Hey, don't ask me. I know what I'd do if an offer like that dropped into my lap." He held his hands up. "But that's me. Like I said, the Phactory will be here for you. It's yours too, now."

"We're still planning to record here," Seb said.

Richie's eyes lit up. "It's a done deal?"

"Yeah. It's a fantastic facility, state-of-the-art. It has tons of history, and the girls are comfortable here." He looked around, nodding. "New York has its perks, but there's something to be said about the slower pace down here. And the lack of paps following you around."

"We've had to deal with that before," Richie said. "I have a security company on speed dial. You only need to say the word."

"Good to know," Seb said.

"You think they will be as...aggressive, now that Candi is gone?" Toni asked.

Seb shrugged. "Maybe not as much, but with the band's star on the rise and you being four gorgeous, talented women, it's bound to happen. The Lillys are going to intimidate people. Some are going to try to tear the band down just for being who they are."

Toni bit her lip. "Yeah... Shit."

Fame. It was everything she hated about the music business. She had grown to appreciate the rush of playing onstage for an adoring crowd, but she'd never thought of herself as the kind of girl to get stars in her eyes. She didn't think she could ever get used to living in a spotlight, or under a microscope.

"I know what you're thinking," Seb said, stepping into her space. "You're worried you'll lose yourself, who you are, to the media, the fans."

"I love playing with the girls. I just don't know if I can handle the rest," Toni said honestly.

"You can make it whatever you want it to be, Nia. It doesn't have to be a circus. I can help it not be one." He took her hands in his and Toni's pulse tripped all over itself.

She was transported back nearly ten years. Prom night, when he'd held her hands and looked into her eyes exactly like this. If only she'd known then what she knew now.

Seb smiled.

Richie cleared his throat, mumbled "I, uh…need to go grab… something," and left the room.

Toni chuckled. "Subtle."

"Very," Seb agreed, grinning. He searched her eyes. "I see you, you know."

"Oh yeah?"

He nodded. "Always have, just like you've always seen me."

"You're pretty easy to read."

"Only for you," he said softly, then frowned. "I don't want you to feel pressured into saying yes to this, to them. If you want to be with the band, *really* want it, then I'll support you all the way. But if you don't…"

He smoothed a hand over her hair and his scent washed over her—sandalwood, fresh grass, and Sebastian. "Nia…" He took a breath. "I'd only ever loved one person before I met you, and she died before I realized how lucky I was to have her. It wasn't… It wasn't until I met you, until you started following me around and bugging the hell out of me…"

Toni chuckled. "You're so bad at this."

He flashed a grin, but it melted away.

"I fucking love you, Antonia Bennette," Seb declared fiercely. He cupped her face in his hands. "This was years in the making, you and me, but whatever you want, whatever you decide, it's up to you. I want you, I want this, if *you* want it. Want me."

A tear slipped down her cheek before she could catch it. "Christ, Seb, how thick are you? I've been in love with you since I was fourteen, probably have been since the day we met. I could probably pinpoint the exact moment I fell in love with you."

"I didn't fall in love with you," Seb replied, his voice thick. "I sort of...sank into it. Fuck, I didn't even know it was happening until I was already underwater, and then it was all I could do not to tell you every time I saw you. There were times I literally had to *bite my tongue* to keep it from spilling out. I didn't want to spook you. Part of me was afraid you'd laugh or, worse, leave. It's not like I wouldn't deserve it."

"Seb, no." Toni's heart broke for him right then, that he'd been carrying so much for so long.

He carded his fingers through his hair. "I'm just a fucked-up guy with a fucked-up past, and you..."

"My past is just as fucked up," Toni countered. "Mo? Mary? I don't come from much myself."

Seb shook his head. "Nah, Nia. No. You're...you're fucking *everything*. To me, you're everything. Take all of this away, all of it—the-the-the band and the music—all of it. If I had you, I'd still have everything."

"You have me, Seb." Toni bit her lip because she didn't trust anything else she might say.

He leaned forward and touched his forehead to hers, pulling her to him by her waist. "Thank you," he whispered against her lips. "Thank you."

A giggle bubbled up from Toni's throat. "This is all terribly romantic, but we might have a problem."

Seb leaned back and frowned down at her. "What problem? Living in different cities? That's easy enough to fix. Whenever we get to that point, I mean."

And, oh. Toni filed that away for later.

"No, I meant the no-fraternization clause."

Seb's grip tightened, his thumb brushing back and forth over her skin. "You're not under contract anymore."

"True, true," Toni said, nodding. "But what if I sign a new contract?"

Seb went still. A slow smile crept across his mouth. "Well... then...in that case, you should probably make sure Jordan doesn't put one in. Make it a deal-breaker."

Toni's brows rose. "A deal-breaker, wow. You think you're worth it?"

"I hope so." His eyes went dark. Toni's pulse quickened, a Pavlovian response to the promise in them.

"We'll see," she said.

"We'll see," Seb echoed, his smile more of a smirk.

"And what about your contract? Don't you have one too?"

Seb's smile fell. "I do, yeah. Guess I'll have to take care of that."

"Guess you will," Toni agreed as she slipped her hands into his hair and pulled.

The next kiss was gentle by design. With the girls waiting for them, anything more would have to wait a little while longer.

But it was okay.

They had time.

EPILOGUE.

ONE MONTH LATER

A GUST OF COLD WIND pushed Seb through the front door of the Electric Unicorn. Inside was nice and toasty, thanks both to Elton's aversion to winter and the tightly packed crowd, there to see the official debut of the Lillys' new lineup.

Seb spotted Elton right away, directing traffic behind the bar like a beat cop. He waved when he saw Seb. The club was so full, it took a few minutes for Seb to wind his way down to him.

"Be right with you, mate," he called out.

"No rush."

A few heads turned his way.

"Hey, Seb," one guy said. The face looked familiar, but Seb couldn't place the name.

"Hey."

"We met a few weeks ago when Toni sat in on my session."

"Oh, yeah," Seb replied. "Owen, right?"

"Yep," Owen said, reaching out and shaking Seb's hand.

"What are you still doing in town? Thought you were hitting the road or something."

"Yeah, tour starts next week." Owen gestured toward the stage. "I asked Toni to come out on the European leg. She turned me down, said she already had a band. I had to come check it out."

"Ah," Seb said, grinning. The guy was in for a hell of a show.

"Nice turnout, eh?" Elton said when he finally reached Seb. "There must be a hundred people here. We're going to have to start turning people away at the door soon, or the fire marshal will shut me down."

Seb looked around. The place was absolutely packed, standing room only.

"I knew she'd make something of herself," Elton said, nodding toward the stage, no small note of pride in his voice.

"Antonia was always something," Seb corrected him.

Elton nodded firmly and smiled like a proud dad. "Right you are, lad. Right you are."

Seb frowned at the mass of bodies between him and the door to the dressing room. "I don't know how I'm going to make it through that."

Elton patted his shoulder and leaned in close. "Go outside and turn left, walk to the small side street, and take the alley to the back door. Bang twice. Someone'll let you in."

"Cool, thanks."

Moments later, Seb stepped inside the warmth of the club for the second time that night, and the backstage area was blessedly clear. He bounded up the few steps to the dressing room, but found it empty, so he headed down to the stage where he found Kayla tightening her drums and Tiff restringing her bass.

The band had splurged on the velvet curtains that hung in front of the stage, renting them from a local theatrical supply company. They were rigged to drop to the floor in a dramatic reveal when the show started. Elton had liked the drama of it so much during the sound check that he said he might buy them.

"Hey, gang."

"Sebastian!" Tiff leaned over and smacked a wet kiss on his cheek, no doubt smearing it with her bright-green lipstick. "Did you see that crowd out there? Philly is wildin' out."

"Yeah, it's a good one."

"This is going to be fun," Kayla said, running through her stretches. It was part of her pre-gig routine.

Seb turned to where Lilly sat perched on one of the speakers. "Hey."

"Seb," she replied absentmindedly as she scribbled something on the set list. When she finished, she looked up. "You okay?"

"Me? I'm fine," Seb answered truthfully. "Great, actually. How are you? Feeling good about this?"

Lilly nodded. "Getting there."

She looked around the stage and Seb followed her gaze. It was a cramped space, but they'd made it work. And Elton had a killer sound system. It was going to be a great show.

"Anything I can do?"

She studied him for a moment before shaking her head. "You've done enough, I think."

Seb frowned. "Meaning?"

Lilly shook her head again and stood. Thanks to her Viking DNA, they were nearly eye to eye. Seb saw a myriad of emotions cross her face as she watched the others.

The smallest of frowns creased her forehead and she let out a breath. "I thought all of this would look different," she said. "Feel different, somehow. I dunno."

"I miss her too," he said, believing he'd read her right. "The old Candi, the one I introduced to you at that dank little bar in SoHo."

"Simpler times," she said, her voice barely above a whisper. "Or maybe more complicated." Lilly searched his eyes. "I wouldn't call it fate, but I think everything is as it should be. Every*one* is where they should be. For now."

Seb leaned in, matching her tone. "I'm sorry if we hurt you. I..." He swallowed. "I didn't know."

Lilly nodded again, seeming to mull over her thoughts. "Neither did I. It was the three of us. You know? And then, suddenly, I was...alone. Again. You had each other, and I..."

"Oh, Lil..." Seb reached down and took her hand. "You're not alone—I'm here. Always. And sooner or later, Candi will realize what she threw away."

"Maybe." Lilly looked down at their joined hands and laced their fingers together, squeezing his tight. "She texted me this morning. She's taking time for herself, says she needs to sort through some things. Wished us all luck."

"She texted me too," Seb said and smiled. "All is not lost. Give it time."

"She made her choice," she said at last. "And we made ours."

The sound of a guitar being tuned echoed from the other side of the stage, and Lilly turned her head in that direction.

Seb turned too and spotted Toni in the shadows.

"Are you two together now? Finished dancing around each other?"

"I think so," he said, drinking in the sight of the woman he loved beyond reason. Seb turned back to Lilly. "I hope so."

Lilly searched his face. "You know you were both in breach of your contracts."

Seb swallowed, still a little guilty about that. "Yeah."

"Good thing we tore those up and started over, then." Her smile didn't quite reach her eyes, but it washed over him like a ray of sunshine. For Lilly, it was as good as a benediction. "It's something real, what you have with her. Isn't it?"

It wasn't really a question but Seb answered anyway.

"Yeah. We... Yeah."

Something moved behind her eyes before she dropped his hand and looked away, a small frown on her forehead.

"I trust you," she said quietly. "Not to fuck it up, and not fuck *us* up."

"I won't, Lil," Seb said with as much sincerity as he could. "I promise."

"Don't promise," she replied, not looking at him. "Be better this time. And don't hurt her."

With that, Lilly walked over to Tiff and Kayla.

Seb watched them for a moment before making his way to the other side of the stage. Toni had her eyes closed, and he decided to give her a moment to compose herself. He needed to have a chat with the sound staff anyway. He wanted tonight to be perfect. For all of them.

***

Toni peeked through a slit where the curtains gaped open. The bar teemed with people, every table in the front of the house crowded with chairs and standing room only in the back.

An arm slid around her waist, the familiarity of the touch unmistakable, and Toni leaned back into the warm, hard body behind her.

"Good turnout," Seb said, his breath tickling the shell of her ear.

Toni turned her head to plant a kiss on his cheek. His five-o'clock shadow grazed her lips as he turned his head to press their mouths together.

Seb made a sound of satisfaction that Toni felt in her toes. What a difference a few months could make.

"Hi," she whispered into the space between them.

"Hey," Seb replied, his eyes twinkling as he studied her. "You sure you're gonna be okay with all of this? People are gonna know your name. They're gonna want to know all about you."

"I know. And to be honest, I don't know if I'll ever be okay with it," she answered. "I just know I'd regret it if I walked away now."

Seb bent and kissed her cheek.

Toni turned back to the gap in the curtains. There were more people packed into the Unicorn than she'd ever seen. Many unfamiliar faces, but a lot of people she knew as well.

Yvette was there, of course, and—*ohhh, hey now*—Richie sat beside her, and they seemed…friendly.

"Huh," she mused.

"What?" Seb rested his chin on her shoulder and wrapped both arms around her waist.

Toni grabbed his forearms and pulled him in tighter, nodding toward her discovery.

"I wonder when that happened."

Seb smirked. "You're kidding, right?"

Toni leaned away to look at him. "What did I miss?"

Seb laughed and the sound of it made her belly quiver. She had always loved his laugh. At least that hadn't changed. Not much had, as it turned out.

"Those two are always all over each other at the Phactory," Seb said, grinning like a kid with a juicy secret. "Didn't Tiff tell you she found them making out like teenagers in one of the empty iso booths?"

Toni cracked a laugh before covering her mouth with her hand. Her head whipped back around, and she watched as Richie draped his arm along the back of Yvette's chair. It was a subtle move, but it spoke volumes.

"That witch! She hasn't said a word to me," Toni groused. She was happy for both of them but a little put out at being the last one to know. Then again, she'd done the same thing.

"I think they look good together," Seb commented. "Besides, you've been…preoccupied."

He wasn't wrong. And Yvette was glowing. The ever-present dark circles under her eyes had receded, and her smile was bright. She deserved a good person by her side, and Richie was one of the best.

"Yeah," Toni agreed at last. "They do."

"I think we look good together too," Seb added, his voice a low growl in her ear.

Asshole. He knew exactly what that did to her, and her body went soft in anticipation.

Toni closed her eyes and leaned her head back against him. "I think so too."

She sighed when he placed a warm kiss against the curve of her neck and shivered when he followed it up with a soft bite.

Seb hummed against her skin, nipped at her throat.

"Seb," Toni warned when she felt his half-hard arousal pressing against her ass. "Seb," she said louder, giggling. "What are you doing?"

He squeezed her tighter before letting her go. "I was being bad, but I'll be good."

As she turned around, he stepped away and spread his arms wide.

"See? I can be good." He winked.

"Miss Bennette?"

Toni turned, surprised to see Daniel Herbots approaching. Though he and Andre were twins, there was a softness to Daniel's carriage that she recognized. "Mr. Herbots."

He smiled warmly. "Daniel."

Seb moved to her side, his gaze searching the area. "I didn't expect to see you and Andre here."

Daniel let out a soft laugh but there was a touch of bitterness in it and a tinge of an accent Toni still couldn't put her finger on.

"My brother isn't here. Andre has…a new pet project to keep him occupied." His face brightened. "But I wouldn't miss this. I've really been looking forward to it."

Seb relaxed and met the man's gaze. "Ah, I see."

Daniel's brow creased. "I–I hope it's all right that I'm here. I don't mean to cause a distraction."

Toni smiled. "We appreciate the support of our label." *Our label.* That still seemed like such a foreign concept.

Daniel's smile returned. "Good, good. I'm definitely here to support. Do you need anything?"

Seb tilted his head, regarding him. "I think we're all set, but thank you. Like Toni said, we appreciate the support."

Daniel gave him a sharp nod. "Again, it is my pleasure. If you don't mind, I'll go find a seat. You have a great crowd tonight."

"I think there's room at our table," Seb offered. "Look for Jordan. He'll take care of you."

Daniel tilted his head in thanks. "I shall do that." He turned to Toni. "Break a leg? I believe that is the expression."

"Thanks," Toni said, smiling.

After one more nod, Daniel was off.

"Well…" Seb began. "That was a thing that happened."

Toni laughed.

"Hey, Toni! You ready for this?" Tiff called over.

She stood in front of her amp, her ruby-red bass in hand. It gleamed, even in the low light. Tiff set it gently down on the stand, then strolled over, her hair a shiny black curtain of braids that hung down her back. She wore a leather bustier over a sheer mesh tee, with matching stockings and a stretchy black miniskirt that hugged her ample curves.

She looked incredible and she knew it.

"Sebster."

"Tiff-monster."

"I want a cool name," Toni mock-pouted.

"Dude, your name is Toni-freakin-Bennette," Tiff said, arching a perfect eyebrow. "Doesn't get much cooler than that."

"Oh, I dunno," Seb said, draping an arm across Toni's shoulder. "Sebastian Quick has a cool ring to it too."

"True that," Tiff agreed.

"I'm going to grab a seat. I want to be in the crowd for this. Knock 'em dead, ladies." Seb kissed Toni's forehead and bounded off the stage.

Kayla took her place behind the drums, tuning and tightening and whatever else she did to make the kit sound like Odin's chariot when she played them.

The overhead lights flashed, signaling their start time, and Toni picked up her guitar, settling the strap on her shoulder.

Lilly strolled to the microphone, which stood dead center, and turned her back to the curtain. She looked at each of them—Kayla, Tiff, and finally Toni.

Toni smiled at her.

Lilly's blink was slow, like a cat. She seemed to be off in her own world.

"Philadelphia, New York, and parts in between," Elton's voice boomed over the PA. "The Electric Unicorn is very proud to present the Lillys!"

Lilly's gaze dropped to the floor.

The curtain dropped, and Luca gathered it up and quickly pulled it away.

Kayla's foot hit the kick drum in a pounding rhythm that Toni felt in her gut. Tiff's bass kicked in to replace her pulse.

Toni positioned her fingers on Minx's strings and let the opening chords flow from her fingertips. She looked back up at Lilly who still stood with her back to the audience, which clapped and stomped in time with the kick drum.

The cue for the first verse was coming up at the top of the next measure. Lilly showed no awareness of what was happening.

Toni glanced at Tiff who shook her head as if to say *This is common* and repeated the intro, leaning even harder into the groove. Toni followed her lead and Kayla did too.

Just before Lilly's cue came up again, she lifted her eyes to the lights in the rafters.

Watching the transformation from Lilliana Langeland into Lilly, the rising star, filled Toni with so much awe she felt privileged to witness it. To be a part of this.

She searched the crowd for Seb, spotting him dead center, arms folded, with all of his attention on her.

I love you, he mouthed and then screamed along with the crowd, grinning like a loon.

Toni laughed and winked at him.

Behind him, a familiar figure pushed into the light, and Toni had never been more grateful to know a song inside and out. Otherwise, she would have lost her place entirely.

As it was, she blinked fast, both to clear her vision and to ensure she wasn't, in fact, hallucinating.

Mo raised his hand in an aborted wave before shoving both of them into the pockets of his coat.

Toni watched as Seb looked over his shoulder, standing when he realized who was there.

The two men exchanged an awkward handshake before Seb offered Mo his chair.

Toni's father sat down and turned back to her, something akin to pride on his face.

She would not cry. Would *not*.

Standing behind Mo, Seb smiled up at her.

He knew. He always knew.

The song looped around to the top again, and Toni refocused.

Locked in.

Held her breath.

Then Lilly turned to the microphone, opened her golden throat, and changed all of their lives forever.

ACKNOWLEDGMENTS

A huge thank you to my new Sourcebooks family, especially my angel of an editor, Mary Altman, and Christa Soulé Désir. You both not only understood and supported my vision but held my hand and helped me to realize it. Helped me make it sing.

Thanks also to Denny S. Bryce and Dena Heilik for pushing me to start my publishing journey, and to Cat Clyne for starting the Lillys on theirs. And an enormous thank you to my agent, Nalini Akolekar, for taking a chance and jumping into the mosh pit with me.

Susan Scott Shelley, you've been a sounding board, a cheerleader, and a voice of reason. You were there when the Lillys were just a concept. Thank you for your friendship. I owe you a metric ton of chocolate. And coffee. Lots of coffee.

I also need to thank a few of the authors and friends who have lifted me up and carried me on their wings. Kristan, Ms. Bev, Sonali, Priscilla, Laura, Susanna, Grace, Roan, Veronica, Robin, and Avery, you and so many others gave generously of your time and expertise to a fledgling author who didn't know a trope from a tripod. I can't thank you enough.

Thank you to my family for always supporting my dreams, one after the other.

And finally, all of my gratitude, appreciation, and love to my other half, Mr. X. This song is for you, babe.

ABOUT THE AUTHOR

Xio Axelrod is a *USA Today* bestselling author. She writes different flavors of contemporary romance and what she likes to call "strange, twisted tales."

Xio grew up in the recording industry and began performing at a very young age. As a result, her knowledge of popular music is nearly encyclopedic. Seriously, look her up on quiz night. She might even be up for some karaoke!

A completely unapologetic, badge-wearing, fic-writing fangirl, Xio finds inspiration in everything around her. From her quirky neighbors to the lyrics of whatever song she currently has on repeat, to the latest clips from her favorite TV series, *Skam*, Xio weaves her passions into her books.

(And if you're curious about *Skam*, ask her about it. Just be prepared to settle in for the long haul.)

When she isn't working on the next story, Xio can be found behind a microphone in a studio, writing songs in her bedroom-turned-recording-booth, or performing on international stages under a different, not-so-secret name.

She lives in complete denial of the last five minutes of *Buffy* with one very patient full-time indoor husband, and several part-time supremely pampered outdoor cats.

BONUS MATERIAL

Enjoy your exclusive VIP backstage pass as Xio Axelrod takes you on a tour of the world of the Lillys, including:

1. About the Band + links to their music

2. Sheet music for an original song written and performed by Xio

3. Questions for your next book club meeting

4. A conversation with Xio about her dual life as a musician and an author

5. A sneak peek at what's next for the Lillys

ABOUT THE BAND

Ask any fan of the Lillys to describe them, and you'll hear words like "hypnotic," "fierce," and "unapologetic." This uber enigmatic, all-female unit isn't interested in labels. They are utterly unconcerned with image, status, or style.

The four members of the Lillys—Kayla Whitman on drums, Tiffany Kim on bass, Candi Fair on guitar, and Lilly Langeland on lead vocals—came together through chance and no small amount of karmic intervention.

Some think the Lillys exploded onto the New York music scene with their cover of the Toadies alt-rock classic, "I Burn," but they first paid their dues playing in small clubs and dive bars. Known for their raw and raucous performances, fans have wondered aloud what will happen to the band's signature sound now that they've been picked up by a major label like YMI. Rest assured, the Lillys are here to melt your brain and upend any preconceived notions you may have about girl-bands. These women rock.

To learn more (and to hear their smash hit cover of *I Burn*), follow the Lillys on:

THEIR WEBSITE:

thelillysrock.com

TWITTER:

twitter.com/thelillysrock

INSTAGRAM:

instagram.com/thelillysrock

FACEBOOK:

facebook.com/thelillysrock

SPOTIFY:

open.spotify.com/artist/4V486OYFT1uMhptcFhsqzX?si
=pVLpwhrATD-cr2XrECdYzg

APPLE:

music.apple.com/us/album/i-burn/1522235703?i=1522235704

YOUTUBE:

youtube.com/channel/UCjGFyubZIxpN_k5hFNRs8Dw

Hurt (U)

READING GROUP GUIDE

1. The first few years of Toni's life were spent on the road with her mother, Mary. How do you think being raised around dive bars and clubs influenced Toni as she grew?

2. What do you think drew Toni and Seb to each other when they first met outside Mo's bar? What made Seb decide to talk to Toni?

3. Seb and Toni's friendship blossoms over a shared love of 90s alt-rock, which they carry with them into their adulthood. What is the music that most shaped you growing up? How does it feel to listen to those songs now?

4. Both Mary and Mo claim the Gibson *Minx* was theirs. What do you think the backstory is there? Why did Mary let Toni take such an expensive instrument, and why did Mo let her have it back years later?

5. Seb, Candi, and Lilly have a complicated history together. What do you think happened between them, and how has it impacted their current relationship?

6. Toni both seems to crave and be repelled by the spotlight. Why do you think that is? What makes her so adamant that she doesn't want to be the center of attention?

7. The relationship between all five Lillys is complicated, thanks to Candi. Why do they keep giving her more chances? What would have been the final straw for you?

8. Is Candi being honest when she says she cares about the Lillys? Does she really want to change, or is she manipulating the Lillys into believing she will?

9. Seb left Toni behind without a word when he was forced to flee their small town. Was what he did justified? Would you have forgiven Seb for leaving if you were in Toni's position?

10. We see multiple instances of men in the industry (other artists, executives, and so on) trying to gaslight or control Toni B. and the Lillys. Do you think this is an accurate portrayal of the music industry? What do you think it's like for young women in music?

11. In their final performance, a clearly intoxicated Candi is thrust out onto the stage. Why did the executives want her there? If you were Toni, would you have agreed to dub over her music from backstage, knowing you were being used?

12. The future looks bright for Toni, Seb, and the Lillys, but there's a long road ahead of the band. What do you think is in store for them? How will their complicated relationship with Candi play into their future?

A CONVERSATION WITH THE AUTHOR

What was the inspiration for *The Girl with Stars in Her Eyes*? What did you draw on as you developed the story?

A: There's a long answer and a short answer to this question.

The long answer is that I grew up in the music industry. I've seen—first-hand—how it operates on almost every level.

As a performer trying to carve a path in an industry that didn't want to take me seriously, I fought to be seen and heard. I watched people close to me rise to the very top and vicariously experienced all of the trappings that came with that level of worldwide acclaim and notoriety. I think it gave me a firm grasp on the realities of the business of music.

With all of that knowledge and experience swimming in my head, it was probably just a matter of time before it spilled into my writing.

Okay, that's the long answer.

The short answer is that I came across two photographs— one of Taylor Momsen performing on stage in cutoff jeans and ripped fishnets, and one of a young (maybe twelve-year-old?) Jurnee Smollett cradling an acoustic guitar—and I had one of those "what if" moments we writers are known to have. What if these two lives, these two worlds, collided?

Music obviously plays an important part in Toni B's life. What role has it played in your life? What are the songs and bands that shaped you as an artist?

A: To answer the first question, music is my life. I'm what you would call a melophile. Unless I am actively listening to something (or watching something), I have a constant soundtrack running in my head.

As for the second question, that's a big one. I grew up listening to whatever my family had lying around. My father wrote and produced a lot of R&B, Soul, and Disco for artists like the O'Jays, the Spinners, and the Village People. He was a big part of the Sound of Philadelphia in the seventies. I don't think I was aware of any other genre—except for, maybe, Broadway and classical—until I was about eleven or twelve years old.

Around that time, I discovered classic rock, and it was like waking up to a whole, new world. There were so many bands I'd never heard before—Led Zeppelin, the Beatles, the Who, Genesis, the Police, Steely Dan—and I remember being devastated that most of them weren't around anymore. It hurt to know I'd have little chance to see them in concert.

Of course, there were groups like Radiohead, Pearl Jam, and Soundgarden, and, later, Muse, the Arctic Monkeys, Cage the Elephant, Tool, etc. I live for live music, and I've been to over four hundred shows.

Asked to point out any direct influences, my answer might seem a bit all over the place. And it would probably change the next time I was asked, but I'd cite artists like Dead Can Dance, Ella Fitzgerald, Bloc Party, the Cocteau Twins, the Psychedelic Furs, Bjork, XTC, Jeff Buckley, David Bowie, the Noisettes PJ Harvey, the Yeah Yeah Yeahs... It is an ever-growing list.

At the top, though, there's always seems to be what I call the three M's: Metric, Mutemath, and Massive Attack.

You're a recording artist, as well as an author. Do you see any connection between your two arts?

A: People have told me I have a lyrical quality to my prose, which I have decided to accept as a high compliment. It isn't intentional. My writing style is truly a happy accident. I've just found a different way to express myself. I found my *other* voice, I guess.

I admit it is kind of freeing to think I might approach a novel like a song—with an intro, several verses, a bridge, a chorus, and an outro. The way songs ebb and flow, I suppose it fits the narrative. And since I tend to pants my way through my books, it's all improvisation anyway. Haha!

I also listen to music when I write. In fact, I find it hard to work without it. I know that's not the case for some authors, and that amazes me. Like, how? I need music to focus. I often sleep with it on.

What are some of the instruments you play? Toni B also has an interest in producing—is this an area you have experience in?

A: After voice, my primary instrument is piano. I played regularly for a long time but not so much anymore. I still use a keyboard to compose, and I have pretty good tonal memory that extends to other instruments. For instance, although I am not a guitarist, I can pick one up and play a simple line to record a demo or to covey to my band what I hear in my head. To that end, I own several instruments, including a few guitars, a couple of bass guitars, a full-sized keyboard, a toy piano, a Celtic drum, a melodica, and a bunch of percussive accessories. My favorite instrument is one I don't own—yet: the cello. I'm also fond of the hammered dulcimer, and I would love to get a drum kit, but I think Mr. X would toss it out in the middle of the night!

My most prized possessions are a vintage Fender Rhodes Mark I stage piano and a vintage Gibson ES 355 guitar similar to

Minx, the one Toni plays in Gwishi. (For you gearheads, Minx is the more valuable ES 335.)

These instruments used to belong to my dad, and both have some serious musical history behind them.

As for the second question, I've produced all of my own stuff and a little bit for my siblings. Production is something I hope to delve into more someday. I know quite a few producers, and none of them are women.

You recorded a cover of the song "I Burn" for this series. What made you choose that song for the Lillys? What's the history of that song?

A: I wish I had an answer to this question that made sense to anyone but me!

"I Burn" is a relatively obscure song, but it's one that has floated through my head, off and on, since the very first time I heard it. In fact, that entire album—*Rubberneck* by the Toadies— haunts me.

There are conflicting accounts of how those songs came to be, and I'd love to know all of the secrets behind those lyrics because there's a *lot* going on there.

"I Burn" somehow became Lilly's anthem. I could see and hear her performing it very clearly, in my mind. When I put together my Spotify playlist for Gwishi (the Girl with Stars in Her Eyes), it was the first song I added. I would listen to it on repeat, for hours at a time, while the scenes from the book coalesced in my imagination. Much later, it occurred to me that I could record the song with my own band—as the Lillys—and that's what I did.

You also used one of your original songs for the Lillys. What was the inspiration there? Tell us the story behind "Hurt (U)."

A: Actually, two of my songs are referenced in Gwishi. The

first one is "Butterflies," which is the track from the fictional band, Caspian's Ghost, that Toni and Seb sing together at the Electric Unicorn. (Don't ask me where that band name came from. I wish I'd thought of it sooner. I would have used it myself.)

"Hurt (U)" was on my last full-length album, *Stranger,* and it was a total outlier in a tracklist full of outliers. I wanted to be a rock-and-roll girl *so badly*, but I couldn't get my foot in that particular door, no matter how hard I tried. "Hurt (U)" is my quirky, indie-pop-rock anthem, and it's one of my favorite songs to perform live. My band likes to tease me because I always want to speed it up when we play it. Really rock it out.

I thought the song fit the Lillys' sound and dynamic. The lyrics are about hurting the people you love and being hurt by them, despite everyone having the best of intentions. It's almost as if I wrote the song for the Lillys themselves. It fits so well.

Toni starts the book as a "hired gun" musician. What does that mean, and what does a typical job look like for a hired gun?

A: A hired gun is a musician who is brought in to fill a position, either in a live band or in a studio setting. They aren't official members of the bands they work with, and it's often a thankless job. There's no fame in it, the money varies, and you usually never know when or where your next gig will be.

Think of them as contract workers. Most contracts are short-lived. You could work with someone on one album or tour, but they might not call you in for the next one, or there might be a scheduling conflict.

Some hired guns do manage to stay with an artist or a band for years. Decades, even. If you're really good—look up bass player Gail Ann Dorsey, for instance—you'll develop a reputation in the industry, and people will seek you out. Gail is a great example, actually. She's had some fantastic residencies with artists like Tears for Fears, The National, and Lenny Kravitz, but she played with David Bowie for over twenty years. They had an incredible working partnership. Incidentally, she's from Philly, too.

What advice would you give to young writers or musicians out there?

A: No matter what your medium is, be confident in your voice. People seem to find it easy, even comfortable, to put things in neat, little boxes. Don't be afraid to spill over the sides. Take up all the space your talent demands, and don't let anyone tell you there's only one path to get where you want to go. Someone always has to go first. Why not you?

THE GIRL WITH RHYTHM IN HER HEART

When Kayla Whitman was fifteen, the pressure to be perfect nearly broke her. Then she picked up a pair of drumsticks, altering the entire rhythm of her life. Since then, she's fought hard to keep her past a secret. But when she meets a man whose heart beats the same tempo as hers, she can't help but want to share the most hidden parts of herself. With her star on the rise and her band's reputation in the balance, can Kayla pursue her dream without destroying everyone around her?

COMING SOON